The Sweet Sister

I am probably not in C. David Belt's target audience. I don't read much in the horror-fantasy genre, and I've never been to ComiCon. I don't even dress up for Halloween. But I do love a great story. And *The Sweet Sister* is a great story. It is one of those can't-put-it-down page-turners that keeps you up late. What's more, it dares to be a clear-cut story about the battle between Good and Evil, devoid of the moral hand-wringing that characterizes so much postmodern storytelling.

Belt casts his heroes and heroines, not in the mold of Tolkien's epic figures, but as utterly relatable everymen. There is nothing special about them except that they want to do the right thing. They succeed using their own modest talents, despite their mortal foibles and self-doubt.

Whether or not you are a fan of the emerging "LDS Fantasy-Horror" genre, if you are looking for a good read with a satisfying conclusion, *The Sweet Sister* is a can't-miss choice.

Devon Asay - Orem, UT

The Sweet Sister by C. David Belt is proof Horror is not a genre only for those who enjoy a terror-induced adrenaline rush. C. David Belt's voice, multi-character POV, abundance of pop culture, and intriguing prose drew me in from the first paragraph and continued to hook me until the last page. True to its genre, some areas are frightening, but the balance of the character's unique faith, makes this a fun and inspirational read.

Loury Trader - Helena, MT

The Sweet Sister is a spooky, suspenseful ride that seamlessly blends the present and the past. It impressively blends the myths and legends of many different cultures into an incredible tapestry that is both satisfying and fascinating. I really enjoyed the quirky, relatable protagonist, and the many great twists in the plot. Highly recommended!

Michael Young, author of *The Hunger*, *The Last Archangel*, and *The Canticle Kingdome* - Eagle Mountain, UT

The Sweet Sister was nothing I was expecting; in fact, I honestly didn't know what to expect from a genre new to me, LDS Horror. There were scary moments where I wanted to cover my eyes but couldn't stop turning pages; sweet moments filled with wonder, hope, and romance; and educational moments where I learned so much about our world's history. This book keeps you on your toes, jumping from each character's vantage point, unveiling clue by clue, until the reader has witnessed the full journey alongside the heroine. Well-written and expertly crafted, this book opened my eyes to the wonder of fiction, of escaping into an alternate reality, and somehow of finding a sense of normalcy therein.

Staci Meacham - Layton, UT

The Sweet

Sister

To Cheryl,

True beauty is found within!

C. David Belt

C. David Belt

Cover design: Ben Savage

PARABLES
Walkersville, MD
http://www.parablespub.com
parables@parablespub.com

For Cindy,
Always

Magic mirror on the wall, who is the fairest one of all?

Queen – Snow White and the Seven Dwarfs

Life is composed of lights and shadows, and we would be untruthful, insincere, and saccharine if we tried to pretend there are no shadows.

Walt Disney

Author's note

This is not the story I intended to tell, at least not at first. The concept for this story started off as a fairly simple one. Then I started to do my research, and my mind was officially blown. There is such a richness and depth to the backdrop for *The Sweet Sister* — the mythologies, religious practices and rituals, and the actual historical events — that I knew I'd scratch only the surface. If I tried to include all the details I was learning, the book would occupy several volumes (and probably be far too slow-paced for a contemporary horror novel). I'd study and research late into the night, and begrudge the time when I finally forced myself to go to bed. Then I'd count the days until I would next go to the Tabernacle on Temple Square.

You see, I'm a member of the Mormon Tabernacle Choir (at least as of this writing). During rehearsals, I would give myself over to the sacred music. In those moments when I was not singing, I'd gaze out from the Choir loft into the vast expanse of the domed ceiling. And the inspiration would come.

Now, I'm not trying to claim divine revelation for my horror stories, but I definitely received help. As I'd stare out into that sacred space, bits of the tale would crystallize in my mind. This phenomenon has occurred during every rehearsal and performance over the past fifteen months — I would go to Choir — and I'd have an epiphany. After one rehearsal, another Choir member asked me how I was doing. I responded with great enthusiasm, "I'm doing great! I know exactly how to describe that grisly ritual murder now! I can't wait to get home and write it down!" He gave me a quizzical (and somewhat horrified) look as I bade him good-night and hurried off to my car.

So this tale grew, as all good tales do, in the telling. It blossomed like flowers on a fruit tree. But I'm getting ahead of myself . . .

While I have added fictional details to the historical events described, many of the people and events were very real. History is

3

typically written by the victors, so I had to rely on accounts about the conquered relayed by the conquerors. And in many cases, recent archeology has validated the victors' accounts. However, I must apologize to Wilhelm the Pious for *possibly* impugning his character. As far as I know, there is no evidence to support how I depicted him in the story. If I meet him in the next life, I may need to apologize to him in person.

A couple of pronunciation notes: in Welsh, "dd" is pronounced "th," and in Gaelic, "dh" is pronounced "v."

Lastly, in Mormon culture, the phrase "sweet sister" is often used to refer to a young (or not so young) woman who is "beautiful on the inside," but not on the surface. I believe that true beauty starts within. No amount of physical loveliness can mask ugliness within. However, a woman who is beautiful on the inside cannot help but reflect that beauty in her eyes, her smile, and her Christlike compassion for others. "Who can find a virtuous woman? for her price is far above rubies" (Proverbs 31:10). Woman is God's crowning creation. I am profoundly grateful for the precious women in my life, most especially my dear, sweet, and beautiful eternal companion. She and they inspire me to do better, to be better.

C. David Belt
March, 2016
unwillingchild@hotmail.com

I

The world had turned to blood.

Light from a trio of smoking braziers danced along the walls of unhewn stone, capering like a host of tiny demons. Even as his mind swam through an ocean of gore, struggling back to consciousness, Jerry knew the light should be yellow. Or orange.

But not red.

And not upside down.

The braziers hung on tripods, hanging from the ceiling, their flames and smoke descending to the floor.

It's not the room, he thought, fighting the grogginess. *It's not the room. I'm upside down.* The realization jolted Jerry back to full consciousness.

To terror.

I can't move! Why can't I move?

His arms hung below his head. Jerry tried to lift them, but they were too heavy. And they hurt like hell. So did his skull. It pounded like when that RPG had exploded near his head back in Afghanistan.

He twisted his body, trying to raise himself, but he didn't have the strength. And that terrified him even more.

Jerry was a big guy—a weightlifter, a college fullback at the University of Utah, a U.S. Army Ranger. He was used to being strong and powerful.

And he couldn't even lift his arms.

Whimpering in pain, he tried again ... and failed. His hands looked swollen—crimson surgical gloves inflated like balloons. He flexed his fingers, sending lances of agony through them. The pain shot up his hands and arms, twisting and clenching his back.

Jerry fought to draw in enough oxygen. Breathing was difficult, laborious. Wrong.

He smelled smoke.

And he tasted blood.

1

He couldn't feel his feet. Or his legs.

With a grunt of agony, he lifted his head slightly, trying to get a look at his feet. He couldn't see them.

But he could see the rope.

The thick rope led up to a group of pulleys dangling from the apex of a wooden frame.

And every bit of it was the color of blood.

Hanging by my feet. Like a hog in a slaughterhouse.

Blood pooling in my hands. My brain. My eyes.

"That's why . . . everything's . . . red," he mumbled aloud.

"Jerry?" The voice was soft, barely a whisper. "Jerry? Are you awake? Are . . . Are you all right?"

A shadow moved on the wall, man-shaped—or was it an antlered stag? Jerry blinked, trying to clear his blurred, blood-red vision—and even that was painful. The shadow resolved into a silhouette—a petite, feminine figure wearing a too-wide skirt. The shape of the girl, the dress, the hair was odd and old-fashioned, like something out of an old *Twilight Zone* episode. Not black-and-white, but black-and-red.

He'd seen her before. He'd been out jogging. At night. In the benches above American Fork. He'd practically run into her, almost knocking her down. She appeared so lost, so out of place. He instinctively wanted to help her, to protect her. He apologized for nearly bowling her over. She had such a dazzling smile in the moonlight. Such a pretty face. She laughed—a delightfully female sound—and dismissed his apology. She'd extended a hand and told him her name . . .

"E-Elaine?" he croaked. "Is that you?"

She took a step toward him. The brazier light illuminated one side of her face, the other was cast in shadow. The half he could see was pretty, the face he'd seen in the moonlight. For a moment, Jerry thought he saw that dazzling smile again, but it vanished.

Another step forward, and the other side of her face was revealed in the firelight. On that half of the face, the flesh sagged as if paralyzed, the eyelid drooping over a malevolent gaze, the lips hanging loose and lifeless.

Jerry wondered how he'd ever mistaken this creature for the pretty girl he'd run into.

"Elaine's not here," the woman said, shaking her head and glaring at Jerry with disgust and loathing. "You couldn't just pass her by. You couldn't just leave her alone."

Jerry shook his head. "I-I didn't do anything."

2

"You followed her," the woman said with exaggerated enunciation, the paralyzed side of her mouth unmoving. Drool spilled from her sagging lip. "You spoke with her. You were going to hurt her. You *all* desire to hurt her."

"No!" Jerry tried to twist, to shy away from the figure advancing toward him. "We just talked! I didn't touch her. I just wanted to help!"

The woman halted. She held up a knife. The blade was long and thick, gleaming a wicked red in the brazier light.

"I didn't touch her! I swear!"

The woman's shoulders sagged, and she nodded once. "I believe you, warrior."

Relief surged through Jerry, shaking him so violently he thought he might wet himself. "Th-thank you. I didn't hurt her. I didn't."

"If I cut you down," the woman said, "if I let you go, you must leave this place at once. Never return. Never speak of it. Never speak of Elaine again."

"Yes!" Jerry wept, tears streaming down his forehead. "Yes! Please let me go. I won't tell a soul!"

The woman stepped closer, raising the knife. Then she froze, turning her head as if listening.

"It's too late," said different voice, ancient and cruel — the rustling of spiders on grave clothes. "He is strong."

"But he weeps like a babe," the woman protested. "Surely he is not suitable."

"They all weep at this stage of the ritual," said the cold voice, "even the bravest of warriors. When they cannot resist, when they cannot fight back, they cry out for their mothers, for the arms that carried them, for the breasts that nourished them, for the lips that sang them to sleep. They cry out, but their mothers never come. Yet, there is courage in his blood. It will make the house strong. It will keep the invaders out."

The woman nodded. "As you say." She looked down at Jerry, and for a moment, her good eye softened — the other as expressionless as the eye of a corpse. "Good-bye, brave warrior." She turned and walked back into the shadows.

"No! Wait!" Jerry sobbed. "Come back! I . . . I'm not brave. Let me go!" He twisted, desperately, futilely trying to free himself. "Please! I just wanna go home."

A figure stepped into the firelight — not Elaine or the woman with the drooping face. The figure wore a long robe and its face was hidden inside a cowl. A large, black bird perched on its shoulder. The bird croaked once, like a black harbinger of death.

The cloaked and hooded figure walked with halting step and stooped posture. It carried a large bucket which looked like an old-fashioned tin washtub. The figure placed the tub below Jerry's head and hands.

Jerry tried to bat the tub away, but it was out of his reach. Excruciating pain and the pressure in his hands and head caused him to wail. Still he struggled to raise his hands enough to defend himself, to strike at the bent figure.

The ancient figure straightened a bit, cackling at Jerry's feeble efforts. "You *are* a fighter," it said in an aged female voice. The old woman raised a gleaming knife. "Your blood will make the house a fortress. Call for your mother, warrior."

And Jerry did.

The old woman grabbed Jerry's arm and slid the cold blade across his wrist. Jerry heard the sound of his blood spattering like thick drops of rain into the tub.

And Jerry felt a very strange thing. The pain, the agony in his hand and arm drained away. The relief, the sudden absence of pain, at least in that arm, was exquisite.

The hooded figure slit Jerry's other wrist, causing the pain in that arm to evaporate as well.

Then the crone raised the knife to Jerry's throat. She executed a quick, practiced movement.

Jerry saw a flash of metal glinting red in the firelight.

And the world turned to blood.

II

Peggy decided to check her pointed ears one more time. As she waited in the visitor parking at Derek's condo, she adjusted her Dodge's rearview mirror until she could see her own reflection. The elven ears were the most delicate part of her costume.

Delicate and *itchy*. The latex itched, like bees crawling on the backs and edges of her ears.

Ignoring the sensation, she turned and tilted her head, inspecting the ears in the mirror. Out of her long, flat, brown hair, the latex ears rose to pronounced but graceful points. The makeup blended well against her fair skin. The ears looked almost natural . . . for elf ears, at least.

Pretty good, even if I do say so myself, she thought.

She smiled, but that made her ears — her *real* ears — pull against the latex, pinching slightly. She winced at the discomfort, and the movement pinched even more.

Sighing and attempting to adopt an expression of elven serenity that she didn't feel, Peggy looked straight into the mirror. The makeup around her eyes was perfect — not too heavy, and just enough to highlight her best feature: her brown eyes. *My best feature?* she mused. *How about my* only *feature?* Pretty eyes in an otherwise plain face. *Plain as an old bucket . . . and getting plainer every year.*

Besides, whoever heard of a plain-looking elf? Or one that looks like she's on the wrong side of thirty? Or one that's "big-boned"?

Peggy wasn't fat — not even husky — but she'd never be mistaken for slender.

At least my ears turned out well.

And my eyes are killer*!*

When she was a little girl, she'd been told that her eyes were pretty. "Doe eyes," her daddy called them. "My pretty, doe-eyed Bambi," he said.

"Bambi's a *boy's* name," she said aloud at the sweet memory, her

5

cheeks coloring slightly, as they had when she was a child.

Her daddy would wink and gently poke the end of her nose. "No *boy* ever had such pretty eyes."

The recollection made her smile. A little. Then the latex pinched her ears again, and she smoothed her face.

Save the smiles for later. For Derek.

She sighed. *Not that he'll ever notice.*

She growled softly in self-reproach. *You're pathetic, Peggy.*

But I love him . . . even if he is making us late.

She checked the clock on the dashboard and pursed her lips in annoyance. "Come on, Derek," she muttered through clenched teeth in a low singsong voice. She drummed her fingers on the steering wheel. "The line is going to be naaaasty."

Maybe I should call him again. Or text.

Or maybe . . .

She snatched the keys from the ignition and shoved them into her satchel—the dark-forest green canvas bag she'd bought just for this outfit—and climbed out of the car (with decidedly less-than-elven grace). From the backseat, she retrieved the two long, curving, elven knives. They were the polypropylene movie-prop versions, not the steel versions she'd left at home—because convention security didn't allow *actual* weapons inside, no matter how cool they were. She slid the knives into the scabbards strapped to her back. She slipped on the quiver of arrows—once again props with rubber tips—and grabbed her elven recurve bow.

At least the bow is the "real deal."

Peggy closed and locked the car, took a moment to smooth out the wrinkles in her costume, and carefully brushed her hair behind her pointed ears. She took a deep breath, trying to muster an air of confidence.

Derek will never know what hit him!

She sighed. *Yeah, right.*

Peggy strode to the door of Derek's condo and rang the doorbell. She took a deep breath and got "into character." The truth was she'd been practicing her opening line for weeks. She'd waffled between quotes and near-quotes from the latest Tolkien movie, hoping to select the perfect words for Derek's first impression of her as Tauriel, the elven captain of the guard—a character that wasn't even in the book, but should've been, in Peggy's not-so-humble opinion.

First impressions are important. Maybe—just maybe—it'll make Derek see me in a whole new light.

See me, Derek.

She wiped her sweaty palms on her pants.

See me.

She forced a smile on her face, pinching her ears horribly. She ignored the pain.

Then the door opened, and Peggy's heart fluttered in anticipation. And there he was.

Derek stood in the doorway, dressed as a dwarf. And not just any dwarf—Derek was dressed as Kili, Tauriel's dwarfish love interest in the movie. Tauriel and Kili—a tragic love story, worthy of Shakespeare.

Peggy had made no secret of what she intended to wear. But Derek had just said, "One of the dwarves."

And he had chosen Kili.

Kili to her Tauriel.

Oh, please let it mean . . . what I hope it means!

"Wow!" Derek said, looking her over appreciatively. "You look . . . Wow!" He nodded, then shook his head. "Evangeline Lilly has nothing on you."

Peggy's smile transformed from forced to genuine. She bowed her head in acknowledgement. "You look great, yourself, Master Kili."

He chuckled and shook his head. "Not as great as you. Your costume is amazing! Mine looks cheesy compared to yours."

It was true, at least partially—Derek's costume, though good, wasn't nearly as authentic as Peggy's. She had sewn her own outfit, painstakingly replicating every detail from the movie. His was probably ordered off the Internet. And he hadn't paid a lot of attention to detail. For one thing, his short hair wasn't long enough. He hadn't bothered with a wig. But still, he was Derek, and that meant he was gorgeous.

"I think you look perfect," she said.

"How much did you spend?" he asked, still staring at her in awe.

Peggy opened her mouth to reply, but in that moment she realized he was looking at her costume—not at her.

Not at her face.

The pleasure that had filled Peggy at the sight of Derek-as-Kili drained from her like water from a wrung-out rag, causing the edges of the smile to droop. But she maintained a forced grin. *See me, Derek. Please see* me. She swallowed, took a calming breath. "Ready to go?"

"Sure. Just let me grab my sword." He turned and grabbed an altogether unconvincing plastic sword. He looked at her for just a moment longer. "Nice ears."

Peggy's smile brightened. A little.

As Peggy drove from Derek's condo toward the freeway, the conversation consisted of the typical light banter they engaged in at work—trivial, familiar, and comfortable, like the chatter of good friends who just happen to work in adjoining cubicles. Once they merged onto the interstate, heading north toward Salt Lake City and the convention, Peggy concentrated on her driving, and Derek grew silent. She glanced over at him.

He'd dozed off.

Peggy sighed in annoyance.

She drove in silence for several minutes, until another car made an abrupt lane change right in front of them. Peggy tapped on the brakes to avoid a collision, and the sudden change in momentum jolted Derek back awake.

He rubbed his eyes and yawned. "Sorry. I was up late."

She glanced at him sideways. "Video-game?"

"Reading." Derek shook his head. "Besides, you've been known to do a few marathon gaming sessions, yourself."

Peggy laughed and nodded. "Okay! I'm not one to talk about video-games. But today is the *con!*" She imbued that last word with all the awe and mystery such a magical gathering deserved.

"Yeah." Derek scratched at his scraggly beard.

"So . . . whatchya readin'?" Whatever it was, Peggy was going to make darn sure she read it too. *So we'll have that in common as well.*

"Can't tell you." He lifted one corner of his mouth in a sly smile. "If I did—"

"You'd have to kill me," Peggy deadpanned, finishing the tired, familiar joke.

Derek grinned. "That's right, Carter."

Carson, she mentally corrected. *Not Peggy* Carter. *Not the comic book character. Peggy* Carson.

Another old joke between them—Peggy Carter. Tauriel.

See me, *Derek. Please see* me.

"It's"—Derek winced sheepishly—"I'm reading the diaries."

Peggy almost hit the brakes. She looked over at him in shock. Her ears pulled painfully as her mouth opened wide. "You're accessing the docs from *home?*"

Derek shook his head, looking horribly affronted. "No way, Carter! You know that's against the rules. That's a contract violation!" He raised his nose to the sky and sniffed dramatically. "How could you even suggest such a thing?"

Peggy exhaled audibly. "Well, that's a relief!" All the documents she and Derek were digitizing at work for the current client were highly confidential. "Not only would it be a huge contract violation, but our client happens to be a *law firm.*" She let the last two words sink in before stating what should've been obvious. "If we access the files outside the office, they could sue us for every penny we have and every penny we would ever make for the rest of our lives. And they'd win."

She looked over at Derek. "You're not accessing the files from home, are you?"

Although he wore a guilty expression, Derek shook his head vehemently. "No."

"Then why do you look like a little boy who just got caught with his hand in the cookie jar?"

He shrugged. Then his lips curled up in a sheepish half-grin. "I . . . brought the diaries home. You know — the actual books."

"You did *what?*" Peggy was shocked. No, she was more than shocked; she was angry. And frightened. "Why?"

Derek raised his hands in a placating gesture. "Don't be upset."

"Upset?" The word didn't even begin to describe how she felt. "How could you . . . ? We could all be . . ." She pounded a fist against the steering wheel. Her ears pinched sharply. And on top of everything, she was fighting tears of frustration that could ruin her makeup. *Really, Peggy? Worried about your makeup?* She waved a hand, fanning her eyes to dry the tears before they could spill. She tried to calm her breathing.

"Let me explain." Derek looked genuinely contrite. "I mean, I know I shouldn't have, but —"

"You're darn right, you shouldn't have!" Peggy couldn't recall a time she'd ever been so angry with him. *What a stupid, selfish, impulsive thing to do!* The betrayal stung the worst.

"I'm really sorry." He sounded so pitiful. "Please let me explain."

Peggy's heart softened. She was still upset, but . . . this was Derek. He could be oblivious, heedless of consequences, blind — he was certainly blind to her feelings for him — but he was a good man, with good intentions. He was her best friend. And she loved him. She had to give him the benefit of the doubt.

She sighed. "Okay. So, explain. But it better be good." She tried to give him a stern look. She wanted to show him she was still mad, that she hadn't already forgiven him, that he was still in trouble.

And of course, she failed completely.

Derek grinned—his big, unpretentious, joyous, innocent smile, all gleaming teeth and bright, shining blue eyes. And Peggy's heart melted. The last drops of her anger evaporated like dew before the sun of Derek's smile.

You're pathetic, Peggy.

"So," he began slowly, cautiously as if he realized that he was treading on thin ice, but at the same time just bursting to share something wonderful, "you know how I said the handwriting in the diaries was really, really similar?"

That was Derek's job: he wrote and tweaked the algorithms that allowed the company's software to decipher handwriting in the physical documents they were digitizing. Every person's handwriting was unique, and to ensure accuracy, each document required slight adjustments. Unless the handwriting was already in the database.

Peggy nodded. "Sure. You're analyzing a few diaries with similar handwriting. So?"

"Yeah! Well, it's not just similar—it's *identical*." He paused as if he were waiting for her to arrive at some epiphany on her own. When she said nothing, he repeated, "I-den-ti-cal."

Peggy glanced over at him. "So?"

"I ran the preliminary scan on one of the diaries, and I got an *exact* match."

"So? That happens, doesn't it? What's the big deal?"

"The big deal is that this only happens if the same person is doing the writing both times. Given a large enough sample, even a master forger deviates from the original. And that means the same person wrote the diaries!"

Peggy pursed her lips in annoyance. *So what?* "Okay. So, you've got a couple of diaries written by the same person."

Derek shook his head, a crooked smile on his face—a crooked smile that made Peggy's heart skip a beat. "Not just *two*, Carter. There are *six*."

"So what? I've managed to fill a number of journals myself. At least that many. You wanna read 'em?" *The last couple contain a lot about you, Derek. Not that I'd ever show them to you.* Peggy glanced at him again.

He bobbed his eyebrows a few times. Peggy couldn't decide if he reminded her more of Groucho Marx or David Tennant—silly or sexy or both. "Are *your* journals"—Derek paused dramatically—"each spaced sixty years apart?"

Peggy gave a scoffing laugh. "No." She looked at him quizzically.

10

"Sixty years?" Peggy opened her mouth to say more, but her breath caught. *Sixty years? Six of them?* "That's a span of . . . three hundred years."

Derek chuckled and nodded slowly. "Uh-huh. And all written by the *same person.*" He raised his eyebrows again and began to sing *The Twilight Zone* theme song. "Doo-doo-doo-doo, doo-doo-doo-doo."

A tremor ran through Peggy, part excitement, part vague terror. "Are you sure?"

"Yep. That's why I took them home. I *had* to be sure. She—the writer, that is—says the same types of things in each book, but the vocabulary changes. She talks about the city, the people, the flowers, the birds—she loves *crows*, of all things—'the glorious beauty of the world,' she says. She starts in the early spring—lots of talk about butterflies, trees, and flowers—and ends in the late autumn. Sometimes she changes cities, sometimes it's the same city. But she's describing different *eras.* The latest one was late 1950s or early '60s. Can't be sure. She *never* mentions the exact year. It's like she—"

Peggy shook her head emphatically. She scowled, and her ears pinched badly. She ignored the pain. "Just hold the phone!" *He's pulling my leg. He* has *to be.* "You want me to believe you've stumbled onto the diaries of—what? A time-traveler?"

Derek nodded vigorously. "Yeah! Something like that. Like . . . like a time-traveling princess."

"You can't be serious."

"I know what it sounds like, but I don't know how else to explain it."

"You're serious."

"Peggy, I need you to believe me." Derek almost *never* called her Peggy—it was always "Carter"—unless he was in trouble. "I'm not kidding you. This is like the coolest thing ever. And . . . I need to share it with . . . with . . . my best friend."

Peggy wanted to melt right there in the driver's seat. *His best friend. Not, "I love you." Not yet. But I'll take "best friend."*

For now.

"Okay," she said. "Let's say I believe you, and you're *not* just messing with my mind."

Derek grinned from ear to ear. "I knew I could count on you, Carter."

She rolled her eyes. "So what do you think she is? A female Doctor Who with a time machine that looks like a British police box?"

"I don't know. She never mentions anything about time-travel. She just always seems amazed at how wonderful everything is. And her latest beau. She falls in love in the spring. New guy each time. And she talks about whatever's new and popular. In the last diary, she was going on and on about TV and *I Love Lucy*. It was like she'd never conceived of such a thing as television. Before that, it was the latest plays by — and I quote — 'that scandalous Oscar Wilde.' I looked him up. I mean, I know he was a playwright a while back, but I couldn't've told you when. Oscar Wilde went to prison for being gay in 1895. 1895! I just barely started really reading the diary before that one. She mentions house slaves and the — "

"Hold on a second," Peggy said. "How do you know it's not just some kind of . . . elaborate hoax?"

Derek opened his mouth as if to say something, then snapped it shut. He scowled. His expression soon shifted from sullen to hurt. "Why would anybody do that?"

Peggy sighed. "Because they *can*."

"But that's just . . . *mean*."

"It's evil. It's like the people who write computer viruses. People who write viruses are as bad as pedophiles, in my opinion."

"But it seemed so real." Derek looked crestfallen. "And the stuff she talks about — I had to Google a lot of it." He paused. "And what good is a hoax buried in a bunch of papers nobody's supposed to look at? I mean it's all just going into a database. You tweak the algorithm, scan the book, digitize it, store it — that's it. Nobody's going to look at it ever again. Nobody's going to take the time to read the whole book, and definitely not more than one of them. Nobody's going to make the connection. I mean what're the odds anybody's going to see it?"

Peggy frowned dubiously. Her ears pinched. "It does seem like a lot of trouble to . . . It can't be real, can it?" *What's more likely — a hoax or a time-traveler?*

A hoax, obviously.

"If it is," Derek said, "it'd be the coolest thing ever!"

"Just promise me you won't go posting about it online, okay? Don't talk to *anybody* about it. We'd be in so much trouble if you did. Okay?"

Derek smiled. "Yeah. It'll be our secret. Just you and me, Carter."

"Just the two of us." She sighed. *Even if it is just a hoax, the secret will be a bond between us.* She smiled at the thought.

The smile pinched her ears painfully, and she winced.

But what if it's not a hoax?

III

Time-travelers were everywhere.

Normally, Peggy reveled in the frivolous fun of glorious geekiness characterized by a huge sci-fi/fantasy/comic convention. As they wandered down the aisles of the numerous artists and vendors, Peggy and Derek encountered orcs, dwarves, hobbits, elves—even a couple of Tauriels, though none nearly as authentic as Peggy herself—Jedi, Disney princesses—and one Disney prince—superheroes and heroines, steam-punk, anime, and of course, video-game characters. The quality of the costumes ran the gamut from wretched to sublime.

However, there seemed to be a glut of the various incarnations of the time-traveling Doctor and his female companions. Peggy was as much a Doctor Who devotee—known affectionately in geek circles as a "Whovian"—as the next fan-girl, but given the subject matter she and Derek had discussed on the drive from Orem to Salt Lake, the sight of time-traveler wannabes made Peggy uneasy.

"Can't be real," she muttered. "It can't."

"What'd you say?" Derek asked.

Peggy was surprised that Derek had been able to hear her over the din coming from the dense throng of convention attendees. The last thing she wanted to do at that moment was bring up the diaries again, not while she was trying to enjoy the con—and she'd done just that. "Nothing," she said, raising her voice to be heard.

"You're thinking about the diaries, aren't ya?"

She made a chopping gesture. "Not here!"

Derek grimaced. "Yeah. Sorry."

"Excuse me." A hand touched Peggy's shoulder lightly and timidly. "Captain Tauriel?"

Peggy turned to see a couple of teenage boys. Both were short—shorter than Peggy at least—and while neither of them wore costumes, they wore delightfully geeky T-shirts. One shirt featured a picture of Bilbo the hobbit, but was captioned with a *Star Wars* quote, "Judge me

13

by my size, do you?" The other shirt sported a picture of Kili with the caption, "Elf chicks dig me."

Peggy couldn't suppress a smile, even though the smile pinched her ears. "Cool shirts, guys."

One of them—the one in the Kili shirt—actually blushed. *He's cute,* Peggy thought, *for a kid.*

"Could we take a picture with you?" asked the boy with the spots of crimson in his cheeks.

"Absolutely!" Peggy smiled, ignoring the pain in her ears.

"Cool!" Kili-Boy grinned and fiddled with his cell phone, getting it ready to snap a picture.

The teenager in the Bilbo/Yoda shirt moved in on Peggy's right side. Derek, standing on Peggy's left, struck a pose.

However, Kili-Boy had a different plan. He handed his phone to Derek, saying. "Just tap this icon."

Derek stared at the phone, an expression of supreme annoyance twisting his face. Then he seemed to shake it off and stepped in front as Kili-Boy sidled up on Peggy's left. The three of them posed, with Peggy assuming a subtle (and less painful) "Mona Lisa" smile.

Derek aimed the phone. "On three. One. Two. Three." He glanced at the phone, checking the resulting snapshot, and grinned. "Here you go!" He extended the phone back to Kili-Boy.

"Thanks!" the kid said, taking the phone. He turned to Peggy, gave an almost courtly bow, and extended his hand, palm up. "And thank you, my fair Lady Tauriel."

Peggy laid her fingers on the boy's hand. It had been a long time—or never—since any male had called her a "fair lady." She nodded her head toward the kid. "My pleasure, young master."

The boy pulled her hand to his lips and planted a kiss on her knuckles.

Peggy gasped in shock.

"Whoo-oo!" the other boy catcalled. "Go, Jason!"

Kili-Boy—Jason—released Peggy's hand and stood, grinning mischievously. In a moment, both boys were walking away, ogling the picture on the phone.

Peggy stared after them, her shocked expression slowly changing to a genuine smile. *That was cool.*

"That was creepy," Derek said, sidling close to Peggy. His proximity bespoke both protection and territorial possessiveness.

Peggy reveled in Derek's attention, but said, "I thought it was sweet."

He stared at her, disgust souring his expression. "They're half your age."

Peggy pursed her lips and scowled. "Nice."

He winced apologetically. "You know what I mean."

Yeah, she thought, bile churning in her stomach. *I do. But I'm only four years older than you. Thirty to your twenty-six. I'm not that old. I'm not.*

She sighed. *You're pathetic, Peggy. That's your mantra – the story of your life.*

Without warning, she was fighting back tears. *Not now. Don't let him see you cry. Don't be pathetic in his eyes.*

She desperately needed to focus on something, anything else.

"Aw, gee," Derek muttered. "Not these guys again!"

Grateful for the distraction, Peggy surreptitiously waved a hand in front of her eyes to dry them. She turned and focused on the objects of Derek's disdain – a man and a woman, both in their thirties, dressed in new age garb. The pair stood in front of a table, listening as a vendor – a local LDS horror novelist – enthusiastically performed his sales pitch.

Six months before, at the fall convention, Peggy and Derek encountered the same couple. The four of them, Peggy, Derek, and the couple listened to the same vendor's pitch. When the author finished telling them about his books, Peggy was about to purchase one. However, the man, staring down his nose at the vendor, announced, "I am a pagan." He then proceeded to lecture the LDS author on the evils of Christianity, while extolling the superiority of paganism. Peggy got a very creepy vibe from the couple, and she chose to walk away, leaving the author to fend for himself.

Afterward, she wished she'd stayed. She wished she'd had some terribly clever thing to say in order to counter the neopagan's blather. She wished she'd stood up to the man. But she hadn't. She simply walked away, and Derek followed.

The unpleasant experience left a sour taste in both Peggy's and Derek's mouths, and it took many water-cooler conversations over the following week to wash it away.

But here they were again: the same two people, the same clothes, and the same hapless vendor. The identical irritating scenario was playing out just as it had half a year ago.

The LDS horror author, a gray-haired, portly man who talked with his hands like a Bronx Italian, finished his spiel with a leading question, "Could there be a path to redemption?" It was, of course, the same ending she'd heard the last time. His sales pitch complete, the author let his hands fall to his sides, and waited with a broad, expectant smile while the couple stared at him.

The woman wore a long, sleeveless dress of green fabric, embroidered with a bewildering muddle of Celtic and Wiccan symbols. Her long brown hair flowed down her back to the metallic-green shawl tied at her slender waist. Her features were delicate, her eyes brown. She would've been pretty — with an ethereal, almost elven beauty — if her face weren't frozen in a haughty, scornful expression. And though she was shorter than the vendor, she eyed the man with a condescension that left no doubt she was looking down on him.

Her companion had his blonde hair pulled back in a medium-length ponytail. He sported a goatee — very popular in Utah, although Peggy found that style of facial hair annoying and pretentious — especially on that particular face. The man wore a wide-shouldered doublet of green and gold over a white, lace-up shirt with billowing sleeves. Although his expression was a study in practiced *ennui*, he stared at the author with contemptuous, unblinking eyes.

After a long, awkward moment of silence, the author nodded deferentially. "Thank you for stopping—"

"I'm a pagan." The goateed man's tone was that of an aristocrat condescending to address a particularly malodorous peasant. "Redemption, sin, and guilt are false concepts, moral whips used to enslave the ignorant."

Peggy knew she should keep her mouth shut. She knew it was worse than useless to argue with people like that. She knew the only way to convey spiritual truth was to teach by the power of the Holy Spirit, and the Spirit did not abide contention. But she wanted so badly to put the guy in his place!

She opened her mouth to say something caustic, something she'd regret later, but Derek beat her to it. "I'll take one," he said.

The self-styled pagan's lips twitched. He grunted in audible irritation.

The author smiled at Derek. "To whom shall I inscribe it?"

"Make it to Peggy, please." Derek grinned and winked at her. Then he faced the couple. "Why do you do it? You stopped by last year. I saw you. I was there. You asked the man to tell you about his book — again. You listened to the man talk" — Derek pointed a thumb at the author signing the book — "then went into your 'I-am-a-pagan' shtick. If you're not going to buy a book off the guy, why pester him?"

Derek turned back to the vendor and paid for the book. "Thanks!"

"I assume you're Peggy?" The author smiled at her. She nodded and the author handed her the book. "I hope you enjoy it."

Derek smiled, then once more turned to the pagan. "Is that what your gods teach you to do, huh? Be a jerk? Or does it just come naturally?"

The goateed man bared his teeth. "You son of a b—"

"What'd you call him?" Derek scratched at his beard. "What'd you call your god? Carno-something . . . Carrot-Nose? Was that it? The great god Carrot-Nose?"

Peggy grinned surreptitiously, pinching her ears. *Derek's in fine form today.* She laid a hand on Derek's arm, leaned to whisper in his ear. "That's enough. You've made your point."

The woman snarled at Derek. "May Cernunnos make your phallus rot off!"

"Whoa!" Derek chuckled at the woman. "Hey, I thought Wicca was all about live-and-let-live. My bad."

This is getting ugly fast. Peggy grabbed Derek's hand. "Let's go." She began pulling him away from the escalating confrontation. "Come on."

Derek allowed himself to be led away. "Sorry. I shouldn't have done that."

"You didn't say anything I wasn't thinking."

Stewing in their own thoughts, they walked in silence down the row of vendors, pretending to look at the various wares.

It wasn't until they stopped to look at some oddly fascinating artwork featuring roller-skating zombies that Derek seemed to remember they were still holding hands. He twitched as if startled, then worked his hand free of Peggy's.

I don't have cooties, for crying out loud. She sighed. *Well, it was nice while it lasted.*

Derek looked at his hand—the one that had been in Peggy's only a moment before. He scratched his head, as if that had been the reason for pulling his hand free. "Uh, thanks for getting me out of there."

Peggy smiled. It was a sad smile. Her ears hurt. And her heart ached. She nodded once. "That's what best friends do." *And that's all I'll ever be to you, isn't it? See me, Derek. Why won't you see me? Why can't you see how much I love you?*

"You're the best, Carter." He put his arm around Peggy and gave her a chummy squeeze. "The best."

Peggy's heart pounded in her chest as if it were trying to escape, trying to get closer to Derek. "Derek, I . . ." *Not here. Not now.*

Maybe not ever.

"Ignorant Mormon trash!" A familiar voice.

Peggy glanced to the side. *They're baaack!*

With a sigh, she and Derek turned to face the pagan couple.

"Give it a rest," Derek said. "We just wanna enjoy the con. You go dance naked in the woods or whatever."

"You know nothing of the old gods!" the ponytailed man spat.

"Actually," Peggy said, "I probably know more than you. Cernunnos, right?"

The man glared daggers at her.

A small crowd had gathered around them, like schoolyard children anticipating a fight.

"Cernunnos," Peggy recited, as if challenging one of her more pompous professors back at BYU, "sometimes called Kernunno or Hu Gadarn, is the Celtic god of virility, fertility, animals, forests, life-in-general, and, of course, the underworld. The Horned God, consort of the triune Goddess. He's often promoted by neopagans as benevolent, but archeological evidence points to human sacrifice." She paused, savagely delighting in the crimson blossoming in the man's cheeks. "So tell me, Sir Pagan, do you build a wicker man each year and burn a loved one alive? I mean, that's what the Horned God demands to ensure a good harvest, right?"

The pagan's eyes widened in shock, then narrowed to slits of rage.

A few of the people surrounding them grinned. One of them—a man with a face that seemed oddly familiar to Peggy—actually applauded.

Derek clapped as well. "Way to go, Carter!"

Peggy grinned, ignoring her ears. *I'm going to regret this later, but that . . . felt . . . good!* "Told ya." She bowed mockingly to the Wiccan couple. "Now if you'll excuse us, good sir and lady, we'd like to get back to the con." She waved and tilted her head. "You two, have a nice day!"

The goateed man uttered a particularly vile oath. He balled his hand into a fist and raised it as if to strike her.

Peggy gasped and pulled back. Derek cried, "Hey!" and scrambled to get in front of Peggy.

The pagan bared his teeth and cocked his arm, but before he could punch Peggy full in the face, a strong hand reached out of the crowd and grabbed the pagan's wrist, freezing it mid-swing.

"Seriously, dude?" said the man who had applauded a moment before. "You're gonna hit a girl?" The man with the familiar face locked eyes with the pagan. For two very long seconds they stared at each other, the newcomer holding the pagan's wrist. Then the newcomer forced the pagan's arm down, twisting it.

The ponytailed man grunted in pain.

"You wanna hit somebody, take a swing at me." The newcomer released the pagan's wrist. "Otherwise, take your fancy-pants, girl-beating, tree-worshipping butt and walk away . . . while you still can."

The pagan growled and rubbed his shoulder. "You'll regret this. May Cernunnos—"

"Yeah, yeah," said the newcomer. "I'm sweating in my little Mormon booties. Now, go on. Get out of here."

The pagan woman let out a stream of profanity that made Peggy's pointed ears burn.

Peggy's defender shook his head in disgust and pointed at the woman. "She kiss you with that mouth?" he asked her companion. He turned back to the woman and said, "Luckily for you, lady, unlike your boyfriend here, I don't hit women."

The woman opened her mouth to respond, perhaps with another vile retort, when her companion grabbed her by the arm and ushered her away. She continued to pollute the air with high-pitched, four-letter words as she and her husband were swallowed by the crowds.

A muscular but rotund man wearing a convention security T-shirt that was at least two sizes too small and sporty a bushy beard and a mane of red hair walked up to Peggy, Derek, and the newcomer. "Everything okay here?"

Peggy's defender nodded. "Yep. Just a couple of village idiots getting schooled by a wise elf-maiden." He winked at Peggy. "We're cool, man."

"Okay." The security guard sounded disappointed that he'd missed the opportunity to break up a fight. "Enjoy the con." He turned and walked away.

"Thank you," Peggy said.

"You okay, Peggy?" her rescuer asked. "It *is* Peggy Carson, right?"

Peggy's jaw dropped. "Do I . . . know you?" She squinted at him. *He looks familiar, but . . .*

The man chuckled. "It's Todd. Todd Cavetto? We used to play D&D together back at BYU? You, me, Chancey, Christy, Paul, Steve? Half the time, you were the Dungeon Master, because you came up with the greatest quests."

The floodgates of memory opened, spilling images into Peggy's mind like water through a dam. Friday nights in the Wilkinson Student Center on campus, playing Dungeons & Dragons until security kicked them out when the building closed at midnight. Todd Cavetto was tall, handsome, with gorgeous blue eyes. Not the best player, but fun to hang out with. He was always yelling corny stuff like, "To arms, me buckos! Show the buzzards what for!"

She smiled wide, and she didn't care that her ears hurt. "Todd?" She threw her arms around his neck and hugged him tight. "It's so good to see you!"

Todd hugged her back. "Good to see you too, Peggy. It's been a long time."

Derek cleared his throat.

Peggy pulled away from the hug. *Man! His arms! They're all muscle!*

She gestured at Todd. "Derek, this is Todd. We were D&D adventurers back at the Y." She pointed at Derek. "Todd, this is Derek Rasmussen. We're . . ."

"Friends. Best friends." Derek shook Todd's outstretched hand, but stood as close to Peggy as possible. "Pleased to meet you."

To Peggy's ears, something in Derek's tone said he wasn't all that pleased.

"Pleased to meet you too," Todd replied. He looked at Peggy appraisingly. "Hey, you look fantastic! Tauriel, right?"

Peggy blushed. "You look great yourself." Todd wasn't dressed up—just jeans and a T-shirt, but he'd always looked hot to Peggy. Black hair, blue eyes, square jaw, tall, and solidly built. But he'd also never had eyes for her. He'd married Christy from their D&D group. "How's Christy?"

Todd's smile vanished. "She's gone. Left me. Left the Church. We're divorced."

"I'm so sorry." But part of her wasn't entirely sorry. *You love Derek, Peggy.*

I know.

Todd shrugged. "It's okay. *I'm* okay. No kids. Christy didn't want any, so . . . yeah." His face was impassive, but his tone couldn't quite hide the hurt.

Suddenly Peggy wanted to cry. *That's so sad. They were so in love. So happy. She attended their wedding in the Salt Lake Temple.* "Well"—she tried to clear the lump in her throat—"what brings you back to Utah?"

"I'm here with the Air National Guard on deployment for a couple of weeks. Hey, have you seen Chancey around here? We were supposed to meet up at the con today." Todd scanned the crowd.

"Chancey?" Peggy couldn't place the name.

"You know," Todd said, "from D&D. He was only with us winter semester, 'cause of football." He snapped his fingers. "No, wait a minute. We only called him that in the military. Back then it was just Jerry. Jerry DeChance."

Peggy nodded. "Jerry. Yeah, I remember him." *Nobody could forget Jerry DeChance – big, athletic, boisterous, funny, flirty, life-of-the-party Jerry. Played football at the U, but came down on Friday nights to play with our group, because he and Todd were missionary companions. Jerry wasn't interested in me – not in that way – but he was always nice to me.*

Todd looked at her hopefully. "Have you seen him?"

"Not since college. I'm sorry." As Todd turned his attention back to scanning the crowd, Peggy asked, "Is something wrong?"

Todd nodded, still searching the convention goers. "Yeah. He's active-duty Army. His unit was deployed down here TDY. We always chatted online. I know it's stupid, but I never got his cell number. We were gonna meet up here at the con after my deployment, so I took a chance. Problem is, he didn't show up for the last couple of days of duty. He's AWOL. And that's not like him."

He looked Peggy in the eye. "Peggy, I'm worried. I've got a really bad feeling. I'm afraid something must've happened to him."

IV

Derek just wanted to go home.

He wanted to get back to reading the diaries, to solving the mystery of the time-traveler. And besides, the day had been a total bust.

It was bad enough when that Todd guy showed up and ruined the con, making Peggy and Derek spend virtually the whole day looking for some guy named Jerry—who was a complete no-show, by the way—whom Derek had never met and Derek had no clue what the guy even looked like. That was bad enough, sure, but to top it all off, Peggy had practically ignored Derek all stinking day. She'd barely talked to him, spending most of her time going on and on about Jerry or catching up with Todd.

Why does that bother me so much? Derek wondered. *It's not like Peggy and I are dating or anything. It's not like I'm jealous, right?*

But that was just it. Derek *was* jealous and he knew it.

He tried not to glare at Todd as the three of them sat in a Provo restaurant eating Korean food—Todd's idea—the interloper on one side of the booth, and Peggy and Derek on the other. Peggy and Todd continued to alternate between reminiscing about college and marathon D&D quests and talking about the absent Jerry.

Todd tapped his chopsticks against his plate. "Jerry has an uncle in Pleasant Grove, I think. Maybe he went to visit him." Todd expertly picked a piece of kimchi out of one of the communal bowls and shoved it in his mouth. "I'll start there tomorrow. My guard unit flew out this morning. I got permission to stay behind for the con so I could meet up with Jerry. Well, that, and 'cause I actually live in Spokane and don't particularly want to fly all the way back to Alaska—that's where my unit, the 210th Rescue Squadron, is based—and *then* all the way back to Spokane."

"Spokane?" Peggy asked. "As in Washington? Your military unit is in Alaska, but you live in Washington State?"

Todd shrugged. "A lot of us don't actually *live* in Alaska—we just have to live somewhere close enough to fly from. When I can't catch a space-A military flight, I rack up a lot of frequent-flyer miles on Alaska Airlines." He paused. "Anyway . . . as long as I'm still here in Utah, I'll take another day or two and see what I can find out." He chewed his kimchi in thoughtful silence for a moment. "I just hope he's okay."

"Me too." Peggy took a bite of kimchi as well.

How can they eat that stuff? Derek tried not to wrinkle his nose in disgust. *It's rotten cabbage, for crying out loud! Okay, okay, it's* fermented, *like sauerkraut, as Carter would say, but it's still disgusting.* He fished some bean sprouts out of one of the small vegetable bowls. Unlike the various forms of kimchi on the table, at least the sprouts weren't fermented. They seemed fresh, if boring.

Why am I being such a selfish jerk? He was pretty sure he wasn't showing it on the outside—pretty sure—but his attitude definitely sucked. *It's not their fault. Just not great timing. Besides, if it were Peggy who was missing, I'd be . . .*

Still, if they're so worried about this Jerry guy, how come they're both wolfing down dinner like they don't have a care in the world?

Peggy picked up a piece of kimchi with her chopsticks and regarded it with a thoughtful expression. "You know, I always wondered—how do you know when kimchi goes bad?"

Without missing a beat, Todd replied, "When it starts holding up liquor stores."

Peggy snorted, then laughed out loud—her obnoxious, snorting laugh. When she really got going, she alternated between sounding like Goofy and a snuffling pig.

Derek had always thought of that laugh as annoying, but Todd was grinning from ear to ear. *He likes her laugh!*

Weird.

Peggy calmed down, her laughter diminishing to an almost girlish giggle. "You always did have an odd sense of humor." She sighed wistfully. "Hey," she said, setting her chopsticks down and placing her hand on Todd's arm, "I don't think I ever thanked you for coming to my rescue back there."

Todd shrugged and nodded in Derek's direction. "I saw Derek on the move to intercept that jerk. I was just in a better position."

Derek was surprised by the man's graciousness. It seemed genuine enough, but it had the effect of making Derek resent Todd all the more.

Cut it out! He seems like a really good guy. And besides, Peggy likes him. And maybe that's the problem.

Peggy turned her head and favored Derek with a smile. "Yeah. I saw you moving. Thank you, Derek."

He smiled back weakly but felt color rising in his cheeks. "I didn't actually *do* anything." When Peggy smiled like that, her whole face brightened and her eyes sparkled. When she smiled like that, she was almost . . . pretty. Derek focused on the bean sprouts again as if they were the most important things in the world.

"But you were *going* to do something," she said, "and I appreciate it." She lifted her napkin from her lap and dabbed at her mouth. "Now if you two gallant defenders of elven womanhood will excuse me, I'm going to visit the elven ladies room."

She slid out of the booth and walked away. Derek watched her leave — *Is she swaying her hips?* — then looked across the table at Todd. The guy stared after Peggy with what appeared to be a wistful expression.

Todd clicked his tongue. "You're a lucky man."

Is he talking to me? "What'd you say?"

Todd turned his face toward Derek and looked him straight in the eye. "You. You're a lucky man."

"What are you talking about?"

Todd jerked his head in the direction Peggy had taken.

Derek stared at him stupidly for a couple of seconds before he realized what Todd was implying. *Peggy and me? He thinks we're . . . a couple?* He glanced toward the ladies room. No sign of Peggy. He chuckled nervously and shook his head. "Nah. No way. She's not . . . We're not . . . Uh-uh. We're just friends. We work together."

Todd shook his head and grinned. "So you said, but . . . I've seen the way she looks at you, especially when she thinks you're not looking back."

Derek shook his head again and grimaced. "No. It's not like that. Peggy doesn't . . . And even if she did, she's not . . ." *Not what? Not pretty enough?* "She's not . . . my type."

Todd rolled his eyes. "You're an idiot."

"Hey!" Derek *really* didn't like the guy.

Todd pointed his chopsticks at Derek. "Listen. If a woman like *that* looked at me that way . . ." He shrugged. "Just sayin'."

Derek felt color intensifying in his cheeks again, but for a completely different reason. "If you think Peggy's so hot, why didn't you just snatch her up back in college?"

Todd grinned and tilted his head. "Because *I* was an idiot. And I never said she was hot."

You are seriously weird, fella.

Todd shoved a piece of spicy pork into his mouth.

How can he eat that stuff? "So . . . if you're worried about your friend Jerry, how come you're still hungry? I mean, excuse me for saying it, but if it was Peggy who was missing, I don't think I could keep anything down."

Todd shrugged and looked down at his nearly empty plate. "I'm a soldier. I've . . . lost friends before. You never get used to it, but . . . you've got to keep your strength up anyway. That's one thing you learn in a war zone where you never know if today might be your last day on earth . . . or your friend's last day. And if I'm going to look for Jerry tomorrow . . . I guess we all handle it in our own way."

I really am being a jerk! "Oh man, I'm sorry. That was a stupid thing to say."

Todd looked up from his plate and locked eyes with Derek. "Don't worry about it. Peggy's not showing it, but she has a tender heart. She tries to hide it. She's good at hiding her feelings . . . most of the time. She hasn't seen Jerry in years, but . . . she's feeling it too. And she'll feel it more as time goes on . . . as the *certainty* sets in. I'm glad she has you for a friend."

Wow. I sure haven't been much of a friend today. "You really think he's . . . ?"

Todd shrugged. "The Army's CID would've checked the hospitals already. They would've contacted the local police. If he's been AWOL this long . . . Well, no news is . . . probably bad news."

"You two look pretty serious," Peggy said, walking up to the table. "What'd I miss?" She settled in next to Derek.

And to Derek, it seemed like she sidled close to him—closer than she'd been all night.

He laid a hand on top of hers. "I'm sorry about your friend."

Peggy set her other hand atop Derek's, sandwiching his between the two of hers. She smiled at him. Her eyes were tender, soft, and glistening with the hint of threatening tears. "I'm sure he's okay. He has to be. Jerry's such a good guy." She turned her gaze to Todd. "Todd'll find him."

Derek looked at the man across the table, the man Peggy trusted. Derek felt a slithering of something ugly and dark in his heart. Then shame displaced the jealousy, shoving it aside—but not entirely.

He had a sudden desire to be a better friend, to *be there* for Peggy. "Hey, Todd," he said. "Where are you staying? Up at Hill Air Force Base?"

Todd shook his head. "Nope. We were actually deployed in the field—you know, in tents. I'm going to get a hotel for a couple days."

"Why don't you stay at my place?" Derek suggested. "I don't have an extra bed, but I've got a pretty decent couch."

Peggy squeezed Derek's hand. "That's so nice of you!"

Todd turned his attention to Derek. "That's okay. You hardly know me and . . ."

Derek gave him a lopsided grin. "Yeah, well, it's not for you, anyway. It's for Peggy. But any friend of Peggy's . . ."

Peggy squeezed his hand again, then she leaned over and kissed his cheek.

Derek's lopsided grin grew into a full smile.

It's good to be a friend.

🝊 🝊 🝊

With Todd settled in the living room and snoring softly on the couch, Derek was at last able to sequester himself in his bedroom with the wondrous diaries. He felt an electric thrill in his head. "'You're about to enter . . . the Twilight Zone,'" he said. He kicked off his boots and propped himself up on his bed. With trembling and eager fingers, Derek opened the fourth book.

The writer—who maddeningly, but perhaps understandably, never revealed her own name—had mentioned house slaves and some unrest "up in Massachusetts" with the British. Derek was fairly certain that meant the year was 1775, just before the Revolutionary War. *The Revolutionary War!*

Every sixty years. Like clockwork.

Four diaries—4 x 60. That's two hundred and forty years. That means she should be here now.

This year.

Here? Where's here? She could be in Boise or Tallahassee for all I know.

If she's real.

He shook himself. *She's real. And she's out there.*

He picked up where he'd left off, reading the delicate, feminine script.

Yestereve, I found a crow in our garden. Its wing was broken. Bran and Badh were pecking at it. By the time I shooed them away, the poor creature was bloodied in a dozen places. How it got into the garden, I do not know. Perhaps it broke its wing in the garden and couldn't escape.

I captured it and bound its wing with a silken kerchief so I could feed it. It didn't peck at me, even when I handled its broken wing. I gave it a bit of the dried fruit. No one saw me. (Oh, I hope my sister never reads this. She must never know. If she ever reads my diary, I will be undone! Undone! I know exactly what to do. I will entrust my diary to our solicitor before the harvest. I cannot leave it where Morgaise might find it.) While the crow slept, I reset its wing and rebound it. I think it shall mend properly now. I didn't need to use a leaf to revive it, because birds sleep no longer than a few moments. But the time I had was sufficient for what needed to be done.

The creature has bonded to me. It perches on my finger and allows me to feed it so long as I hold the proffered morsel between my lips. It makes such a delightful caw when it speaks. Of course, it cannot truly speak, nor even mimic as Badh or Bran do. I sing to it, and it caws happily to my song. It has become very dear to me.

I think I shall call it Percival.

I asked Morgaise—

A name! *Okay. So it's not* her *name,* Derek thought, *but it must be the older sister!*

I asked Morgaise if I could keep it. At first, she refused. However, in the end, she surrendered to my entreaties. She took one of the pair of stand-perches from the parlor, the ones the ravens use, and placed it in my boudoir. (How very fashionable French has become! I must say that "boudoir" is a silly word for bedchamber. Even now, I am laughing as I say it over and over. Boudoir! Boudoir! How very droll!) Percival looks quite contented indeed atop his perch in my chamber. The ravens will share a roost in the parlor until such time as we can procure another stand-perch. (I do not think they mind so very much.)

My sister is so good to me. She said that I am an overindulged child, but her tone spoke more of sisterly affection than of malice or resentment.

How would I live without her?

The answer is quite simple. I could not!

Again with the crows! What is it with this chick and crows? Derek had already gathered that the older sister kept a pair of ravens as pets. *Bran and Badh. How the heck do you pronounce "Badh?" "Bad" or "Bath" maybe?*

Derek thought the writer's kindness to the wounded crow was adorable. *It's like she's Snow White . . . only with crows instead of bluebirds.*

When he was little, Derek's family went to Disneyland. Six-year-old Derek was so in love with Snow White—he watched the movie *at least* once a day that year—he and his daddy stood in line for an hour, just so little Derek could meet her. And when they *finally* got to the front of the line and it was their turn to meet the young woman dressed as Snow White, Derek, who had whined and pleaded and fussed and jumped up and down trying to get the attention of the first, the original Disney princess, was suddenly so painfully shy, he hid his face in his father's chest and wouldn't respond when Snow White smiled and greeted him.

The photo (which his mom took, and Derek still treasured) showed a beautiful princess with fair skin, raven-black hair, and a dazzling smile, standing next to a rather embarrassed and frustrated father, holding a little boy in his arms—a little boy who wouldn't look at the camera. When at last his daddy shrugged, apologized, and walked away from Snow White, little Derek panicked. He screamed, wriggled out of his father's arms, jumped to the ground, and ran crying back to hug his beloved Disney princess.

The Fairest One of All smiled sweetly and bestowed a kiss on Derek's forehead, leaving the boy wide-eyed and openmouthed, blushing furiously, and solemnly swearing never to wash his forehead again.

Now why couldn't you get a picture of that, *huh, Mom?* He grinned widely at the memory, then plunged back into the diary.

My sister summoned our solicitor, Mr. Abbot, to the house today. She was very cross with him, the poor fellow. I know she is displeased with the house. The form of it is not quite suitable, I fear. Of course it's unsuitable, but what is to be done? Shall he arrange the purchase of another, more exact house? She quite took the man to task. He perspired profusely, had such a dreadful pallor to his countenance, and quaked so violently as he dabbed with a pocket handkerchief at his balding pate that I feared he might swoon or die right there in the parlor. He fell to his knees like a supplicant before a throne and begged for mercy. I could no longer watch the exchange and so fled the room.

I felt such pity for him, but the house should have been more exact.

Derek scratched his whiskered face. *What was wrong with the house? "More exact?" What does that mean? This Morgaise lady sounds like a real nasty character—like the Evil Queen in the fairy tale. I wouldn't want to cross her.*

But the truth was he fantasized about rescuing Snow White from the Evil Queen. *What would that make me? Prince Charming? A latter-day Prince Charming saving a time-traveling Snow White from her Sleeping Death?*

Yeah, right. Even if you know the when *— sort of — you don't know the* where.

Brushing his fantasy aside (for the moment), Derek turned his attention back to the diary.

After the solicitor departed, I—

The solicitor. That's like a lawyer, right?
The lawyer bought the house for them. The lawyer.
The law firm purchased that house.
Derek gasped loudly.

He snapped the diary closed with a loud smack and leapt off the bed. He tore his costume from his body, pulled on his jeans, and transferred his wallet and keys to his pockets. He yanked on a T-shirt.

Derek bolted from his room, slamming the door behind himself. He flipped on the living room lights.

From the couch came the sharp inhalation of snoring cut short. Todd scrambled off the couch and to his feet, staring at Derek in confusion.

I forgot about Todd!

"Everything okay?" his guest asked, looking quite alert for a man who'd been sawing logs just two seconds before. In fact, from his stance, he looked ready for a fight.

"Yeah. Sorry." Derek shoved his sockless feet into his tennis shoes. "Gotta go to work. Emergency. Make yourself — you know — at home. Eat whatever's in the fridge. Lock the door when you leave."

"Okay." Todd nodded and settled himself back on the couch.

Derek was out the door and dashing to his car, a single thought galloping through his head like Prince Philip racing to Princess Aurora's rescue.

The law firm buys the house!

V

Winslow Abbot nursed his fury. Anger was something he was used to. Anger was something he knew how to use. He could stoke his rage, heating it like magma in a volcano that always *threatened* to erupt, but never did.

"Keep your anger contained, but let it bubble near the surface," his grandfather would say. "Let them know that they must never cross you. Never. Make them absolutely certain that if you were to unleash your fury upon them, they would be utterly and violently consumed."

Winslow knew how to use his anger to great effect, especially in front of a jury or in a negotiation. In court, his closing arguments were persuasive, powerful, and nothing short of legendary.

Yes, anger he controlled. But not fear.

Fear was alien to Winslow, at least in himself. Fear was something he planted, cultivated, nurtured, and harvested in others. Other attorneys feared him. Judges feared him. Congressmen feared him. They knew what he could do to them. They knew the power he wielded, the power of secrets purchased with obscene wealth. They knew he *owned* them. They knew he could destroy them. Yes, people feared *him*, not the other way around.

But Winslow was terrified. And fear meant a loss of control. And that was something he simply could not tolerate.

And he knew just who to blame.

Storming into his grandfather's office in the old man's grand mansion, Winslow slapped the Sunday edition of the *Salt Lake Tribune* on the mahogany desk. He jabbed a finger at an article on page five of the "Local" section.

"Have you seen this?" He pounded his fist on the desk.

The old man glared at Winslow from under bushy white brows. He didn't even glance at the newspaper. Fury — the renowned Abbot fury — smoldered in his ancient eyes. His gnarled and age-spotted hand did not tremble in the slightest as it raised a cup of tea to his lips.

Thurgood Abbot sipped his tea serenely, but his eyes never blinked, never wavered from his grandson's.

Winslow glared back, absolutely resolute that his gaze would not be the first to falter, that he would not blink, that he would stare the nonagenarian down.

The two formidable lawyers stared at each other like statues, and time slowed to a crawl. Minutes could have passed. Hours. Eons. The sun could have gone nova, and neither would have noticed. All that mattered was the contest of wills.

That is, until a bead of sweat ran down Winslow's brow and into his eye. He blinked.

He had lost.

"Sit down," his grandfather said in a quiet voice—quiet, but brimming with peril.

Winslow collapsed into a chair in front of the desk. He looked around his grandfather's office, his eyes flitting from shelves of law books ancient and modern to priceless *objects d'art* to a huge map of the world studded with pushpins linked together with string—anywhere but at his redoubtable grandfather.

The elder Abbot said nothing, but Winslow could hear Thurgood sipping his tea. The sipping sound, the ticking of the grandfather clock, and the blood pounding in Winslow's ears, were the only sounds in the room.

When at last the old man serenely placed his teacup back in the saucer, he spoke. "Have I seen what?"

Winslow met his grandfather's gaze. Winslow's fury was gone. The old man's wrinkled face was kindly, indulgent. "Go on, boy." He waved at the newspaper on his desk. "Show me the reason you burst in here to interrupt my lovely Sunday morning."

Winslow nodded and pointed at a small headline.

Catholic Bishop Missing, Feared Dead

The old man nodded slightly, chewing at his lower lip. "I see. That was to be expected."

A chill froze Winslow's spine. "You knew?"

Thurgood shrugged. "I did not *know*. I anticipated. I still do not *know*, and neither do you."

"But his name was on that list!" Winslow spluttered.

"You mean the list that does not exist?"

Winslow threw up his hands in exasperation. "Yes, of course! The list of corrupt clergy and politicians who might be vulnerable to a-a-a . . ."

"A honey trap?" the old man completed.

Winslow nodded.

"What did you expect? You were asked to provide such a list, which you never did, of course. What did you think would happen?"

"Influence, manipulation, control—what we always do," Winslow said. "But not murder!"

The old man drew his lips into a thin smile. "If such a list existed—and it does not—and if we provided said list to our client—"

"*The* Client," Winslow interrupted.

The old man nodded. "If we provided it to our special client—and we did not—we have no control whatsoever over what the client does with such a list, assuming it exists, which it does not."

"But you knew it would be used for that!"

"I *knew* no such thing."

"But you anticipated."

Thurgood shrugged. "That would be consistent with the pattern." He waved vaguely in the direction of the map with its pushpins and connected points.

"If this ever gets linked back to us . . ." Winslow couldn't even finish the thought.

"It won't. And even if it did somehow, that would be far better than the alternative."

"What alternative?"

Thurgood Abbot looked his grandson directly in the eye. "Disappointing this particular client."

"Why? Is it the money? I know there's a lot of money involved—an incredible amount—but we have more than enough wealth to last us for generations."

Thurgood laughed. It was a harsh, bitter sound, utterly devoid of mirth. "You really have no idea, boy. This client's money *built* our firm and our family fortune many times over—and has for centuries. But it's not the money. It hasn't been about the money for generations. If it were simply the money, we would have—"

A knock at the door interrupted the old man.

"Come in," Thurgood said.

A thin man wearing the livery of a butler entered the office. He had gray hair, gray eyes, and an expression of constant indignation at the stupidity of the world. In a very proper and clipped British accent, he said, "I'm very sorry to interrupt, sir, but you have a visitor. She is *very* insistent. A Miss Morgan to see you, sir."

Thurgood sighed. "James, I don't entertain unexpected visitors at home on Sunday mornings. You know that. I don't care how insistent she is. Send her away. What do I pay you for, man?"

The butler glanced behind himself, listened for a moment, said something quietly to whoever was behind the door, and then turned to his employer. "She says to inform you that she is your client, that you will indeed see her at once, and that the name is Morrigan, not Morgan."

The color drained from Thurgood Abbot's face. "Y-Yes, yes, of course. By all means. Show her in, James, and . . . fetch us some tea and-and-and cookies." He stood and came around from behind his desk. "Yes. That's the very thing!"

The servant scowled, not even attempting to hide his disdain. "Tea . . . and . . . cookies. Very good, sir." He opened the door and stepped aside to admit the visitor.

She wore a wide-brimmed black hat and veil that completely shrouded her head, reminding Winslow of a beekeeper. Her floor-length, long-sleeved dress was all black—as if she were in mourning—and of a style that struck Winslow as something out of a Victorian funeral or ghost story. Except for her pale, dainty hands, not an inch of flesh was showing. She carried a small black handbag in one hand and a newspaper-wrapped parcel in the other. She wasn't tall—barely over five feet—and slightly built. Yet she was imposing, as if she were used to commanding attention . . . and obedience.

Winslow sat, staring at the woman and her strange garb, until his grandfather nearly shoved him from his chair.

"Get up, boy," the elder Abbot snapped. "Show some respect."

Winslow stumbled to his feet. Thurgood stood at the back of the chair Winslow had so unceremoniously vacated.

"Please, Your Majesty," the old man said, inclining his head deferentially. "Please make yourself c-c-comfortable. How may I serve you?"

The visitor turned her veiled head toward Thurgood. However, she extended the parcel toward Winslow.

"Remember, boy," his grandfather said. "Right hand only, and palm up."

This is The *Client?* Winslow remembered the oft-repeated instruction about receiving anything from The Client. He extended his right hand, palm up, and took the item from her. The parcel was long—nearly two feet—and about four inches in diameter, but surprisingly light. Winslow judged it to be around two pounds. Part of it felt wet, tacky. Winslow placed the parcel on his grandfather's desk. He looked at his hand. A dark, reddish-brown, viscous liquid smeared his fingers.

Blood!

He stared at the parcel in horror as he imagined a severed arm, hand, or foot inside the newspaper.

Is that thing *from . . . part of the missing bishop?*

He turned his gaze on the veiled face of the woman in black, unable to disguise the revulsion on his own countenance.

The woman sat in the proffered chair, her back regally erect, and placed her handbag in her lap. "'Your Majesty' is a title for a queen. I am not the Queen." Her accent sounded British—almost, but not quite. She opened the bag and retrieved a moist towelette from somewhere inside. She proceeded to wipe the blood from her fingers. "Pray that you never meet the Queen." She handed the gore-smeared towelette to Winslow.

He took the wet thing with trembling fingers. He quickly dropped the disgusting item atop the parcel.

"Yes, Y-Your Highness," Thurgood said, bowing to the woman. The old man tilted his head, looking to her expectantly, as if for approval.

The woman nodded slightly.

Winslow realized that bowing must be painful for his grandfather at that age—and Winslow had never seen the old man bow to anyone. It was difficult to recognize his powerful and imperious grandfather in the obsequious creature bowing before him.

"How may I serve you, Your Highness?" the old man said, straightening painfully. "Is the house not to your liking? The servants? The clothes? The list?"

The veiled woman waved a hand—the freshly cleaned hand—dismissively. "The house is *exact*. The servants will do for the moment, but only for the moment. You will find more suitable ones, servants whose devotion is more heartfelt than mercenary. The cost is not relevant, you understand. Their hearts are not right. You will correct this. Quickly."

Thurgood bowed again, although less deeply than before. "Yes, Your Highness. I will begin today."

The woman nodded.

Winslow tore his eyes away from the veiled face. He glanced out the window. A large, black car sat at the curb. A liveried chauffeur leaned against the car. Winslow had hired the staff for the house himself. They came very highly recommended. He was well aware the "chauffeur" doubled as an armed bodyguard.

"More heartfelt?" What was that supposed to mean?

"However," the woman said, "that is not why I am here." She pointed at the parcel on the table with the used towelette atop it. "Open it."

Winslow and his grandfather looked at each other, hesitating for the most fleeting of moments, but Winslow knew to whom the command — yes, "command" was the right word — was directed.

He turned to the desk and the ghastly roll of newspaper.

We gave her the bishop's name. And now he's dead. And there's some part of him inside. It's an arm. A forearm, maybe. It's long enough to be a forearm.

Winslow didn't want to open the package. He wanted to be anywhere but there, looking at that bloody parcel. He'd heard the rumors, of course — the half-whispered dark warnings, like ghost stories to frighten children. He'd heard his grandfather's oft-repeated instructions. The frequency of those instructions had increased dramatically in the past year. He could hear his grandfather's voice. *Never cross the Client! Follow the instructions to the letter! To the letter! Never, ever disappoint the Client!*

His hands shook as he flicked the bloody towelette aside and picked up the parcel. Not just his hands — his whole body trembled. *It's just a bit of flesh. Dead tissue. You wanted to be a doctor before your father forced you into law school. You can do it. Just unwrap it!*

He peeled back the newspaper, getting blood on both hands.

Whatever was inside, it wasn't the pale color of human flesh. *The bishop was a white guy, wasn't he?* It was black as night. Soft to the touch, yet rigid at the same time.

Feathers?

It was a large, black bird. Dead.

As he finished unwrapping the bird, the creature's head fell off and dropped to the desk. The black, clouded, lifeless eye stared at him.

A bird. Not a human body part.

Winslow stifled a hysterical laugh.

Just a bird.

"That is not Bov," the woman said.

Winslow set the bird's headless corpse back on the desk.

He turned to face her, or at least to face her veil. "I don't understand." He realized he was sweating profusely, breathing rapidly. And he still had an almost irresistible urge to laugh with relief. "What . . . What's Bov?"

"That, you simpleton, is not Bov." The woman's voice was cold, stern, but somehow not threatening. She sounded like a schoolteacher correcting a particularly slow student. "You were to provide two ravens."

Understanding dawned in Winslow's mind. The urge to laugh vanished. *One of the many, many odd requirements for the Client.* "Yes, two ravens, trained to talk or mimic. A mated pair. A male named Bran and a female named Badh." He pronounced the second name "Bad."

"It's p-pronounced 'Bov,'" Thurgood corrected.

Winslow nodded. "Bran and" —he cleared his throat—"Badh." He used the correct pronunciation.

The woman in black pointed a finger at the black corpse on the desk. "That is not Badh. That is not a raven. It is at best a craven. Do you know what a craven is, boy?"

Winslow shook his head.

The veiled woman sighed audibly. "A craven is a mongrel—a crossbreed between a raven and a crow."

Winslow's mouth was dry. *Don't disappoint the Client.* "I'll procure another . . . Badh."

"That is impossible," she replied. "Ravens mate for life. You will secure another mated pair, another Bran and Badh."

How in the world am I supposed to do that? We ordered those birds two years ago! Did the breeders have backups? "I don't . . ." Winslow glanced at his grandfather for support. The old man was shaking his head vigorously. He looked horrified at the very suggestion that Winslow might be unable to fulfill the command.

Winslow swallowed. "I will see to it immediately."

"Do not fail again." She gestured at the elder Abbot. "Explain to him the price of failure."

The old man flinched as if struck. He turned his face to his grandson, but his eyes were lowered. He let out a bone-weary sigh and raised his eyes to look at his grandson. Those ancient eyes looked haunted, dead. "Men came to our home in the middle of the night." His voice was lifeless as well. "My wife . . . your grandmother . . . my three daughters . . . my beautiful little girls . . ." He drew a hitching, deep breath. "As this year—the year we've prepared for all your life—as it drew near, your father . . . he couldn't face it. Not again. That's why he shot himself."

Never, ever disappoint the Client! Winslow thought he might be sick. His father's suicide had been hushed up. It had required enormous payoffs, but the man's death had been ruled an accident. *Gun-cleaning accident.* He'd swallowed the barrel of a Smith & Wesson.

Winslow shuddered. He thought of his own wife, of his two daughters. He turned to the veiled woman. "I will not fail you." His voice barely shook as he said it.

"Then you have gained wisdom this day," she replied. "Be grateful and thank the Goddess."

"Thank you," muttered the old man.

A knock at the door. James, the butler, entered, bearing a silver tray. "Tea and cookies, sir."

"Wonderful," the woman said. "I'm actually quite peckish."

She lifted her veil. Sunlight streaming through the window suddenly illuminated her face.

Thurgood's eyes widened in horror as if he were seeing a nightmare made flesh. "You!"

Winslow gasped.

One side of the woman's face was young, beautiful— with one shining grass green eye. Her lips were pink and full, her skin unblemished and fair, her cheekbone high and well defined. The other side sagged as if paralyzed or drooping with extreme age. It was as if a line had been drawn right down the middle of her face. On one side, loveliness and youth—on the other, lifeless flesh. She looked at the old man with one sparkling green eye and one doleful eyeball half covered by a drooping eyelid.

Thurgood Abbot shook violently as he stared, wide-eyed and openmouthed, at the woman. A dark stain blossomed on his pants, near the crotch. The wet stain widened and then ran down his leg.

Half of the woman's face smiled at the old man. "Hello, Thurgood. I'm so pleased you remember me. I certainly remember you."

VI

The parking lot at work was full. And that annoyed Peggy. It wasn't that she minded the walk of a couple of Provo city blocks. The walk wasn't even going to make her late for work. The spring weather was beautiful—a clear sky the color of a robin's egg, cool, but not brisk—even the air smelled of peach and pear blossoms.

No, the problem was that she had to walk by *the house*. It was that or walk all the way around the block. And that was something she definitely did *not* have time for. So, it was either walk by *the house* or be late for work.

Just go for it, she thought. *Don't be such a baby.*

As she approached the dreaded house, she tried to keep her eyes straight ahead and step as quietly as she could in her three-inch heels. *Why did I have to pick today to wear heels?* But she knew the answer—because Derek had only complimented her on her shoes once, and she'd been wearing heels that day. And this Monday felt like a *let's-try-to-catch-Derek's-eye* day.

Not that he'd notice anyway. That one time was months ago.

She'd worn a skirt and pumps at least once a week since then, but Derek had never complimented that or any other look since.

You're pathetic, Peggy.

Out of the corner of her eye, she saw that she was almost to the chain-link fence. There was no sign of *the beast*—the huge pit bull that patrolled the brown, pitted yard like a lion pacing in his cage at the zoo. Peggy had seen lions and heard them roar. Compared to *the beast*, they were harmless kittens, at least in Peggy's mind.

Peggy had always been afraid of dogs, ever since her parents gave her a boxer when she was a little girl. The dog never took to her—perhaps sensing her fear. It chased her, barking and snapping at her heels whenever she tried to feed it. She knew her fear was irrational, especially when it came to small, yappy dogs.

But *the beast* was no little boxer. That massive creature, with its

38

powerful jaws, really could tear her apart, leaving her horribly scarred, maimed, or dead.

Is it too late to pull off my shoes and make a run for it? She didn't care if she looked ridiculous, running flat-out in a skirt, but she didn't want to arrive at work with torn pantyhose. *What would Derek think of that?*

At least you might get there alive.

She was almost to the gate in the middle of the fence. *Almost halfway. You can make it, Peggy. Keep your eyes straight ahead.*

She passed the gate.

Maybe the beast is asleep. Maybe it doesn't know I'm out here. I put on too much perfume today. I just know I did.

It's not your perfume that monster can smell. It's your fear.

Out of the corner of her eye, she spied the far end of the fence. She quickened her pace.

Almost there. Almost there.

A flicker of movement from the back of the yard.

Peggy froze. She wanted to run, to flee, but she was rooted to the sidewalk as if her feet had been cemented there.

The dog never barked or growled to warn of its approach. It just charged.

In moments, the beast was up on its hind legs, clawing at the fence. Drool dripped from its fangs.

And then it barked.

Peggy's heart pounded like a sledgehammer striking from within, trying to burst out of her chest. She felt as if a scream was clawing its way up her throat, but her throat was clenched so tight, no sound could escape.

The beast snarled and barked and snapped—fury and murderous rage incarnate.

And Peggy was absolutely certain, in spite of all historical evidence, that *this* time the fence wouldn't be high enough or strong enough, that *this* time *the beast* would tear its way through or over and . . .

Peggy became aware that she'd dropped to a defensive stance, her knees bent, her left arm out to ward off the rending teeth of the dog— the dog that was on the other side of the fence, and had never once actually escaped, never gotten to her, never been able to attack her.

She fumbled in her purse for the small can of pepper spray. She couldn't find it. *Where is it? Where is it?*

Then she had the can in her hand, pointing it at the beast. Her hand was shaking so badly, she didn't think she could've pressed the button at the top of the canister, even if she'd actually needed to.

It can't get you! It can't. You're safe.

The huge dog continued to bark and snarl and claw at the fence.

Quaking like the leaves on an aspen, Peggy forced herself to turn and walk away. She wobbled on her high heels. In spite of her terror, she couldn't force her legs to go faster.

I'm gonna fall, and it's gonna get me.

It can't get you. You're safe. Just keep walking.

She forced herself to look at the last fence post.

Just have to get past the fence. It can't follow me once I get past the end of the fence.

It's like the bridge in Sleepy Hollow. Once I get over the bridge, the Headless Horseman can't get me.

The beast *can't get me.*

She counted the steps, wobbling all the way.

Inside the fence, the beast followed her.

When Peggy reached eleven steps, she at last got to the end of the fence. And then she was past it. She could hear the dog barking at her as she walked — faster now — but the sound faded. Somehow, having her back turned to the animal felt comforting.

Abruptly the barking ceased.

It's not behind me. It didn't get over the fence. It's not running silently at me. It's not going to attack me from behind.

Say it enough times and maybe you'll believe it.

When she was past the next house, she dared to glance back. The dog was back to prowling around its yard. *The beast* took no further interest in her.

Peggy forced her fingers to unclench from around the pepper spray can. She was actually surprised she hadn't dented it. Her fingers barely trembled as she stuffed the canister back into her purse.

Gotta find a better place for this thing. Someplace where I can get to it when I need it.

But spraying the dog wouldn't have helped. Peggy knew this from her research. She was always researching something, looking up things that crossed her mind, anything and everything, like useless facts about ancient Celtic gods. And she had spent a lot of time researching pit bull terriers.

Pit bulls were unusually insensitive to pain. That was one reason they got used in dogfights, because they didn't give up. And while most breeds of dog shied away from a human that had inflicted pain in the past, pit bulls didn't.

"I hate dogs!" she muttered. *Not just* the beast. *I hate the whole rotten species.*

When it comes time to go home, I'm definitely walking around the block.

When she arrived in the office, she hurried straight to the ladies room to check her appearance. The encounter with *the beast* had taken its toll. She was pale. Her hair looked windblown. And her eyes were swollen as if she'd been crying.

She hadn't—her makeup wasn't smudged—but she looked awful just the same.

At least I don't have pit-stains. She dried her sweaty palms on a paper towel.

So much for "Impress Derek Day." Can't a girl catch a break?

She dug her brush out of her purse and tried to salvage her hair with ferocious brushstrokes. She had only moments to beat her hair into submission, to work a miracle, and of course, a miracle didn't happen. She stuffed the brush back in her purse and frowned at her reflection.

Can't make a silk purse out of sow's ear.

It was a line from a play she'd performed in college. She'd been good in it too.

Yeah. You played a fat chick. Or at least a plain one. Now tell me that wasn't typecasting.

By the time she got to her cubicle, she realized that she needn't have bothered fussing over her appearance: Derek wasn't in his cube, the one next to hers.

I guess he's running late.

No, wait. His screen's on. Derek's current screensaver—a slideshow of images from the latest Tolkien movie—was running.

He's been here recently.

She looked down the row of the cubicle farm.

No Derek.

Peggy sighed and sat at her desk.

She logged in and began reading her morning messages.

"Hey, Carter! You okay?"

She turned her chair to face Derek, putting on her best smile. She was about to deliver a cheerful greeting, but it stuck in her throat as she got a good look at him.

Derek looked terrible. Dark circles rimmed his red eyes. He still hadn't shaved the scruffy beard he'd grown for the con. He looked like he hadn't slept in days.

And in his hand was a bottle of diet cola.

41

He's probably been up all night.
Derek said, "You look awful. You see a ghost or something?"
So much for that. "You don't look so great yourself. Bad night?"
He shrugged. "Frustrating night. I've been here for hours. Couldn't sleep."
"I'm sorry."
"Not your fault."
She smirked. "I'm commiserating, not apologizing."
He grinned back at the old joke. Then he took a long swig from his caffeinated soda, burped quietly, and muttered, "Excuse me."
"No excuse for ya."
Derek rested a hand atop the cubicle wall that separated his and Peggy's workspaces. "So what happened? You have another run-in with the hellhound?"
Peggy grinned sheepishly.
Derek shook his head. "He can't hurt you, ya know."
It was Peggy's turn to shrug.
"You gotta face your fears, Carter. You should just go stand in front of that fence and stare him down."
Peggy rolled her eyes. "That doesn't work with pit bulls." *Or any dog, where I'm concerned.* "So what's keeping you up? Is Todd a loud snorer?"
"Naw. Least not that I can tell. I left before he got up."
Peggy frowned. "I thought military guys got up at the crack of dawn."
Derek shrugged his shoulders again and took another sip of his soda. "Like I said, I've been here for hours."
That doesn't sound like you. "We're on schedule. You shouldn't have to be working extra hours to catch up." She squinted at him. "What's going on?"
Derek leaned his head out of the cube and glanced up and down the row, as if looking for prying ears.
Oh, no! It's more about those wretched diaries!
Derek placed his soda bottle on Peggy's desk, put a hand on the back of her chair, and leaned in toward her ear. "It's the time-traveler." His voice dropped to a barely audible whisper. "She's *here*."
Peggy's head snapped toward him. "In the office?" She felt as if the temperature suddenly dropped by twenty degrees.
Derek glanced around again, then leaned back in. "No, stupid. Here in Utah. Now."
"No way!"

"Yeah!" His whispering rose in volume as his excitement mounted. "It's been the sixty years. And I figured out that Abbot and Sons purchases the house the traveler lives in. The firm keeps moving around the country, opening new offices every sixty to a hundred and twenty years or so. I found a couple of memos from last year about purchasing a house here in Utah County. If I can find the real estate contract, I'll know where the traveler lives!"

Peggy groaned. *Why can't you just leave this alone, Derek? I've got a bad feeling about this. Or maybe, I'm just jealous.* "Okay, assuming you're right, assuming she's real" — Peggy held up a hand, silencing the protest she saw building in Derek's face — "why are you so hot to find this girl?" *I'm right here. See me. See how much I love you. Why do you need to find some girl you've never met? Some girl who might not even exist?*

I'm right here. In front of you.

I'm real.

Derek's face twisted into a grimace of frustration. "I don't know! Maybe, because it's *cool*. Isn't that enough?"

Peggy shrugged.

Derek's eyes were pleading. "If you'd read the diaries, maybe you'd see what I see."

Peggy felt suddenly tired, defeated. "And what's that? What would I see?"

"She's in trouble."

Peggy scanned his eyes, probing them, trying to understand his need. "What do you mean? If she's really traveling in time, wouldn't she — I don't know — escape from danger? Could that be why she's traveling?"

His eyes brightened. "It's her sister — her older sister. She's *evil*. I mean, the princess — the traveler — she thinks the *world* of her big sister. At least, on the surface. But reading between the lines . . . I just think the sister is . . ." He threw up his hands. "Evil. There's no other word for it. And she's *scary*. It's like she's the Evil Queen, and the . . . traveler, well, she's like Snow White."

Peggy waved her hands, causing Derek to step back. She stood, grabbed him by the arm, and began dragging him out of her cubicle. "Come on," she said.

Derek held up a hand, breaking free of her grip. "Okay. Just let me grab my soda."

Peggy led the way to the server room, not *intentionally* swaying her hips, but very conscious of the fact she couldn't help it in three-inch heels.

As they approached the room filled with racks of computers, Derek scurried past her, set his soda bottle on a table outside the server room—no liquids allowed in there—and held the door for her, grinning impishly.

Peggy suppressed a smile of her own. She was still upset with him, but he'd made a big deal about holding the door, and that gave her a small flutter of pleasure.

Following her inside, Derek shut the door. They were immediately cocooned in the dry coolness and ever-present white noise of the climate-controlled server room. Peggy walked the length of the room, glancing down the aisles between the racks of servers to ensure they were alone. Once she was certain, she stepped into the first aisle, motioning for Derek to follow. Although the room was all windows on two sides—allowing anyone walking by to see them—the noise of the air conditioners, dehumidifiers, and the servers themselves would allow them to speak without fear of being overheard.

Derek joined her, a mischievous smile on his face. "Ya know, Carter, people are gonna think we're making out in here."

Peggy almost slapped him. *You can be so infuriating sometimes!* Sneaking a kiss with Derek in the illicit, relative privacy of the server room was actually one of her favorite recurring daydreams. She looked away from him, fighting the sudden urge to cry.

"Sorry," he said. "I guess that's not funny."

If only you had a clue!

Struggling to contain a tear, she'd almost forgotten why she'd brought Derek in there. She cleared her throat, trying to clear her thoughts. But all she could see in her mind was the mental image of Derek's face close to hers as he took her in his arms. She cleared her throat again. *You've got this, Peggy.*

She turned her face back to his. If her eyes were red, so be it. "Please tell me you don't have some wild adolescent fantasy in your thick head about rushing in and rescuing your time-traveling princess from her evil stepsister!" Her voice was steadier than she'd imagined possible, given the emotions roiling inside her like dark, tear-filled storm clouds threatening to burst. But there was an edge to her voice as well—a harshness, even a bit of anger. "You have no idea what you're dealing with. You have no idea if she's even real."

"Peggy ..." His eyes communicated pain, confusion, even betrayal.

"And," she continued, rushing on, desperate to soothe his bruised male ego and, at the same time, to avoid causing him pain, "and ... it could be . . . dangerous. You said she has a new beau each time. What happens to them?"

Please, Derek. Let this go!

He looked confused. "I don't . . ."

She gently put a hand on his shoulder. She'd almost reached for his face. "I know you. I know the thought of meeting a real time-traveler is fascinating and cool and downright irresistible. But please, Derek, please—I don't know—just back off a little. Give yourself time to breathe. Promise me you won't rush off and do something stupid." *Something stupid and impetuous and dangerous and . . . romantic. Something romantic that doesn't include . . . me.* "You said she sticks around till the fall, right?"

Derek nodded. His giddy enthusiasm seemed to have deflated like a popped balloon. "Yeah. She stays till the harvest."

"Okay." Peggy tried to smile, not entirely succeeding. "So there's no rush."

Derek gave her a half-smile. "No rush."

"Okay, then. Let's get back to work, before somebody . . . gets the wrong idea."

Derek's smile widened. "Wouldn't want any rumors getting started."

Peggy turned and walked away before Derek could see her tears.

"Hey, Carter," Derek called after her, his tone suddenly serious. "Any word on your friend Jerry?"

Peggy quickly and surreptitiously dashed away a tear, before turning back. "No. But Todd's picking me up for lunch. Maybe, he'll have some news."

Derek wasn't frowning, not exactly, but he didn't look happy. "Todd, huh? Is that why you got all dolled up today?"

Peggy huffed in exasperation. "No!" *It was for you, you blind idiot.* "I dress like this once or twice a week. But thanks for noticing."

Derek shrugged. "You look . . . nice." He glanced away as if embarrassed.

Peggy smiled. She turned and walked toward the server room door.

And that time, it didn't bother her one bit that her hips swayed as she walked.

Not one bit.

♦ ♦ ♦

Todd twirled his fork without enthusiasm, wrapping pasta noodles into a spiral around it. Although there'd been some reminiscing and catching up, Todd and Peggy had waited until the "endless" pasta bowls had been served before talking about Jerry. Peggy intuited that, had the news been good, Todd would've told her right away, instead of waiting. In spite of all-you-can-eat Italian food, neither Todd nor Peggy had much of an appetite.

"I checked with his uncle," Todd said at last. "Jerry did stop by for a visit, but that's the last anybody's seen of him. CID's not talking, but that's pretty much standard operation procedure during an ongoing investigation."

"I'm sorry." She laid a hand on his arm.

"It's not like Jerry and I've been super close over the years. After BYU, we were at Fort Rucker together. That's where Air Force and Army helicopter pilots go for training. We've been facebook friends over the years, but that doesn't amount to much, not really. But when I read on facebook that he was going TDY — you know, Temporary Duty Yonder — to Utah about the same time as me, I reached out, arranged a meet-up at the convention. Still . . ." He paused, set down his fork, and placed a hand over Peggy's. "Thanks for listening. You always were a good listener." He locked eyes with her.

Todd's eyes were so blue. He had wrinkles around those eyes, as if he'd seen a lot trouble in his life.

He's been to war. And his wife left him. That's trouble enough for one lifetime.

Still, they're beautiful eyes. A girl could get lost in . . .

She looked away, embarrassed. "So" — she cleared her throat — "you really think Jerry's . . ."

"Yeah. I'm afraid so."

Peggy glanced back at him. He wasn't looking at her anymore.

Whatever that moment had meant — if it'd meant anything — the moment had passed.

Peggy stabbed at her food. "So now what?"

Todd shrugged. "Now I head home to Spokane. I have to go back to my civilian job. The Army's CID has resources I don't. A helo pilot is a valuable asset, a huge investment. They'll keep digging. But I've done all I can here."

"When do you leave?"

"I fly out this evening." He picked up his fork and shoved the spiral of pasta into his mouth. He chewed joylessly and swallowed. "I might come down this way and try again. I used half my civilian vacation days for this deployment. Civilian employers are supposed to give you the time off to serve, but the guard doesn't pay all that well.

So, I use vacation and get paid twice. But I'll stay in touch and let you know if I find out anything. I gotta say, I'm not holding out a lot of hope for a happy ending though."

Peggy bit her lip. "Jerry was always nice to me."

"Yeah." He looked up at her. "It's sure been good to see you again, Peggy. I wish it were under — you know — happier circumstances."

She smiled sadly. "Yeah. If you come to Utah again, look me up."

Todd returned the smile. "I'd like that." Their eyes locked once more.

And for just a moment, all thoughts of Jerry disappeared. For a moment, she wasn't even thinking about Derek.

Peggy's cell phone chimed out the title theme from *Star Wars*.

Text from Derek. She was mildly surprised that she resented the interruption.

She opened Derek's message and read:

FOUND IT!
Abbot and Sons didn't buy house.
They had it built!
I KNOW WHERE SHE LIVES!!!!

VII

The house was . . . *weird*. There was no better word for it.

Or perhaps, Derek thought, *there is . . .*

Exact?

Is this what "Snow White" meant by an "exact" house?

He sat in his car, parked at the side of a two-lane road in the rural Hobble Creek section of Mapleton near the mouth of the canyon. He stared down the slope at the strange house below. The house stood on a large grassy lot dotted with flowering trees. Derek scratched at his scraggly beard. He *had* intended to shave it off Sunday morning before church, but he'd been distracted, of course.

He'd also intended to simply drive by the house, just to verify its existence—just to prove *she* was real.

But once he got there and saw the architectural oddity of the building, he was unable to just drive on by.

Whoever designed this place must've been on some serious drugs. Is that a steeple or a belfry or what?

The house was a large, two-story, wooden structure, with a small tower in the middle of the roof. A lightning rod topped the tower. Twin circular structures, like silos, stood on either side of the house. A series of windows were placed around the silos at increasing levels.

Must be spiral staircases inside. That's the only thing that makes sense.

Not that anything makes sense about this place.

However, the staircases weren't the most bizarre aspect of the house, at least not to Derek's eye. The first story had two extensions jutting out at twenty-degree angles on either side of the front door. These extensions were longer than the house was wide. At first, Derek thought they might be twin garages, but he could see no garage doors and no driveways leading to them. In fact, the only vehicle that Derek could see—a large, black car nearly as big as a limousine—sat in front of the house in the circular driveway. A walkway went from the driveway to the house. There was no other pavement on the property.

48

Nowhere to park the car, except out front. Not even an unattached garage or barn.

Both the extensions and the entryway between them were covered by a gradually sloping roof. All the many windows — every single one of them — were secured with iron bars.

It's a fortress.

No, it's a cage.

It's a strange, butt-ugly cage.

Derek's gaze shifted to the tower. The rest of the monstrosity was dotted with windows, but not the tower itself. The tower had only a single window facing the front.

Is she up there? Is that her chamber? Her "boudoir?" Or is it her cell?

A princess imprisoned in a tower by the Evil Queen — the older sister which she praises to the stars in her diaries. But I can tell she's hiding something — something sinister. She's gotta be —

And there she was.

A lone figure strolled across the wooded back lawn. She wore a white, sleeveless dress with a full, mid-length skirt. Her long, flowing hair was a dark, tawny yellow, falling in waves to her slender waist. Her skin was pale, as if she rarely exposed it to the sun. She appeared to be barefoot, but from that distance, Derek couldn't be sure.

As she walked, she gripped her skirt in one hand and swayed it back and forth. The other hand waved in the air as if she were listening to music . . . or singing. She began to skip like a child. She pirouetted like a ballerina, her dress and hair whirling about her.

She's real. She's real!

Derek was enraptured, enthralled at the sight of her. He felt as if he'd stepped over a mystical bridge, through an enchanted portal, and into Faery — and was gazing at a fairy princess.

She was real, and he had found her.

The princess continued to dance and skip across the grass as if she hadn't a care in this or any other world.

She certainly doesn't look like a prisoner. She doesn't look like she's in any danger.

As elated and exhilarated as he was at the sight of the sweet vision before him, Derek realized he was also disappointed. This was not a princess in need of a valiant knight riding on a white charger to rescue her. This was no damsel in distress. This was a grown woman, obviously at home and comfortable in her own element.

His heroic, romantic fantasy slowly evaporating like the mists of Eden, Derek still couldn't tear his eyes away. He watched as the princess—she was still a princess in his mind, even if she didn't need him to save her—danced toward a ring of tall, standing stones. The circle appeared to be about three yards in diameter, with an earthen mound in the center. Just outside the ring, sat a huge black boulder.

What kind of stone is that? Black marble? Maybe it's a statue of some kind. Hard to tell from—

The stone came to life.

It moved, unfolding, rising up on four legs.

Bear!

Derek fumbled desperately with his seatbelt. *Gotta get to her! Gotta save her!* He had no idea what he could do—he was so far away—but he had to try.

But as soon as he scrambled out of his car, ready to charge down the slope to the rescue, he froze, shocked and puzzled by the scene below him.

The princess *hugged* the bear.

Only, it wasn't a bear. The creature—whatever it was—was huge, but it didn't rear up on its hind legs.

And it appeared to be licking her face.

A dog!

A massive black dog, bigger than any dog Derek had ever seen. Even with the animal standing on all fours, the princess hardly needed to bend in order to put her arms around the beast's neck. She wasn't afraid, and the dog appeared to pose no threat to her.

That thing is huge!

Unless she's really just a child . . .

No. She's got the curves of a grown woman.

"What do you think you're doing?"

Derek nearly jumped out of his skin. He uttered a very unmanly yelp and whirled to the left, toward the source of the question.

Peggy stood next to her own car, slamming the door. She planted her hands on her hips, looking furious. "Honestly, Derek! What do you think you're doing?"

"How did you find me?" he demanded. He was angry, embarrassed, and frustrated. "What're you doing here?" *You'll spoil everything!*

Peggy opened her mouth to say something, then snapped it shut. She crossed her arms under her breasts. "You said it was new construction, right? I'm supposed to be the database guru on our team—emphasis on *team*." She paused, then shook her head slightly. "It wasn't hard to find a contract for construction, not to mention a dozen or so memos. I *can* look stuff up in the DB. I'm not stupid. It's what I'm good at."

"I know you're not stupid. It's just . . ." Derek looked away from the woman right in front of him and focused on the enchanting vision below. The princess was sitting on the grass, the massive dog resting beside her. A huge black bird perched on her hand. It was too big to be a crow. *Maybe a raven? Bran or Badh or whatever?* The princess appeared to be singing to it, but Derek couldn't hear anything at that distance.

And for Derek, the image of Snow White solidified in his mind, like a Disney animated movie come to life. *Instead of a deer and bunnies lying beside her, it's a gigantic dog. And instead of a bluebird or a robin, it's a raven. And instead of jet black hair, it's golden brown.*

But it's her.

"Look at her, Carter," he said, his voice full of wonder. "She's real. Just like Snow White."

Peggy gasped. Derek looked at her and saw that she was pale. *Like she's seen a ghost. Or a dog.* "It's okay. I know it's big, but it's very gentle, at least with her."

"That's . . . a-a dog?"

"Yeah. I think so."

"Oh my, Derek. You were . . . right." There was an odd note to Peggy's voice. Instead of wonder or awe, Derek heard sadness, defeat.

He looked at his best friend. She *did* seem sad and tired. Derek felt a sudden urge to put his arm around her. "What's wrong? You should be happy. This is like . . ."

". . . the coolest thing ever," she finished. Her expression belied her words.

"Yeah." Derek turned his attention back to the princess. She appeared to be looking in their direction. Abruptly, the bird took flight and flapped off toward the house. The girl rose to her feet and waved her hand.

Derek's heart leapt. *Is she waving at me?* With palms that were suddenly slick with sweat, he shyly waved back.

The princess waved more enthusiastically.

She is waving at me!

He grinned like an idiot and waved with matching gusto.

The girl stopped waving and clapped her hands to her face as if in wonder or joy. Then she abruptly turned and ran toward the house, skipping as she went.

Derek watched as she disappeared into the odd structure. "Coolest . . . thing . . . ever."

"We should go," Peggy said.

Derek nodded. "Yeah, we should. I gotta go home. Get cleaned up. Shave."

"You're not seriously thinking of coming back, are you?" She was no longer sad — she was back to angry.

"Yeah." He was puzzled by her reaction. "What's wrong with you, Carter?"

"Wrong with me? Are you kidding? You have no freaking idea what you're getting yourself into! This is bad, Derek. *She's* bad. I can feel it. We need to get out of here. Now."

"What's with you, Carter?"

Movement below caught his attention. The black car was leaving.

Is she in that car?

Derek gestured toward the house. "You saw her. She was sweet, innocent." *Real.*

"And how would you know?" Peggy snapped. "You could barely see her from here."

"I *know* her," he said, "from the diaries. I know all about her. I know her innermost thoughts. I know . . . her *soul*. She's sweet. Perfect."

The car left the driveway and entered the road.

"Will you listen to yourself? You sound like some lovesick preteen, mooning over the latest movie space bimbo!"

Derek wheeled toward her. "Oh, yeah? You told me you used to have a huge crush on Han Solo. Or was it Chewbacca? I forget. What's the matter, Carter? You act like you're — I don't know — jealous or something."

Peggy stomped her foot and snarled.

"Careful, Carter. You'll break a heel."

Peggy wiped savagely at the corner of her eye.

Is she . . . crying?

"Hey." He took a step toward her, his tone softer than before. "I'm sorry. I didn't mean to . . ."

But Peggy wasn't looking at him. She stared past him, an expression of worry or even fear on her face.

Derek halted. He turned around to see the black car pulling off the road beside them. *The* black car.

In a moment, Peggy was at his side. She grabbed hold of his arm.

Derek wasn't sure if she was seeking protection . . . or protecting him.

The driver's door opened, and a man emerged from the car. He wore a black suit, white shirt, black tie, and sunglasses. To Derek's eye, the man was obviously meant to be a chauffeur, but he was big — tall and thickly built. He didn't look like a man who drove a limo for a living — more like a wrestler or an NFL linebacker or a body builder.

Or a bodyguard.

The man closed the driver's door.

He stood there for a moment, looking at them in silence from behind his dark sunglasses. Derek got the distinct impression the guy was assessing them, sizing them up, determining how much of a threat either of them posed.

Keeping his shaded eyes on them, the imposing chauffeur stepped backward and opened the rear door of the car.

"The Lady Elaine wishes to meet you."

When neither Peggy nor Derek moved, the man said, "You may leave your vehicles here, if you like, and ride back with me. Otherwise, you may follow in your vehicles."

Peggy tugged on Derek's arm. "Let's get out of here," she whispered.

Elaine! Her name's Elaine.

Pretty name.

"We'll" — Derek cleared his throat, feeling like a teenager addressing the father of his prom date — "We'll follow you."

The burly chauffeur nodded. "As you wish. If you will please follow me?" The man bowed deferentially, but Derek was certain that, while he was being offered a choice on *how* to get to the party, attendance was *not* optional.

Not that Derek would *dream* of missing his chance to meet "the Lady Elaine."

He scratched at his beard.

Wish I'd shaved.

VIII

The dog is not in the house! The dog is in the backyard!

Peggy's hands shook as she gripped the steering wheel.

But there's no fence to keep it in the backyard!

It could be right outside the car.

Peggy looked around in a barely controlled panic. She could see Derek's car parked just ahead of hers in the circular drive. She could see the black car. She could see the house.

But no dog.

It's crouching down, waiting for me. The instant I open the door . . .

Something tapped at her window.

Peggy screeched.

But it was only Derek. "You coming, Carter?"

Am I coming? Am I going to get out of the safety of this car?

She nodded, still gripping the steering wheel with white knuckles.

Why, Peggy? Why are you going to leave this car? Why are you going to brave that monstrous dog?

For Derek.

For Derek? He doesn't love you. He wants her.

Because I love him. Because I'm afraid for him. I'm afraid of what she'll do to him.

How can you hope to compete against a time-traveling princess?

He needs me. He needs me, even if he doesn't realize it.

He doesn't realize you exist.

I know. But if I love him – if I really love him – I need to be there for him. I need to make sure he's safe.

You? Protect him? As if. You're pathetic, Peggy.

"Carter?"

"I'm coming." She peeled her hands from their death grip on the wheel and turned off the car. She stuffed the keys into her purse, missing on the first try and jamming them in on the second. She unbuckled her seat belt, took a deep, trembling breath, and opened the door.

54

Derek offered his hand to help her out, but she refused it.

Why, Peggy? Because you're mad at him?

She managed to stand on legs that felt like rubber.

Though Peggy avoided meeting Derek's eyes, she could still see a shadow of hurt darken his features. Then it was gone. As he looked away from her, toward the house, his face brightened with eager anticipation.

He needs me. He does.

She nervously scanned the yard for the dog, but saw no sign of the beast. She reached inside her purse and, finding the can of pepper spray, gripped it tightly inside the bag.

The hulking bodyguard pointed toward the house. "If you will follow me, please."

To Peggy's ears, it sounded like an order.

The chauffeur/bodyguard led the way. Derek followed, with Peggy close behind.

Peggy hadn't paid much attention to the house up to that point. She'd barely noticed its odd shape, but when she looked up at it, all thoughts of giant dogs and comely time-travelers were washed away by a wave of *déjà vu* and nebulous fear. In some way she couldn't articulate, the house reminded her of the Shinto monkey Jizo statues she'd seen while serving as a missionary in Tokyo. And at the same time, it also reminded her of "Night on Bald Mountain" in Disney's *Fantasia*. She almost expected the house to unfold and transform into a massive Chernabog, the dark Slavic demon-god from that part of the movie.

As they entered the dark shade under the entryway roof between the two wings of the house, her nameless fear grew. The entryway was not lit, except by ambient light coming from behind them. Ahead, all was shadow and gloom. Peggy had never before in her life felt claustrophobic, but at that moment, she felt entombed, as if the two wings on either side of the entryway would slam together, trapping them inside. The space between the walls narrowed toward the dark-ness of the door, funneling them toward a portal she could barely see.

Goosebumps covered her arms, and she felt chilled to her core. It seemed as if she had a great weight on her chest, as if breathing was difficult. She wanted to turn and run—back to the safety of her car, away from this sinister house with its barred windows—away from the dog. She wanted to grab Derek and flee for their lives.

This place — it just feels . . . evil.

So go. Leave. Now.

I can't. I won't leave without Derek.

The bodyguard opened the front door and held it for them. Inside the door, she could see more light, but that light was far from inviting.

Derek stepped across the threshold without the slightest hint of hesitation.

But Peggy froze.

Run! Just go!

She gripped her purse and her pepper spray more tightly, took another deep, shuddering breath, and followed. She crossed the threshold, moving from darkness into dim light.

Once she was inside the relative brightness of the house, the oppressive fear that had gripped her eased somewhat. Compared to the bizarre exterior of the house, the foyer looked . . . ordinary.

A vase of fresh daisies adorned a small table, above which hung a painting of a woodland scene. The floor was hardwood of some kind. A wooden bench sat beside the door. Although she knew the house was freshly constructed, Peggy had half-expected antique furniture. However, everything looked very modern and very expensive.

Did you think a time-traveler would bring her furniture along?

The bodyguard closed the door behind them, shutting them in. However, Peggy shuddered in relief. *At least the dog is outside.*

The man pointed off to the right. "Please wait in the parlor. The Lady Elaine will receive you shortly."

Peggy followed Derek into a large sitting room. Sunlight entered through a pair of barred windows, dispelling the gloom. A wooden chair was placed under each window. In the center of the room sat a sofa and a loveseat, both of which faced a large, stuffed, wingback chair. Paintings of nature scenes were placed at intervals on the walls.

Paintings, but no photographs, no portraits.

No history.

The bodyguard took up a position near the window. He leaned against the wall with the practiced nonchalance of a cat watching mice. "Make yourselves comfortable."

Derek took a seat on the couch. He looked over at Peggy and patted the spot next to him.

Peggy, however, sat on the loveseat, deliberately placing herself where she could see Derek, the wingback chair, and the casually menacing guardian.

Near the windows, a doorway opened onto a spiral staircase. Peggy suspected that "the Lady Elaine" would enter from that direction. She glanced from Derek to the bodyguard and back again. Then her eyes were drawn to the staircase.

Derek appeared to be staring in that direction as well.

Time crawled as they waited in silence. The vague fear began to grow again, gnawing at Peggy's gut. And still the silence dragged on. Peggy's chest felt heavy again, and the air seemed to gel into an unbreathable mass.

Just grab Derek and go!

"Derek," she whispered, "I think we should . . ."

She saw the dog before she heard it.

The gigantic, black beast emerged from the stairwell doorway, padding silently on massive paws. It stood at least four feet tall at its powerfully muscled shoulders.

Terror froze the air in Peggy's lungs. She felt as if a scream were trapped in her clenched throat. She couldn't move a muscle.

The dog sniffed in her direction and then in Derek's, but didn't advance toward them. It simply waited in the doorway, watching them in silence.

"Gaius, *sede!*" The voice came from the direction of the stairs, from behind the dog. It was a strong female voice—the voice of a woman who expected and received obedience.

The dog sat on its haunches, but it did not turn its head toward the voice. It continued to stare at Peggy and Derek. It licked its jowls with a great, red tongue.

Peggy was absolutely certain that if she moved a muscle, if she even twitched, the beast would be on her in a heartbeat, tearing out her throat with its fearsome jaws.

"Do not be afraid of Gaius," said the voice. "She won't hurt anyone unless I tell her to."

Peggy ripped her eyes away from the dog and beheld the source of the commanding voice.

The woman was short, barely a foot taller than the dog. She entered the room from the stairway entrance, crossed to the wingback chair, and sat. She wore a floor-length black dress, loosely fitted around her slender frame.

But the woman's dress and her height barely registered in Peggy's mind. Peggy's attention was riveted to the woman's face.

Half of the face was young and pretty—or might've been pretty if she smiled. The other half sagged as if dead. Both green eyes—one bright and intense, the other expressionless—regarded Peggy for a second or two. The woman looked puzzled, as if she wasn't sure what to make of Peggy. Her nose wrinkled, and her lip—on the good side of her face—curled in distaste.

Peggy felt like a bug under a magnifying glass—a bug of no particular interest.

Then the woman's uneven gaze shifted to Derek.

Relief washed over Peggy the instant she was no longer being examined and weighed—and, she suspected, found wanting.

It's like half her face is . . . paralyzed. Peggy knew she should have compassion for the woman, but it was all she could do to keep her lunch down. *And her eye!* The eye moved, but it was devoid of emotion.

"Who are you and why are you here?" The woman's voice wasn't loud, but it was firm. The accent was vaguely European, but Peggy couldn't place it.

Derek stared at the woman openmouthed, looking more than a little panicked. "Uh . . . I'm Derek"—he swallowed hard—"Derek Rasmussen. And, uh, I'm here, because the Lady Elaine invited—"

The woman in black sighed impatiently, rolling her eyes. "Yes, yes, I know Elaine desires to meet you. But why are you here? Why were you spying on my sister?"

Derek looked at Peggy as if seeking her help. Then he turned his eyes back to the woman. "I . . . I saw her. I just wanted to . . . I saw her strolling in the yard. I just . . . I want to meet her."

The woman stared at Derek, her good eye narrowing. "You want to meet her. Why? Because she is beautiful? Because you desire her?"

Derek bit his lip. "I . . . I don't know. I've never seen her. Not up close. I was . . ."

The woman frowned, half her face twisting in contempt, danger smoldering in her good eye.

Help him!

"He was"—Peggy hesitated, sure she had to say something, terrified to say the wrong thing, terrified of angering the woman in black—"Derek was concerned for her safety."

The woman turned her split countenance toward Peggy. "Who are *you?*"

Peggy couldn't suppress a shudder as she came under that gaze of the unreadable eye. "I'm Peggy C-Carson. I'm h-his . . . I'm his friend." She struggled to keep a tremor out of her voice . . . and failed miserably.

The woman sniffed haughtily. "I despise nicknames. They diminish a woman. Your real name would be Margaret?"

Peggy shook her head quickly. "No. It's Peggy, not Margaret. My parents named me Peggy."

"I see. And why were you concerned for my sister's safety?"

Peggy shrugged nervously. "We saw the dog. Thought it was . . . a bear . . . or something."

Half of the woman's face smiled. "Ah. You saw Suetonius." She gestured toward the dog. It rose from its station by the stair entrance and padded over to sit by the woman's chair. "He could no more harm Elaine than could Gaius here." She patted Gaius on its head, scratching behind its ears.

The dog licked her hand.

Two dogs? There are two *of them?*

Derek laughed nervously. "Yeah. My mistake. I nearly ran down the hill to — you know — save her."

The woman in black raised one eyebrow. "Indeed? That would have been foolish. Suetonius would have torn you in pieces, young man. Molossii are lethal in battle."

Molossii? Is that the name of the breed? Peggy had compulsively researched dog breeds — she'd thought of it as trying to face her fear — and she'd never heard of molossii. *Is that Latin?* But then, she'd never heard of a dog that looked to be at least three hundred pounds and four feet tall at the shoulder.

"Foolish," the woman said, "but very brave."

A smile brightened Derek's face.

Even with a monstrous dog watching her every move, even sitting in a house which made Peggy feel so uneasy, even being in the presence of a frightening woman with a disfigured face, Peggy's heart skipped a beat at the sight of Derek's smile.

"Very well, Derek and Peggy," said the woman, "you gave me your names. I shall give you mine. I am Morgaise Morrigan. I am grateful, young man, for your courage — misguided and unnecessary though it was."

Morgaise? Isn't that a name from fantasy? From Arthurian lore?

Derek shrugged, grinning sheepishly. "Uh, thanks, uh, Morgaise. But, I didn't do anything."

"Nevertheless, you were willing to lay down your life for Elaine. Therefore, I will give you one piece of kindly advice: leave. Leave and never return. *I* protect Elaine."

Yes, Derek! Let's leave. Now. While we still can.

Derek looked stricken. "No. Please. Please let me just meet her. I . . ."

Morgaise shrugged, and an expression of sorrow passed across the good half of her face — passed and vanished as if it had never been there. Her good eye blinked, like a witch's wink. "Very well. Elaine desires to meet you as well." She rose to her feet. "I shall summon her. You may wait here. Gaius, *mane!*"

The dog glanced at its mistress, then turned its attention back to Peggy and Derek. It huffed once, flapping its mastiff-like jowls. Then it lay down where it was.

"Shawn," Morgaise said, "you may attend to your duties."

The bodyguard nodded. "Yes, my lady." He smirked maliciously at Derek and Peggy, then strode purposefully out of the room.

No! Don't leave us alone with that thing!

But Morgaise was already climbing the staircase.

When the woman in black was out of sight, Derek leaned over and whispered, "That's one big dog. You okay, Carter?"

No! I am most certainly not okay. I'm as far from okay as it's possible to be. I'm not even on the same planet as okay.

"Carter?" He was looking at her. And he looked worried.

For a brief moment, their eyes locked.

You care, don't you, Derek? But you'll never care for me that way.

"I'm fine." She wanted to plead with him to leave, to flee that house. But she knew it would be futile. *He has to meet his princess.*

Aren't you even a little bit curious, Peggy? Don't you want to meet a real-live time-traveler?

And part of her—a small part—was curious.

"Sorry about the dog," Derek said. "Why don't you come sit with me? I might not be much protection, but . . ."

Peggy shook her head quickly. "I'm fine. Just . . . promise me we'll—"

"Do you hear that?" Derek waved her to silence and turned his attention to the stairway.

Singing.

A soprano voice—high, clear, and ethereal—floated down the stairs as if born on wings of perfect song. Peggy couldn't make out the words—she wasn't even sure they were English—but the tune was vaguely familiar.

The dog lifted its head and turned it in the direction of the singing, panting eagerly.

As the singing grew louder, closer, Peggy recognized the tune. *"If You Could Hie to Kolob." But it sounds different, happier. And that's definitely not English.*

"Here she comes," Derek whispered in a tone of almost reverential awe as he rose to his feet.

Elaine swept into the room, finishing the last notes of her song. She was barefoot and wore the white sundress Peggy had seen before.

And she was lovely.

Long, luscious, tawny hair framed a youthful, pretty face. High cheekbones, bright green eyes, flawless skin, and a genuine, innocent smile so sunny it could melt a glacier. She wore no makeup. She didn't need any.

Peggy hated her instantly.

How could I ever hope to compete with that?

You can't, Peggy. You never could.

Elaine's pretty eyes widened with childlike delight as they alighted on Derek. She glided over to him, moving as gracefully as a ballerina. "Are you my daring knight in shining armor? The man who was ready to charge down the hill and brave a molossus to save me?" Her voice was musical, with a charming British accent. But the accent sounded slightly *off*, as if it not quite natural.

She sounds like Lindsay Lohan in that Disney movie.

Derek grinned like the proverbial village idiot. "I" — his voice squeaked like an adolescent boy's, and he cleared his throat — "I . . . Yeah, that was me."

Elaine extended her hand. "I'm Elaine. I'm just pleased as punch to meet you!"

Pleased as punch?

"I'm Derek." He took her hand as if to shake it, hesitated, and then bowed, lifted the dainty hand to his lips, and kissed it. His movements and posture were as awkward and unpracticed as those of the boy who'd kissed Peggy's hand at the convention.

But Elaine was delighted.

She giggled and blushed. "Oh, my! Aren't you the perfect gentleman! I thought true chivalry was dead in this century."

It was Derek's turn to blush.

Elaine favored him with a broad smile.

Peggy noticed for the first time that Elaine's teeth were slightly crooked. It didn't detract from her beauty — not one bit.

She's never been anywhere — or any when — *long enough to get braces. Did they even have braces in the fifties? That was the last time she . . . surfaced, wasn't it?*

Peggy's teeth were perfectly straight. She'd gone through the pain and humiliation of orthodontia all through middle school.

More than anything else, it was the imperfect smile that convinced Peggy they were dealing with someone who hopping through time.

With the kind of wealth this ugly house represents, any normal girl her age would've had braces — at least nowadays.

How old is she really?
When was she born?

Elaine looked to be around twenty—a grown woman, though still young. But she *acted* like a girl of fifteen—all innocent smiles and giggles and unpretentious sweetness. She turned her guileless, radiant smile on Peggy.

"And you must be Peggy! Not Margaret. Just Peggy. My sister told me." Elaine curtsied. "I'm so very pleased to meet you, Peggy."

Elaine extended both her hands toward Peggy. It was obvious that she wanted Peggy to take her hands. Peggy was forced to let go of her purse and the can of pepper spray inside. Elaine took hold of Peggy's hands.

A nervous laugh escaped Peggy. "Nice to meet you, Elaine."

She curtsied! Who does that?
Someone from another era, that's who.

Elaine squeezed Peggy's hands warmly, released them, and turned back to Derek. "It's lovely to make new friends, isn't it? We haven't been in town long, and I simply don't know anyone here. Do you two live in town?"

"Peggy and I live up in Orem," Derek said. "Uh, not together." He chuckled nervously. "It's not far."

Peggy saw an opening, a chance to get some answers. "Where'd you live before . . . before you moved to Mapleton?"

Confusion erased the smile from Elaine's face. "I . . ." She frowned and gathered her long hair in her hands. "I don't remember." She tugged at her hair. "Isn't that silly of me? How could I . . . forget . . . where I lived . . . before?" Confusion morphed into concern. "I should . . . be able to remember."

The huge dog, apparently sensing Elaine's distress, raised its head, causing Peggy to jump. It didn't growl, but its body tensed as if it was ready to spring up and defend its mistress.

Elaine shook her head abruptly, her countenance brightening. "I know! Let's have tea! Just the three of us. Oh, wouldn't that be delightful?"

Once Elaine was ebullient again, the dog relaxed, resting its head on its paws.

Derek shook his head and grinned sheepishly. "No. We can't. No tea. We're Mormons. We don't drink tea."

Elaine looked confused again. "No tea?"

Derek shrugged. "Sorry."

Elaine looked at Peggy. "No tea?"

Peggy forced herself not to stare at the dog. She managed a weak smile. "No. Thank you." *Wherever she was before, it apparently wasn't Utah.*

"Perhaps lemonade?" Elaine looked at each of them expectantly.

Derek nodded. "Sure. That'd be nice."

"Thank you," Peggy said.

Elaine squealed with delight. "I'll have Cook prepare some. But we simply can't sip lemonade inside on such a lovely day. Let me show you around the grounds. Won't that be fun?"

Her eyes went to Peggy's shoes. Elaine wagged a finger at her. "Oh, but you'll want to go barefooted, Peggy. The grounds simply won't do for heels, I'm afraid. You'll sink right in!"

Okay. The shoes were a bad idea all around, but I'll shred my pantyhose. And we need to leave!

And that might be the perfect excuse! "I don't think—"

"Oh, and your stockings too," Elaine said. She pointed back toward the front door. "There's a washroom just down the hall on your right. Can't miss it!"

No, no, no, no, no!

Peggy forced a polite smile, nodded, and turned away from Derek, Elaine, and the monster dog, Gaius. She literally bit her tongue as she strode down the hall to keep from muttering under her breath in frustration.

I hate her! She's too pretty, too clever, too . . . everything!

And she's dangerous. What happened to the other boyfriends? Derek doesn't stand a chance.

Is that the real reason, Peggy?

Does it matter? So what if I'm insanely jealous? Derek's still in danger!

🌢 🌢 🌢

As the three of them strolled through the backyard, Elaine extended the hand holding her glass of lemonade—the other was entwined in the crook of Derek's elbow—and pointed at an apple tree covered in fragrant white and pink blossoms. "That's Drusilla." She pointed at another tree. "And that's Abigail."

Derek raised an eyebrow and looked at her quizzically. "You gave the trees names?"

Elaine looked at him askance as if he'd uttered the most scandalous thing she'd ever heard. "Of course not! I didn't name them. What an odd thing to say!"

Derek sipped his lemonade as if buying time to think of a response.

Peggy, walking barefoot a couple of paces behind the others, hardly spared a glance at the trees with their all-too-human names. Her eyes were riveted on the dog. Gaius, the female, had remained in the house. But the male lay just outside the ring of standing stones. The dog's head was raised, its eyes watching them, watching Peggy — vigilant and alert. The beast was ready to attack at any moment, Peggy was certain.

"Okay," Derek said, "I give up. If you didn't name the trees, who did?"

Peggy forced herself to look at Derek and Elaine. The dog scared the living bat-snot out of her, but the sight of Elaine and Derek flirting tore at her heart.

"Why *they* did, silly goose." Elaine looked amused and puzzled at the same time.

"Who did?" Derek asked.

"The trees," Elaine replied. "All living things have names. Don't you believe that?"

"I suppose, but . . . how did you learn their names? Did they . . . tell you or something?"

Elaine shrugged. "Oh, not in words, perhaps, but I can feel it. I have an affinity with trees and birds and dogs. When a tree is ready to tell me her name, I can simply feel it."

"Do you know all their names?"

Elaine laughed. "Oh, no! Not all of them. Most of them haven't given up their secrets. Every girl has secrets, you know." She grinned impishly and winked at him. "It's what makes us so *mysterious*." She giggled.

Derek grinned at her stupidly, obviously enchanted with her.

"Speaking of names," Peggy interjected, "you said the dog inside — the female — was named Gaius. Latin, isn't it? Isn't that a masculine name? Wouldn't the feminine form be Gaia?"

"Oh, Peggy!" Elaine beamed her. "How clever of you! Yes, of course it would."

"But why call her Gaius? Did she . . . tell you her name?"

Elaine shook her head. "Of course not! Dogs can't speak. She's called Gaius, because . . . Well, it's a joke, you see. She's named after someone."

"Named after whom?" Peggy asked.

Elaine looked confused again. "I . . . I don't remember. I'm sorry."

Like she couldn't remember where she lived before.

"It's okay," Derek said, shooting Peggy a reproachful look.

Peggy stared back at him, openmouthed. *What did I do?*

Elaine's face brightened once more. "Do you want to meet Suetonius?"

Peggy shook her head vehemently. *No!*

But Elaine was no longer looking at her. Elaine's eyes were on Derek. When Derek hesitated, she said, "Oh, don't be silly. Suetonius is just a big teddy bear!"

She handed Derek her glass and skipped over toward the ring of stones and the "teddy bear."

At her approach, the beast stood up. Elaine bent slightly and threw her arms around the monster's thick neck. The dog, however, continued to stare at Derek and Peggy.

"You're just a big old teddy bear, aren't you, Suetonius?" Elaine said in a childlike voice. "You wouldn't hurt anyone, would you, laddie?"

She straightened, turned toward Derek and Peggy, and scratched the dog behind its floppy ears. She beckoned Derek and Peggy to come closer.

Derek glanced back at Peggy. He looked concerned.

Peggy's heart leapt. *He's worried about me. He knows I'm scared. He'll stay with me. He'll —*

Derek turned and walked toward Elaine and her giant dog.

Suddenly fighting back tears, Peggy followed.

"Suetonius, *sede!*" Elaine said.

The dog sat.

"*Sede!*" Elaine repeated.

The dog lay down.

It sounds like she's giving commands in Latin. Who does that?

Yeah, yeah, I know. A time-traveler.

Avoiding the dog, Peggy took a good look at the ring of standing stones. The stones were of varying heights, between seven and ten feet high. *They look like something from the British Isles. Like Stonehenge, only cruder — and no top pieces.*

And she names the trees.

Is she a Druid? Is that how she's jumping forward in time? Druid magic?

There's no such thing. It's gotta be something else. Something more rational.

And time-travel is rational?

Derek was petting the dog.

Peggy tried to look past that, to focus on something, anything else. She focused on the mound of dirt in the middle of the stone circle.

The mound was long—at least seven feet—but only about three

feet wide. It rose about half a foot above the grass. Out of the center of the mound sprouted a thin tree, perhaps a couple of feet tall. Peggy had the oddest feeling she'd seen that mound or something like it— minus the sapling—before. It hadn't been inside a ring of standing stones, but it had been . . .

. . . in a cemetery. It's like a freshly covered grave.

Peggy shuddered violently and dropped her glass of lemonade. The glass didn't break, but the lemonade spilled on the grass.

"Hey, Carter!" Derek called. "You okay?"

"I'm fine," Peggy lied. She bent her knees and waist and retrieved the fallen glass.

"Dogs make her nervous," Derek explained to Elaine. "She's scared of them."

"Oh, you poor dear!" Elaine started toward her.

Peggy held up a hand to stop her. "No, I'm fine. Really." She pointed toward the house. The back door opened onto a small wooden patio on which sat a small bench. "I'm going to sit down, if that's okay."

"Of course, it's okay," Elaine said. "But remember to mind your step. Gaius and Suetonius leave their gifts all over the yard."

Peggy turned and walked toward the house on wobbling legs. *Turn my back on Monster-Dog, and I still have to watch out for dog poop!*

As she walked toward the house, Peggy could hear Elaine giggling. *Honestly. I don't know what he sees in her. Other than she's beautiful and charming and dainty and a time-traveler. Everything I'm not.*

She stumbled, almost stepped in one of the piles of dog "gift," and her foot managed to come down on another pile.

Her face twisted in disgust. *Ew! Ew! Ew!* She pulled her foot from the brown, gooey mess and began wiping the foot on the grass.

I hate dogs!

Her eyes went to the impression her foot had made in the mess.

And saw a glint of gold in the midst of fecal brown.

Peggy bent to get a closer look. It was definitely gold.

You're not really going to touch it, are you?

Maybe not with my hands . . .

Cringing at the thought of what she was doing, she used her dirty toes to pull the metal free. Then she recommenced furiously rubbing her toes on the grass. As she did so, she took a better look at the gold.

It's a ring! Big, like a man's ring. It's badly scratched, but that's what it looks like.

She fought down a wave of nausea as she bent and picked up the gold with trembling fingers. She rubbed it on the grass and soon she was able to distinguish the markings on the ring.

A large "U," and above that, "2007."

A University of Utah 2007 class ring.

Peggy wiped her fingers on the grass, then walked quickly to the patio and the bench. Placing her glass on the bench, she sat with her back to Derek and Elaine.

U of U Class of 2007. Why does that sound familiar?

She stared at the single letter and the four digits, but found no answers. She looked up at the house looming above her. Then she looked down at the patio.

And something else caught her eye.

Dots of reddish brown on the visible part of the house's foundation.

She looked to her left and then to her right, her eyes following the concrete foundation. Dots of varying sizes were sprinkled all along it.

It looks like blood — blood sprinkled on the foundation of the house.

Blood. And a U of U 2007 man's ring.

Understanding bloomed in her mind, and terror seized her heart like a massive dog sinking its fangs into her.

She leapt to her feet, clenching the filthy ring in one hand. "Derek!" she yelled. "Can you come here?" She tried to keep her voice steady, to keep her legs from trembling, afraid they'd give way. "Please, Derek!"

Derek came trotting over. "What's up, Carter? You look like you've seen a ghost."

Peggy grabbed his arm with her free hand, squeezing hard. She lowered her voice to a whisper. "We have get out of here right now!"

Derek looked confused and angry. "What? No! We just met her. We can't leave—"

"Derek, please." She glanced back at the monster dog, keenly aware another dog lurked inside the house. And that didn't help her maintain any semblance of control. "Listen to me. Trust me. We have to leave!" She tried to pull him toward the house—the house guarded by a dog, the house where she'd foolishly left her purse, her keys, her pepper spray, and her shoes—but Derek was having none of it.

He tried to pull free, but she held on. "Why?" he asked. "Why do we have to leave?"

"Derek, please! I know what happened to Jerry!"

IX

The *dogs* ate him?" Derek's cheeks were flushed, his eyes blazing. "Honestly, Carter! That's the best you can come up with?"

Peggy looked around the office parking lot. One of their co-workers was a dozen yards away, walking to his car. From the way the guy stared at them, Peggy guessed he must've heard the two of them arguing. "Will you please keep your voice down?"

Derek snapped his mouth shut and scowled at her, then folded his arms and shook his head. "You drag me through Elaine's house, making lame excuses about having to get back to work—'It's an emergency,' you said—and when I ask you to explain, you say you can't talk about it till we get back here. Then you wouldn't answer your phone while we were driving. Well, now we're here, and all you have to say is, 'The dogs ate Jerry.' I know you're petrified of dogs, Carter, but come on!"

Peggy glanced in the direction of the nosy co-worker, but the man was nowhere to be seen. *Probably already in his car.* "It's more complicated than that."

"So . . . what? Jerry wandered onto the property and got eaten by big, scary Suetonius and Gaius? What proof do you have?"

Peggy opened her hand and showed him the golden ring. She'd done her best to wipe it with facial tissues on the drive back, but it still had bits of brown feces in several places. Worse than that, both her hands stank.

Derek stared at the contents of her hand. "What's that?" He wrinkled his nose. "And what's that smell?" He lowered his head slightly and sniffed at her hand, then snapped his head back in revulsion. "Gross, Carter! Is that dog crap?"

Peggy nodded, grimacing both in apology and disgust. "It was in a pile of the stuff."

"That's sick!"

"I stepped on it with my bare foot." She shuddered anew at the

68

memory. "Anyway, it's Jerry's. At least, I think it is. It's the right year, and Jerry went to the U. See the way the ring's all scratched up? I think those are tooth marks."

"So one of the dogs swallowed a ring. Dogs swallow lots of weird stuff. On my mission, I once had to pull a bologna wrapper out of a dog's butt. That doesn't prove anything."

"There's more." She closed her fist around the ring.

"If it involves more dog crap, I don't wanna see it. 'Cause that's what this is — a big, steaming pile of crap."

"Please, Derek! Please hear me out."

Derek's mouth twitched, and he turned his face away from her. Some of the anger bled out of his expression, only to be replaced by impatience. "Okay. What else you got?"

"There was blood sprinkled all over the foundation of the house."

That got his attention. "Blood? Are you sure?"

Peggy shrugged sheepishly. "That's what it looked like." *At least he's listening now.*

"You sure it wasn't just . . . red paint or something?"

"Who sprinkles paint on a concrete foundation?"

Derek rolled his eyes at that. "Who sprinkles *blood*? Are you saying the dogs ate Jerry and then spattered his blood everywhere? That makes no sense."

"Not the dogs. I think Jerry was killed first, and his blood was sprinkled on the foundation. Then the dogs ate his body." When Derek didn't respond, she continued. "Bones, ring, and all. Dogs eat bones, especially big dogs." *And those are big dogs!*

Derek's face showed his confusion. "So . . . you're saying they're— What? Practicing voodoo or something?"

"Not voodoo." She paused, knowing how the next part would sound. "Derek, I think they're Druids."

"Druids?"

"Yeah. Think about it. Elaine talks to the trees. Well, she gives them names at least. The Druids venerated trees. Then there were those standing stones."

Derek grimaced. He uncrossed his arms and scratched his beard. "Yeah. That was weird." Then he shook his head. "But Druids? In Utah?"

"Yeah. And there's the blood on the foundation. I remember reading that, in ancient Britain, the Celts used to put the blood of a warrior on the foundation of a castle or fortress. Jerry was in the army, so he was a warrior. Don't you see? And besides, do you think the idea of Druids in Utah is any more farfetched than time-traveling princesses?"

Derek nodded slowly, thoughtfully.

He's really considering it! Please, Derek! Please listen to me.

See me!

Not now, Peggy. Your love life isn't what's important here. His life-life is more important.

"Okay," he said. "Maybe you're right. But what about that mound inside the stones? It looked fresh. If you're right, and Jerry is dead, and Morgaise killed him . . . why not just bury him there? I mean, it *did* kinda look like a grave — a grave with a tree planted on it."

Morgaise killed him, but not Elaine? Well, it's a start. Peggy nodded. "That's what I thought, but I found the ring *in* the dog poop, so the dogs must've eaten part of him at least." *Poor Jerry! What an awful way to go!*

"But it doesn't make sense," Derek said. "Why not just let the dogs have *all* of him? I mean, that's one way to dispose of a body. And, that mound is out in plain sight."

"Maybe there's something else — some*one* else — buried there. Maybe it's just a really special tree. I don't know." *He's listening. He's really listening.* "Should we call the police?"

He shook his head. "And tell them what? That a time-traveling evil queen murdered your old D&D pal and fed him to her colossal dogs?"

Peggy shrugged. "We could leave out the part about the time-travel."

"What we've got so far is pretty flimsy. Just a scratched-up ring, some red dots that might just be paint" — a raindrop hit his face — "and if it's blood, it'll get washed away when it rains." Another couple of drops struck him. "So, a ring, spots, and a wild theory. That's not much."

"You're right," she said. A few drops hit her as well. *When did the sky get so dark? It was sunny when we were at Elaine's house.* "It's not much. But I should call Todd at least, and let him know what we've got."

"Whoa!" Derek grabbed her by the shoulders. "You can't do that!" His voice took on a pleading tone. "It's *our* secret, Carter. Just you and me, remember?" The hint of a smile lifted the corners of his mouth.

An answering smile tugged at her mouth as well. Peggy almost relented. *But Todd needs to know.* "Even if I don't tell Todd about the time-travel, he still has a right to know about Jerry."

Derek looked horrified. "No! They'll come and . . . take Elaine away."

"But if they killed Jerry—"

Derek shook his head emphatically. "Elaine had nothing to do with that! It was all that creepy woman—that Morgaise."

Peggy stepped back, freeing herself from Derek's hands. "You don't know that. Elaine's part of it too. She has to be. There's no way—"

"No way! You met her. She's so sweet and innocent. She wouldn't hurt a fly."

He sounds like Norman Bates in Psycho. "Derek, you don't know that! What happened to the other boyfriends? What happened to *them*, huh?"

"Isn't it obvious? *Morgaise* killed them. She probably fed *them* to the dogs too." He paused and looked up, away from Peggy. Resolution hardened his features as more raindrops drizzled his face. "I've got to get Elaine away from that evil witch!"

"What?" Peggy couldn't believe what she was hearing. "You can't be serious!"

"Oh, yes. I'm deadly serious." He lowered his face back to Peggy's. "I told you I could sense Elaine was hiding something in her diaries. She's afraid of her sister. I *know* she is. And I'm going to save her!"

"No! You can't go back there. You need to stay away. Listen, I'll call Todd and—"

Derek's face twisted in disgust. "Oh ... my ... gosh! Todd was right!"

"What? What are you talking about?"

Derek nodded, and his expression darkened. "You're *jealous*! You just want to keep me away from Elaine. Todd said you were in love with me. I didn't want to believe it. But you are!" He scowled. "Well, give it up, Peggy. It's *not* going to happen."

Tears spilled from Peggy's eyes, mingling with the rain spattering her face. "Derek, please! Don't go back there. Please! She's dangerous!" She reached for him with her empty hand, but Derek took a step back.

He lifted his chin and stared at her with contempt. "You'd say *anything* to keep me away from Elaine."

"Derek, please!" She was sobbing, desperately pleading with him. "Please don't go back there. She'll kill you!"

"You're pathetic, Peggy."

Peggy recoiled as if he'd struck her. To hear those words—the words she so often repeated in her own mind—coming from Derek's mouth — it was as if he'd reached down her throat and ripped her heart out.

His rain-drenched features could have been made of granite. "Stay away from Elaine. And stay away from *me*." With that, Derek spun on his heel and walked back to his car through the pouring rain — rain that was washing away any trace of blood on the foundation of Elaine's strange house and taking with it all vestige of Peggy's hope.

Peggy gazed at his retreating back, making no attempt to control her tears or her ragged, hitching sobs. She mouthed his name, but she didn't call after him. Derek's parting words reverberated in her mind, tearing at her heart, chilling her soul. *Stay away from me.*

As Derek drove past her, he didn't spare her a glance. He just stared straight ahead.

She had become invisible to him.

You're pathetic, Peggy.

X

1955: Outside Portland, Oregon

Thurgood Abbot stepped on the shovel, attempting to drive it deeper into the soil. As he felt and heard the scrape of the shovel blade against yet another rock, he cursed softly.

"Mind your language, Thurgood." Morgaise Morrigan sounded amused, rather than remonstrative. "After all, you are in the presence of the holy father."

With quaking hands, Thurgood repositioned the shovel and continued to dig. "Yes, mistress."

"I suggest you apologize to Father Malloy," Morgaise's quiet, even tone made it abundantly clear that disregarding any such *suggestion* would be extremely ill-advised.

Thurgood paused digging and leaned on his shovel. He turned his head slightly—not enough to see anything behind himself, but merely to give the illusion of attention. Instead, he looked up at the full moon, at the stars in the clear night sky—a rarity in Portland—at the ring of standing stones that surrounded and towered above Thurgood and his nocturnal excavation—anywhere but at the woman with the half-dead face . . . or at the priest. "Forgive me, father"—Thurgood's voice was flat and expressionless—"for I have sinned."

The priest responded with a muffled whimper.

From the radio in the house behind him, Thurgood could hear the sweet harmony of the Chordettes as they sang their recent hit, "Mr. Sandman"—the very song Father Malloy had lambasted in his sermon that morning. The good father had pounded his pulpit, shouting, "The Devil's evil music, with its gyrating rhythms and suggestive lyrics will inflame the youth of our parish with the deadly sin of lust!"

Laughter born of mounting fear, hysteria, and irony threatened to rip from Thurgood. *And all the while, the holy father's been corrupting the morals of any pretty teenager he could lure into the rectory – anything with a ponytail, poodle skirt, bobby socks, and lipstick.*

But I knew that. I knew what he was doing, and I looked the other way.

And that's why I'm here tonight, isn't it? Because Hank Malloy couldn't keep his cassock on . . . and I pretended not to know.

Thurgood pictured his oldest daughter, barely twelve years old – too young for Father Malloy's taste. Thurgood shuddered.

But it would never have come to that. The priest would never have set his eye on Marietta, because we're leaving Portland. The new place has been chosen. After this abominable Covenant year is over, we're moving to Utah. All of us.

And the cycle will start all over again.

But I won't be around to see it. I'll never live to see ninety-five. Never live to see the Morrigans again.

Never again.

Thank God.

And which god would that be, counselor?

Thurgood resumed digging. *Don't think about that. Don't think about why you're here. Don't think about what you're doing. Just do what you're told. And look the other way.*

You're simply digging a hole in the ground. Nothing more.

Simply doing what the Client wants.

Don't disappoint the Client. Never disappoint the Client!

But Thurgood had done precisely that – he had failed. Worse than that, he had willfully disobeyed.

And the Client wasn't about to let him forget it.

"I made a simple request, Thurgood," Morgaise said.

"Yes, my Lady."

"And what was that request?"

As he continued to dig, he answered mechanically, "A list of local clergymen, preferably Roman Catholic, who . . ." Thurgood felt hot, moist air on his face. He looked up, and uttered a decidedly unmanly screech.

Directly in front of him, at the edge of the shallow pit, lay a massive, black monster, a deeper shadow against the blackness of the night. And out of the midst of the shadow, a pair of huge, dark eyes stared at him. The air suddenly stank of raw meat and sour breath.

The beast had made no sound, and Thurgood had been completely unaware of its approach. It was just suddenly *there*, staring at him, breathing on him.

And licking its jaws.

"Suetonius! *Immo!*" Morgaise snapped. "He is not for you."

The black beast huffed, flapping massive jowls, and lowered its head.

"Good dog," Morgaise said more softly.

Dog? Thurgood stared at the beast openmouthed. *The thing's as big as a bear!*

"Good boy," Morgaise said. "*Ede tuum bellatorem.*"

Thurgood froze. *Did she just say, "Eat your . . . warrior?" I can't have heard that right. I can't have!*

The beast commenced chewing on something white and vaguely spherical in shape.

Latin's a bit rusty. I must've heard wrong. That's it.

Thurgood didn't want to look—he was well practiced at not looking when it came to his clients, especially *that* client—but he couldn't tear his eyes away. He watched with mounting dread as the massive beast crunched into the white object. Thurgood recognized the familiar shape.

A human skull.

A second dog, nearly as large as the first, trotted into the circle and plopped down beside its mate. The newly arrived creature carried in its jaws a partial forearm with a hand still attached.

Thurgood fought the urge to retch.

Don't think about it. Just look away. Dig.

But he couldn't look away as the two giant dogs noisily devoured the remains of some nameless human being. *A warrior. Eat your warrior.* Thurgood felt as if he were cursed, under an evil spell, unable to do anything except watch the offal being consumed—including the bones—by a pair of ebony demons straight from the Bottomless Pit.

Muffled screaming from behind him broke the spell, and Thurgood ripped his eyes away from the ghastly scene. He turned around and gazed at last on Father Malloy. Anything would be better than the grim feast taking place a mere couple of feet behind him.

The priest was trussed up like a pig going to slaughter, his wrists and ankles bound with rope. A rope was also tied around his neck, but it didn't appear tight enough to strangle. He was gagged with a cloth stuffed in his mouth. Tears streamed from eyes wide with terror. With his back to the dogs, Thurgood could smell the sour stench of urine.

He's wet himself.

The good father was sobbing, pleading with his eyes, piteously importuning Thurgood for succor—and there was nothing Thurgood could do for him.

Impotent as a eunuch.

And above the wretched man in the putrid cassock stood Morgaise Morrigan, cloaked in her customary midnight black. The moonlight lent deeper shadows to the cadaverous side of her face. "I asked you a question, Thurgood."

A question? What was the question? He thrashed about in his mind like a man flailing his arms, teetering on a razor blade of sanity. The crunching sounds behind him and the muffled, frantic begging from the priest scattered Thurgood's thoughts like feathers on the light breeze. "Yes, mistress," was all he could manage.

What question?

Never disappoint the Client!

Keep the Covenant at all costs!

Morgaise sighed. "And you lawyers pride yourselves on your sharp minds. Very well. I shall refresh your memory. I made a simple request of you, Thurgood. What was that request?"

That was it! That's why I'm here digging the wretched hole while being slobbered over by man-eating beasts!

Thurgood swallowed hard, then recited, "A list of local clergymen, preferably Roman Catholic, who have a penchant for seducing young women. Or failing that, a list of bankers with the same predilection."

"And did you fulfill that request?"

Thurgood shook his head. "Not exactly. I supplied you with a list of bankers and clergy." He stared into the eyes of Father Malloy. "However, I purposely omitted the name of my parish priest."

The hogtied cleric whimpered.

"And why, oh why, Thurgood?" Morgaise asked. "Why would you do such a thing? Why would you ever consider betraying me? After all I have done for you?"

Why, indeed? "Because ... Because Hank Malloy is ... my friend. No, not even that. He's a fishing buddy. And I wanted to protect him." *Because my girls aren't old enough to catch his eye yet.* But as he watched the pathetic creature mewling and sobbing at him, Thurgood realized that he despised the lecherous cleric. He hated the man with every molecule in his body. *It's because of you I'm here digging this bloody hole.*

Thurgood's mouth was dry. He tried to work up a mouthful of saliva to spit at the holy father, but he couldn't. He settled for a contemptuous scowl. "All you had to do was keep your pants zipped." He turned his back on Father Malloy, doing his utmost to avoid looking at the monsters chomping noisily in front of him. He recommenced his digging. *I'm digging your grave, Hank.*

Nearly done. Not big enough for both of us, is it? Is it?
And it's so shallow. Why so shallow? It'll be sticking up above the ground.
I don't want to know. I just want to survive the night.
She won't kill me. She needs me. Doesn't she?

The larger dog, having finished consuming its ghastly repast, seemed to be eyeing Thurgood hungrily.

I don't want to die! Despite being a churchgoing man—the Abbots had been practicing Catholics for many, many generations—Thurgood Abbot was not a praying or believing man. But for the first time in his life of privilege and power and obscene wealth, Thurgood wanted to pray.

Please, God, don't let me die!
Don't let me be eaten by those creatures!

To his horror, Thurgood realized he'd said those words aloud. He froze, not daring to turn around. He began to dig with a speed born of panic and terror and lawyerly denial. He attacked the earth, stabbing it with his shovel. His heart pounded in his chest—a violent staccato rhythm keeping time with his desperate grave digging.

Morgaise laughed. Her laughter was neither cruel nor mad. Incredibly, she sounded as if she were genuinely amused. And she laughed heartily.

Thurgood continued to dig. At any moment he expected her to say, *Ede advocatum!*

Eat the lawyer.

When Morgaise's laughter died away, she sighed. "Oh, Thurgood! I thank you. I have not laughed so much in centuries." She chuckled once more. "I'm not going to *kill* you, stupid man. I've never killed anyone. I would *never* kill anyone—especially not you. You are . . . *useful* to me." Her voice hardened. "You are useful to me as long as you serve me *faithfully*—as long as your service protects Elaine." She paused. "You may stop digging. The hole is big enough. It is *exact*."

Thurgood planted his shovel in the ground and leaned on it, panting as if he'd just run three miles. He looked up just in time to see the last bits of what had once been a human hand disappear with a sickening crunch into the maw of the second beast.

She's never killed anyone? Does she mean personally? *Does she mean the* dogs *do the killing?*

"Why?" he began, but stopped. *Don't ask questions!*

"Why what, Thurgood?" Morgaise asked.

Idiot! Keep your mouth shut! Plausible deniability! He shook his head.

"It's nothing. I don't . . . Forgive me."

"Ask your question. I command it."

Fool! "Why . . . Why d-dig a grave if you're just" — he forced down the bile that suddenly filled his mouth — "going to feed him . . . t-to the dogs?"

"Very well, since you asked, and since I commanded you to ask . . . The first sacrifice is an offering of blood. The blood of a strong warrior — in this case, one Deputy Sheriff Jeffery Hallowell — is sprinkled on the foundation of the house, making the house strong and impenetrable. The warrior's blood keeps us safe. The warrior's flesh? Well, that is but meat for Gaius and Suetonius. The second sacrifice is a sacrifice of blood, flesh, and lust. A corrupt priest or banker — thus, the holy father here — is offered to the Horned King as nourishment for the sacred Tree of Life. Now, the third sacrifice — "

Father Malloy screamed again, cutting off Morgaise's grisly list. Thurgood heard a thud, most likely a savage kick to the man's gut. The muffled screaming ceased, only to be replaced by the priest whimpering once again.

"Silence," said a new voice, barely audible above the sobbing of the priest and the panting of the dogs. The voice was dry and cold and ancient, like the voice of something long dead, something that abhorred all living things. "You have said enough, Morgaise."

"Yes, Morgana." Morgaise sounded humbled, chastened.

"Go inside, child," said the terrible voice. "You do not need to witness this. Go and fetch the seed."

The seed?

"Yes, Morgana," Morgaise said.

"And you, lawyer," said the one called Morgana. "Do not turn around. It is death to gaze upon the face of the Queen."

Thurgood had no intention of turning around. Not then. Not ever. Not if he had to stand there for a century. He was certain he would gouge out his own eyes rather than turn and look upon the source of that cruel voice.

"Forget what you have seen and heard this night," said the voice. "Never speak of it. Not to your sons or your sons' sons. Not if you wish to live. Not if you wish for your sons to grow up to be" — a malevolent chuckle — "*men* like yourself."

"Y-yes, mistress."

"Cernunnos!" croaked the voice, "*Lig an Rómhánach cothaigh an crann na beatha!*"

A thump, then a muffled scream, cutting off abruptly, replaced by a sound that reminded Thurgood of someone gargling with mouth-wash . . . or blood.

And from the distant radio, the Penguins sang "Earth Angel."

Thurgood shut his eyes tight. Frantically, he chanted, "Hail Mary, full of g-grace. The Lord is with thee. B-blessed art thou amongst women, and blessed —"

The hideous voice chuckled. "You pray to the wrong goddess, lawyer."

Something heavy struck Thurgood from behind, knocking him down, forcing his face into the dirt. Ululating incoherently in unbridled panic, he flailed and kicked and clawed to free himself from the weight that pinned him in the open grave.

But he couldn't get purchase in the dirt. The mass atop him was wet, slippery.

At last, he forced his way clear to the edge of the pit. He flipped over to see what had held him down.

The priest. Or rather the priest's corpse.

Hank Malloy's lifeless eyes stared up at the moon. His throat had been sliced open. His cassock was soaked with dark blood and covered with wet earth.

One of the dogs sniffed at the corpse.

"Gaius, *Immo!*" snapped a voice.

Thurgood jerked his head toward the speaker.

Morgaise stood at the edge of the pit. And she stood alone.

The *other*, the source of the ancient voice, was no longer there.

Thurgood sobbed in relief. *It's not her! It's not . . . the Queen.*

Compared to what Thurgood's frantic imagination had conjured at the voice of the unseen *other*, Morgaise's half-dead visage was almost comforting. Thurgood dared not look around to see where the other woman had gone.

"Straighten him up," Morgaise commanded. "Straighten his arms and legs. And get the shovel out from under him."

Barely able to force his legs to support him or his arms and hands to obey his will, Thurgood did as he was told.

I didn't kill him. I didn't see him killed. I don't know anything. He glanced at his hands. They were covered with blood and dirt. *My hands are clean.*

"Clean your hands," Morgaise commanded. "Ensure there is no blood on them."

Thurgood wiped his hands against his pants. He examined them in the moonlight. "No blood," he whispered. *No blood on my hands. My hands are clean.*

"Here," Morgaise said, extending a hand toward him. "Place this on his belly. Be certain to place it in the blood."

In her open palm, Thurgood saw a tiny, dark object.

A seed?

"Take it," she commanded. "Be very careful. Be *exact*. Be quick. And stop shaking!"

He forced his hands to be still and took the seed from her palm. It looked like an apple seed, small and dark and wizened.

He turned around, and under the attentive gaze of the canine guardians, Thurgood placed the seed atop the corpse's blood-soaked belly.

The seed *twitched* between his fingertips.

He cried out, dropped the seed in the gore, and jumped back.

Before his eyes, the seed sprouted tendrils. The tendrils expanded, becoming roots that bored into the gore-soaked body of the priest as if they were soaking up the blood.

"Bury it," Morgaise said. "Be quick, man!"

Thurgood snatched up the shovel. He heaped dirt onto the seed, hiding it from sight. As he continued to entomb the carcass, it seemed to him as if the corpse began to dry up and desiccate before his eyes. The face shriveled like the face of an Egyptian mummy.

Thurgood scooped dirt over the face.

In an adrenaline-and-terror-fueled frenzy, he buried the corpse of his erstwhile friend, raising a mound of earth over the fresh grave.

And when Thurgood stepped back and leaned against one of the great standing stones, having finished his funereal task, he watched in horror as the center of the mound opened slightly, over the spot where the seed was planted. A thin sapling emerged. It sprouted leaves, growing impossibly fast. When it reached a height of six inches, the sapling's growth seemed to slow and then stop.

How could it grow so fast? Feeding on blood? What kind of tree is that?

"It is done," Morgaise said. Her tone was reverential, as if she were praying.

She called it "the sacred Tree of Life."

"You may go now," Morgaise said.

Relief washed over Thurgood like a warm rain, and his legs threatened to give way. He looked into her eyes, one stern, the other expressionless. "Th-thank you, mistress."

Half her face smiled. "Oh, do not thank me, Thurgood. You have disappointed me."

He sank to his knees and extended his hands to her in supplication. "I'm s-s-sorry! So sorry! Please d-don't kill me! Please, please don't kill me!"

She shook her head, one side of her mouth still smiling. "I told you, Thurgood. I won't kill you. I don't kill. However, there is a price to be paid." She licked her lips hungrily—both the living side and the lifeless side. "And perhaps, when that price has been exacted, you will think that your death would have been a mercy."

She lowered her voice to a whisper, pregnant with menace. "But you will *never* disappoint me again."

XI

Hi. This is Todd Cavetto. Yeah, you've got the right number, unless, of course, you were looking for somebody else. Either way, for some probably inexcusable reason, I can't take your call right now. So wait for the beep, and . . . Well, you know the drill."

Peggy had already listened to the message four times, always disconnecting before the beep. *Stop being such a coward,* she scolded. *Todd deserves to know.* When the beep sounded in her ear, she took a deep breath, opened her mouth to speak . . . and hung up once more.

He's probably on the plane back to Spokane. I'll call him later.

Coward.

She set her cell phone down on the coffee table and stared at it, shivering. *Get off the couch and dry your hair. That would warm you up.* Instead, she wrapped the blanket more tightly around herself.

How long did you stand there in the rain? Honestly, Peggy! Who do you think you are? Some tragic Jane Austen heroine, like Marianne Dashwood standing in the storm, pathetically calling the name "Willoughby" over and over? Lamenting rejection from a man who was never yours — a man who never even saw you as a woman?

The rain had been cold, drenching her hair and her clothes, chilling her flesh, leeching the warmth from the depths of her soul.

When she got home, she didn't bother to turn on the lights. She left her waterlogged clothes strewn about the condo, lying wherever they fell. Then she took a long, hot shower, sitting on the floor of the stall, sobbing. She sat there, tears running down the drain along with the hot water. She cried till she had no tears left. And when the hot water was depleted, she toweled off and wrapped herself in a blanket.

As the stormy gloom outside her condo faded into dark, tempestuous night, the light inside her faded as well. Shattered dreams gave way to despair.

So, Peggy, was he worth it?

I was trying to save him!

But he doesn't want *you to save him. He doesn't want your help – not anymore. He doesn't want your love. He doesn't even want your friendship.*

But I can't just . . . abandon him. I can't simply let her *have him.* Even in her own head, her protestations sounded weak – clutching at mental straws.

You're pathetic, Peggy. Pathetic and useless.

Shut up, will you?

She let out a short, bitter laugh. "Listen to me," she said aloud. "I sound like Gollum – arguing with myself."

Yessss, Preciousssss!

The ghost of a smile threatened to raise the corners of her mouth. *That's it. I'm going insane.*

Going? You've already lost it.

Her phone played the *Indiana Jones* theme, startling Peggy out of her dark thoughts.

Daddy?

She picked up the phone. "Dad?"

"Hey, Bambi." The strong, familiar voice carried a note of tender concern. "Are you all right, sweetie?"

Peggy swallowed hard, trying to steady her voice. "It's got to be – what? – three in the morning there in Kiev? How come you're calling now?"

Her father chuckled weakly. "You know we mission presidents never get any sleep. Besides, I . . . I had a prompting. The Spirit said, 'Peggy's in trouble.' And your mother had a dream too. And you know I put a lot of stock in your mother's dreams. So . . . what's going on?"

"Nothing. I'm okay." She tried to sound convincing.

"You know, Bambi-Girl, you're a woman of many and varied talents, but *lying* isn't one of them."

"I'm okay. Really, I am."

"Spill, kiddo. Come on."

Even though her father couldn't see her, Peggy squirmed on the couch. "There's nothing you can do from Ukraine. You can't come home. And I don't want Mom coming home either."

"Okay. Fair enough. But I can pray. I can fast." He paused. "And I can listen."

But I can't tell you everything. "My friend – he's in trouble." *He's in danger.*

"Is this Derek you're talking about – the one you mention in all your emails?"

Is it that obvious?

Apparently to everyone but Derek.

"Yeah," she said. "He's . . . He's gotten mixed up with . . . some really bad people."

"Another woman?"

"No. Well, yes, but . . . It's more complicated than that. He's in danger, Daddy."

"Danger?" Her father paused. "Physical or spiritual?"

"Physical . . . mostly."

"I see. Can you tell me about it?"

Peggy bit her lip. *I wish I could tell you!* "Not . . . really. But it's . . . bad." *What a lame word!* "I think his life's in danger."

"Are *you* in danger, Peggy?"

"Me?" *Why would I be in danger?* "No. I . . . don't think so."

"Are you sure?"

I'm not the one she's after. "Derek's the one in danger."

A moment of silence, and then, "Be careful, sweetie."

"Okay, Daddy."

"Did you call the police?"

And tell them what? Giant, man-eating dogs? Time-traveling-Druid serial killers? They'd lock me up.

And Derek would still *be in danger.* "I can't call the police. I can't prove anything." *All I've got is a mangled class ring I found in a pile of dog poop.* "And Derek—he won't listen to me. We had a . . . a fight."

"I see." Her father paused, sighed. "And you've done your best to warn him?"

"Yes, Daddy, but—"

"Sweetie, you can't save someone who doesn't want to be saved. It's like when you were a missionary. All you can do is warn him."

But I love him! "I can't just stand by and watch."

"Peggy, every fiber of my being is *screaming*, telling me to go home right now and protect my little girl."

"Daddy, I'm okay. Really, you don't—"

"I want to come home and protect you, but I have to stand and watch." He paused. "I know you, Bambi. I know you're not telling me everything. I know you're holding something back. And I don't know why, but . . . I feel strongly, *strongly* impressed to tell you two things."

He fell silent.

"What two things, Daddy?"

"First, my sweet, beautiful, intelligent, precious girl, you are more—*more* than what this Derek sees. You are more than what *any* man sees."

"Daddy, I—"

"Let me finish. You've spent your whole life, ever since you were—forgive me for saying this—a socially awkward twelve-year-old girl, worrying about how boys, how *men* saw you, or . . . or *didn't* see you. When the other girls were going on lots of dates, when they had boyfriends . . . when you didn't get asked to the prom . . . when the only guys who asked you out were boys I didn't approve of—or they were . . ." His voice trailed off.

You can say it, Daddy — they were nerds . . . like me.

"Well," he continued, "they weren't the boys you were sweet on . . ."

But Derek is perfect. He's gorgeous and smart, and he's a geek like me.

"What I'm trying to say, Bambi, is that you need to stop measuring yourself by what they see or don't see. You are *not* what they see. You are not what Derek sees. You are *more*."

Tears spilled from Peggy's eyes, startling her. She wiped at her cheeks and stared in shock at the glistening moisture on her hand. *Honestly, Peggy! Did you actually think there were no tears left?*

"You still there, sweetie?"

She swallowed, trying to keep the ragged edge out of her voice. "Yeah, Daddy. I'm still here." *You're my Daddy. No other man is ever going to see me the way you do.*

I'm always going to be invisible . . . and alone.

"Okay," her father said, "second thing—you are *not* alone. Talk to someone—a friend, your home teachers, your bishop, your visiting teachers. Talk to your Father in Heaven. He's always there for you. He will not abandon you. But find someone to confide in. This burden you're carrying—this fear for Derek—you don't have to carry it by yourself. You *shouldn't* carry it by yourself. You know, you can always call me, but . . . promise me you'll talk to *somebody*?"

Peggy cleared her throat. "I promise."

"That's my girl." He paused again. "Well, I've said my piece. You know I'm only a phone call away, even in Ukraine."

"I know."

"I love you, Bambi."

"I love you too, Daddy." She smiled. "Thank you. Thank you for being my dad."

"Remember, talk to someone."

"Okay." *Who?*

"Bye, sweetie."

"Bye."

The Sweet Sister

Peggy heard the simulated click. She held the phone in front of her, staring at it until the screen went dark.

You are more than what he sees.

And you are not alone.

Her phone lit up and played the *Star Wars* theme.

Text from Derek?

She opened the message.

I'm sorry. I was a jerk.

Peggy was certain her heart would leap out of her chest and dance an Irish jig on the coffee table. *He's sorry!* Her thumbs trembled as she began to type a reply, but her elation evaporated when the next message appeared.

I still want to be friends.

Friends. She sent, I want that too.

Liar.

The *Star Wars* theme played again.

I know you want more than that, but I just don't feel the same. I'm sorry I hurt you. I really am.

But you're wrong about Elaine. I'll prove it to you. I'm going to save her.

Oh, Derek! She's part of it. Why can't you see that?

Derek texted, See you tomorrow, Carter?

At least he's talking to me again. That means there's still a chance.

A chance for what? To get him to fall in love with you?

No. I can't . . . He won't . . . There's still a chance to save him.

She sent, Of course. See you tomorrow.

You sound like a battered woman, going back to an abusive boyfriend.

You are more than what he sees.

Her phone rang. The caller ID displayed, "Todd Cavetto."

And you are not alone.

Peggy answered the phone. "Todd?"

"Hey, I forgot to turn my phone back on after the plane landed. You called?"

"Yeah. A few times."

He chuckled. "So I gathered. So what's up? Miss me already?"

That actually brought a small smile to Peggy's face. "Is this a good time? Can we talk?"

"Affirmative, I just walked in the door."

"Oh." Her courage, like a lonely candle flame exposed to a sudden breeze, flickered and threatened to die. "You can call me back when you're settled . . . if you want."

"That's a big negative. Talk to me. I'm all yours."

"Okay." *How much can I tell him?* "It's about Jerry. I'm . . . pretty sure he's dead. And I . . . I think I know who murdered him."

"You definitely have my attention now."

Time-traveling-Druid serial killers sounds so stupid, like the plot of an Ed Wood movie. "Plan 10 from Druidia." Todd's not gonna believe you. "It's gonna sound completely nuts, but hear me out, okay?" *You are not alone.*

"Peggy, tell me what you know."

And she did.

She told him everything.

🜚 🜚 🜚

Bran perched on Elaine's arm and uttered a doleful croak. The bird's voice seemed to echo around the bedchamber. Elaine kissed the tip of the raven's beak, then parted her lips invitingly. The bird nipped playfully at her lower lip, making a noise that sounded remarkably like a kiss. It fluttered its long wings and said, "Badh!"

Elaine gave the raven a sad, sweet smile. "I'm so sorry about your Badh. You look so lonely without her, poor thing. But we just couldn't keep her, because—well, because she wasn't *nice*. Oh, no. She wasn't nice at all."

"Elaine, that word no longer has such a meaning," Morgaise said. "'Nice' hasn't meant 'exact' or 'specific' for centuries. In this day, it means 'pleasant' or 'kind'—like you, my sweet."

Elaine grinned for her sister. "I didn't hear you come in."

"You know I will never be far away—not since Bavaria."

Elaine's smile vanished. "I'm sorry. I won't ever . . . do that again."

Half of Morgaise's face lifted in a warm, tender smile. "I know. I'm as much to blame as anyone." She sighed. "But let's not speak of that."

Elaine's countenance brightened. Then she bit her lower lip. "Uh, Morgaise?"

"Yes, little one?"

"When the new ravens come—the new Bran and Badh—may I please keep this one?"

Morgaise shook her head. "That is not the way. You know this. There can only be two ravens."

87

"I know, but—he'll be my pet. I'll keep him here in my room, away from the others. Please, may I keep him?"

"He'll pine for his mate. He'll die of grief."

"Please, let me try?"

Morgaise rolled her eyes. "Very well. I can deny you nothing." Half her face smiled. "You are incorrigible."

Elaine winked at the bird joyfully. She ran her hand down the raven's back, eliciting a happy croak. "Do you hear that, Bran? You're going to live with me. And I will care for you and love you and try to fill the hole in your heart."

"I love you," said the bird, bobbing its head. "Pretty bird."

Elaine gently scratched Bran behind its head. "Yes, indeed, you are a pretty bird." She pursed her lips and regarded the bird with a thoughtful expression. "But you can no longer be Bran, can you? Perhaps, I shall call you . . . Percy." She smiled again. "I once had a pet crow named Percy. Now you shall be Percy. Percy. Percy."

"Percy," said the raven.

"Do you see, Morgaise? He likes the name. Percy. Percy."

Morgaise nodded. "So . . . what do you think of this young man— this Derek?"

Elaine's cheeks flushed crimson. "I like him. He's so sweet and"— she sighed—"handsome! I'm so pleased beards are back in fashion. He looks so manly with his unkempt beard. And so gallant!" She dropped her voice down an octave. "So brave!" She giggled with girlish delight. "He was going to save me from Suetonius. Can you imagine? Suetonius hurt someone?" She moved her arm, bringing the raven close. "Isn't that just the silliest thing, Percy?"

"Percy," said the bird.

"That's right. You're Percy now. Such a clever bird!" She kissed the raven's beak again.

Percy croaked, spread its wings, and flapped over to a stand-perch. It sidled over to its food bowl and fished around for a tasty tidbit, like a greedy boy on Halloween, rummaging through his bag for the prize candy bar of the night. Croaking triumphantly, the raven plucked an eyeball from the bowl. Raising its head, the bird opened wide its beak and gulped the grisly morsel down.

"Good boy!" Elaine clapped her hands. "At least he has a healthy appetite."

"Yes," Morgaise said. "Perhaps he may survive after all—at least until the harvest."

"Oh, that would be lovely!" Elaine sat in front of her vanity mirror, picked up a brush, and began stroking her long, tawny hair. Seeing her sister in the mirror, Elaine gasped in surprise and delight. "Why, Morgaise, you have your hair down! It looks lovely. You should wear it down more often."

Morgaise scowled bitterly, both sides of her mouth momentarily symmetrical. "It doesn't matter what I do with my hair." She pointed at the lifeless half of her face. "No man will ever be able to see past this!"

"I'm sorry," Elaine said, a tear spilling from her eye. "I didn't mean to be cruel. Forgive me."

"I can *never* have what you have. No man will ever caress my cheek or kiss me tenderly or hold me in a loving embrace." Morgaise wiped away a tear, then forced a smile. "So I must live through you, dear sister."

Elaine nodded. "And so you shall."

"So you like this Derek?"

"Yes, I do." Elaine sighed happily. "He's so — what was that word they used on the TV? — Oh, yes! Dreamy!" She sighed. "Derek is dreamy."

"Yes," Morgaise whispered, "he is that."

"I know I only met him today, but . . . I think . . . I hope he might be . . . the one."

Morgaise nodded. "That would be . . . convenient." She stood. "Good-night, sweet Elaine."

Elaine blew a kiss. "Good-night."

🌢 🌢 🌢

Morgaise left Elaine's bedroom through the side door and into the small, unadorned room beyond. To the right were the steep stairs leading into the tower. Straight across was the door that connected to her own bedchamber.

As soon as Morgaise closed her bedroom door behind herself, she heard Morgana whisper in a voice dry as grave cerements, "So it will be that man?"

"Yes," Morgaise replied. "It has begun again."

"I assume you contacted the solicitor?"

"Yes, I did. And they have already responded."

"So quickly?"

Morgaise nodded. "They are able to gather information very quickly through their machines — computers and Internet they are called."

Morgana uttered a sound like the low growl of a dying predator.

"They are clever, these modern Romans. And what have you learned?"

"The young man is suitable. He has no—the term is 'criminal history.' And no immediate connections."

"Good."

Morgaise frowned. "However, his companion—the woman named Peggy—she is . . . problematic."

Morgana growled again. "She has a criminal history?"

"No. Quite the opposite. However, she has deduced or guessed something. She dragged the young man out of here quite abruptly. I believe she may be a threat."

"Then remove the threat."

Morgaise nodded. "It shall be as you say."

Morgana's laugh was low and soft, like a jackal's death rattle.

XII

CID's no longer pursuing the case!" Even through the cell phone Peggy could sense Todd's frustration and anger. "They've just written Jerry off."

Peggy put her phone into speaker mode and set it on the passenger seat of her car, next to her shoes. Parking was hard enough one-handed, but the rain made it more difficult. "How can that be? I thought you said helicopter pilots were . . . 'valuable assets.'"

"Yeah, well, it's only been a couple of weeks, but my buddy in the CID . . . Sorry. That's the Army's Criminal Investigative Division. Anyway, my buddy in the CID confirmed it — the investigation is *over*. But it gets worse."

"Worse? Hold on a sec." A car was parked in Peggy's covered parking spot — her *reserved* spot. *Figures. Pouring rain.* She pulled into an uncovered visitor spot. *With my luck, the condo manager will have my car towed.* The rain crashed against the windshield with all the fury of a spring storm. *Only six-thirty, and it's already dark.* She knew the gloom outside was brought on by the storm, but without the light of the streetlights, the narrow road in front of her condo seemed as dark as a downtown alleyway. *And I'm gonna get soaked.*

As if to punctuate that thought, a man in a hoodie walked through the downpour right in front of the car. *Yep, soaked like that poor guy.* Peggy kept the car running, but turned off the wipers. "You said it gets worse. How?"

"My friend in the CID says they were *ordered* to close the investigation."

"Ordered?"

"Yeah. That means somebody — somebody high up the chain of command — just wants all this to go away."

Peggy shivered with a chill that had nothing to do with the raging tempest outside. "What are you saying? Why would somebody in the Army do that?"

91

"I think it's got to have something to do with your time-travelers."

"You think somehow the Morrigans—what?—shut down the investigation?"

"Them or their lawyers."

"But how?"

"I don't know, Peggy. But these women obviously have money—a *lot* of money. That kind of money means power. They can bribe people—blackmail people."

"I thought I was being paranoid. I thought . . ." Peggy wiped away a sudden tear. "Todd . . . I'm so glad you . . . believe me. Without you . . ." *I'd be all alone.*

"Hey, I wish I could do more."

"Just having someone to talk to . . ." *Even if he is in Spokane. But right now, I really need . . . What do I need?*

"Sure," Todd said. "Always. You know that."

"Thanks." Peggy's feet ached. *That's what I get for wearing heels all week. And for what? To show Derek what he's missing? As if!* She looked at the shoes in the seat beside her with no small degree of resentment. "So what's our next move?"

"I don't know what to do. If the Army has given up on him, there's no other law-enforcement option. He's just a missing person and not high on the priority list, as far as the civilian police are concerned. There's no real evidence of a crime. And we certainly can't tell them your theory."

Peggy winced. *Nope.* "What if they searched Elaine's house? Wouldn't they find Jerry's DNA or something?"

"Maybe. I don't know. It's been a while. And they'd need a warrant. My anonymous tip doesn't appear to have done any good. What about on your end? Any progress?"

Peggy groaned. "Not with Derek. I mean, he talks to me—sort of—but only about work or trivial stuff. Every time *I* try to talk about Elaine, he changes the subject. But *he* talks about her all the time. He's over there *every night.*" Peggy tried and failed to keep the bitterness and hurt out of her voice. "He makes a point of telling me about the movies he and Elaine go to see, where he takes her for dinner, the plays . . ." *All the stuff he doesn't do with me.*

The man in the hoodie had taken refuge in the covered parking area—*At least he's out of the rain.*—standing next to the car in Peggy's reserved parking spot. *Is he . . . watching me? Or am I just being paranoid?* A bolt of lightning turned gloom into electric brilliance, but the area under the parking cover was cast into darkness. And when the retinal afterimage dissipated, Hoodie-Man was gone.

Drive away, Peggy. Just come back later.

A massive crash of thunder, followed by another blinding flash.

There he is! Hoodie-Man was across the street—a little farther away. *Okay, I'm just being paranoid. He's not really after me. He's not. Still gonna get out my pepper spray.* Thunder boomed, startling her. *Now's my chance!*

"Hang on, Todd." She shoved her phone into her purse, grabbed her can of pepper spray, and zipped the purse shut. Holding her purse and her pepper spray in one hand, she grabbed her shoes in the other. *To heck with my pantyhose!*

She pulled the keys from the ignition, opened the car door, hit the lock button on her keys, and bolted from the safety of the vehicle, slamming the door behind herself. Water splashed up her legs, soaking her hose, skirt, and slip as she dashed toward her condo, key and pepper spray in hand, held like weapons. She wished she had one of her elven knives—the real ones she displayed on her bedroom wall, not the polystyrene movie props sitting on her coffee table—instead of just a handful of keys and pepper spray.

And as she pelted through the storm, she saw Hoodie-Man break into a run.

Terror-spiked adrenaline drove her forward, heart pounding, breath coming in frantic gasps. *Don't trip!* She reached her door, fumbled with the key, trying to force it into the deadbolt lock. *Don't break the key!* She turned the key, wrenched it out, and jammed it into the doorknob lock. As she turned the knob, she risked a glance back. Hoodie-Man had closed only half the distance. He'd stopped running and was standing more than a dozen yards away in the rain.

A lightning flash illuminated his face. He was leering at her, his smile a rictus of demonic triumph.

I know him. She was certain of it, but she wasn't sure from where.

Still staring at Hoodie-Man, Peggy opened the door.

Something slammed into her from behind, shoving her inside her condo.

She fell forward, hitting the floor hard. The air exploded from her lungs. *Can't breathe!* Her lungs seemed as if they were held in a vise. She couldn't suck in anything.

She heard the door close and the deadbolt being locked. She tried to force herself to her knees. *Breathe!*

A savage kick caught her in the side and rolled her onto her back. *Breathe!*

The vise on her lungs unlocked, and she sucked in air with a loud gasp. She managed two heaving breaths, drew in a third so she could scream, but her attacker threw himself on top of her, forcing the air from her lungs again.

She felt something pressed against her neck.

Something sharp.

She stopped struggling, except for her attempts to draw in ragged breaths.

"Not so smart, are ya, bitch? Not without your men?"

"P-please." Her plea was barely a pained whimper.

She remembered the can of pepper spray. But it was no longer in her right hand. She still clutched the straps of her purse, but the pepper spray was gone. Her keys were still in the doorknob.

She tried to swing her purse around to strike at the man, but he caught her forearm. "Drop it, or I'll kill you right now."

She complied. She felt her purse straps wrenched out of her hand.

"That's better."

Peggy looked into the face of her attacker. It was right above hers, of course, but until that point she hadn't looked at him.

And she knew him.

It wasn't Hoodie-Man, but she knew him.

Cold blue eyes. Pretentious goatee.

She didn't have to see the blonde ponytail.

The pagan from the convention.

He bared his teeth in an evil smile. "You recognize me, don't you, bitch?"

"Please don't hurt me." She felt tears streaming down the sides of her face. "I-I'm sorry."

The pagan licked his lips. "That depends on how much you fight me. You gonna fight me?"

Fight him! She could feel his hot, sour breath. She could smell alcohol.

Peggy shook her head. "No."

He inclined his face toward hers and leered. "Are you a virgin?" His lips almost touched hers in an obscene kiss.

The question surprised and confused her. "What?"

"Of course, you are. All you Mormon whores are virgins."

Although Peggy could smell drink on him, there was no slurring of his speech.

His leer transformed into a contemptuous smirk. "You *reek* of virginity."

Lie to him! Tell him you're not a virgin. "Wh-what difference does it make?"

He chuckled. Peggy could feel the quiver of his laughter against her stomach. "Oh, it makes a lot of difference. If you're a virgin, I get to . . . *initiate* you. If not?" He shrugged. "I get to strip and flog you. Commandment of the Goddess." He leered at her again. "Which is it?"

Even in her panic, the man's words struck her as odd. *What does that mean? Think, Peggy!* "Why?" she asked. *Buy time.*

"You're a virgin," he pronounced. He forced her legs apart with his knees.

"You're going to kill me either way." It was a statement of fact.

He chuckled again. "I guess you *are* smart." He closed his eyes as if in prayer. "Cernunnos and the Goddess, accept this offering."

Yes, Peggy, you are smart. Use that. Think! What do you have to fight him with?

And she remembered her shoes. One of them was still gripped in her left hand.

If I fight him, he'll kill me.

If I don't, I'm dead anyway.

He shifted, pawing at her skirt with his free hand.

The pressure of the blade on her neck lessened.

She swung her shoe at him. She struck him hard on the head with the heel.

He roared in pain and rolled slightly off her.

She shoved hard with her right hand and struck him again with her left — with the heel of her shoe.

He rolled off her completely, clawing at the side of his head. Blood streamed from between his fingers. "Bitch!"

Peggy tried to get to her feet, but her attacker clutched at her foot. She tried to crawl away, scrabbling at the carpet, trying to get purchase. The coffee table was within reach. She latched onto the table with her free hand — she still clutched her shoe in her left — and pulled the table toward herself.

Her attacker yanked on her foot, pulling her back toward himself. The coffee table tipped, and the two fake elven knives fell to the carpet. Peggy reached for the nearest, snagging it.

The pagan began to claw his way up her legs, one of his hands slick with blood.

Peggy rolled, sat up, and stabbed at him with both her weapons. She missed with the shoe, but connected with the prop knife, stabbing his back. The plastic didn't pierce his skin, but Peggy struck him again with all her fury and terror. She hit him so hard, the polypropylene blade snapped.

He yelped, lost his grip, and rolled over on his back.

Peggy struck him with her shoe. The heel gouged his cheek. She struck again, and the heel sunk into his eye.

He screamed—a high-pitched sound that seemed to fill the world with his agony.

And that scream completely unnerved Peggy.

She let go of the shoe, leaving it protruding from the man's eye, and scrambled to her feet. She fled to the bedroom.

She slammed the door behind herself and locked it.

That won't keep him out.

Like most bedroom doors, it was flimsy—two thin layers of plywood—a barrier for privacy, not protection against a raping, murderous pagan.

The screaming from the other room continued, but it altered, dropping in pitch and intensity.

"Bitch! I'll kill you!"

Peggy looked about frantically, panic threatening to overwhelm her again. *He'll be through that door any second!*

Her eyes lighted on the window on the other side of the room. She scrambled toward it and opened the shades.

Lightning flashed, silhouetting a figure outside.

A hooded figure.

Two of them!

No escape!

Thunder crashed. Then she heard a thud against the bedroom door.

A second thud, and a large hole appeared in the door.

No escape!

So, fight!

Her legs and hands trembling, she prepared to stand her ground. "Don't come in here! I'm armed." She brandished the broken prop knife.

Mad laughter came through the hole in the door. "Yeah, you dropped your damn shoe. All you got is a broken toy knife."

"I . . . I've got more shoes!" *Do you know how lame that sounds?*

The pagan laughed again—a hyena closing in. He slammed against the splintered door and forced his arm and head through the hole. "Here's Johnny, bitch!" He flashed his teeth in an insane grin below the ruin of his eye.

"I don't want to kill you!" Peggy's voice quavered with terror, but at the moment she wasn't sure she was telling the truth. And that uncertainty scared her almost as much as the thought of the man's forcing his way into the room. *Maybe I don't want to kill him. But I want him gone!*

"Go away!" she cried.

Madness blazed in his good eye as he stared at her. He reached for the doorknob.

Peggy dropped the useless prop knife and turned toward her closet to grab another shoe. Then her eyes lighted on the wall display of Tauriel's elven knives.

She snatched a knife from the wall. "This knife is real—not plastic. Go away!"

He turned the knob. "Not fooling me!" The door began to open. Grinning at her like the comic book Joker, the man began to extricate himself from the hole in the door.

Peggy gripped the knife in both hands and raised it. She lunged forward and stabbed at his shoulder.

She missed.

Her knife sank into the door.

The pagan's good eye narrowed in fury. He snarled like a feral animal. Still halfway through the door, he shoved the door open, breaking Peggy's grip on her knife.

She backed away, watching in horror as her attacker ripped his arm free from the hole. He raised his knife.

Peggy snatched the second knife from the display and wheeled to face him.

He roared and leapt at her.

Peggy's weapon caught him in the gut.

He knocked her to the floor, landing atop her.

His face, twisted in rage, was poised above hers. The rage vanished, replaced by confusion. He made a noise halfway between a wheeze and a groan. He looked as if he was struggling for breath.

Peggy shoved at the man and managed to roll him off herself. She scrambled to her feet and backed away.

He looked at her, his good eye wide with terror, his mouth working soundlessly. He reached a hand toward her, as if pleading for help.

Peggy's eyes were drawn to the knife. Only the butt of the handle was visible, sticking out of the gore of his abdomen.

Pierced his diaphragm. And so much blood. Maybe if I performed CPR . . . No. He's a dead man.

"I-I'm sorry." And she was. She knew the moment would haunt her for the rest of her life. "There's nothing I can do."

His hand dropped to his side. He mouthed, "Mormon bitch." His eyes rolled up, and his face went slack.

Peggy stared at the corpse, her eyes riveted to the dead face.

I killed him. I killed someone. "Heavenly Father, I . . ."

Peggy's prayer was interrupted by a sound that drove fresh horror into her like a knife, nearly sending her to her knees — the sound of an unlocking deadbolt.

A quick glance out her window confirmed what she already knew in her heart — the mortal certainty of just who was on the other side of the door.

Hoodie-Man.

XIII

Help!" Peggy screamed. "Help me!"

Whoever was on the other side of the front door—Hoodie-Man, she was sure—must have hesitated, because the door did not open immediately.

Peggy continued to scream for help, trying to buy a few seconds. She knew her cries wouldn't keep him out for long.

Nobody's going to hear me in this storm. I'm alone.

She needed a weapon. Peggy glanced at the knife sticking out of the pagan's abdomen, then at the elven knife embedded in the splintered remains of her bedroom door.

She chose the knife that wasn't slick with the dead man's blood. Still calling for help—although with less conviction—she wrenched the knife from the broken door.

Her next scream died in her throat as the front door flew open. A soaking-wet Hoodie-Man stood illuminated in the doorway.

He aimed a handgun at her.

He slogged into the condo, pushing the door closed with a gloved hand. He tossed the keys aside—the keys Peggy had left in the doorknob when she was attacked. Peggy could see only the lower half of his face, veiled as it was in the shadow of the hood. But what she could see looked angry.

"Drop the knife." Despite his scowl, his voice was calm . . . and familiar.

Peggy *almost* complied. Her knife was no use against a gun.

But why hasn't he used it?

"Why?" Her voice was raw from screaming. "You're going to kill me anyway, aren't you?"

His mouth twitched. Then his scowl tightened into a thin-lipped smirk.

His expression tugged at Peggy's memory, but she couldn't quite make the connection.

"Okay," he said, "we'll do this the hard way. You wanna dance, lady? Let's dance." His grin widened, and he bared gleaming teeth. "You could say it's your funeral."

He strode toward her, still aiming the gun—still not shooting.

Peggy backed away, retreating farther into the bedroom, brandishing the knife—*I killed a man!*—like a magic talisman—*As if I stand a chance against that gun!*—taking care not to trip over the corpse. When her feet squished into the blood-soaked carpet, she recoiled and nearly lost her footing.

Hoodie-Man quickly closed the distance, entering the bedroom. "There's nowhere to run."

Why hasn't he shot me yet? "A-are you going to rape me?"

He chuckled. "Not my style." Then he shook his head. "And not my job."

Peggy's legs threatened to buckle. She almost laughed out loud. *I'm still going to die, but at least I won't have to endure being raped first.* "No, I guess that was y-your friend's job."

Peggy couldn't see the man's eyes, but his head turned slightly in the direction of the dead would-be rapist, and his mouth twisted in apparent disgust. "Not my friend." He entered the bedroom. "Just a tool." He grinned again. "You can take your pick of definitions for that word." He gave the blood and body a wide berth.

He doesn't want to step in the blood.

He doesn't want to leave any evidence of his presence.

"Stay back!" Peggy slashed at the shrinking space between them. "I called the police! They're on their way."

He hesitated for a moment, then shook his head. "You didn't have your phone out in the rain. And you haven't had a chance since lover-boy jumped you."

Peggy yelped as her back bumped against the closet door. *Trapped!*

"Just drop the knife," the man said. He was barely six feet away. "If you do, I'll make it quick—one shot to the head. You make me work for it . . ."

Peggy responded by lunging forward, slashing at his arm.

He stepped into her lunge, caught her wrist deftly with his free hand, and twisted her arm. Hard.

Peggy cried out in pain, and the knife fell from her fingers.

In an instant, Hoodie-Man yanked her arm up behind her back. He shoved her toward the floor.

She landed face first in the blood.

Recoiling in horror, she attempted to get to her knees, but she slipped in the gore. No matter how she moved, she seemed to edge closer and closer to the corpse.

"On your knees and turn around." He didn't sound angry or excited. He was composed, businesslike. He wasn't even breathing hard.

He knows what he's doing, unlike . . .

In spite of her terror, Peggy tried to calm herself. She forced her trembling to stop. *Think, Peggy! Why does he want you to turn around?*

She managed to get to her knees, but she kept her back to him.

"Turn around," he repeated.

"No." She was almost proud of herself—her voice barely shook.

"Turn around. I *could* rough you up. At least that'd be consistent. But I don't want to. So make it easy on both of us. Just turn around."

What does he mean? Consistent? Then she understood. *He's staging a scene—one in which the pagan shoots me when I get the better of him—one in which there is only one attacker, not two.* She shook her head. "No. You won't step in the b-blood. That means you d-don't want to leave any evidence—no evidence you've been here. That's why you didn't break the window. That would show someone else was here, b-because the glass would be inside."

"Turn around." There was an edge to his voice.

That did it. He's angry now.

"But you already screwed up," she said. "You left your wet f-footprints on the c-carpet."

"Turn around!"

"I don't know who you are," she said. But in that instant, she realized she *did* know him—the hulking bodyguard-chauffeur from Elaine's house. *This is Elaine's doing! Elaine and her horrid sister sent them to rape and kill me!* A cold anger began to supplant Peggy's fear. And that fury gave her strength to calm her trembling voice. "Leave now, and I won't be able to identify you. It's your only ch—"

"I said, turn around! Now!"

"'I am disinclined to acquiesce to your request,'" she said, quoting from a favorite pirate movie. She even affected a cockney accent. Her voice was calm, but her gore-slick hands trembled with rage. However, the anger—the realization of just who the enemy was—gave her a clarity of mind. *Maybe he'll still kill me, but he doesn't want to get caught. He doesn't want this to be traced back to his employer. Use that, Peggy.* "You need me to turn around so you can put a bullet in me with an *upward* trajectory, as if your friend fired it while lying on his back. You're going to have to kneel down to get that shot, aren't you?" She

101

shook her head. "You wanna kill me? Well, you're just going to have to shoot me in the back—in the back like the coward you are."

Thunder boomed, shaking the walls.

Avoiding the blood, the bodyguard circled around until he was standing in front of her.

"How's this?" she said, forcing herself to lie facedown in the blood, deliberately placing herself beside the pagan's corpse. "You shoot me while I'm lying like this, and the police will know for certain that a second man was here."

He grabbed a fistful of her hair and yanked, forcing her head up. "You think you're pretty smart, don't you?" He put the cold barrel of the gun against her forehead, right between her eyes. Peggy could smell the gun oil. "Well," he growled, "pretty smart doesn't make up for being an ugly chick."

In spite of the pain from her savagely pulled hair, she almost laughed. "Really?" she said, tears of pain streaming down her blood-covered face. "That's all you've got? The big, strong man with the gun. You have all the power . . . and you still go for the 'ugly chick' remark? What's the matter, big man? Smart girls scare you?"

He jerked her up higher, making her cry out.

She fought him then, clawing at his arm, trying to loosen the punishing grip on her hair. "No! Let me go!"

And abruptly, he *did* let go of her. He stood up and stepped back.

As Peggy scrambled away, she saw the man's head tilt up as if he was listening to something.

And then she heard it too—distant, as if coming from miles away through the storm.

A siren. More than one.

With a grunt and a muttered oath, Morgaise and Elaine's bodyguard turned and escaped out the open door and into the storm.

And Peggy was left alone and alive . . . with the corpse.

On wobbling legs, she staggered to the door, slammed it closed, and locked it. Then she collapsed to the floor, curled up into a fetal ball, and sobbed with relief and terror and a roiling mess of other emotions she couldn't identify, blubbering out a nearly incoherent prayer of gratitude.

Through her sobs and the approaching sirens, she became aware of another sound—muffled and indistinct, but urgent—her name, repeated over and over.

She looked around in confusion—and then renewed fear. Was the voice coming . . . from the bedroom? Was the pagan somehow still alive? Peggy lifted her head and looked toward the ruined door. The corpse was clearly visible—and clearly still very dead.

"Peggy!" She heard it again.

It was coming from her purse.

The purse lay on the living room floor where the pagan had tossed it.

"Peggy!"

She sat up partway, rubbing tears and blood—the pagan's blood—from her eyes, as she stared at the bag, blinking without comprehension.

"Peggy!"

My phone?

Todd! I was talking to him before . . .

She crawled over to the purse and fished her phone out with trembling, gory hands.

"Peggy!"

She put the phone to her ear. "Todd?"

"Peggy!" His voice was so loud, she had to pull the phone away from her. "Are you okay? Are you safe?" Todd sounded frantic and relieved at the same time.

Her tears started afresh. "Yeah. I-I'm . . . I'm okay."

"Thank heavens! I was afraid to hang up. So I called nine-one-one on my fax line. The police are on their way."

Todd called the police? A massive sob burst from her. *He saved me!*

"Peggy?"

All the way from Spokane, he saved me. She drew a hitching breath. "You s-saved me . . . saved m-my life. H-he was going to . . . But I stopped him." *I killed him. Blood on my hands.* "But then, there was . . . another . . . with a gun and . . ."

A loud pounding at the door startled her. "Orem Police! Open up!"

"I'm c-coming," she called. "H-hold on, Todd."

Shakily, she got to her feet and lurched toward the door.

Todd saved my life.

♦ ♦ ♦

The bloodstain was huge. At least it seemed huge to Peggy.

She sat on the edge of her bed, staring at the crimson spot. The rusty stench of blood filled her nostrils. She tried not to look at the shattered bedroom door, at the flimsy barrier that had failed to protect her from a man who wanted to rape and murder her.

No better than cardboard.

Never keep anybody out.

Never feel safe again.

So she focused on the bloodstain. While the door symbolized her helplessness, her vulnerability, her physical weakness, the bloodstain symbolized something else.

I killed a man.

You defended yourself, Peggy. Nothing more.

Yes, but I killed him. I stuck a knife into his gut and punctured his diaphragm. Then I watched him bleed to death.

And you apologized *to him — apologized to the man who tried to rape you, the man who tried to kill you!*

I should've tried to save him. I could've tried CPR.

He bled to death. Honestly, Peggy! You couldn't have saved him.

But I didn't even try.

It wouldn't have done any good. Besides, you fought him off! You beat him. He was bigger, stronger. He should've won. But, no! You beat him. You!

Dressed in a long nightshirt — the one she usually saved for cold winter nights — she rubbed at her arms, scrubbed at them.

I'll never get the blood off.

You must've scrubbed half your skin off in the shower. It's gone.

"Not over there," she said aloud, her eyes on the reddened carpet. "That stain will never come out."

Her phone rang. She plucked it from where it sat beside her on the bed, glanced at the caller ID, and smiled. A little.

"Hi, Todd."

"Hey, Peggy," he answered. Peggy could hear a fair amount of white noise in the background. "How're you holding up?"

She sighed. "Well, the police left half an hour ago . . . except for the two cops in the patrol car outside. They said they'd keep a watch in case . . . in case the other guy comes back. But only for the rest of the night. Something about lack of resources and budget cuts. 8:00 A.M. — another hour or so — and I'm on my own." *I'll be alone.*

"At least you're safe for now."

She laughed bitterly. "Safe. For now." *Never be safe again. Hoodie-Man's still out there. Elaine and Morgaise are still out there. Never safe.*

"Hey," Todd said, "one day at a time. Let's see what the morning brings."

Peggy's eyes went back to the bloodstain. "You know what's funny?" she asked in a voice totally devoid of humor.

"My smell? My breath? My looks?" He raised the pitch of his voice an octave and spoke through his nose. "My voice? Tell me if I'm getting close here."

Peggy couldn't suppress a small grin. *He's just trying to cheer me up.* "Well, yeah, those things too, but ... I always assumed that—you know—before the cops left, they would—I don't know—help ... clean up the place. I mean, they took the body and my shoes and my knives, but ..."

"Yeah, Peggy. You've been watching too many cop shows on TV."

"Silly, huh? Cops with carpet cleaners."

"Kinda silly, but understandable. Those shows are all about catching and stopping the bad guy. They don't focus on the victim ... Oh crap! Peggy! I'm sorry! I didn't mean to call you a-a-a ..."

"It's okay. You can say it. I am a *victim.*"

"But you fought him off. That makes you a *fighter,* at least in my book."

"I didn't fight off the second one."

"He had a gun. You couldn't have—"

"That's not what I meant," she said. "What I meant was ... *you* stopped that one."

"All I did was make a phone call."

Tears spilled from Peggy's eyes again. "Yeah, well ... it saved me. You ... stayed with me."

"I wish I could've done more. I wish I'd been there."

"You were ... there for me."

An uncomfortable silence followed, eating away at the tender feelings Peggy wished she could articulate. Saying, *Thank you,* for the thousandth time that night was simply not enough. Finally, to fill the void, she laughed nervously. "I guess I should let you get some sleep. We've both been up all night. At least it's Saturday." She yawned. "I really need to sleep, but ... you keep calling me."

"I'm worried about you, Peggy. And with good reason."

"Yeah, but if you keep calling, people will talk."

Todd said nothing.

"That was a joke," she said. *But I'm really, really grateful that you keep calling.*

"I just ..." He sighed. "I just don't think you should be alone."

"There're two policemen outside, sitting in their police car. I'm not alone."

"You're in danger. You told me it was the Morrigans' bodyguard."

Peggy couldn't resist a fearful glance at the window with its closed blinds keeping out the Saturday morning light. "He won't be coming back. Not today." *You don't know that! Never be safe. Never again!*

"I still think you shouldn't be alone."

"That's sweet of you, Todd" — *Really sweet!* — "but there's nothing more you can do."

"Yeah," Todd said, drawing out the word, lading it with guilt, "about that . . . Don't be mad, but . . . I called Derek."

"Derek?"

"Yeah. He's on his way over. He said he'd stay there today, just to keep you safe."

"Derek?!?" It was nearly a shriek. "He's on his way *here*?"

"Yeah, but . . ."

"I gotta go!"

Peggy hung up, hating herself as she did it. *He saved your life! He deserves better than this.*

But Derek's coming. Here. To be with me.

She stripped out of her nightgown, tossing it into her closet. She jerked on a pair of jeans and a nicer top. Then it was into the bathroom to unbraid her hair and yank a hairbrush through it.

Already brushed my teeth. Do I put on makeup?

Of course, but . . . how much?

A little eyeliner, mascara, blush. Lipstick?

Too much!

Lip gloss.

Her phone rang, and she jumped, smearing the lip gloss. She didn't recognize the phone number, but she answered it anyway. "Hello?"

"Miss Carson? This is officer Newsome. There's somebody to see you. The man's name is Derek Rasmussen and — "

"Yes! Let him come in."

"You have to let them in, Miss."

"Yes. I will. Thank you!"

She hung up and then savagely wiped the smeared lip gloss away.

She barely got the lip gloss reapplied — after two more tries — when she heard the knock.

"Hey, Carter! You in there?"

He's here! When I needed him, he came!

She ran out of her bathroom, leapt over the bloodstain as nimbly as if she hadn't been assaulted and almost murdered and been photographed by the police forensics unit with *and* without her clothes, and questioned by detectives for hours and had her condo combed over by the forensics team and been up all flipping night. None of that mattered. Not at that moment.

Derek had come. For her.

She flung open the door.

And there he was. Derek. Gorgeous Derek. And he looked worried. Worried for her. And he was carrying a rental carpet cleaner.

"Carter," he said, biting his lower lip, "I'm so sorry. Are you okay?" He dropped the carpet cleaner and opened his arms.

"Derek!" Peggy was about to fling herself into his open arms when she saw who stood behind him, looking radiant in the early morning light.

Elaine.

XIV

What is *she* doing here?" Peggy stared at Elaine as if the time-traveler were a viper, coiled and ready to strike. *Elaine tried to kill me!*

Elaine shrank back at Peggy's words, hanging her head and wringing her hands.

"What gives, Carter?" Derek demanded. "Elaine's here to help!"

"She sent those men to rape me! To kill me!" Peggy couldn't believe Derek would bring Elaine along. *I thought you were here for* me, *Derek.* Peggy's eyes teared up again, but she wasn't sure if it was rage or hurt behind those tears.

"What are you talking about?" Derek sounded confused and angry, but Peggy couldn't spare him a glance. "How could you say—"

"It was Shawn," Elaine said, "wasn't it?" She burst into tears and buried her face in her delicate hands.

"Shawn?" Derek asked. "Who's Shawn?

"Our driver," Elaine said, her face still in her hands. "Or h-he was. Morgaise dismissed him yesterday. She said he made such a horrible scene! He is a bad, bad man."

Without warning, Elaine dropped her hands and launched herself at Peggy. Peggy was so startled, she didn't step back or bring her own hands up in defense. Before Peggy could stop her, Elaine had wrapped her arms around Peggy's neck and clung to her, sobbing. "Oh, Peggy! I'm sorry. It's all my fault!"

Peggy stood with her arms at her sides, torn between the contradictory urges to shove Elaine away and to comfort someone in such obvious distress. From the sobs shook Elaine's small frame, it seemed to Peggy as if Elaine was genuinely upset.

Upset because Shawn didn't *kill me? Or upset because he* tried?

In the only previous encounter between Peggy and Elaine, the girl had come across as utterly guileless, completely unable to lie. *But she's lying now! She has to be!*

Derek stood, biting his lip and looking totally flummoxed. "How could it possibly be your fault?"

"It was me!" Elaine wailed. "I . . . I told Morgaise that . . . Shawn frightened me. Morgaise sacked him. I . . . I had no idea he would do this! I mean, I sensed he was violent, but . . ." Elaine pulled back, releasing Peggy. She looked straight into Peggy's eyes. The girl's eyes were red, and tears streaked her pretty face. "Please forgive me! I didn't know."

Morgaise is behind the attack. I know she is! She must've ordered it. But . . . could it be possible Elaine didn't know? She had to know, right?

She's the enemy. Of course she had to know.

And I don't believe — not for a New York minute — that Shawn — or whatever his name is — got fired. He was here on Morgaise's orders. And even if he did get fired, why would he come after me?

No. Elaine had to know.

Peggy looked at Derek, willing him to see the obvious.

He glanced at Elaine, then back at Peggy, hesitated, and then inserted himself between the two women. He put his arms around Peggy and hugged her . . . tentatively. "I'm sorry, Peggy," he said. "I . . . don't know what to say. Are you . . . okay?"

Peggy returned the embrace cautiously, vainly wishing it signified more than simple comfort — knowing full well it didn't. She kept her eyes locked on Elaine who had gone back to wringing her hands. "I . . ." *What do I say? I'm not okay, but . . . that's not what Derek needs to hear right now. It's like he feels . . . guilty. Does he feel guilty? Maybe so.*

And he wants absolution.

For a brief moment, she considered withholding that forgiveness. She considered punishing him.

A very brief moment.

She sighed. "I'm okay." She squeezed her eyes shut and held Derek tight. It felt so good to hold him, to be held by him, even under those circumstances. Even though he didn't mean it *that way.*

Even though he doesn't love me.

He squeezed back gently. "Don't be mad," he whispered in her ear — and the feathery brushing of his lips against her ear sent a shiver through her — "but I *believe* her."

Of course you do. But in her heart, Peggy believed Elaine too. *Somehow, Elaine didn't know.*

Peggy opened her eyes and regarded the younger-looking, prettier woman again. The girl was pleading with her bloodshot eyes. Elaine mouthed, "My fault."

Peggy closed her eyes again. She felt as if she could melt in Derek's arms. He was so strong, so comforting. He smelled so good. Even the scratchy roughness of his beard felt comforting against her cheek.

He doesn't love you. He never will. He loves her.

Shut up and let me dream . . . just for a moment longer.

Her knees threatened to give way, and suddenly she was leaning on him, nearly toppling them both.

Derek pulled out of the embrace, still supporting Peggy, but no longer *holding* her. Peggy felt hollow, as if something vital had been ripped from her. *Derek! I love you!*

"Come on, Carter," he said. "You must be exhausted."

Peggy nodded. She was tired—bone tired, utterly drained—and suddenly chilled without Derek's warm arms holding her. *Sweep me up in your arms, Derek. Carry me inside.*

"Let's get you inside." Derek put his arm around her shoulders.

Giving me a shoulder to lean on.

Like a friend. Like a buddy.

She allowed herself to be led inside the condo.

Derek took her to the couch. "You sit down, and we'll clean the carpet." After Peggy collapsed on the sofa, Derek laid a hand on her shoulder and squeezed gently. He favored her with the lopsided grin—the grin that always turned her wits to mush. "You can sack out here on the sofa, if you want to."

Peggy smiled up at him. She almost felt as if she could go to sleep right there—and might have, if not for the presence of Elaine. Instead, Peggy sat and watched as Elaine entered the front door, awkwardly dragging the carpet cleaner.

I'll bet she's never even seen one before.

Derek looked in Elaine's direction. He let go of Peggy's shoulder, and in an instant, he was at Elaine's side, relieving her of the machine—abandoning Peggy at the first sign Elaine was in distress. "Here. I've got that. It's really just a one-man job anyway."

So why did you bring her along?

Elaine beamed at him with a smile so sweet it made Peggy want to hate her. Elaine shrugged her shoulders and tilted her head coquettishly. "I really don't know a thing about that contraption." Then she clapped her hands with delight. "I know! I'll make you something warm to drink, Peggy. I know you don't drink tea or coffee—Derek has put me off those myself—but maybe I could make us all some hot cocoa?"

Peggy started to protest. *Innocent or not, I don't want you here. Not now. Not ever. And I don't want your wretched cocoa.* But Peggy decided she was just too tired to fight against Elaine's terminal cheeriness. "It's in the cupboard"—she yawned so wide it felt as if she might dislocate her jaw—"above the stove."

While Elaine danced into the kitchen, Derek prepped the carpet cleaner. "That sounds like a great idea! I was teaching Elaine how to drive a car this morning, but then Todd called and . . ." His voice trailed off. Peggy looked at him and noticed he was staring at the pulverized bedroom door . . . and the ugly bloodstain beyond it. "Holy . . . Todd told me about it . . . said it was bad, but . . . Wow. Carter, I'm so, so sorry."

Elaine emerged from the kitchen, wearing a horrified expression and clutching the can of hot chocolate mix to her breast. She reminded Peggy of a frightened little girl clinging to a teddy bear as if it were a talisman of protection. "Y-you fought him off?" she asked. "By your-self?"

I killed him. "Yeah. Th-the first one. The second one . . ."

"Shawn," Elaine whispered.

"Yeah," Peggy said. "Shawn. He would've killed me, if not for . . . for Todd calling the police." *Todd saved my life, and I hung up on him. Because Derek was coming over. With her.*

Elaine set the hot chocolate mix canister on the coffee table, then knelt in front of Peggy. Elaine wrapped her arms around Peggy's legs, just below the knees, and laid her head in Peggy's lap. Peggy fought the urge to push the girl away. It was such an odd gesture, but something about it tugged at Peggy's memory. *It's an old way of begging forgiveness, isn't it? Or was it protection? A custom from . . . another time?*

"You're so brave." Elaine's voice was muffled, soft. "I wish I were brave . . . like you." She began to shake, and Peggy realized the girl was sobbing. "If I were brave, maybe I could . . ."

Could what?

Derek worked his way around the coffee table and knelt beside Elaine. He put his hand on the girl's back and rubbed it gently, tenderly. "She wants to escape," he said, gazing at Elaine with a tenderness that broke Peggy's heart, "from Morgaise, from the endless cycle of . . . whatever it is . . . however it is they keep jumping forward in time."

He lifted his gaze to Peggy, his eyes begging for understanding.

Peggy was stunned. "She knows . . . that *you* know?"

Elaine moved her head in Peggy's lap, nodding . . . and snuffling, getting tears and snot on Peggy's jeans.

"But," Peggy said, shaking her own head in wonder, "you still don't know how . . . how she travels in time? Or why?"

Derek shrugged his shoulders and shook his head.

"To escape," Elaine said.

"What?" both Peggy and Derek asked in chorus.

"Escape from what?" Derek asked. "From whom?"

"I . . ." Elaine squeezed Peggy's legs even tighter. "I don't know. Morgaise is afraid of . . . of something . . . or someone. I just don't know." A tremor shook her body.

To Peggy, it sounded as if Elaine truly was afraid. *Of what? This unnamed person or persons pursuing her and her sister through time? Or maybe it's just the* not knowing *that scares her . . . or the not remembering.*

"Elaine," Peggy said. She had the sudden urge to stroke Elaine's hair, to comfort the girl clinging to her like a frightened child clinging to her mother's legs. Peggy resisted that urge. Barely. "Elaine, what year is it?"

"Nineteen fifty-five," Elaine replied, then abruptly shook her head. "No, that's not right. That's silly. Um, it's . . . twenty . . . fifteen?"

"Elaine," Peggy continued, "do you remember nineteen fifty-five? Do you remember . . . before . . . this year?"

Elaine squeezed Peggy's legs again. "No. I . . . don't think so. I remember . . . I remember music. *Mr. Sandman?* Is that right? I . . . like . . . I *liked* that song. I wore . . . my hair in a ponytail."

"What else do you remember?" Peggy asked.

"I . . . no." She shook her head. "I don't remember." Elaine sounded frustrated. "Just jumbled . . . pictures. Snatches of songs, music. I know we lived in Bavaria once—Morgaise mentions that. And something bad must've happened there—something bad I did. But I . . . don't remember. "

"I showed her the diaries," Derek said, shaking his head. "It's her handwriting, but she doesn't remember anything that happened."

"I'm frightened," Elaine said. "I *should* remember. I know I should. But I just don't. Those diaries . . . those words—they sound like my words, but the memories . . . they're like the memories of someone else —a total stranger."

"Peggy . . ." Derek grimaced and shook his head as if to warn her not to venture further into dangerous territory.

Peggy ignored him. *Could she be telling the truth?* "Elaine, do you remember being a little girl?"

Elaine shook her head rapidly. "No! Nothing!" Her voice was the wail of a lost and terrified child—a lost child who had no memory of her childhood.

With a start, Peggy realized she was indeed stroking Elaine's hair, trying to comfort the girl. *When did I start doing that?* She paused, about to remove her hand, then she resumed running her fingers through Elaine's tawny tresses. *It's as if the urge to protect her, to shield her is irresistible. She's the enemy. No, that's not the right word. My rival? She took Derek away.*

Peggy looked at Derek, at the man she loved so desperately, so hopelessly — the man gazing at Elaine. And Peggy could see fear, concern, and love in his eyes, in his face — all for the girl clinging to Peggy's legs — the lovely, time-traveling princess. The irresistible damsel in distress.

His Snow White.

He doesn't love you, Peggy. And he never, ever will.

I know. I do. But he's in danger, *because he loves her. I can't just watch him . . . what? Die? Be killed?*

What happened to those other men — the other men who once loved Elaine? What happened to them?

Elaine grew still, her crying ceased. "I do remember . . . a dog . . . no, a-a wolf. Father carved it for me." Then she shook herself and squeezed so hard that Peggy's legs hurt. "No! I can't! Please." Her voice dropped to a whisper. "Peggy, I'm scared. So scared. Please. Please help me. Help me to be *brave.*"

Elaine tilted and turned her head till she was looking up at Peggy with red, moist, frightened eyes. "I want to be brave . . . like you."

$$\blacklozenge \ \blacklozenge \ \blacklozenge$$

"I thought that stain would never come out." Derek stared at his handiwork. The bedroom carpet was wet, but there was no visible sign of blood. "Just had to keep going over and over it."

Peggy sat on the edge of her bed, watching him. "Thank you. I don't know how I would've been able to sleep with that smell in here." *It's still here. Not as strong, but I can still smell the blood. How can I ever feel safe here again?*

The police had left half an hour earlier, with barely a phone call as a last check-in. Derek's presence was a comfort, but he and Elaine would be leaving soon, since the carpet was cleaned. *He'll leave, and I'll be all alone here . . . with that stench.*

The blood of the man I killed.

"I'm glad I could help." Derek took the discharge tank from the machine and headed toward the bathroom to empty it for the last time.

Peggy stared at the wet spot. *Never be safe.* She heard the tank being emptied into the toilet, then the toilet flushing. She looked toward the bathroom door in time to see Derek emerging. Their eyes met briefly, then Derek looked away. "Listen, Carter. I'm sorry I've been such a jerk lately." He glanced out of the bedroom toward the living room and the kitchen.

Peggy could hear Elaine clattering around in the kitchen, washing dishes, cleaning . . . being annoyingly nice. And she was singing. Peggy didn't recognize the song, but the language sounded like German. *I wonder how many languages she speaks.* The song was pretty and melancholy and Elaine's voice was angelic, ethereal.

Why can't I bring myself to hate her?

Because that's not who you are. And besides, how could you hate someone you feel pity for?

Derek knelt beside the carpet cleaner and wrapped the power cord around it. "I took her to see a psychiatrist yesterday." He looked guilty, as if he were betraying a confidence.

"A psychiatrist?"

"You know, a hypnotherapist—to try and recover her memories of the past."

"And?"

He shook his head and looked in Elaine's direction. "Elaine couldn't relax enough to be hypnotized. She tried—I mean, she tried really hard, but . . . I don't know. It was as if part of her was fighting it." He shrugged. "Anyway, the bottom line is it didn't work. She reads the diaries, but nothing happens—no recognition, no memories. Nothing. It's like she's a blank slate. Completely innocent. I . . . want to help her. I need to save her, but . . . I have to be careful. She loves her sister, so I can't push too hard, but—"

"Morgaise did this," Peggy hissed, still keeping her voice down so Elaine wouldn't hear. "She's behind it."

Derek nodded. "I believe it. I haven't seen her except for that one time—when you were there. But that woman . . . She's seriously creepy. However, I believe Elaine is innocent."

Peggy brushed away a sudden tear. "I . . . do too. But, Derek, be careful. You're in danger too."

He looked at Peggy in confusion. "Me?" He frowned and shook his head. "Nah. Elaine's the victim here. She's . . ." Suddenly, he looked utterly stricken and horrified, as if he'd realized what he'd said. "Peggy, I'm sorry. I'm such a moron. Of course, you—"

A knock at the door.

Peggy froze. All the terror and trauma she'd suppressed erupted to the surface. *It's him! It's Shawn!*

No, you idiot! Shawn wouldn't knock.

Elaine stopped singing. "I'll get it!"

"No!" Derek was on his feet, racing to stop her.

The knock came again, followed by, "Hey, Peggy! You in there?"

That voice! Impossible. He's . . .

Peggy leapt to her feet. She dashed through the shattered bedroom doorway, past a startled Derek and Elaine.

She flung open the door, revealing the last person she ever expected to see.

He looked disheveled and unshaven. In fact, he looked as if he had driven all through the night.

Todd.

XV

Todd!" Peggy's mind swirled with countless questions, but all she managed was, "You're here."

Todd's eyes scanned her. Peggy felt as if he was assessing her condition. Then his gazed shifted to Derek—briefly—and then to Elaine. He stared at the girl intently, his eyes moving from her golden-brown hair to her modest, knee-length dress—which, though not tight, emphasized her slender curves—to her sandaled feet. Todd's eyes then returned to Elaine's face . . . and he smiled.

He set the large duffle bag he carried down and extended a hand. "Hi, I'm Todd Cavetto. I'm an old friend of Peggy's."

Elaine smiled prettily, her eyes bright and gleaming, as she curtsied. She took his hand. "I'm Elaine. I'm Derek's friend." She glanced at Peggy and gave her an uncertain, questioning smile. "Peggy's too."

Peggy nodded . . . reluctantly.

Elaine grinned widely, showing her not-quite-straight teeth, and turned her attention back to Todd.

Derek's face twisted into an almost scowl. "I, uh . . . We got the carpet cleaned. The police left a while ago. So, um . . ."

Todd let go of Elaine's hand and grasped Derek's. He shook it warmly. "Thanks. I'll take it from here."

"That's okay." Derek let go of Todd's hand. To Peggy's surprise, he sidled closer to her. "We can stick around for a bit."

Todd shook his head and smiled. "I got this. You two go ahead and enjoy the rest of your day. You've done great. I really appreciate you taking care of things here. But, I'll take it from here." He patted a weapon holstered on his right hip.

He has a gun. To protect me.

Todd picked his duffle bag up again and focused his gaze on Peggy. He gave her a warm smile. And as haggard and wrung out as he looked, he was ruggedly handsome when he smiled. "Mind if I come in?"

116

He came here – all the way from Spokane – to protect me.
He came for me.
"Yeah," she said. *He saved my life. Then he dropped everything . . . for me.* "Sure."

Todd's grin widened, but he looked so tired. His face was lined and unshaven. Dark circles rimmed bloodshot blue eyes. However, those eyes sparkled. "Great! Elaine, it was a pleasure to meet you. Derek, thanks again."

Todd put his arm around Peggy's shoulders and gently, but firmly turned her around. He guided her toward her bedroom. "You go on and get ready for bed. I'll watch over you while you sleep." Then he whispered, "Let me get rid of them, and we'll talk. Or you can just sack out." He let go of her and stopped short of her shattered bedroom door.

Peggy nodded and went to her closet. She was so tired and dizzy, she almost fell over when she retrieved her nightgown from the closet floor – where she'd unceremoniously tossed it the instant she'd heard Derek was on the way. *Derek came, but he brought Elaine. But Todd dropped everything and came all the way from Washington. For me.* As she was about to enter the bathroom to change, she looked back.

Todd was cheerfully and insistently ushering Derek, Elaine, and the carpet cleaner out the front door. The carpet cleaner, of course, was indifferent to the polite yet firm dismissal, but Elaine looked confused, and Derek wore a scowl of annoyance.

As she closed and locked the bathroom door, Peggy didn't even attempt to suppress a smile.

She washed off her makeup and repeated her facial regimen – or rather, the shorter variation she employed when she was really tired – and then she took a good look at herself in the mirror as she braided her hair.

You look tired, Peggy.
Tired and plain and old.
How old is Elaine really? She looks . . . maybe twenty, but even with her jumping forward in time every sixty years, whenever she appears for six months or so, she has to live through those months. She has to age during that time, doesn't she? How can she look so young – so young and so pretty?
How many times has she done this?
How old is she?
She scowled at her cosmetic-free reflection. *I don't want Todd to see me like this.*
Why do you care, Peggy? He's not Derek.

No, he's not Derek. He's Todd — the one who came to protect you.

Exactly. That's why I don't want him to see me like this.

Come on, Peggy! Give yourself a break! You just survived an attempted rape and two murder attempts. You're entitled. Nobody expects you to look, well, your best after that.

Yeah. Besides, Todd doesn't care how I look. He's not interested in me that way. He's just a friend.

Yeah, a very good friend. The best kind of friend. He doesn't care what you look like. He's just there when you need him.

Peggy slipped on her long nightgown, then examined her face in the mirror once more. She frowned and growled at her image. Then she stuck out her tongue.

Say good-bye to your last shred of dignity.

When she entered her bedroom, she stared in shock. The covers and sheets had been stripped from the bed. But a greater shock awaited her in the living room.

Todd had rearranged the furniture. At that moment, he was in the process of laying her dining room table on its side in front of the door. Her single easy chair was up against the wall, facing toward the bedroom.

Only the sofa remained in its normal place, but Todd had converted it into a bed. Her pillows and comforter covered it. She assumed that underneath she'd find her sheets as well, neatly tucked in. *If he's going to sleep on the sofa, does he expect me to sleep with nothing?*

Or is the couch for me?

"Todd?" she said, confused and unsure if she liked the idea of him having completely taken charge of her home.

Having finished barricading the door, Todd turned around and smiled apologetically. "I know it's a bit presumptuous of me, but it's for your protection. We're on the ground floor, you see. The bed makes you an easy target. All somebody has to do is to shoot through the bedroom window. If he fires off enough rounds quickly, he's bound to hit you." He pointed at the sofa. "The couch is below the window, so he can't get the same angle. So you're gonna sleep on the couch."

"O . . . kay. Where are *you* gonna sleep?"

He shrugged and shook his head. "I'm not. I'll stay alert as long as I can."

Peggy's eyes filled with tears. "But you just drove all night." Her voice shook.

He nodded. "Yeah, but I can go a few more hours at least. I've got some caffeine pills. I can keep going a bit longer. And I haven't . . . been through what you've been through. So you sleep." He patted the holstered gun on his hip. "I'll stand guard." He pointed at the easy chair. "Maybe I'll *sit* guard."

As the tears spilled from her eyes, Peggy rushed forward and hugged him. She was very conscious that she wasn't wearing a bra under her nightgown—she never wore one to bed—but at that moment, she didn't care. She laid her head on his shoulder. "Thank you."

After a second's hesitation, Todd put his strong arms around her and held her tight. "My pleasure, pretty lady."

Pretty lady? Is he . . . hitting on me? Now? After all I've endured? We're alone and . . . I'm defenseless.

And what if he is? What if he is hitting on you? Would that be so bad?

Not now. Not today.

She pulled back, not fully breaking the embrace, but making sure there was a somewhat more *appropriate* distance between her chest and his. She looked up at him with confusion and more than a little concern. "'Pretty lady?' Nobody's ever called me that."

He smiled, his bloodshot, blue eyes staring into hers. "You have the prettiest eyes I've ever seen. And when you smile . . ." Then his jaw dropped, his eyes widened, and his face flushed. "Oh, Peggy, I-I'm sorry. That was"—he looked away—"completely inappropriate. I'm sorry." He pulled back from her, cleared his throat, and pointed at the sofa. "You get some sleep. You're safe. You can . . . trust me. Really, you can."

Peggy crossed her arms protectively over her chest. She lowered her head and nodded, not looking at him. And as she slipped into the bed he'd made for her on the couch, she turned her back to him. Wrapping the comforter and sheet around herself protectively, as if the layers of bedclothes were armor, she squeezed her eyes shut, trying to contain the maelstrom of emotions swirling inside her.

He was hitting on me. Why would he do that? Because I'm vulnerable and alone?

Peggy, the man dropped everything and drove all night just to be here with you. Isn't it obvious?

But, he can't be . . . He can't have . . . feelings for me. He's just my old friend, my D&D buddy. And to be honest, right now is not . . .

Okay, so his timing is awful, but is it so hard to believe that he could . . .

Yes! That's the problem—it is hard to believe. I'm nothing like Christy, the girl he married. I'm not pretty. I'm not vivacious and charming and desirable. I'm geeky and nerdy and plain. I'm not the kind of woman a man like that wants. I'm not the kind of woman any man wants . . . unless he's just looking for an easy . . . conquest.

Stop it. You're not being fair to him. Todd saved your life.

Yes, he did.

You should at least give him the benefit of the doubt.

I guess so.

And if he does have feelings for you . . . What then?

I don't know. I'm not sure of anything anymore. Nothing makes sense. Could Todd really have feelings for me?

And with those unanswered questions bouncing around her brain, exhaustion finally claimed her.

◢ ◢ ◢

Something cold and sharp pressed against Peggy's throat. Her eyes snapped open. A hooded man hovered above her, the face cast in shadow. In the dim light, she could see only the man's gleaming teeth. "Just go along with it, bitch. Maybe you'll enjoy it, huh? Anyway, it'll all be over soon." Keeping the knife at her throat, the hooded man climbed on top of her, his weight crushing her into the sofa cushions. His sour breath smelled of alcohol.

No! Not again! In spite of the heavy body crushing her, she drew in a lungful of air to scream.

"Scream, and I'll slit your throat right now."

The cry died in her throat.

Hoodie-Man pawed at her, ripping her nightgown.

"Please," she whimpered. "Please don't do this! Please! No!"

"Piggy-Peggy," he said. "That's what the kids used to call you, right? When you were a little girl? Well, maybe you weren't so *little* then, huh, Piggy-Peggy?"

How could he know that name?

"Please don't!"

He chuckled—an evil, malicious sound.

Fight him!

I can't! He's too strong! And I'm so weak. Helpless.

Pathetic.

Todd! Help me please, Todd.

"W-where's Todd?" she blubbered.

The vicious grin widened. "I'm right here."

Hoodie-Man pulled off his hood, revealing Todd's face, leering down at her. "Squeal for me, Piggy-Peggy."

And Peggy screamed.

120

"Whoa!" Todd said. "I'm sorry. I didn't mean to scare you."

The crushing weight was gone. Nobody was on top of her. She wasn't being raped.

Todd stood beside the couch.

A dream. Just a nightmare.

"You okay?" Todd asked. He looked worried and contrite. "I called your name, but you didn't respond, so I shook your shoulder. I'm sorry I scared you."

Quaking like a leaf in a windstorm, Peggy sat up on the couch. "I'm okay." *It wasn't Todd. He's here to help me.*

For one brief moment, she needed to be held. She needed *Todd* to hold her. And she almost reached for him.

Instead, she looked at the blinds covering the window. *Still daylight.* "What time is it?"

"Nearly two in the afternoon. I'm sorry. I just had to wake you up. I'm losing it here. Can't stay alert anymore. Just need a couple hours of shut-eye. Sorry."

"No." Peggy shook her head, mostly to clear the cobwebs and the nightmare images out of her brain. "That's okay. You take the couch. Let me . . . uh . . . stand watch."

Todd unholstered his sidearm, checked the safety, and handed the gun to Peggy, grip-first. "You know how to use one of these?"

Peggy nodded. "My dad took me to a gun range a few times when I was a teenager." She took the weapon. She checked the safety, felt the weight of it, and examined the gun. "Glock-17, semiautomatic. Nine millimeter."

Todd smiled and ran a hand through his hair. "The lady knows her guns. There are fifteen hollow-point rounds in the magazine. If you have to shoot somebody, empty the clip. Aim for the chest."

Peggy smiled wistfully. "You sound like my dad."

"So, your dad is a smart man too, huh?" He yawned long and loud. "Really losing it here."

Peggy got off the couch. "My turn." She sat in the chair. It was warm. *Todd has been sitting here for hours. Watching over me.*

Todd was already on the sofa, wrapped in the comforter. "So, did you get any intel from the enemy?"

"The enemy?"

"Elaine. What did you learn from talking to her?"

"Mostly that she seems really nice. Darn it. Genuine. I think she might be innocent in all this."

"Hm. You think so?"

Peggy set the gun on the coffee table in front of her. "I *want* to hate her. You don't know how much I *want* to hate her. But I just can't. She's so sweet. And she's scared. And she doesn't really remember anything about her previous jumps in time. As stupid as it sounds, I think she's as much a victim here as . . ." *As me.*

"Did you ask her about . . . talking to trees?" He sounded like he was drifting off.

Peggy chuckled. "Actually, I did. She says *she* does all the talking. She just imagines what the trees might say back."

"Huh. Just a couple hours. Two hours. No more . . . more'n that. I mean it. Promise?"

"Promise."

Todd began to snore softly.

Peggy smiled. *You really are one of the good ones, Todd Cavetto. Christy is a fool.*

♦ ♦ ♦

Shawn O'Rourke watched the giant dog as it lay just inside the circle of standing stones. Suetonius rested its head on its massive paws. Blacker than the moonless night, the beast was almost invisible—a darker shadow among dark shadows. Only the huge dog's eyes were visible.

And those eyes stared right back at Shawn.

For the tenth time in the last couple of minutes, Shawn wrapped his fingers around the grip of the Smith & Wesson forty-five semiauto in the shoulder holster. He was making sure the gun was loose and ready to draw. Very few things in the world scared Shawn, but the molossii did. Perhaps "scared" wasn't the right word, but Suetonius and its mate, Gaius, definitely made Shawn very nervous.

And Gaius was pregnant.

More of those monsters on the way, Shawn thought.

He leaned against one of the tall stones, trying to look casually indifferent to the molossus' presence . . . and checked his weapon yet again. "'Meet at the Tree at midnight,' she says." He checked the time on his cell phone. "Well, it's fifteen minutes past. Where the hell is she?"

The dog huffed, as if expressing impatience of its own.

"One of you two beasts are always out here, aren't you? Guarding this 'sacred tree,' right? I looked you up, you know. Molossus—an extinct breed of Roman war dog, known for its ferocity in battle and its massive size." He glared at the dog. "Well, you're massive all right."

The thing about the dogs that spooked Shawn the most was the fact that they were virtually silent. They never barked or growled. The huffing noise was about as loud as they ever got. "Could sneak right up on a guy, and he'd never know you were there."

Shawn could see his breath. The air was chilly, and he almost regretted ditching the hooded sweatshirt he'd worn earlier. Almost. The Carson woman had surely given that particular detail to the police. "Probably still soaking wet, anyway."

"You failed me, Shawn."

Shawn nearly jumped out of his shoes. He spun around, uttering a particularly choice oath. "You gotta quit sneaking up on me!" *How does she do that?*

Morgaise stood just outside the circle wearing her customary black, floor-length dress. And the nonparalyzed half of her face looked royally pissed. "Language, Shawn. There is no excuse for foul language, and I will not tolerate it in my presence."

Okay, I'll play your game, lady. Just a bit longer—just till I get paid. Then I'm out of this freak show.

He inclined his head deferentially. "Forgive me, my Lady."

"For the language, yes. For the failure, no."

"Hey, it wasn't me that"—he picked a different word from the one he was about to use—"messed up. It was that prissy little disciple of yours. I set it all up for him. I did the legwork. I got him in the door. But he couldn't handle it. She kicked his . . . She killed him."

Morgaise glared at him with her good eye. "And your job was to ensure Evan's success. You failed me."

"Look, I wanted to just ice her, but no. You had to have your blessed *ritual*. Well, this wouldn't've happened if you'd listened to me. So just pay me, and I'll disappear."

Morgaise regarded him in silence for a moment. Then she nodded. "As you say. Wait here. My sister will return with your payment."

Elaine? The younger girl never seemed to get involved in the messy stuff. "Yeah, well, hurry it up."

Morgaise turned and walked briskly back toward the house.

Shawn watched her go. "Never should've taken this gig. Abbot's a damned fool. The money's good, but these crazy women . . ."

Morgaise was no longer in sight. *If I never have to see that ugly half-face again, it'll be too soon.* Shawn had little use for women in the first place—except for *one* use, that was—but ugly women made him want to puke. *And this butt-ugly house!*

He looked at Suetonius. "Ugly dog too."

Suetonius huffed again.

Yeah, you don't like me either.

Now, that Elaine chick — I wouldn't kick her outta bed.

Shawn looked at the tree growing out of the top of the mound at the center of the stone circle. It was a lot bigger than it'd been the last time he saw it. *That was just a couple days ago. I swear it's grown two feet. I thought they just planted it . . . What? A few weeks ago?* The "sacred tree" had reached a height of seven feet. *Who ever heard of a tree that grows that fast? It's like a sunflower . . . or one of those* Invasion of the Body Snatchers *pod-things.*

He shrugged. "What do I know about trees? Nothing."

Looking back toward the house, he saw a figure dressed in a white robe and hood walking slowly toward him. Shawn had never seen Elaine walk anywhere without skipping or dancing. *And since when does Elaine go in for all the white-robe disciple stuff they do around here, chanting in the moonlight?* He'd never seen the pretty sister participate in the rituals with the acolytes and disciples.

He checked his weapon again, then forced his hand to his side. *Don't look nervous. Never wanna look nervous around the Morrigan sisters. Or their dogs.*

Once Elaine got within a few paces, Shawn noticed that Gaius was walking beside her, the dog's belly and teats swollen with pregnancy.

She's got both dogs. Well, a hollow-point round in the chest will stop those monsters . . . if it comes to that.

Elaine halted a yard in front of him. Gaius sat on its haunches beside her. Elaine kept her head down, the hood hiding her face. She stood unmoving, holding a bag in her left hand.

Shawn stared at her uncomprehendingly for a moment. *What's she waiting for?* Then he remembered. Morgaise always insisted that he accept his pay with his right hand—and *only* his right hand. *Another damned ritual.*

He extended his right hand in the prescribed manner, palm up.

Elaine's hand shot out and swiped across his wrist. Her movement was so quick, that Shawn didn't realize what had happened—not until the blood began to spurt from his wrist and his right hand hung limp and useless.

She'd severed the arteries in his wrist. And the tendons.

With a cry of pain and horror, he reached for his gun, but his right hand wouldn't respond. He stepped back, grasping for his weapon with his left hand, but couldn't quite reach the holster under his left armpit.

Another flash of gold, and the bronze knife sliced his throat open.

He fell to his knees, clutching at his neck with his good left hand. Blood streamed through his fingers.

The white-robed figure kicked him in the chest, and he fell on his back. Elaine stepped closer and leaned down. She pulled back her hood, and Shawn saw that it was *not* Elaine. The woman's face was lifeless, like the visage of a corpse.

As his blood soaked into the mound and his thoughts grew dim, Shawn heard a sound as of wood creaking. Above him, blossoms burst out all over the tree.

The dead lips moved, and a voice whispered, cold and dry, like stale air escaping the long-sealed tomb of some ancient queen. "The children here sing a song—*Popcorn Popping on the Apricot Tree*." The crone cackled softly. "Perhaps we shall have an early harvest." She straightened up. "Suetonius, Gaius—*Ede*."

Both dogs moved in silently and sank their teeth into Shawn's flesh.

XVI

1595: Bayerischer Wald (Bavarian Forest), Bavaria

It was the kiss that woke her, the soft brush of lips against hers — skin on skin, flesh on flesh. Love's first kiss. And it was sweet.

Her eyes fluttered open.

Roland leaned over her, blocking the torchlight. And though his face was cast in wobbling shadow, she could see that he was smiling.

Skuld thought she might die of happiness. She smiled back at him. "You found me."

"Schneewittchen, my love! You live! I thought you were dead. Your lips . . . they were so cold."

She shook her head slightly, rolling it on the soft pillow. "My lips are warm now."

"Schneewittchen!" He bent and kissed her again.

And Skuld reveled in the touch of his lips against hers. *Schneewittchen! Because of my fair skin — skin as white as snow, they say. I do so prefer that name to Skuld. Yes, I shall be Schneewittchen from now on. And I shall be with my beloved Roland.*

She kissed him again and sighed happily.

You may not be a prince, my love — only the unlanded, bastard son of Duke Wilhelm the Pious — but you are prince enough for me. And we shall be wed in the church — the Roman church, yes, but it must be so. And we shall leave this land and flee to a faraway country, where no one will ever find us — not the Romans and not . . .

Her head began to throb. *No. I will not think of it. Not now. Not when I am so happy.*

Roland's face clouded over with worry. "My love?"

She smiled up at him. "I am well."

Roland reached into the long box of glass and copper in which Skuld lay, put his arms around her, and lifted her out. From Skuld's

126

hand fell a golden fruit, in shape very much like an apple, with a single bite missing.

Roland set Skuld on her feet on the cavern floor. Then he encircled her in his strong arms. "I love you, my fairest of the fair, my Schnee-wittchen."

Skuld closed her eyes and trembled in his embrace. *And we shall leave all fear behind us. And I will bear you strong sons and beautiful daughters. And we shall be safe at last.* "And I shall love you, my prince, to the end of my days."

A cheer rose up around them, echoing off the walls of the cavern. "She lives! Schneewittchen lives!"

Skuld opened her eyes and beheld her loyal friends surrounding her and Roland—seven elderly men, some of them holding torches, all of them kneeling and waving their hats in celebration.

"My dear friends!" Skuld broke away from her beloved Roland's arms, clapping her hands in delight. "You stood watch over me."

Wolfgang, the eldest, bowed his bald head. "Yes, Princess." He wiped away a tear with short, round fingers, more reminiscent of sausages than the clever, skilled fingers of the artisan he was.

Skuld bent and laid a hand on the short man's head as if bestowing a royal blessing. "You have my eternal gratitude, dear Wolfie." She moved her hand from Wolfgang's pate to his chin. Tenderly, she raised his bowed head. "I can never hope to fully express my gratitude or repay the debt I owe"—she looked into the faces of each of Wolfgang's brothers—"to each and all of you." The aged faces—more lined and wrinkled than Skuld remembered—beamed in the reflected light of her love and approbation. "Rise, my dear friends. You sheltered me. You hid me from my enemies. You cherished me as you would a daughter."

"It was nothing," said Ulf, the youngest of the brothers, smiling through his long, gray beard. "You were never a burden. You brought such joy into our lives. You were the bright star of our twilight days."

Skuld glided toward Ulf. As she moved around the glass coffin, her steps were light and graceful, as if she were dancing. She placed a delicate hand on either side of his gray head and tilted it down. And although both she and Ulf were standing, she had to bow to bestow a kiss on the little man's head. "And you have all been as fathers to me."

She danced around the circle and kissed the head of each brother in turn, pronouncing words of daughterly affection.

Then Skuld turned her gaze back to her beloved Roland. Even in the flickering light of the torches, he cut an impressive, manly figure.

Has he grown taller, or is it merely a trick of the torchlight? "And you found my Roland."

"We searched for eleven winters, Princess," said Johann—though not the youngest, he was the most spry of the brethren. "Two of us were ever at your side, two continued our craft, but the other three, led by myself—we searched far and—"

Skuld felt as if she might faint. "Eleven winters? *Eleven?*"

Johann bowed his head in shame. "Yes, Princess. You have slept for more than ten years."

Then I did not imagine it. Roland is taller.

Roland stepped toward her. He took her small hand in both of his and knelt on one knee. His flesh was so warm. "Yes, my love. I am no longer the youth you agreed to marry. I have traveled many leagues and seen many things since we were parted . . . since I thought I'd lost you forever." His brown eyes glistened in the flickering light, brimming with unshed tears. "But now we are reunited. Will you still consent to be my bride, my life's companion?"

A collective gasp rose from the seven brothers, and even Roland's eyes grew wide, as Skuld knelt before him. She placed her free hand atop his and looked up—he was most assuredly taller than he had been—up into his eyes. "Roland Wittelsbach von Bayern, I will marry you."

Roland bent down and kissed her.

And the seven brothers cheered once again.

And joy welled up in Skuld till she thought she might faint again.

Then her head began to throb. She moaned and pulled away from Roland.

Worry clouded his features. "Schneewittchen? My love?"

Skuld released his hands and put her fists to her head. The cave spun, so she closed her eyes tightly. "We must go," she said.

"Go?"

Her eyes flew open, and she took his hands in hers once more, squeezing them hard. "We must flee! Now!"

"Go?" cried her friends. "Now?"

"We must go now!" Skuld looked about frantically. "Where are the hounds? Where are Paulinus and Quintus?"

"They sleep still," said Wolfgang, his eyes cast down as if with guilt.

"How is that possible?" Skuld did not understand. "They should have awakened before me." *At the first scent of mankind.* Panic filled her, driving away all reason. "They always awaken before me."

"We . . ." Wolfgang twisted his hat in his hands, definitely guilt-ridden. "Forgive us, Princess, but we . . . deceived them. We gave them pieces of the fruit, mixed with sausage—as you instructed—but we fed them in another chamber of the cavern. They would not allow us to watch over you. They kept waking whenever we approached your casket. So we . . . lured them away." He bowed his head. "Forgive us."

Skuld smiled, deeply touched by the love and devotion of her adopted fathers. "All is forgiven, my friends. But please guide me to them. Hurry. Roland and I must depart immediately."

"But," said Roland, "it is madness to enter the forest at night. There are bandits . . . and my father's game wardens."

Skuld rubbed her aching temples. "We must go, before we are discovered."

Roland nodded. "Then let us be away."

♦ ♦ ♦

The two massive hounds padded silently along the game trail, leading the way through the dark forest. They sniffed the ground and the air for danger, then halted, looking back at the lovers following slowly behind.

Skuld clung to Roland's arm with one hand as they walked, picking their way slowly over the dark trail. In her right hand, she clutched a bronze knife. She held the weapon awkwardly, unaccustomed as she was to wielding knives except for cooking. Roland carried a dagger in his left hand, reflecting the light of the occasional star. Skuld knew Roland was taking the utmost care that they should not stumble and injure themselves. And yet Skuld wished they could travel faster. Peril was close at hand, even at their heels.

In her vivid imagination, every noise of the dark forest portended danger. The hoot of an owl became a ghostly cry. The rustling of leaves became the sound of a hundred pursuing footsteps. The flapping of bats became the beating of demons' wings. Even the branches of the trees grasped at her cloak and hair with skeletal fingers.

"The dwarves," Roland said in a low voice, providing Skuld with a welcome distraction from her waking nightmare, "they were . . . good to you?"

"Yes, and I loved them all dearly." The parting had been bitter-sweet—the more so, because it had been so hurried. "They discovered me alone and terrified, hiding in their woodland cottage. At first, they feared me, because they knew I had run away from . . . the castle. But they became my protectors. And when I realized that discovery was imminent, I partook of the fruit"—nervously, she patted her satchel and the precious, wooden box it contained—"and I slept. I slept, knowing they would hide me and watch over me . . . and search for you." She looked up at the dim outline of his face. "And they brought you back to—"

Skuld stifled a scream. She stood as still as a stone, listening intently to the night sounds. "What was that?" she hissed.

After a moment, Roland whispered. "I hear nothing but the sounds of the forest."

"Can you not hear it?" Skuld looked around, searching the trees, the shadows within shadows. A chill like a winter wind shook her.

She is here!

Roland pulled his arm free from her grasp. "Wait here!"

"Roland, no!" she whispered, clutching after him, her fingers closing on nothing but air.

"The hounds will protect you," he said. "Call them."

"Paulinus!" she hissed as loud as she dared. "Quintus!"

In the space of two beats from her pounding heart, the black dogs were on either side of her. She placed a hand on Paulinus, seeking comfort in the beast's warmth, in its strength.

She could no longer see Roland. She could no longer discern anything in the blackness. All she had were her ears. So she closed her eyes and listened with all her being.

And she heard the sound of footsteps on the path.

"I see nothing," Roland said. "There is no—"

His voice stopped mid-word.

Skuld opened her eyes.

Roland stood before her, a dark man shape in the blackness. He said nothing, but made a sound like a gurgling spring. His knife fell to the ground, and Roland crumpled to his knees, clutching at his throat.

"Roland!" she screamed.

He toppled onto his back, and Skuld dropped to her knees beside him. "Roland! Roland!" She sobbed his name and ran her hands over his face, his neck, his chest. She felt the hot blood spurting, smelled its coppery scent, but she could not see it in the night. She clamped her hands over his throat as if with the power of her love she might close the wound and stop his life's blood from escaping.

In seconds, the pulsing flow of his blood lessened.

"Roland!" She wrapped her arms around him, shook him, but he did not respond. "Roland!" Blood soaked into her cloak and her gown and drenched her hair.

And she wept, her tears mingling with the gore.

The hounds sat on either side of Skuld, panting, sniffing.

"It is done," said an ancient voice—the phantom substance of nightmares—a voice Skuld had never heard in the waking world. "Did you think to elude us forever, child? And look at you. You have aged, child. Every time you do this foolishness, you *age*." The voice imbued the word with utter contempt. "You have aged an entire year."

"That is enough, Urd," said another voice—a kindly voice—a voice Skuld had hoped never to hear again. "Allow her a moment's grief. Allow her to mourn her loss."

Urd growled, then remained silent.

"Why, Verdandi?" Skuld wailed. "Why? I was happy! We were happy! Why could you not simply leave us in peace?"

"Why?" Verdandi laughed as if Skuld had asked the most foolish question in the entire history of foolish questions. "Why, sister? You know the answer."

And Skuld did know the answer. In a voice as hollow as her empty, broken heart, she recited the litany, "We are in danger. The Romans control this world, and we must flee to the next. And someday, Rome and all its might will be dust. And we will be truly safe."

Skuld took Roland's bloody face in her hands. She kissed his lips, the lips that had awakened her from the long slumber. Those lips were cold—and covered with blood. "Good-bye, my love," she whispered.

"Come, sweet Skuld," Verdandi said. "We must flee."

"Where shall we go?" Skuld asked, wiping the blood from her lips with her sleeve. "Where in this world can we go?"

"Back to England," her sister replied. "Elizabeth Tudor has driven the Romans and their minions from her land. We shall be safe there . . . for a time."

"We shall never be safe," Skuld said, rising to her feet. She began to shuffle down the path, as lifeless as a revenant.

"Mind your step, sister," said Verdandi, wiping the drool from the dead side of her mouth. "We would not want you to break your ankle."

"Yes, sister," Skuld replied. "You are so good to me." However, her tone belied the gratitude of her words. She felt as dead as the drooping side of her sister's face.

"When we return to England," Verdandi said, "we shall visit the Abbot family. We shall remind them of their oath and obligation. They shall serve us again, just as they did long ago."

"Yes, Verdandi," Skuld said. *And all shall be as it was. As it shall ever be.*

"And it is time, I think," Verdandi continued, "for us to take new names. The names of the three Norns will not serve us on our native soil. No, they will not. We can no longer be Skuld, Verdandi, and Urd. Perhaps something from the age of Artos and Myrddn. But they call them Arthur and Merlin now, do they not? Yes, Merlin's triple goddess, sorceress, and temptress. That will do." Half of her face smiled. "You, Urd, shall be Morgana. I shall be Morgause. No, *Morgaise* is better. Yes, Morgaise. I shall be Morgaise. And you, my sweet sister—you shall be Elaine." Morgaise, who had been known and feared by many such names, sighed contently. "And we shall be together. And we shall be safe."

Skuld, who had briefly been known as Schneewittchen, and who would thereafter be Elaine, shook her head and wiped away a tear—the last tear she would ever shed for Roland. *When next I awaken, will I even remember my dearest Roland? No. I think not. Roland shall be lost to me, not even the dimmest memory.*

And I shall be alone.

No, not alone—I shall have my sisters.

I shall always have my sisters.

"And we shall all be safe."

XVII

Aw, come on!" Todd groaned. "That's a *videogame* character, for Pete's sake!"

Peggy bit her lower lip, trying — sincerely trying, and yet still failing — to suppress a smile.

The object of Todd's disdain, a teenage boy, costumed in the quasi-medieval green garb of a popular digital hero, walked alongside a teenage girl wearing a purple-and-white princess dress and matching tiara. Both sported long, pointed, and very fake-looking ears. The boy carried a Styrofoam shield and a large plastic sword.

Todd lowered his voice to a disgruntled mutter. "How's *that* supposed to be authentic?"

Peggy squeezed the crook of his elbow. "Hey, not everybody dresses authentically for a Renaissance faire. Some people just come in shorts and T-shirts. At least they're authentic-*ish*."

"No such thing." Todd drummed his fingers on the basket-hilt of his sword — his *authentic* Scottish basket-hilt claymore, forged of real, high-carbon steel.

"It's not every man who can *rock* a kilt like you!" *And you do look fantastic in that Scottish costume, great-kilt and all. Especially the kilt.* "You look like you stepped right out of the sixteenth century."

Todd snorted. "I look like an idiot." Then he grinned. "But at least I look like an *authentic* idiot."

"Well," Peggy said, "I think you look ..." *Sexy. Hot.* "... magnificent."

Todd raised a very Spock-like, quizzical eyebrow. "You know, I could think of about a dozen adjectives to describe how I look right now, but 'magnificent' would not be among them. I don't think *anyone* in their right mind — at least if they were sober — would use that word to describe *me* in a kilt."

He sighed, and looked straight ahead, his expression taking on an air of forced innocence. "Besides, I guarantee nobody is wasting a moment looking at me, no matter how ridiculous I look. If their eyes happen to glance this way, they'll be riveted to the lovely princess on my arm."

Peggy felt her cheeks flush. *I wish I knew how to read you, Todd Cavetto — you and your compliments.*

Todd was *never* stingy with his compliments — not with her, not since the day he arrived two months earlier. However, physically at least, he kept a respectful distance since that day — since the day he told her she had the prettiest eyes he'd ever seen. She was never sure if he was flirting or simply being nice.

She bent her knees in a fair, if somewhat ungraceful, curtsey. *Good thing I have Todd to hold on to. I'd probably fall on my butt.* "Thank you, milord."

Todd inclined his head in acknowledgement, a smile playing at the edge of his lips. "I still can hardly believe you made that gown yourself. And I watched you sew it!"

Peggy grinned happily. "Well, I can't take *all* the credit."

He gave her a skeptical look. "You've gotta be kidding me. You did it all yourself. You forget, milady — I was there."

She squeezed his arm. "Exactly. You were *there*. You went to the fabric store with me." *You haven't left my side since you arrived.* "You helped me pick out the pattern and the fabrics. You helped measure and cut the cloth. And you kept me company while I sewed."

"I sat at your dining table and worked remote on my laptop. I wasn't great company. Mostly, I tried not to make a nuisance of myself."

"But you were there." *Watching over me.* "You're always there." *And you were* never *a nuisance.* A tear threatened at the corner of her eye.

"So," Todd said, drawing out the word, "what you're saying is . . . I'm beginning to get on your nerves." He pulled his right hand against his chest, curling the hand upward into a claw as if it were paralyzed. He arched his back, lifting one shoulder above the other. Then he bent his head and turned it toward Peggy, twisting his face into a comical grimace, as he dragged his right foot behind him. "Tell me truthfully," he said in his best Peter Lorre impersonation. "Isss it the way I walk? Isss it my voice? Giff me another chance! I can change!"

"Stop it!" Peggy cried, slapping playfully at his curled claw-hand. She tried to give him a mortified look, but succeeded only in bursting into laughter.

Todd straightened his body, but it was too late — the damage was done. Peggy was laughing uncontrollably. In moments, her laugh had transformed into her "goofy" laugh. And the more she laughed, the worse she got. It was embarrassing—or it should have been—but Todd was laughing too—with her, not at her.

He likes . . . my laugh?

After their mutual hilarity slowly quieted, they both wiped at their eyes.

"That's it," Todd said with a nod. "You should smile more often. It lights up your whole face." He looked as if he were about to say more, but then he turned and strolled along again, at least ostensibly scanning the crowd of fairegoers.

Peggy suppressed a sigh. *I really* don't *know how to read you, Todd Cavetto.*

But I have to admit, you're in an awkward situation.

We're both *in an awkward situation.*

The gossip was vicious, of course, with some of the women in her singles ward chattering on like canaries on caffeine.

She could still hear Cassie Woodruff and Tanya Smoot in the ladies room at church on Sunday, unaware of Peggy's presence in the restroom stall.

"They're living together!" Cassie said. "No other way to put it. She says he sleeps in the spare bedroom — as if! I visit teach her — or I used to before she requested someone else. Anyway, I've been in her place, and that so-called 'spare bedroom' is her home office. There's no bed in there, I tell you. I told the bishop about my concerns, and he says it's unusual, but it's" — she paused as if making air quotes — "'for her protection.' I mean, I heard she was attacked and all, but it's been like two months! And it's those clothes she wears, if you ask me. I mean, they're modest and all, but they're too form-fitting. And she's always wearing pantyhose and heels — even to work. Who wears pantyhose anymore? And the way she sways her hips when she walks! I'm not saying she had it coming, but . . . well, don't you think she bears some responsibility?"

Peggy had heard such vile comments before, but had never responded to the backbiting — not out loud, at least. But the insinuations always stung like angry wasps in her ears. And though she had resolved to simply wait silently until long after Cassie and Tanya left, it was Tanya's response that shattered her forbearance.

"If you ask me," Tanya said, "I'm wondering why a hunk like that would be with her? I heard he paid for an expensive security system, complete with cameras and motion-sensor lights, and . . . who-knows-what-else. Why would

he do that? He must be getting something from her. And you know exactly what I mean."

At that point, Peggy burst from the bathroom stall. For a moment, both Tanya and Cassie's eyes widened, the color draining from their faces. Then they both narrowed their eyes in contempt as they stared down their raised noses at her.

Tears of rage threatened to spill from Peggy's eyes. "You can say whatever you like about me," she'd growled through clenched teeth. "Say any vicious, nasty thing you want about me — even if you don't have the guts to say it to my face. But you have no right to even suggest those awful things about Todd. He's the nicest, sweetest man I've ever met. And for your information, he has NEVER touched me."

She pushed between the stunned, self-righteous harpies and stormed out of the restroom.

Peggy felt her cheeks burning at the memory, but to be honest, as awkward and unseemly as it might be to have Todd staying with her, she was beginning to wonder how she would bear it if Todd were suddenly . . . *not* always there.

From that first night, he'd kept her safe. He installed a door — a heavy, solid door with a deadbolt — on her bedroom. The next day — a Sunday — he accompanied her to church, and they met with her bishop to explain the unusual situation. They didn't tell him *everything*, of course — no mention of time-travelers or Druids or giant, supposedly extinct, man-eating war dogs — just enough to explain the danger. And Bishop Iyamba agreed, and after some prayer, of course, even gave the arrangement his cautious blessing — along with some stern counsel. On the following Monday — two days after his arrival — Todd drove Peggy to work and walked her to the entrance. And while she was at work, he purchased and installed the security system.

And then he *apologized* profusely for his presumption. Apologized! As if she might be offended at his caring for her, even if he was taking over so many aspects of her life.

Peggy felt many confusing and conflicting, warm and tingly, and frustrating emotions when it came to Todd, but she was not offended.

But he kept his distance, especially when they were at home alone. He was the perfect gentleman, of course. Perhaps, too much the perfect gentleman.

She squeezed Todd's arm as they strolled through the faire. "Thank you."

Todd paused, drumming his fingers on the hilt of his sword, and looked at her quizzically. "For what?"

She smiled at him and shrugged. "Everything."

He let go of the sword and placed his left hand atop hers. "It is both my pleasure and privilege to be of service, milady." He paused and drew a deep breath. "Peggy, I . . . Well, there's something we should . . ."

Peggy felt as if they stood at the edge of a bridge, each with one foot poised, ready to cross—and once they stepped onto that bridge, they had to cross all the way to the other side. There could be no going back. And she both hoped for and feared what might lie on that other side. She bit her lip, waiting for Todd to continue, but he didn't.

"You were saying . . ." she prompted.

Todd shook himself. "Uh, maybe the Ren Faire wasn't such a great idea."

That's not what you were going to say, was it? She sighed—half in exasperation, half in relief. "Just remember, this whole thing was *your* idea."

Todd scanned the fairegoers dubiously. "I know. But it's so . . . *inauthentic.* Too many anachronisms. Whatever reaction we were hoping for from Elaine, whatever memory we were hoping to trigger—I don't think it's going to work—not here."

Peggy shrugged. "Maybe not. But it doesn't have to be a total bust. We could just . . . have fun." *Just the two of us.* Peggy and Todd had spent a lot of time with Derek and Elaine over the past two months. Derek called the outings double dates, but Todd treated each occasion as a "reconnaissance mission," an opportunity to gather intelligence on the "enemy."

Is Elaine the enemy? Peggy wasn't so sure anymore. *Morgaise, yes. But Elaine?* The more she got to know the pretty time-traveler, the harder it was for Peggy to hate her. *She's just so darn sweet and likeable! I hate that she's so likeable! She takes delight in* everything, *in every little aspect of life.*

It's annoying . . . and contagious.

As they wandered through the faire, Todd continued to express his irritation at the many anachronisms. "Up in Spokane, there's a great Ren Faire where each year is a specific year during the reign of Henry the VIII. I mean, they have fun stuff—like a living chessboard and jousting—but the costumes and characters, even the political intrigues are specific to the time. Here, you've got a hodgepodge of everything. Look." He pointed at a tall man a dozen yards away, wearing a red doublet and sporting a gray goatee. "That guy's supposed to be William Shakespeare! He's even wearing a nametag that says, 'My name is Will,' for crying out loud. And there." He pointed at a man in pirate regalia, sauntering along as if he were half-drunk. "That's supposed to be Jack Sparrow! And that guy's supposed to be Merlin, I suppose." He threw up his hands in defeat.

Peggy smiled mischievously. "So, I suppose it's not a good idea to point out the Roman legion at the other side of the faire." She pointed vaguely in the direction of the jousting field known as the Links. The tent housing the Roman Military Historical Society wasn't clearly visible from their vantage point, but she'd read that the "Legion" would be displaying armor and weapons, as well as performing military maneuvers and a mock battle during the faire.

Todd stared at her in shock. "Romans?" Then he shrugged and shook his head. "Nope. Not one of my better ideas. I should've done my research." He turned his face toward Peggy. "You're *always* researching things . . . random stuff. You probably read all about the faire. Did you know all the . . . inaccuracies we'd run into? I mean, you've been to this faire before, in previous years?"

With Derek. "Yes, but it was *never* going to be accurate. You knew that. I mean, if it were really, truly authentic, there'd be sewage everywhere, right? When you boil it all down—the concept, not the sewage—it's all just a fantasy. It's all just for fun." *Can't we just have fun? Can't we just, for one afternoon, forget about Elaine and Morgaise and molossii?*

And what about Derek? Are you forgetting about Derek?

Todd frowned. "Yeah, but I had hoped we might learn *something*—trigger some memory."

Peggy sighed. *It would've been nice to just have one fun afternoon. With you.*

Even if I don't know how you really feel.

"So," she said, "you and my dad talked for a long time the other day."

Todd snorted. "We talk *every* week. More like, he calls, grills me, and I give him my report. Reminds me of my squadron commander up in Alaska. And I assure him you're safe, I'm behaving myself, and Morgaise and Elaine—" He cut off abruptly.

"Tally ho," he whispered. He nodded slightly off to their left. "Eleven o'clock."

Peggy looked in the direction of his nod.

Speak of the devil, and she shall appear.

Holding hands like high school sweethearts, Derek and Elaine strolled across the faireground, past the huge Styrofoam Celtic cross at the center of the field. And Peggy, in spite of Todd's presence at her side, experienced an ugly flash of anger and a sour twinge of jealousy.

I want to hate you. I do. You took Derek from me.

And Derek's still in danger.

The "harvest" is coming – whatever that means. That's when this all ends – one way or the other.

Elaine wore the costume of a fairy-tale princess. And she looked lovely.

Almost like Disney's Snow White. Not quite, but . . . That's just too creepy.

Derek wore his Kili costume.

Not authentic, but not too out of place.

"Smile," Todd said. "It's showtime." He grinned and waved at the approaching couple.

The ease with which Todd slipped into "intel-mode" disturbed Peggy. He *seemed* so natural, so much the happy, silly man she'd known in college. *He's hard inside. He doesn't trust Elaine. But he seems so casual, so genuine.*

So who's the real Todd? The soft, tender, considerate gentleman? Or the hardened warrior?

Peggy forced a smile. *You're good at that, Peggy – forcing a smile.* She waved as well.

Derek waved back, but Elaine let go of Derek's hand and began bouncing up and down, waving with both hands like an enthusiastic, utterly unselfconscious child. She cried, "Peggy!" Then she gathered her skirts in her hands and skipped gracefully across the green.

She looks like she's dancing.

Elaine grinned joyfully, innocently as she collided with Peggy, embracing her and nearly knocking them both to the grass. "Oh, Peggy! Isn't it wonderful? There are so many things to see. The artwork, the handcrafts. And the music!" Elaine pulled out of the hug. She clapped her hands and danced around in a circle. "I simply love the music!"

Derek trotted up and stood beside her, beaming his adorable, lopsided grin. "I think she's having fun."

"Oh, yes!" Elaine spun in a circle with her hands in the air. "So much fun!"

Imagine Elaine at Disneyland. She'd probably explode. Literally explode.

Maybe I should suggest a trip to California?

Stop it. She may be the victim here.

And I'm not?

Elaine stopped twirling. She grabbed Peggy's free hand in hers. "Oh, Peggy! There's a storyteller in that tent over there! Come on! Let's go!"

And with that, she began to drag Derek, Peggy, and—because Peggy still held Todd's arm—Todd toward the storyteller's tent.

♦ ♦ ♦

The storyteller, a grandmotherly woman, wore a green bodice and split cotton skirt over a muslin underdress—a simple peasant costume. She had long, wavy, white hair adorned with ribbons and a wreath of flowers, sparkling gray eyes, rosy cheeks, and an infectious smile.

And she held her audience enthralled as if by magic. Her hands and face were animated and expressive, and she used a distinct voice for each character in the story. As she spoke, she plucked at a small, twelve-string harp and sang snatches of song to punctuate her tale with music and sound effects. And as she narrated, her voice carried the musical lilt of a very authentic-sounding Irish brogue.

Peggy could think of only one word, one title to adequately describe the woman—*bard*.

Sitting between Peggy and Derek, Elaine was enraptured, her face the epitome of childlike wonder, as she listened to "The Fisherman and His Wife." Elaine laughed with delight, clapped her hands, and cheered at all the appropriate places—right along with the children.

When the story reached its conclusion, the storyteller rose from her stool and curtsied. Elaine leapt to her feet and applauded. Peggy felt compelled to do the same, not simply because Elaine was giving the woman a standing ovation, but also because the storyteller had earned the accolade.

"Oh, she's wonderful!" Elaine said, turning her head to Peggy. "I've never seen a lady bard before. Who could have imagined such a thing?"

Todd leaned across Peggy and asked Elaine, "Don't they have female storytellers where you come from?" His question sounded innocent, but Peggy understood exactly what he was trying to do. *Trying to trigger a memory, to catch her off guard.*

"Oh, no!" Elaine responded, her face still a vision of wonder. "In my day, women were never allowed to study the bardic arts. It would've been unseemly."

"Really?" Todd said. "And when was that?"

On the other side of Elaine, Derek shook his head vehemently.

An all-too-familiar look of confusion and worry clouded Elaine's pretty face. "I . . . I don't . . . remember."

140

Derek put his arm around her protectively. "It's okay, sweetheart. It's okay." His tone was soothing, but he glared at Todd.

"And now," the storyteller said, sitting atop her stool once again, "the tale of" — she paused and plucked at her harp — "the Sleeping Beauty!" She began to play Tchaikovsky's familiar "Sleeping Beauty Waltz."

Peggy could hear the words of the Disney song, "Once Upon a Dream," running through her mind. She smiled. *This is one of my favorites!*

Elaine, however, looked distraught. She whispered in Peggy's ear, "This is not an appropriate story to tell to children."

Yep. The original story is pretty dirty.

"Don't worry," Peggy assured her. "Disney cleaned it up."

Elaine blinked at her in confusion. Then her face lit up. "Oh, you mean that Walt Disney on the television. Disneyland?"

Peggy nodded. "He's the one. I love that movie!"

Elaine looked horrified. "He made a movie of . . . that story?"

"Uh-huh," Derek said. "Let's sit down and listen. It'll be all right."

The four of them sat, but Elaine looked decidedly unhappy. Derek held her hand and rubbed her back, but as Elaine listened to the story, masterfully told by the bard though it was, she became increasingly agitated.

"That's not right," Elaine muttered. "There was no evil fairy. No fairies at all."

Peggy stole a glance at her. Elaine was pouting. *No, it's more of a scowl.* Peggy turned to look at Todd. His expression was passive, but Peggy could feel tension in the muscles of his arm.

And he kept stealing glances at Elaine.

"It wasn't a dragon," Elaine said, a little louder that time. "There was no dragon protecting her." She paused. "It was a pair of dogs."

Todd's whole body tensed.

Dogs? Molossii? She was there? Elaine was . . . Sleeping Beauty?

"It's okay," Derek whispered.

"No!" Elaine said, not even attempting to keep her voice down. "It is *not* okay!"

The storyteller paused, startled, her hand poised above the harp. "Is something wrong?" The Irish accent was gone. "Are you all right?"

Elaine jumped off the bench. "No! You've got it all wrong. Why are you telling lies? Lies to children?"

Members of the audience gasped. A couple of small children began to cry.

"What's wrong, miss?" the storyteller asked, visibly upset. "I-I mean, milady?" The brogue had returned, if a bit shakily.

Derek pulled on Elaine's hand, trying to get her to sit again. "Calm down!"

"No! You've got it all wrong." Elaine pulled her hand free from Derek's and stamped her foot. Tears spilled from her eyes. "It wasn't an evil fairy. It was her sister. And she wasn't evil. She was only trying to protect the princess. And that *prince!*" she snarled, imbuing the word with loathing. "*He* was the one who was evil. He didn't *kiss* her. He tried to *rape* her! But her sister awoke first! She killed him! She cut his throat and fed his carcass to the dogs!"

"Okay," Derek said, standing and grabbing Elaine's arm. "Let's go!" He began pulling Elaine out of the tent.

Elaine allowed herself to be led, but she kept glaring back at the storyteller with contempt. "You are no bard!"

The sight of Elaine's pretty face twisted in rage and hatred was so unnerving, so horrifying, that Peggy didn't follow them. She sat where she was, staring after Elaine.

Elaine was Sleeping Beauty. The prince tried to rape her?

And Morgaise killed him.

Peggy recalled Morgaise's words. "*I protect Elaine.*" She shivered. *The prince tried to rape her.*

"My lords and ladies," the storyteller said, "I apologize for the interruption. P-perhaps another tale. 'The Shoemaker and the Elves.'" She plucked the strings of her harp. "Once upon a time . . ."

Todd stood and grabbed Peggy's hand. "Come on."

Derek and Elaine stood a dozen yards away. Elaine had her head buried in Derek's chest. Her small body shook with sobs. Derek held her close, running his fingers soothingly through her golden-brown hair.

"That puts her in Europe," Todd said, keeping his voice low, "France or Germany, probably the Middle Ages. How old is she, I wonder?"

"The prince tried to rape her." Peggy thought she might be sick. And she had the sudden, sympathetic urge to hug Elaine, to comfort her. *The poor girl!*

"And it's not time-travel at all," Todd continued. "It's some sort of sleeping. Suspended animation, maybe."

"Suspended animation? That makes sense . . . I guess." *He tried to rape her. She's been assaulted.*

Like me.

142

As they got closer, Peggy could hear Derek's calming words. "I'm sorry," he said. "You're safe now. I'm here."

And Peggy felt a bitter pang of jealousy. *You never said that to me — not when I was . . .*

Elaine broke free from Derek's embrace. "Oh, Peggy!" She threw herself at Peggy and wrapped her arms around her.

Peggy put one arm around Elaine — and realized with a start that Todd was holding her hand. *He's never held my hand before. I know he was just pulling me out of there, but . . .* Reluctantly, Peggy released Todd's hand and put her other arm around Elaine.

Why is she turning to me for comfort? To me, instead of Derek?

Because she's used to her sister's protection.

Peggy held Elaine tight and patted her back. Elaine laid her head on Peggy's breast and continued to cry.

Peggy looked at Derek and then at Todd. "Why don't you guys give us a minute? You can go get us something to drink, maybe something to eat. Elaine, have you had lunch?"

Elaine shook her head.

Todd nodded, a knowing look on his face. "Good idea."

The hurt was plain on Derek's face, but he nodded as well. "She wanted to see the jousting. We'll meet you there? At the Links? Is that okay, sweetheart?"

He calls her sweetheart. "We'll see you at the Links." *I want to hate her. I just . . . can't.*

The two men turned and walked away in the direction of the food pavilion. Peggy watched them go, unable to sort through the emotions swirling in her heart, unsure which of the two men she would miss the most, if only for a short time.

You're such a basket case, Peggy.

Elaine's sobbing quieted. "Thank you, Peggy." Her voice was still ragged, barely under control. "You understand."

"That was *you*, wasn't it?" Peggy asked. "In that story — that was you."

Elaine shrugged. Then she nodded. "I think so. I can't remember — not really. It's like a . . . half-remembered dream, just out of reach. When I try to remember it, my head hurts. The pain is . . . I just can't . . . I'm sorry."

Peggy nodded. "It's okay." She hesitated. "It must've been . . . traumatic." *That sounds so lame!*

"I don't know. Maybe that's why I can't remember. I *try* to be happy. I really do, for Morgaise, for Derek, but I know something's . . . missing.

143

Something's wrong with me. I'm . . . I'm so scared. Always scared."

Peggy squeezed Elaine. "I know the feeling."

"My raven died."

Her bird? That big black thing Derek saw? "I'm sorry."

"He died this morning."

Maybe that's why she got so upset, with her emotions so close to the surface. "Was he sick?"

"Yes. No. He . . . died of a broken heart." Elaine lifted her head off Peggy's shoulder and looked at her with red eyes. "Ravens are like that. They mate for life. His mate, Badh . . . she died. I renamed him. I named him Percy. I tried to save him." She lowered her eyes. "He just pined away." She sighed. "You know how that is, don't you?" There was nothing cruel about her tone — she had simply stated a fact.

She knows.

Elaine broke the embrace and took Peggy's hand. "We can go now."

Peggy led the way. *She knows.* "We'll go wait for the men at the jousting links."

"We have a new Bran and Badh now," Elaine said as they walked. "A new pair of ravens. They're Morgaise's pets. I miss my Percy. Oh, please don't tell Derek. I don't want to make him sad too. I've . . . already made such a spectacle of myself."

"It's all right," Peggy said.

"Thank you" — Elaine gently squeezed Peggy's hand — "for being my friend. I know it's hard for you. I know how you feel . . . about Derek."

Then you know more than I do. I don't understand what I feel anymore. "Elaine, is Derek . . . in danger?"

Elaine stopped walking. She looked at Peggy, confusion plain in her eyes. Her mouth worked as if she were about to say something but was unsure what to say. She took a deep breath, looked into Peggy's eyes, and said at last, "Yes."

"From Morgaise?"

Elaine's confusion deepened, and she shook her head. "No. I love him. Morgaise would never hurt him. Never."

"From you?"

"No! I would *never* hurt Derek!"

"Then who?"

Elaine bit her lower lip. "I . . . don't know. But I'm afraid. I can't explain it. I'm just afraid. We have to escape. We have to get away from . . . the danger."

"I don't understand. Get away from whom?"

Squeezing her eyes shut tight, Elaine let go of Peggy's hand and gripped her head in both hands as if it might explode. "I . . . don't . . . know. I just know we must escape from . . . I don't know! I can't remember!"

Peggy gripped Elaine's wrists and pulled them down. She put a hand on either side of Elaine's face, forcing the younger, older woman to look her in the eye. "Then go. Go now. Far away. Escape."

"I can't!" Elaine wailed. "Not before the harvest. I've tried before. I know I have, but they always hunt me down."

"Who?" Peggy demanded. "Who hunts you down?"

"I can't remember! But I know . . . if I wait till the harvest . . . if we leave *during* the harvest, they'll be distracted. They won't be able to come after me. I can't explain it, but I must wait till the harvest!"

Peggy took a deep breath, held it for a moment, then let go of Elaine's head. She took Elaine's hands in hers. "All right. When is the harvest? In the fall?"

Elaine nodded. "*Sah-win.*"

Peggy shook her head in confusion. "I don't know that word. Is that the name of a day?"

Elaine nodded again. "Sunset on the last day of October. You call it All Souls Night."

"You mean . . . Halloween?"

"Yes. *Sah-win.* Maybe you pronounce it . . . Samhain."

Samhain! Peggy shuddered. She knew that name. From her recent, obsessive research on all things Druidic. *The ancient festival of the dead, when the gateway to the Otherworld opens.*

"If we wait until Samhain," Elaine said, "we can be far away before they know we're gone."

"Okay. Let's talk about it with the guys."

Elaine smiled. "Yes! Oh, yes! Thank you, Peggy!"

Don't thank me yet. I'm not sure I buy this idea of waiting till the harvest.

Or the idea that Morgaise isn't behind it all.

But Peggy nodded all the same. Then, mostly to avoid Elaine's grateful gaze, she turned back toward the jousting links, and spied an empty bench. She discreetly checked her very inauthentic, anachronistic wristwatch. "The joust won't start for a while. But we can sit and wait. There are supposed to be some mock military maneuvers on the Links starting about now."

And that will give me time to digest what I've learned.

145

Peggy turned and pointed toward the empty bench.

The legion of the Roman Military Historical Society began to march out onto the Links. Numbering about forty or so, they looked impressive, imposing—and to Peggy's eye—magnificent in their polished Roman armor, carrying tall spears and large, oval shields.

This looks like it could be pretty cool.

And that was when Elaine screamed.

XVIII

As Todd ran toward Elaine and Peggy, he reached into the leather pouch at his waist and retrieved the Glock. He thumbed off the safety, but kept his finger pointed down the barrel and away from the trigger. He grabbed his sword so it wouldn't tangle in his legs and dashed on.

Idiot! I let Peggy get too far away!

He was only a couple dozen yards away from the women, but it seemed like a mile. He glanced about for danger, but could discern no threats.

Fairegoers had stopped in their tracks to gape at the screaming girl and the woman she clung to. The men in Roman armor had stopped to stare as well, but no one approached.

There!

Two men wearing light jackets had broken from the crowd and were running toward Peggy and Elaine.

Should've spotted the jackets. Too hot for jackets.

Todd quickened his pace.

A couple of yards away, he abruptly slowed and turned his back to the women. He kept the Glock close to his chest, not brandishing it exactly — not yet — and faced the approaching men.

These guys can see the gun, but don't want to start a panic.

Behind him, Elaine continued to scream, but Todd could hear Peggy trying to calm her as Elaine paused to suck in a breath. "It's okay, Elaine. What's wrong?"

The two jacketed men slowed and stopped ten yards away. As one, they reached into their jackets.

"Don't do it!" Todd yelled, waving his gun in front of his chest, but not pointing at them. "I'm her bodyguard!"

The jacketed men froze, exchanged puzzled, if annoyed, glances, then slowly withdrew their empty hands.

Elaine's screaming died down.

"That's it," Peggy cooed. "You're safe. Todd's here. You're okay."

147

Out of the corner of his eye, Todd saw Derek running up.

These guys might see Derek as a threat! Got to defuse this quickly.

Todd said, "He's with us."

"Michael! Samuel!" Elaine called. "I'm fine." Her voice was shaky, but at least she wasn't screaming anymore. "I'm safe. Go home. Whatever my sister said, don't worry. I'm safe with . . . my friends."

Bodyguards. Watching Elaine from a distance. Sent by Morgaise.

Neither man moved.

"You heard the lady," Todd said. "Go home. We've got this under control."

"But, Lady Elaine," one of them said.

Definitely sent by Morgaise.

And I've seen the tall one before. Via the security camera at Peggy's place.

"Go home." Elaine's voice was stronger now — less like the sweet or perhaps hysterical teenager, but more mature — like someone used to command. "I will speak with Morgaise myself. Leave now — or leave our employ."

Both men looked at her and then at each other uncertainly.

"Leave now!" Elaine said. "I will not say it again."

Even Todd felt the urge to obey her. *When she wants to, she can be pretty forceful.*

One bodyguard turned and walked away. The second hesitated a moment longer, then followed his associate.

Todd watched them go, but as they receded in the direction of the faireground gate, he began to scan the crowds again. Seeing no other immediate threat, he reset the safety on his Glock and stowed it back in his pouch.

And hopefully nobody kicks me out for bringing a firearm onto the grounds. I'd rather not have to prove my Washington concealed-carry permit is applicable in Utah right now, thank you very much.

Besides, this is private property, and firearms are specifically forbidden at the faire, aren't they?

"What happened?" Derek asked.

Todd turned around, still searching for threats, keeping his hand inside the pouch. The various fairegoers were turning away, some in embarrassment, some in boredom.

Nothing to see here, folks. Fun's over.

"I'm sorry," Elaine said, wiping her eyes. "I was startled. It was nothing." She sounded like a girl of fifteen again — perhaps a little shaken, but lighthearted. The air of command and maturity was gone as if it had never been there.

Todd finally turned his attention—at least part of it, as he kept glancing in the direction of the departed bodyguards—to Elaine, Derek, and Peggy.

Peggy stood close by, her face inscrutable. Elaine was in Derek's arms.

"Nothing?" Derek held Elaine close. Over her shoulder, he looked at Peggy with an expression of disbelief and concern. "That didn't sound like nothing. You were screaming your head off."

"I saw something"—she nuzzled her face into Derek's shoulder—"something that frightened me."

"What was it?" Derek asked.

"It doesn't matter now," Elaine said. "It wasn't real."

"Tell me, please." Derek stroked her hair. "No secrets, remember?"

Elaine shrugged her shoulders. "I don't remember."

Don't remember? Or don't want to?

Or just plain lying?

Peggy nodded in Elaine's direction. "She started screaming when she saw the Romans."

Elaine flinched.

Bingo. So what does that mean?

Peggy laid a hand on Elaine's back. "Isn't that right?"

"I don't . . ." Elaine squeezed Derek, clinging to him for support. "I can't . . ." She shook her head against his shoulder. "No. Please. Don't *force* me . . . to remember."

The way she said . . . That's not what she started out to say. I'm sure of it. Don't force *her . . . to what?*

Derek gave Peggy a warning look, but to Elaine, he said, "It's okay. You don't have to remember. Not right now."

Peggy pursed her lips.

She's annoyed.

And why not? We're close. Really close. That's why we came, isn't it? To trigger memories.

Yeah, but Derek doesn't know that.

Todd opened his mouth to press the question just a bit more, but his attention was drawn to a man walking toward them.

A man in Roman armor.

Oh, boy. This could be interesting.

And dicey. Don't want to set off another round of screaming.

The "Roman" carried the plumed helm of a centurion in his left hand. He wore a segmented breastplate over a red tunic. A short sword—a gladius—hung in a baldric at his right hip. From the front of his belt dangled the customary five thin leather strips. At his left hip hung a large dagger.

Todd noted that the centurion's sword and dagger were not tied into their sheaths. Fairegoers—like Todd—were required to keep their weapons "peace-bound."

I guess that doesn't apply to performers. They were going to stage a mock battle, right?

Todd fingered the black leather lacing that held his own sword in its sheath. The dirk that hung at his waist in front was similarly bound. The small knife in his boot—the *sgian dubh*—was not tied in. *Too small to worry about – no bigger than a pocket knife.*

If anybody saw the Glock . . . and had authority to do anything about it, they'd be in my face by now. Well, maybe not in my face, per se, but they'd be asking me to leave.

As Todd watched the Roman approach, he noted the man's military bearing. *This guy walks like a soldier, not just a performer. Maybe retired Army?*

Peggy and Elaine had their backs to the approaching Roman. The man walked up to Todd and tipped his head in Elaine's direction. "Is she okay?"

Todd nodded. "I think so."

Peggy turned around, and her eyes grew huge at the sight of the man. She looked over at Todd, and her expression seemed to say, *Are you sure this is a good idea?*

Todd lifted his shoulders in a slight shrug.

"We're fine," Derek said with an expression that didn't match his words.

Elaine clung to Derek, quivering, her face buried in his shoulder. But one of her eyes was visible through her hair.

And she was watching the centurion.

Intently.

The Roman inclined his head deferentially to Derek, obviously unconvinced. "If you're sure."

Derek nodded emphatically and—to Todd's eyes—ungraciously. "We're sure."

The Roman said, "Sorry, miss. Didn't mean to scare you." He waited a moment as if hoping for an answer. In spite of his warlike accoutrements and military bearing, he had the face of a kindly soul. *Looks like Bishop Morris back home in Spokane, right down to the salt-and-pepper hair and gray eyes.* And he appeared genuinely concerned for Elaine's welfare. "Well, as long as you're all right." The Roman turned to Peggy and smiled apologetically. "I'm really sorry, ma'am."

Peggy's lips twitched.

Elaine is "miss," and Peggy is "ma'am."

That's gotta hurt.

Peggy's smile would've probably seemed genuine to a stranger, but Todd knew it was forced. "We're okay, really. I'm ... We're looking forward to the" — she seemed as if she were searching for the right word — "maneuvers. Thank you for ... your very kind concern." She extended her hand.

The Roman bowed, took her hand and bent as if to kiss it.

Courtly manners. Todd grinned. *That'll almost make up for the "ma'am."*

Elaine exploded out of Derek's arms. *"Immo!"*

Before Todd could react, Elaine had bent and snatched the small knife from Todd's boot. She forced herself between Peggy and the Roman, shoving him backward, away from Peggy.

Peggy uttered a startled cry.

Elaine pressed her back against Peggy and brandished the tiny knife at the Roman.

The startled man took a hurried step back out of reach. "What the — ?"

"Non tangeres eam!" Elaine snarled, her pretty face was twisted into a horrific mask of rage. She swiped the knife in the Roman's direction.

"Hey, hey," Todd said, keeping a safe distance, but putting his hands forward in a placating gesture. "You're okay. Everything's okay. Elaine, give me the knife."

Elaine continued to swipe and stab the three-inch blade at the Roman. Her body shook as if she were terrified, but her expression showed fierce determination. *"Si tetigerit eam, et interficiam te!"*

Is that Latin?

Todd didn't know exactly what Elaine was saying, but the gist was unmistakable. "Elaine," he said, trying to keep his voice calm, but emphatic. "He's not going to hurt Peggy or you. He's not a real Roman. It's just a costume."

"Yeah," the centurion said, his voice remarkably steady, given that an apparent madwoman was attempting to gut him with a knife, "it's just a costume." To the guy's credit, though he kept a safe distance, he hadn't run off. "I'm not going to hurt you or your friend."

"Elaine," Peggy said, "what year is it?"

Elaine's brow wrinkled in confusion. Her knife hand shook violently. *"Tredecim annis et octingentis ab urbe condita."*

151

The Roman shook his head, laughing nervously. "Seriously? You think it's eight-thirteen *ab urbe condita?*" He paused as if thinking something through.

Okay, he understands Latin.

The Roman nodded, apparently coming to some conclusion. "You think it's sixty A. D.?"

Todd felt a chill run down his spine. *Almost two thousand years.*

Todd locked eyes with Peggy. She mouthed, "Wow."

And Elaine's terrified of Romans.

Derek said, "Sweetheart, it's twenty-fifteen."

"Twenty-fifteen?" Elaine looked away from the Roman and toward Derek. Her countenance was stricken, and her lower lip trembled. "It's not ..." She looked back to the Roman. "You're not ... going to ... to hurt us?"

The man with the kindly eyes shook his head. "No, I'm not."

Elaine's eyes lowered to the knife in her hand. She looked as if she might be sick. "I-I did it again."

The knife fell from her trembling fingers, and she dropped to her knees.

Todd bent down quickly and snatched up the *sgian dubh.* He stepped back, and stuck the blade into its boot sheath.

With her face in her hands, Elaine rocked back and forth, sobbing. Derek knelt at her side with his arms around her, shushing and cooing. "You're okay. You're safe. I won't let anybody hurt you."

Elaine shook her head. "Never be safe. Never. They're everywhere. Every age." She rubbed her eyes, then lifted her head to the Roman. "I'm sorry. So sorry."

The Roman said nothing.

Todd looked at the man. He was staring intently at Elaine.

Is that ... recognition?

The Roman took a cautious step forward. When Elaine didn't flinch or pull away, he stepped closer. He extended a hand. "No harm done, miss. My name's Moe. Short for Moses." He winked. "You know, the Deliverer?"

Elaine smiled, but looked away, not meeting the man's gaze.

She doesn't know who Moses is. Maybe she is a Druid.

Elaine took Moe's hand and shook it. "I'm Elaine. Elaine Morrigan."

The Roman bowed slowly, cautiously. He raised Elaine's hand to his lips and kissed it.

Elaine blushed and giggled.

Moe looked her in the eye. "I'm very pleased to meet you, Lady Elaine." His smile seemed warm, but there was something about the way he looked at Elaine that was off. An eager, hungry light burned in his eyes.

He knows something about her.

"Now," Moe said, turning his smile to Peggy, "if you will pardon me, fair ladies, I have a battle to command." He inclined his head to Derek and snapped his fist to his breastplate in a Roman salute. "My lord."

He turned to Todd, still keeping his fist over his heart. "If you will indulge me, my laird, I would be honored if you'd allow me to arrange front-row seats for you and your companions." He locked eyes with Todd. "If you would be so good as to walk a pace with me, sir?"

He wants a word with me . . . in private.

Todd exchanged a knowing glance with Peggy. Todd smiled and affected his best Scottish accent. "Aye, my laird centurion."

Moe bowed and gestured toward the jousting links and the assembled legion.

Todd said as casually as he could, "Derek, you'll guard the ladies?"

"With my life." No accent. No role-play. Simply an earnest pledge.

Todd followed the Roman.

He didn't ask for any of our names. He only needed to know Elaine's.

After they had walked a dozen paces, Todd said. "You recognize her."

"Yes."

Todd felt a thrill run up his spine. "And you know what she is? Where she comes from?"

"It's not so much a question of *where* as it is of *when*."

Todd glanced at the Roman, but Moe kept his eyes forward as they walked, a forced smile on his lips. "Okay," Todd said. "Then you know Elaine's been around for . . ."

"I know the Morrigans have been around for centuries. I only knew for sure they've been surfacing every sixty years since the ninth century, but after that little scene back there, I suspect our pretty Lady Elaine and her disfigured sister have been around since at least the first century — since the Roman Empire."

"How do you know all this — about Elaine?"

"I know, because my family has been enslaved to the Morrigans for over a thousand years. My last name's Abbot, and the Abbots have been — "

Todd almost stumbled. "You're the lawyer?"

Moe raised an eyebrow. "So you know about that."

"I know she has a lawyer named Abbot."

"That'd be my grandfather or my uncle . . . or both. I'm not exactly welcome in the family. Not that I'd want to be. I was raised in an orphanage, out of sight."

"If that's the case, how did you recognize Elaine?"

"I recognized her, because I happen to possess what is probably the only existing photograph of Elaine Morrigan. It's from eighteen-ninety-five."

Todd fished his wallet out of his pouch, and out of the wallet, a business card. "My name's Todd Cavetto. We need to talk." He handed the card to the Roman.

Moe took the card in his fist without looking at it. "I'll be in touch. Tonight."

"Can't you tell me more? Now?"

Moe shook his head firmly. "I've got to run this battle. Don't want to do anything to raise the Morrigans' suspicions."

Todd grabbed the man's arm, forcing him to stop and look him in the eye. "I don't think Elaine is the problem. It's her sister Morgaise."

"You might be right about Elaine, but I'll tell you this. You and your lady friend are in danger. But that young fellow? The one holding Elaine? The one who's so obviously in love with her? And she with him?"

"Derek?"

Moe nodded grimly. "Well, whatever his name is, he's a dead man."

XIX

The Mexican restaurant was the right kind of noisy—loud enough to make eavesdropping difficult, but not so loud one had to shout to be heard across the table. And it was out of the way—located on the outskirts of Springville.

Sitting alone in a corner booth, facing the entrance, Todd scanned the other patrons. Nobody looked suspicious or familiar.

But that doesn't mean a thing. Morgaise's people could be anywhere.

Man! I sound paranoid.

Yeah, but you're not paranoid if they really are out to get you.

He glanced at his watch. *Another minute and he'll be late.*

And that's atypical for a soldier. Even if he was only a—

As if on cue, the door opened, and in strode a man with salt-and-pepper hair and gray eyes. Moe's kindly face was hardened into a grim expression. He scanned the room. Todd waved casually, and Moe's eyes fixed on him. The man nodded and began navigating the crowded restaurant toward Todd.

Todd slid out of the booth and stood. He offered Moe his hand.

Moe shook it.

Nice firm handshake. Almost like a missionary.

The two men locked eyes, like gladiators assessing one another.

"Thanks for meeting me here," Todd said, breaking the handshake and gesturing toward the booth.

They both sat. Moe scanned the room again. "Where's your lady friend?"

He didn't ask about Derek or Elaine. "Somewhere safe."

Moe's grim expression softened. "Yeah, I wouldn't trust me either. Not yet."

Todd shrugged. "My lady friend, as you call her, was attacked a couple months back. There were two men. Both sent by Morgaise. I have reason to believe they were hired by your grandfather."

Moe nodded. "Yeah, that fits the pattern."

155

"The two goons at the Ren Faire were sent by Morgaise as well. I've seen one of them lurking around ... my lady friend's home at night. More than once."

"Morgaise must see your friend as a threat."

"That's my assessment."

Moe's eyes narrowed. "And you're sure she's safe tonight? I assume you've been watching over her."

Todd nodded. "Affirmative on both counts." *As safe as Bishop Iyamba and his impressive collection of firearms can make her.* Peggy was at the bishop's home for the evening, the same as she was every time Todd had to leave her side—like the one weekend each month when he had to go to Alaska for Air National Guard duty.

"Your business card says you're a software engineer," Moe said, "but you sound military."

"Roger that."

"Air Force?"

Todd raised an eyebrow. "Been checking up on me?"

Moe shook his head with a wry grin. "Not exactly. I don't have those kind of resources. I'm just a seminary teacher."

Todd nodded. "Yeah, but you used to be an Air Force chaplain. Catholic." Moe looked at him with surprise that quickly morphed into suspicion, so Todd explained, "I have a friend in the Army's CID. I called in a favor." *And that's pretty much all I know. Let's see if Mr. Moses Abbot fills in any details.*

"Fair enough." The older man chuckled. "Used to be Catholic. Then I befriended a young B-52 pilot and his wife—Mormons. And well, you can guess the rest of the story."

Todd grinned. "Yeah, I can."

"Anyway, once I got baptized, I resigned my commission. Now I teach seminary and the occasional evening institute class. And I tutor in Latin"—he winked at Todd—"for a *Catholic* school."

Todd's grin widened. *I like this guy.*

The waiter arrived with chips and salsa, and asked for their order. Todd deferred to Moe.

Let's see what you order, padre.

Moe ordered a couple of enchiladas—one shredded beef and one cheese. Todd nodded in approval and ordered the same.

Moe eyed him dubiously. "Why do I feel as if I just passed a test?"

Todd narrowed his eyes. "You did."

"What test would that be?"

"The Mexican Chicken Test."

The older man looked at Todd in confusion. "Mexican chicken?"

"Yeah," Todd said, keeping his expression as serious as he could. "Any man who orders chicken in a Mexican restaurant cannot—I repeat—*cannot* be trusted."

"You're kidding me. Aren't you?"

Todd grinned widely. "Maybe. But seriously, chicken in Mexican food is disgusting. Gimme beef or cheese any day."

Moe burst out laughing.

Todd seized the opportunity to scan the other diners. Nobody paid them more attention than normal—and nobody studiously ignored them.

Todd pulled out his cell phone and removed the battery. Then he looked pointedly at Moe.

The former Catholic priest nodded and followed Todd's lead.

"Okay," Todd said. "I think we can talk."

Moe's kindly face hardened. "My grandfather has a lot of power and resources. But I wouldn't have thought he'd have the ability to eavesdrop on us through our phones."

Todd shook his head. "Not taking that chance. Remove the batteries, and the phone can't be used to spy on us. A friend of mine was murdered by the Morrigans. He was an Army officer. *Somebody* had the CID investigation terminated."

Moe nodded and pulled at his chin thoughtfully. "A warrior—his blood sprinkled on the foundations of the house—his body fed to the *molossii*."

"That fits with what we know."

Moe bit his lower lip. "How do I know I can trust *you*?"

"Hey, that goes both ways. The Mexican Chicken Test, I'm sad to say, is only about ninety-five percent reliable."

The seminary teacher gave him a tight-lipped grin. "I guess we'll both have to rely on our respective guts." He sighed. "And the Spirit."

"In that case . . ." Todd drew in a deep breath, held it, listened . . . And nodded. "Let's compare notes."

Moe shook his head. "Uh-uh. Tell me about yourself. I want to know who I'm trusting my life to."

"*Your* life?" Todd glanced at the man's ring finger. He saw a plain gold band. "No wife? No kids?"

Moe smiled. It was sad, sweet, and wistful, like a memory of loss that time had mostly healed. Mostly. "I had a wife. Her name was Joan . . . Joan Archer, before we married. I used to call her my Joan of Arc. She used to be a nun—my Joan—before she joined the Church. We were both orphans — both raised in Catholic orphanages. We . . . found each other . . . later in life. Funny how that goes. Or maybe not, I suppose — similar backgrounds and all. Married in the Provo Temple. We were never blessed with children — just our seminary kids. My Joan — she taught seminary too, you see. Sweetest, most beautiful soul I ever met. She was . . . killed by a drunk driver three years back." He looked up at Todd. His eyes were misty. "So, it's just *my* life now, such as it is. But I intend to spend it well, so I can be worthy of her — so I can be with her when I'm done here."

Sweet story.

And it feels right.

You better be telling me the truth, padre, because I already like you.

Moe chuckled and shook his head. "And here I was asking about you! Now tell me about yourself, son. I can tell you're LDS. You married?"

Todd pulled his lips into a tight grimace. "My story's not so sweet. I . . . was married. Temple marriage, but . . . she left. Left me and the Church. We were struggling, sure. Military life can be hard on a young wife — leaving her family and friends behind. I was in JSUPT Phase 3 — you know, uh . . . helicopter training at Fort Rucker, Alabama. So I was always busy, under a lot of stress. That didn't help. Christy — that's her name — she never connected with the sisters in the ward there, at church. But she did —" Todd shook his head. "Never mind." He shrugged. "Anyway, divorced — no kids."

"I'm sorry."

"Well, life has a way of going on, even when we don't want it to."

"Yeah," the older man said. "Life's funny that way."

"Yep."

"But you have a new lady friend now." Moe grinned. "And from what little I've seen — but then, I *am* a great judge of character — she's a fine one."

Todd said nothing. He dipped another tortilla chip in salsa, paused, then shoved it in his mouth.

Moe grimaced. "Sorry. Sore subject?"

Todd shrugged. "Not really. Just . . . complicated."

Moe raised an eyebrow. "Complicated? I watched you two, during our maneuvers and after. A blind man could see your devotion to the lady. How long have you been dating?"

Todd rolled his eyes. "We're not — not dating, that is."

"What do you call today at the Ren Faire?"

"Recon mission. We're observing Elaine. Gathering intel on the enemy. We're trying to save Derek—at least, that's what Peggy's trying to do." He paused. "Sorry. Peggy. That's her name. But as for me? I'm just trying to keep Peggy safe."

Moe nodded. "Because you love her."

Todd chuckled, but there was no mirth in it. "Because she's my *friend*." He looked at Moe with eyes that were as cold and hard as his voice. "Because Morgaise tried to have her raped and killed. Twice. Because Morgaise's goons keep skulking around Peggy's place late at night. Because Peggy's in love with Derek, and Derek's going to get himself killed trying to rescue Elaine from her sister. And Peggy can't just walk away. She can't abandon her friend, even if he doesn't love her, even if he doesn't *deserve* her. It's just not in her nature to walk away. She has to save Derek, even if it gets her killed. And if with my life I can save *her*, I will."

Todd stared intently into the older man's eyes. "Problem is, I don't know if I *can* save her. I'm afraid. I'm afraid I won't be good enough, strong enough, vigilant enough. Brave enough. Especially when I don't understand the threat we're facing."

The waiter arrived with their food.

Todd dug in, eating with purpose, if not gusto.

Moe took a deep breath. "You said a mouthful."

Todd shrugged and continued the process of refueling his body.

"Listen to me," Moe said. "You pick up certain skills as a Catholic priest. One of those is, as I said, you get to be a good judge of character. And I can tell that you're a good man, Todd Cavetto. Another skill is to listen to what people say. And another, even more important skill is to listen to what people *avoid* saying."

Todd looked up at the former chaplain. "So, what am I avoiding?"

"You love this woman. And it's a selfless love. You'll lay down your life for her, this good woman, and she'll never know how you feel. She deserves to know."

Todd smirked and shook his head. "Negatory. Not gonna happen. It has to stay . . . the way it is . . . at least for now."

"And why is that? Because you think she's in love with this other fellow?"

Todd rolled his eyes again. "Well, for one thing, she *is* in love with him. But . . . I wish it were that simple. At least then I might have a chance."

"Then why not?"

Todd's lips drew into a smirk. "Because, since the attacks, I *live* with her."

Moe's eyes widened in shock. He opened his mouth to speak, but Todd cut him off. "Just as her bodyguard—her bodyguard and *nothing* else. Her bishop's onboard with it. It's *awkward"*—he rolled his eyes again—"but she needs round-the-clock protection. So living with her and all, it simply wouldn't be appropriate for me to . . . let her know how I feel, to put that kind of pressure on her. I need her to trust me, to feel safe—not be worried about me being there."

Todd scratched at his nose and grimaced. "Besides, I *did* make a pass at her, sort of. It was right after the attacks—and the timing was awful. And . . . she didn't . . . respond."

"Ouch," Moe replied.

Todd nodded. "Ouch. But the worst part is, nobody else seems to see how amazing she is. Especially her. She's smart. She's funny. She's compassionate. She's . . . good."

Moe grinned. "I noticed you didn't say, 'She's pretty.'"

Todd returned the smile. "She has her own beauty. Especially when she smiles. Her eyes light up and . . . Well, it simply takes your breath away. But she just doesn't see it. I see it—and I tell her all the time—but she doesn't believe me."

Moe sighed. "The women we love rarely do. And so we must keep right on telling them. And they keep right on doubting us—doubting themselves."

Todd nodded. He looked down at his food. "You know . . . I've had *pretty*. *Pretty* wasn't all it was cracked up to be. Now, I want *good*." Todd grinned. "Besides, when Peggy smiles . . . she is gorgeous."

Moe's smile was broad and genuine. "Amen!" He reached across the table and slapped Todd on the shoulder. "Well said, Brother Cavetto."

Todd tilted his head and looked at him in surprise. "Why the heck am I telling you all this anyway?"

Moe laughed and waved a tortilla chip at him dismissively. "Hey, I used to be a priest! People just open up and confess things to me. They can't help it." His eyes narrowed and sparkled mischievously. "It's like a *superpower*."

Todd grinned. "Yeah. I should call you The Amazing Padre-Man."

"Don't you dare!"

Todd chuckled, then the mirth drained from his face. *Down to business*. "So like I said, let's compare notes. Tell me what you know."

Moe nodded. He glanced around the restaurant. Apparently satisfied nobody was listening, he began. "Okay, here's what I know. Sometime back in tenth-century England—so the story goes—my ancestor, Lucius, was an abbot of the church. But far from keeping his vow of celibacy, he was a notorious seducer of young women — especially young, pretty wives and daughters of the country peasants round about his abbey. And then, of course, there was the occasional nun."

Todd growled. "Sounds like a waste of skin."

Moe nodded. "But I'm getting ahead of myself. Let's get back to Lucius in a minute. Now I know for sure each time the Morrigans appear, there are at least two blood sacrifices. The first is a warrior — like the friend you mentioned."

Jerry. I'm sorry you got involved in all this. "Yeah. Go on."

"His blood is sprinkled on the foundation of the house. This is to make the house strong and safe. The house, by the way, is built to some very exact specifications. I don't know the particulars, but it has something to do with the way the house is laid out. But so far as I know, no two houses look exactly alike."

"You said the blood is used to make the house safe. What are they — Elaine and Morgaise — afraid of, exactly?"

"I would've thought that was obvious from the scene at the Ren Faire today." Moe paused, but Todd said nothing. "Romans," the former priest continued. "Whatever started all this, it seems to be something that goes back at least to the Roman Empire in the first century."

Todd nodded. "Makes sense, I suppose," he said around a mouthful of cheese enchilada.

"The second sacrifice is a lascivious priest or dishonest banker."

Todd looked at him dubiously. "A priest *or* a banker?"

"Yeah. Sounds weird. Not exactly sure how the two are equivalent, but I have a theory. I want to do some more research first. Anyway, my ancestor, Lucius was supposed to be one of these sacrifices. He certainly fit the mold of lascivious priest. The story goes that he was enticed by a pretty young maiden with golden-brown hair."

"Elaine?"

"Yeah, I'm pretty sure it was her, although she didn't go by Elaine back in the tenth century. Back then it was Viviane, I think."

"So she *is* part of it." *And I was actually starting to feel sorry for her.*

Moe dropped his fork into his refried beans, then scratched at his temple. "Well, that's where it gets a little murky — at least for me."

"What do you mean?"

Moe placed his hand on the table. "I'm pretty sure Elaine or Viviane or whatever she calls herself . . ." He paused and clucked his tongue as if uncertain. "I'm pretty sure she *is* the bait in these honey traps, but it's possible . . . maybe . . . that she might not realize how she's being used. Until today, I was certain she and Morgaise were equally guilty, but . . . Well, when I met Elaine today, she seemed so innocent, so utterly guileless, even if she was brandishing that tiny Scottish knife and threatening to kill me — in Latin, no less. By the way, she was *protecting* your lady friend. She said, 'If you touch her, I will kill you.' And like I said, I tend to be a pretty good judge of character. Or at least, I thought I was."

Todd sighed. "Yeah, it looked to me too like she was defending Peggy. Okay, so the jury is still out on Elaine . . . maybe."

"If she *is* complicit, she could be acting out of fear."

"Fear of what?"

"Her sister, mainly, I think. Or Romans . . . or whatever demons drive her."

Well, dang it all. Now I'm back to feeling sorry for her. He rolled his eyes briefly heavenward. *Is it too much to ask to have a clear enemy to fight? Give me Hitler or bin Laden, not some pretty little wisp of a girl.*

"Anyway," Moe continued, "back to Lucius. He was entrapped and about to be sacrificed. But he begged for his life and swore eternal fealty to the Morrigans. And Nimue — that's apparently what Morgaise called herself at the time — spared him, enslaving my family for all future generations."

Todd pointed his fork at Moe. "What about you? You don't appear to be 'enslaved.'"

Moe chuckled. "Well, that's because I'm not officially part of the family."

Todd raised an eyebrow, but waited for Moe to elaborate.

"Okay," the older man said, "so here's where I come into the story. Sixty years ago, my grandfather, Thurgood Abbot, did something that ticked off Morgaise. I never could find out exactly what it was, but the bottom line is he failed Morgaise somehow. And that just can't happen. Failures . . . *true* failures have been rare, but when they occur, the retribution is brutal. It's always the same, like it was back in 1955 in Portland, Oregon."

"What happened?"

"Whenever they appear, the Morrigans gather or attract a cult of followers — fanatical true believers. Don't ask me how these nut jobs find the sisters, but they do. My family handles certain matters, like the house, the massive trust account, and arranging for the household staff and bodyguards. Oh, and a mated pair of ravens." He waved a remonstrative finger at nobody in particular. "Can't forget the ravens. The acolytes provide the rest. They'll do anything for their 'goddesses.' So, after my grandfather committed his trespass, these fanatics came in the middle of the night, invaded my grandfather's house, pulled the whole family out of their beds . . ."

He paused and took a deep breath. Then he took a long drink from his water glass. "Sorry. It's not easy to talk about. And I wasn't even there."

"Take your time."

Moe squared his shoulders. "They dragged my family out into the backyard. They stripped my grandmother naked and tied her to a tree. Then they whipped her till her back was shredded. Then they stripped . . ." He took another drink. He was sweating, and his kindly face was twisted in pain and horror. "They took the three little girls and they . . . they gang-raped them. They made my grandparents and their sons watch it all. And Morgaise was there the whole time—presiding, watching . . . blessing it."

Suddenly, Todd wasn't hungry. He kept his eyes on Moe's. He didn't want to look inward. He didn't want to see the faces of the raped and mutilated and slaughtered children he'd seen in Afghanistan. *Don't close your eyes. Don't see their faces, their broken bodies, the shattered spirits of the survivors.*

So he focused on Moe.

Raw hatred blazed in the former priest's eyes.

Todd knew that hatred. He was intimately acquainted with the horrors religious fanatics could inflict on the innocent.

Moe's voice had dropped to a growl filled with long-suppressed rage. "My mother was twelve years old when she was raped by more than twenty men. And she was the lucky one. Her little sisters, Alexandra and Catherine—they never recovered. Alexandra bled to death. She was four. Catherine was seven. She died in an asylum for the insane before her twelfth birthday. My mother, Marietta, became pregnant as a result of the rapes. My grandfather, in spite of being a practicing—I won't say, 'devout'—Catholic, demanded she have an abortion."

Tears spilled from Moe's eyes. His expression softened as if his rage were draining away with his tears. "She ran away, rather than let someone shred me up with a coat hanger shoved into her womb. She made her way to a convent. After I was born, we were both placed in an orphanage. Later, when she was too old for the orphanage, she stayed on as a volunteer—so she could be near me. She . . . died when I was eight, due to lingering complications from . . . from giving birth at such a young age. She was . . . fragile. She sacrificed her life for mine."

He chuckled—a bitter sound devoid of mirth. "You know, she named me Moses, because she had a *dream*. She said, in her dream, an angel told her that her son would deliver her family from bondage. Moses, the Deliverer. Get it?"

Todd nodded. "Yeah, I get it. So what have you done so far in the way of delivering your family?"

Moe shook his head. "Not much, I'm ashamed to say. Researched the family curse, but that's about it. My mother taught me what she knew, but she ran away from home when she was twelve. Most of what she'd heard were just rumors and spook stories whispered in the dark." He shrugged his shoulders. "I . . . I just didn't know what else I could do."

"So what else can you tell me?"

"Okay, well . . . Elaine always has a beau or fiancé. Every single time. And he disappears. Always around Halloween. I know that sounds dramatic, but that's when the Morrigans disappear. And sixty years later, it starts all over again."

"Yeah," Todd said. "Elaine told us about Halloween herself."

Moe's eyebrow shot up. "Interesting."

"Yeah. She says she wants to escape—to have Derek take her away and . . ."

That guy at the bar. I don't recognize him, but . . .

The man in question—a thin man with flaming red hair—turned casually around on his stool and faced away.

Paranoid.

"You okay?" Moe asked.

"Yeah. Just thought somebody might be watching us."

Moe looked around slowly . . . as if he were trying to hide the fact that he was scanning the room.

A surreptitious smile crept over Todd's lips. *I bet Moe thinks he's being sneaky, but . . . I guess spycraft wasn't exactly part his training as a priest.*

Not that it was part my training either.

I don't know what the spam I'm doing.

Todd pointed his fork at Moe. Bringing the older man's eyes back to him. "So why'd you become a priest?"

"I was sort of pushed into it. I had an anonymous benefactor."

"Anonymous?"

"Yes, and I'm almost certain it was my grandfather. But whoever it was, he paid my university tuition ... on the condition I enter the priesthood." He shrugged. "So I did."

"Your grandfather knew where you were?"

"I'm sure it wasn't hard for him to track my mother and me down, not with the money and power that man wields, but ... he never made contact." Moe smirked and shook his head slightly. "Not once."

The redheaded man at the bar had turned around again.

But that time, Todd spotted something in the man's ear.

He might be listening to us.

Maybe not so paranoid after all. Todd didn't see a microphone or parabolic dish, but that didn't eliminate the possibility of a listening device. Maybe not at the table, but ...

"Listen," Todd said. "I'm gonna pay the check. There's something I want to show you."

Todd got up, went to the cashier, paid the check—leaving a generous tip for the waiter—and motioned for Moe to join him.

The man at the bar was facing away from them, and Todd's eyes bored holes in the back of the fellow's red head. "If it's okay," Todd said when Moe met him near the door, "we'll take your car."

Moe followed the direction of Todd's eyes, then nodded. "Yeah. That's fine."

As they turned to leave, Todd thought, *Let's see if this guy follows.*

As they walked out the door, Todd furtively tapped Moe's arm, then—once he had Moe's attention—made a subtle zipping motion across his lips.

Moe replied with a barely perceptible nod.

Todd pointed to his own car—not Moe's. "Thanks for letting us take your car."

Moe hesitated for just a second, then nodded. "No problem." Then he followed Todd toward *Todd's* car.

Todd quickly glanced back at the restaurant door. *No sign of pursuit.*

In moments, they were in Todd's car, and driving through the dusk, down Main Street into Springville. "Tell me more about your mother," Todd said. He made a spinning motion with his hand. *Come on, padre. Pick up on what I'm really trying to say.*

Moe gave another surreptitious nod. "She was sweet. She would've been pretty, I think, if she weren't so frail."

Todd looked in the mirror. *Nobody following.* "Uh-huh."

"She was—"

"Okay," Todd interrupted. "I think we're out of range. Now I can tell you where we're headed. There's something I need to show you in the Harold B. Lee Library at BYU."

Moe opened his mouth to speak, but Todd shook his head vehemently. He mouthed, "No!"

Todd was certain Moe realized that they were actually headed in the opposite direction. *Keep playing along, padre. Make whoever might still be listening think we're clueless.* "I think we were being bugged." Todd began to pat down his pockets. He motioned for Moe to do the same.

"Bugged?!" Moe said, sounding horribly alarmed—exaggeratedly so. His expression, however, was grim. He nodded his head and checked his own pockets. "That Irish-looking fellow?"

"Yep. But we're out of range now."

"How do you know we're out of range?"

"If he was listening—and I can't be sure he was—he was wearing a garden-variety Bluetooth headset." Todd glanced in the mirror again. *Still no pursuit.* "Very limited range. And not terribly sophisticated."

"Meaning what?" Moe's eyes went wide. He dug in his pocket and slowly pulled out a small cell phone. He held it out so Todd could see it. He mouthed, "Not mine!"

The phone was transmitting on speakerphone.

Somebody else might still be on the other end. Still eavesdropping. Gotta keep up the act until we disable it. Todd nodded. "Meaning, they had one of us bugged, but it was done on the cheap. So it's either an *ad hoc* surveillance mission—improvised and put together in a hurry—"

Moe rolled his eyes nervously. "I know what *ad hoc* means, young man."

"—or the guy spying on us was an amateur." He mouthed, "Mute!"

Moe found the mute button and pushed it.

Todd's shoulders sagged in relief. "Pull the battery."

Moe complied. "How did you know?"

"I didn't. Not till I saw the phone. It's really not a great way to eavesdrop, especially located in your pocket, but like I said, I think it was an *ad hoc* job."

"Then why let them know we were on to them . . . at least partially?"

"Because . . . I screwed up. I'm not used to this clandestine stuff. My clumsy behavior in the restaurant—you know, cutting the conversation short—probably let them know I was aware of the bug. I should have steered us out of there more casually. I was too abrupt."

"Don't beat yourself up about it."

Todd gestured at the phone. "How did that get into your pocket?"

Moe shook his head. "I don't know." Then a horrified expression. "Oh, my! Someone could have slipped it into my pocket back at the Ren Faire—you know, while we were in Roman costumes. We have a support trailer where we change and store our clothes."

"That would mean it was one of your friends in the Historical Society."

Moe shook his head. His expression bespoke profound sadness . . . and betrayal. "One of my cohort."

"Morgaise has someone in your group."

Moe nodded. "Morgaise . . . or my grandfather."

They drove in silence as Todd turned east toward the foothills above Springville and Mapleton. Each man brooded in his own dark thoughts.

After a few minutes, Moe looked around, startled. He peered into the deepening gloom outside. "Where are we going?"

"Recon mission."

"Up here in the mountains?" Moe sounded confused. "Is the Morrigan house up here?"

"Nope. The house is down in Mapleton."

"So what are we doing up here?"

Todd's grin was fierce and determined. "Luckily, the surveillance equipment I've got in the trunk is a bit more sophisticated than that Irish-looking fellow's."

◆ ◆ ◆

"I gotta say, it's one thing to do academic research on these rituals," Moe said, gazing through a pair of high-powered, night-vision binoculars, "but it's another thing entirely to see it happening right before my eyes. And led by an original practitioner! How did you know this would be going on tonight?"

Sitting next to him on the hillside, Todd adjusted a large parabolic eavesdropping dish, trying to capture anything useful from the ceremony playing out below. He wore the headphones with one ear covered and one ear free. "Full moon. Elaine told Derek she had to be home by dusk, and she told him he couldn't hang around there tonight. Easy to put two and two together and equal Druid ceremony tonight. I don't suppose you speak Gaelic or Welsh, do you, padre?"

"No," Moe replied. "And please don't call me that."

"Sorry," Todd said. "Force of habit."

"We've known each other less than a day! How can it be 'force of habit'?"

167

Todd chuckled. "Hey, I started calling you 'padre' in my head as soon as I knew you used to be a Catholic priest. And once I name somebody in my head, they stay named. Be grateful it's not 'Padre-Man.'"

Moe growled something Todd couldn't quite make out, but he was reasonably sure the older guy wasn't expressing gratitude for Todd's discretion.

Todd tweaked the dish a bit more. "I'm not getting much. Chanting, mostly. But what I can hear isn't English. I don't know what language it is. You said the Morrigans might be from first century Roman Britain. So it could be Gaelic or Welsh. I don't think it's Latin." He took off the headphones and offered them to the former priest.

Moe traded the binoculars for the headset.

Todd looked down at the Morrigans' backyard.

Observed through the night-vision binoculars, the distant scene was illuminated by the full moon as if it were high noon—at least high noon if sunlight were a ghostly green. Figures in hooded robes danced slowly, circling the ring of standing stones. Todd couldn't get an exact count since the figures were moving, but he estimated there were fifty to sixty people. *Judging by their relative heights, about an equal mix of men and women.*

He focused on the tree at the center of the ring of stones. *Definitely bigger than last month. A month ago, it was maybe two-thirds that size. And the fruit is bigger too. A lot bigger. From pea-size to plum-size in a month. If I hadn't seen it myself, I wouldn't have believed it. Peggy said it was only a sapling just two months ago.*

What kind of tree grows that fast?

For a brief moment, he considered the possibility that the larger tree had simply been transplanted in place of the smaller one he'd seen at the last full moon. *No. We're dealing with people who've been around for two thousand years. So why not a tree that grows to maturity in a few months?*

"Definitely *not* Latin," Moe said. "Not Germanic, either. That's where English comes from, you know—the language of the Saxons. And I've heard Welsh a few times. This doesn't sound like that. Gaelic would fit the time period, but I don't know what it sounds like."

Where are the dogs? Where are Morgaise and Elaine? "Did you see Morgaise or Elaine down there?"

"I don't think so," Moe replied. "But it's hard to tell with those robes they're . . . Hold on. There's some English. Something about 'harvest.' 'Goddess.'"

168

Tally ho! There she is! A lone, robed figure stepped from under the tree. A huge black bird perched on each of her shoulders—avian blackness contrasted against the blaring whiteness of her robe. At her right side squatted one of the massive hounds. The beast's head came up past the woman's shoulder.

The second dog trotted up to the hooded figure's left side. The slightly less massive beast sat on its haunches and panted at the worshippers outside the stone circle.

That's both dogs accounted for. Molossii—*ancient Roman war dogs. That makes sense now — What the crap are those?*

Smaller shapes scampered out from under the tree. Six of them. They trotted around the smaller *molossus*—the female.

Puppies! Six more of those things? And they're already the size of a regular dog!

Todd thought of the Glock in its holster. *Fifteen rounds. Eight of those monsters. If it comes to it, I can't even put two rounds in each.*

And that's assuming a pair of nine millimeter hollow-points can stop a full-grown molossus. *Frankly, I don't like my odds.*

Note to self: carry extra clips.

Lots of extra clips.

The woman raised her hands, causing the ravens to flutter in order to stay atop her shoulders.

"Earphones!" Todd said urgently. He extended his hand, but Moe placed the earphones over Todd's ears.

Todd heard the woman by the tree cry out. The noise of the worshippers ceased. In a loud voice, she shouted, *"Féach ar an crann na beatha!"*

The procession of robed worshippers halted their slow dance. They turned toward the center of the ring of stones and raised their hands to the sky.

No, Todd thought, *not to the sky. They're pointing at the tree.*

The hooded figure lowered her hands to her head. *"Féach ar do bandia!"* Then she pulled back her hood, revealing Morgaise's split face—the left half so like Elaine's, the right sagging and lifeless.

As one, the worshippers dropped to their knees. They pointed their outstretched, yearning hands toward Morgaise. Some of them writhed on the ground as if possessed by demons or in the throes of religious ecstasy.

And the cries began.

It was not the unified chanting of before. Rather it was a cacophony of pleading, desperate, hungry worship.

Todd caught only an occasional intelligible word. "Goddess!" "Mother!" "Morrigan!"

Half of Morgaise's face smiled, drinking in the adoration. She tilted her head back as if carried away in spiritual rapture, borne on wings of worshipful adulation.

They can't actually think she's a deity, can they?

Though she's certainly playing the part.

Maybe the bigger question is, does Morgaise *think she's a goddess?*

Morgaise shuddered and bowed her head. She raised her hands. Her mouth moved, and a moment later, Todd heard her cry, "Enough!"

It's like watching an old, cheesy horror movie with the sound out of synch.

The worshipers quieted and ceased their euphoric undulations. They stared at Morgaise expectantly.

Looking to their goddess for instruction.

"Let the transgressor step forth!" cried Morgaise.

A robed and hooded figure rose shakily to its feet and separated itself from the other acolytes. Staggering into the ring of standing stones, the figure's unsteady gait suggested it might be intoxicated. As it approached Morgaise, it removed its hood.

The bodyguard from the Ren Faire!

Morgaise took the man by the arm and led him toward the trunk of the tree.

"What's going on?" Moe asked.

Todd glanced up at the older man. Moe was using Todd's night-vision rifle scope—minus the rifle. The magnification wasn't as good as Todd's military-grade NV binoculars—Moe would be able to see the action, but not distinguish the faces.

Todd focused back on the scene below. "I think they're going to punish the bodyguard from the faire. I doubt Morgaise was happy with him."

The man was on his knees near the trunk of the tree. Morgaise stood behind him. At least, Todd assumed it was Morgaise. But the standing figure was hooded again, and no ravens perched on her shoulders.

And the figure stooped, as if bent with age.

Is that a leash?

The woman held what appeared to be a rope in her left hand. The rope wrapped around the bodyguard's neck like a leash and collar.

Not a leash. It's a noose!

The worshippers were chanting again, but Todd couldn't make out the words.

"No!" screamed a voice. "Don't kill him! I promised!"

That sounds like Elaine.

Todd hadn't seen the younger Morrigan, but he wasn't about to take his eyes off the stooping figure and the kneeling bodyguard.

Elaine might be under the tree.

"How many times must I tell you, child?" Morgaise's voice—but Todd was no longer certain Morgaise was the woman holding the noose.

Morgaise could be under the tree as well.

"I do not kill," Morgaise said. "I *never* kill. Now close your eyes with me, child. We do not need to see this."

Still holding the end of the noose, the woman raised an amorphous object above her head.

Is that a rock?

The woman brought the object down and struck the bodyguard on the head. The man swayed, but the woman held his head up firmly with the rope.

Todd heard Moe gasp. "We've gotta stop this!"

"We'd never get there in time." Todd knew it was true, but he still had to fight the urge to run screaming down the hill, firing his weapon. Anything to stop the impending violence below. Images of Afghanistan flashed through his mind. He fought them down. *Not now!* "Never get there in time."

The chanting rose in a feverish, lunatic crescendo. "Hasten the harvest! Hasten the harvest!"

The woman pulled the noose tighter until the bodyguard's head was tilted back. Todd saw a flash of metal, and then a gout of blood sprayed from the man's neck, falling upon the dark earth surrounding the tree.

Todd battled to control his stomach and *not* vomit his cheese and beef enchiladas down the mountainside.

He heard noises beside him—Moe had lost that battle.

I've seen worse. In Afghanistan.

Yeah, but this isn't Afghanistan. This is America. This is Utah.

Below them, the woman released the rope, and the unfettered corpse collapsed at the foot of the tree. She stepped back, and all eight of the dogs moved in to tear at the steaming meat that moments before had been a living human being.

"Hasten the harvest!" the revelers shouted.

171

"The Triple Death," Moe muttered.

Todd couldn't take his eyes off the mass of gigantic dogs and monstrous puppies roiling around their grisly feast. "Triple Death? What are you talking about?"

"The ancient Romans described a Celtic human sacrifice called the Triple Death—strangulation by rope, a blow to the head, then the slitting of the throat while pulling on the rope, creating a spray of blood." Moe sounded as if he might be sick again. "I always . . . I thought it was . . . Roman propaganda—justification for conquest, but . . ."

"No," Todd said, "the Romans were simply reporting the facts. They were describing . . . evil."

Below them, the chant had become a shriek of mass religious hysteria. "Hasten the harvest! Hasten the harvest! Hasten! Hasten!"

The woman raised her hands toward the tree. Todd couldn't see her face, but her posture, the urgency with which her hands reached toward the tree, grasping, clenching, and unclenching, as if she sought to draw power or magic from it . . .

It's as if she expects the tree to . . . do something.

"Hasten! Hasten! Hasten!"

And the tree began to move.

Not moving.

Growing.

In seconds, the tree had expanded, sprouted and grown new leaves, until it obscured the woman and the hell hounds from Todd's sight. The branches reached beyond the circle of stones.

And the fruit was the size of large apples.

"Where is she?" Moe asked. He was looking through the NV scope again. "Where's Morgaise? Is . . . is that tree . . . bigger? It *is* bigger! How?"

It grew. Moe sees it too.

"She fed it blood," Todd said, struggling to believe the evidence of his own eyes. "And it grew."

But it was the image of the slaughtered bodyguard that filled Todd's mind, driving all other images away. He tried to block it out, but it possessed him, filled him with horror . . . and memory.

Afghanistan all over again.

Little girl. Maybe four years old. Gang-raped. Eyes gouged out. Nose and ears bitten off. Tongue ripped out. Nipples and genitals mutilated.

A tiny corpse left for the birds or dogs to eat.

She was the first he'd seen.

But she wasn't the last.

All in the name of a twisted, psychotic religion.

Todd tore off the earphones and set the binoculars down. He sat staring up at the full moon. His hands trembled, and sweat beaded on his face.

How do I fight this?

Heavenly Father, how can I possibly fight this evil? I know I asked for a clear enemy to fight, but . . . What am I supposed to do?

How am I supposed to save Peggy . . . from that?

Run away?

Drag her away from her beloved Derek?

Leave Derek to his fate?

She'll never do it.

She'll . . .

Todd heard a sound behind them.

Footsteps!

He leapt to his feet, reaching for his Glock, spinning around.

And found himself staring into the barrel of a gun.

XX

Drop it!"

Moe Abbot nearly jumped out of his skin. Still trembling and sick with horror at the grisly sights he'd just witnessed, he leapt awkwardly to his feet and tried to turn around. Without the night-vision binoculars or rifle scope, he was almost night-blind. He lost his balance, and with a startled cry, fell to the ground.

His left knee came down hard on the rocky shoulder of the mountain road, forcing a grunt of pain from between clenched teeth.

A bright light hit him in the face.

He shut his eyes and turned his face away from the blinding light. The stench of his own vomit wafted into his nose, causing him to gag anew.

"Easy," he heard Todd say from his left.

Confused, terrified, and queasy, Moe opened his eyes slightly. No longer looking directly into the light—a flashlight, he realized—he found he could see again.

And what he saw wasn't comforting.

To Moe's left, Todd stood in the beam of a second flashlight, gripping a sidearm barely out of its hip holster. The man holding the flashlight pointed a handgun at Todd.

A quick glance in front confirmed that he was in a similar predicament. Moe couldn't see a face, but he could discern a weapon pointed at him.

"I said, drop it!" It was the same voice as before, coming from the man holding Todd at gunpoint.

"If I drop it," Todd said, his voice calm and deliberate, "it could go off."

Todd's gunman hesitated, then said, "Then set it down. Slowly."

Todd nodded cautiously. "Okay. Setting the safety. Easy now." He slowly bent to place the weapon on the ground.

Moe, his knee beginning to throb, remained on his butt, unmoving.

"Who are you?" He took some small satisfaction in the fact that his voice barely shook. "What do you want?"

"Shut up!" snapped the man holding a gun on him.

If they wanted us dead, they'd have shot us by now. "Or what? You'll shoot us?"

"Yeah," replied the unseen figure.

By that time, Moe could discern a little better the man aiming a gun at Todd—not much more than a silhouette, but Moe could make out some features. And he recognized the guy. *The Irish-looking fellow from the restaurant! How'd he find us?* Moe still couldn't see his own gunman.

He stared past the blinding flashlight beam, forced a big grin, and shook his head slowly. "No. I don't think so."

"What?" both gunmen said.

Moe imagined rather than saw the confusion on their faces. "You're not going to kill us." *But I'm not sure, am I? And I'm not only gambling with my life—I'm betting Todd's too.* "You want something— something you can't get if we're dead."

"So what do you want?" Todd asked, apparently taking his cue from Moe.

When neither gunman answered, Moe said, "Please get those lights out of our faces."

"You're not in charge here," snapped his gunman.

"Maybe not," Moe replied, "but you need our cooperation. So, a little *quid pro quo*, if you please."

A bead of sweat formed at Moe's temple. *Please, don't see how bat-crap scared I am!* It wasn't that he'd never looked down the barrel of a loaded gun before—he'd been mugged twice—but that sight was something he could never get used to. *Just a twitch of a finger, and bang—you're dead.*

He held his breath as seconds ticked by with agonizing slug-gishness, like the slowing heartbeats of a dying man.

The beam of light angled downward slightly.

The drop of sweat slid down Moe's cheek, and he tried to release his breath without a telltale shudder. Out of the corner of his eye, he saw the light on Todd lower as well.

Moe nodded his head graciously. "That's better. Thank you." He could almost make out the dim outline of his gunman.

"What do you want?" Todd repeated.

"Just shut up, will you?" Todd's gunman said. The exasperation in the man's voice was obvious.

175

Okay, they're still in control, but the balance has shifted toward our favor. A little.

Moe raised an eyebrow. "So you just want to hold us here? And do what? Wait? Don't say anything? Don't go anywhere?"

His gunman growled softly in frustration. "Just . . . There's someone who wants to talk to you."

I think he means me. Someone wants to talk to me.

And I think I know who.

He nodded again. "So are you going to take us to him, or is he coming up here?"

His gunman motioned with his weapon. "Get up. Go stand with . . . your friend. Slowly. Hands in the air. Both of you, hands up."

Moe got to his feet slowly, cautiously. He raised his hands, then sidestepped toward Todd. He tried to make the movement appear casual—no easy thing, moving sideways like a crab. *A casual crab . . . with an injured knee.*

As soon as he took his place next to Todd, Moe's gunman lowered his flashlight, then activated a cell phone. The man placed the phone to his ear, and his face was bathed in a ghostly light. Dark, perhaps black, hair, plain face, clean-shaven—Moe was sure he'd never seen the guy before. *I wonder if Todd recognizes him?*

After a few seconds, the gunman said, "We have him, sir."

Him. They're only interested in one of us.

Moe was deadly certain it was himself.

"Yes, sir," the man continued. "We have them both. You can come on up." After a pause, he repeated, "Yes, sir." He ended the call and pocketed the phone. Then he pointed his weapon at Moe and Todd again.

And they waited.

Todd shifted his feet. "I don't suppose we can like . . . put our hands on our heads? My shoulders are aching. Besides, I don't think my antiperspirant was designed for a stickup. 'Extra-Dry,' my butt!"

"You trying to be funny?" the Irish-looking gunman asked. He sounded more irritated than angry.

Todd nodded. "Actually, yeah. I was all set for a career in stand-up comedy, but Mom said there was better money in the Air Force. Boy, was she wrong!"

In spite of the danger, the stench of vomit, and the fear, Moe chuckled. *Odd sense of humor. Bravado? Or just covering fear?*

The two gunmen exchanged glances.

"Okay," Moe's gunman said. "Hands on your heads then."

I thank thee, Father, for small blessings. Moe sighed theatrically and lowered his hands, placing them on his head and interlacing his fingers. "Thank you. That's much better. Arthritis, you know." He shook his head. "Never grow old, young man."

Moe's night vision had recovered enough for him to see the gunman sneer at him.

Okay, so it was a fib about the arthritis. Todd's using humor. Maybe I can exploit age bias.

Moe had no intention of making a move against the gunmen, but it wouldn't hurt if their captors could be tricked into underestimating them.

"What's taking so long?" Moe's gunman muttered, peering down the road into the darkness. "You got this for a minute?"

The redhead nodded. "Yeah. I got this."

"Okay. Watch them. I'll be back." He turned and walked off, his flashlight beam preceding his passage into the darkness.

Todd chuckled. "I'll be Bach," he said, using a ridiculously fake Austrian accent. "Either he thinks he's a robotic assassin from the future or a dead classical composer who specialized in organ music."

The remaining gunman groaned in disgust.

Moe, however, grinned wide.

"Maybe," Todd said, "a time-traveling android that plays a killer calliope."

The redhead growled. "Just shut up."

"Hey, buddy," Todd said, pointing with his chin at the man.

"What?" The gunman sounded supremely annoyed.

Todd, on the other hand, seemed thoroughly amused with himself. "Great food at that Mexican place, huh?"

The redhead hesitated. "What of it?"

He didn't realize we spotted him there, did he?

"What'd you order?" Todd asked.

"Just shut up."

Todd shrugged. "Simply making conversation. Simply passing the time. 'Sides, I'm with the padre, here. I don't think you'll shoot us. Not unless we do something stupid."

The redheaded gunman, his arm straight and rigid, pointed the weapon right at Todd's face. "What if I told you that it's just the old guy we want, huh? What if your life isn't worth sh—"

"I bet it was chicken you ordered," Todd said. "Am I right?"

The gunman seemed surprised. "Yeah—chicken. So what?"

"Figures." Todd grimaced as if thoroughly revolted.

The barrel of the gun pressed against Todd's forehead.

You're pushing him too hard, Moe thought, terrified.

The gunman uttered a particularly foul oath. "What the hell's that mean?" He raised the flashlight slightly, not shining it directly in Todd's eyes, but enough to make Todd squint.

Todd chuckled. "You see, it's like this." His tone was suited to casual conversation, as if he were talking to an old friend. "A woman might order a chicken burrito — you know — because she's trying to eat *lite*. But a skinny fella like you?" He frowned and shook his head, rocking the barrel of the gun back and forth slightly and forcing the gunman to pull it back a little. "Naw, you aren't into eating healthy. And chicken in Mexican food is disgusting! But you ordered it anyway. So you know what that means, don't ya?" He laughed — soft, low, and — to Moe's ears — with a just hint of madness.

Has he lost it?

The gunman looked anything but amused. "What?"

Todd laughed again, and his laughter had gained an almost creepy edge, as if his mind had turned a dangerous corner. "Tell him, padre. Tell him what it means."

"Uh, it means . . ." Moe swallowed hard, trying to dispel the sudden lump in his throat. "It means you . . . can't be trusted."

The gunman turned his eyes on Moe. "What the — "

Todd's hands snapped down from atop his head. His right hand clamped on the gunman's wrist, thrusting it and the weapon to the left — away from Todd's face and away from Moe. At the same time, Todd's left hand slammed heel first into the gunman's elbow, thrusting it hard across the man's chest. Moe heard a nauseating crunch and a popping sound as the gunman's arm bent at an angle nature never intended.

The man opened his mouth to scream, but Todd drove his left fist into the man's gut, knocking the wind out of him.

Todd freed the gun from his opponent's grip, then punched him hard on the jaw.

Moe heard another horrible crunch, and the redhead dropped his flashlight, crumpled to the ground, and lay unmoving. The flashlight, pointing at the man's face, revealed an obviously broken jaw.

Todd aimed the weapon at the prone figure and growled, "Get my gun!"

Moe stared in shock at the unconscious man with the horribly twisted arm and shattered jaw.

"Moe!" Todd snapped. "Get my gun. It's in his belt."

Me? "Get your gun?" Moe didn't want to touch the man. He stared at the fallen enemy, his mind clouded with horror. He couldn't quite process what he'd just seen.

Todd just broke his arm and his jaw.

Todd grunted. He placed the gun in Moe's hand. "Cover me."

Acting on numb instinct rather than consciously following Todd's instructions, Moe pointed the weapon at the broken man on the ground.

He watched mutely as Todd knelt and retrieved a handgun from the man's belt. Todd snatched up the flashlight as well, then got back to his feet, asking, "You okay?"

Moe shuddered, breaking out of his horrified paralysis. "Yeah." He blinked. "Y-you okay?"

Todd gave voice to a growl. "About broke my blasted hand." He flexed his left hand in the beam of the flashlight and grimaced. "It'll be okay . . . I think." He shook it. "But it's gonna hurt like the dickens tomorrow."

There was something in Todd's voice that Moe found unsettling. Moe resisted the sudden urge to shine the flashlight beam directly into his ally's face, but he needed to get a closer look. He wasn't a trained psychiatrist, but he'd done enough counseling sessions with troubled servicemen who'd exhibited the same symptoms.

Moe observed Todd's hands—both the one holding the sidearm and the one he'd used to break the redhead's bones.

They were trembling slightly.

Post-Traumatic Stress Disorder. PTSD. Shell-shock. Combat Fatigue.

The trembling hands by themselves weren't enough to confirm the condition, but Moe was certain of one thing—Todd had experienced the horrors of combat close up. He was coping, but he was broken inside.

And with someone to help—a soul in need of healing—Moe's own fear vanished. *Once a priest—always a priest.*

He offered up a silent prayer. *Father in Heaven, help me to help him.*

But first things first. Moe shone the flashlight on the unconscious man's face. "What do we do with him?"

"Leave him. We need to get out of here before the other goon comes back."

Twin pinpoints of light appeared on the road, downhill from their position. *Too late for that.*

Todd growled again, muttering something unintelligible—and most likely unpleasant. The tremor in his hands vanished.

This is how he copes — he fights, he solves problems. He's a Search-And-Rescue pilot. He saves people.

"Okay," Todd said. "New plan. We go cross-country. Get the night-vision—"

Moe laid a hand on Todd's arm. "Actually, I think I know who's in that car. And I want to talk to him as much as he wants to talk to me."

Todd took a deep breath, shook his injured left hand again, and nodded. "Roger that. I think I do too. Only, I want to do it on *our* terms. I don't like having a gun pointed at me . . . or my friends."

Moe raised an eyebrow. "You don't say."

"Okay," Todd said, "here's the plan . . ."

♦ ♦ ♦

As the large SUV pulled to a stop a few yards away on the side of the road, Moe was absolutely certain Todd's plan was *not* going to work. Moe stood with his back to the car, holding a gun on Todd. Moe disliked—no—he *loathed* the feel of the weapon. *Give me a Roman sword, a nice* gladius *any day — even if it's just for reenactments — blunted and just for show — not this heavy, ugly, cowardly thing that can snuff out a life from a distance.* Moe had never pointed a gun at another human being—not until that night. And he was aiming it at his new friend.

My friend who just crippled a man with his bare hands.

Todd stood in front of Moe, facing the car, holding and supporting the redheaded man next to him. Moe watched as Todd shifted his feet and angled the unconscious man's dead weight so that neither the man's lolling head nor his red hair were visible in the bright gleam of the headlights.

Hopefully, nobody'll notice they aren't lifting their hands in the air.

It's not going to work.

Father, please let this work!

He heard a car door open and footsteps on the gravel of the road shoulder. "Betchya thought we weren't coming back!" called the voice of the second gunman cheerily.

Moe looked at Todd, and his friend nodded slightly.

Todd dropped the unconscious redhead to the ground, raised his Glock, and shouted, "Don't move! Hands where I can see them!"

Moe spun around and pointed his weapon and the flashlight at the returning thug. The man already had his hands in the air.

"*Slowly* put your weapon on the ground and step aside," Todd ordered.

The man complied, then raised his hands again. "Is he dead?"

"No," Moe replied, "but he might wish he were when he wakes

up." *Why am I being so flippant? The man's badly hurt!*

"Cover him," Todd said.

"Okay." Moe took a deep breath, trying to steady his aim.

"On your knees," Todd ordered. "Hands on your head." Then he aimed his weapon and flashlight at the vehicle. "You! In the car! Get out slowly and show me your hands!"

The gunman dropped to his knees and placed his hands on his head.

"Get his weapon," Todd said.

It took Moe a moment to realize Todd was talking to him. "Okay." Keeping his gun trained on the kneeling man, Moe awkwardly managed to retrieve the discarded weapon. He checked the safety and stowed the gun in his belt.

The steel felt cold. *Probably go off and hit me in the groin.*

I hate guns.

When he glanced in Todd's direction, he saw Todd pushing a man in front of him. Moe could only assume this was the driver.

Forcing the driver to kneel a few feet away from the gunman, Todd said, "Take off your belts. Then lie down and put your hands behind your backs." Working quickly, Todd soon had both the driver and the gunman with their arms behind their backs, bound tightly at the wrists. The wrists were strapped together by the belts, with the palms flat against each other, the elbows pulled close together, the shoulders rotated back in an awkward position.

That looks painful.

Judging from the grimaces on both the captives' faces, it probably *was* painful.

Todd's done this before. In a combat zone, I'd wager. Improvising. No zipties. No handcuffs. Just belts holding elbows and shoulders on the verge of dislocation.

Even if they manage to get their hands free, their arms will be near useless.

"Where'd you learn to do that?" Moe asked as Todd stood, inspecting his handiwork.

"Afghanistan." Todd's voice sounded dispassionate, as if it were coming from a distance, as far away as that distant, battle-torn country. "We took fire. Had to make a hard landing. Taliban territory. Had to fight our way back. We captured a couple of locals. Thought they might be Taliban sympathizers. Couldn't let them give away our position. Had to improvise. Didn't shoot them. But their eyes—the hatred."

181

Oh my. "Sorry."

"What they did to their own people. Women. Girls. Little boys."

Abruptly, Todd shuddered. He shrugged his shoulders as if casually trying to cast off the weight of a recurring nightmare. Then he turned around and aimed his weapon and flashlight at the car. "You there, in the backseat! Show me your hands!" He shone the light into the backseat and yanked open the door.

"Hey, Moe!" he called over his shoulder. "Come on over. There's someone here who wants to chat with you."

Moe lowered his weapon, breathing a sigh of relief. *If I never have to hold a gun again . . .* The prisoners weren't going anywhere. He joined Todd at the side of the SUV. Peering into the door, Moe saw an ancient face squinting out at him and shielding its eyes with arthritic, age-spotted hands.

Moe smiled at the old man in the backseat, but the ex-priest's eyes held no warmth. Moe knew the man—and he despised him.

"Hello, Grandfather."

XXI

Y ou will get that light out of my face immediately, young man."
Thurgood Abbot's calm, imperious voice conveyed neither fear nor
irritation.

Moe couldn't help but be impressed by the old man's bravado. *He
acts as if he's the one in control, as if he actually expects to be obeyed.*

Seemingly unimpressed, Todd kept the flashlight beam steady and
pointed his Glock at the nonagenarian. "Show me your hands."

His eyes shut tight against the blinding light, Thurgood smiled,
revealing a mouth of impossibly straight and white teeth — a wolf with
perfect dental work. He kept his age-spotted hands in his lap and
wiggled his skeletal fingers. "You can see my hands."

Brave or foolish, Moe thought, *your timing is terrible, Grandfather.*

Quite predictably, Todd was not amused. "I'm normally not a
violent man, but I just crippled one of your men with my bare hands.
The other two are incapacitated. They're all going to need medical
attention soon. Now I know you know who I am. You have threatened
me and my friends. You sent two men to rape and murder — "

Thurgood waved a dismissive hand. "I had nothing to do with — "

"Get your hands up!" Todd snarled.

Moe noticed a slight tremor in Todd's gun hand. Todd's index
finger was pointed down the barrel, but it would take only a second to
place his finger on the trigger. "I think you've pushed him quite far
enough for one night, Grandfather."

Thurgood paused a moment as in careful deliberation, then pursed
his thin lips and nodded slightly. "As you wish." He raised his hands
and pressed them up against the roof of the vehicle. "I hope you don't
expect me to hold this ridiculous pose for very long, young man. I'm
ninety-five years old and — "

"Ninety-five," Todd said, "and still capable of arranging murder,
rape, and general scumbaggery. You sit behind a big desk, like some
mafia godfather. Then you send your thugs out to do your wetwork so

183

you can keep your hands clean. But they're *not* clean."

The old man's mouth twitched.

That got to him, Moe thought. *Something about his hands not being clean . . .*

"Young man," Thurgood said, apparently recovering his composure, "I have no — "

"Search him."

Moe hesitated. "I, uh, doubt he's got a weapon."

"I'm not willing to take that chance," Todd said. "Are you?"

"I guess not."

"So search him."

"Now you listen here!" The elderly lawyer sounded indignant. "I will not allow — "

Todd laughed — a low and sinister sound full of predatory madness.

Like just before he crippled that Irish-looking fellow.

Moe was unable to suppress a shudder. *It's just for show — just to unnerve him. It's certainly unnerving me.*

"You think you're in control, *sir*?" Todd gave the last word a sense of respect and loathing at the same time, like a seasoned and combat-hardened master sergeant addressing a newly commissioned, wet-behind-the-ears-snot-nosed-butter-bar second lieutenant. "You think you're in control? Well, *sir*, you picked the wrong guy to mess with on the wrong bloody night."

Thurgood seemed to consider Todd's words for a moment, then he lifted his chin and looked away, straight ahead. "You won't kill me. You Mormons are — "

Todd's low, chilling laugh stopped Thurgood short.

"You're right," Todd said. "I won't kill you. But you so much as twitch an eyebrow, and I'll blow your kneecap away." Todd aimed the Glock at Thurgood's right knee, then pulled back slightly. The slow, smooth cadence of his voice was the most frightening aspect. He spoke of mayhem as if he were soothing a sick child. "Or maybe a hand. Are you right- or left-handed, Mr. Abbot?"

Thurgood's arrogant composure crumbled like the battlements of a wet sandcastle. He swallowed several times, and looked as if he might be sick. "Right jacket pocket. It's just . . . just a Taser."

Moe felt as if he might be sick too. Again. *That's right. I was supposed to search him.*

But Todd wouldn't really blow away one of his hands, would he?

"Get it," Todd said. "And pat him down anyway. I don't trust him." He placed his flashlight under his armpit, keeping the light more or less on the old man, while freeing up his left hand. "Give me your gun first. I don't want him getting ahold of that. Hey, Moe! You listening?"

It is just an act, right, Todd? Moe handed his weapon to Todd. Then he knelt beside the open car door. *He smells of expensive cologne. No, he reeks of it. Perfume masking feebleness. All the times I imagined this meeting . . .* Moe stuck his hand carefully into the pocket of the old man's expensive suit. His fingers found something hard. *Plastic. Rectangular. Not a gun.* He removed the object and glanced at it. "Taser. Just like he said."

Moe pulled back, out of the car, and set the Taser on the ground by his knee. Then he bent and reached back into the car to continue his search.

Never imagined hugging the man — or even shaking his hand — but this? I imagined telling him off, using words I'd never say out loud — but patting him down? Searching him for weapons?

Moe found a pen and a slim wallet in the left breast pocket, a phone in the right. He withdrew from the door and showed the items to Todd. "What do I do with these?"

"Keep the Taser, but toss the rest into the front seat."

Moe complied, then got to his feet, Taser in hand, and stepped back to stand beside Todd.

"Okay, Mr. Abbot," Todd said. "You can lower your hands."

The old man nodded his head. "Thank you."

"Now sit on them," Todd said. "Sit on your hands. Don't make me bind them."

Thurgood Abbot scowled indignantly, but he shoved his aged hands under his skinny buttocks. He then turned his face straight ahead and assumed an expression of calm indifference.

Todd handed the gun back to Moe. Then he retrieved the flashlight from under his armpit. "That's better." Todd's voice had shed its anger and psychotic edge.

Just an act. Scary. Effective. Very effective.

"He's all yours," Todd said. "Watch him. Tase him if he gets out of line. I'm gonna check on the, uh, prisoners."

Moe nodded and cleared his throat, not trusting his voice. "Sounds good." His hands felt clammy, and the gun felt cold. Gratefully, he set the safety on the gun and stuffed it into his jacket pocket, trading it for the Taser. He turned the device on. In moments, an indicator light showed it was ready to shock. He shone his own flashlight on his grandfather—not directly in the old man's face, but a bit lower.

I want to look him in the eye.

At least, I think I do.

Todd leaned in toward Moe's ear. "Sorry to go all Norman Bates on you. Freaky, but it works . . . in any language. We have to keep this quick. I wasn't kidding about those other guys needing a doctor."

And it seemed to Moe as if Todd shuddered.

Repulsed by the violence. Compassion for the enemy.

Moe felt a warm surge of affection and admiration for his new friend and ally. *Even if he does know how to creep me out.*

Todd turned and walked away.

And Moe was left alone—more or less—with his grandfather.

The feeling of warm affection he'd felt for Todd bled away, and an old and ugly hatred—spawned by decades of being abandoned—throbbed within him.

Thurgood Abbot, however, looked straight ahead, calm and silent—a sphinx, mute with the secrets of the past.

Moe stared at the old man, striving to control his anger. *Coward! You tried to have me erased before I was even born. You drove my mother away into a life of shame and poverty, and into an early grave.* He suppressed the sudden, almost overwhelming urge to drop the Taser and throttle the life out of the old man's decrepit carcass.

Moe drew in a calming breath to steady his voice. "You wanted this little family reunion, so talk."

His gaze fixed ahead, Thurgood exhaled loudly through his nostrils, like an enraged bull barely containing his anger. "Is the barbarian gone?"

"For the moment. But I wouldn't count on him being gone long."

"Very well." The old man turned his face and intense brown eyes toward his grandson.

Surely he can't see me, not with my face in the dark, but . . . It seemed as if the old man's gaze bored right into Moe's eyes, looking into the depths of his soul. *Like he's trying to stare me down.*

"Moses." Thurgood paused as if choosing his words carefully. "This is not how I envisioned our first meeting."

No, you envisioned holding me at gunpoint. Moe wanted to say that—he wanted to say a lot of unpleasant things—but the old priest in him won out, restraining his tongue. *Let him talk.* "So it would seem."

"Yes, well, be that as it may, I have been watching over you for your entire life, Moses. I have been . . . keeping track of you and your progress."

I bet you have.

Thurgood smiled. If Moe hadn't known better, he might have mistaken the softness around the old man's eyes as patriarchal affection. "I paid for your schooling, you know."

"Yes, I know."

The wrinkles around the lawyer's eyes hardened momentarily, and his eyes flashed in irritation or anger.

Guess I wasn't supposed to know that. I bet you're just dying to know how I know.

The old man's eyes softened again. "I shouldn't be surprised, I suppose. There weren't many other . . . suspects, if you will, for your benefactor."

"You must have been very disappointed when I joined the LDS church."

Thurgood shrugged—or tried to, hampered as he was with his hands stuck beneath him. "I had hoped you would make a career of the priesthood. I had hoped you would have done some good in the world."

"I am doing good in the world. I teach the youth in the Church. I've served as a bishop. I married a good woman. I've led a life of dedicated service. And I'm sure my mother is proud of me."

The corner of Thurgood's mouth twitched slightly. A shadow of sorrow passed over his face. "My sweet Marietta."

"You knew where she was—where we were—the whole time, didn't you?"

The old man nodded slowly. "After the first year—after you were born."

"Well, I'm certainly grateful you failed to find her in time to kill me."

Thurgood's sad expression soured, then the mask of calm smoothed his wrinkled features. "I've made . . . many mistakes in my life. But I've tried to—"

Footsteps approached. Moe almost took his eyes off the old man, but forced himself to keep staring at his reluctant grandfather. *Just Todd. Not one of the others.*

I hope.

Thurgood scowled, apparently hearing the footsteps too, and looked straight ahead again.

"Hey, Moe!" Todd said.

Moe almost shuddered in relief. "Yeah?"

"Let me have that Taser for a minute."

Moe pulled the nasty gun out of his pocket, clicked off the safety and pointed it at his grandfather. Then taking his cue from Todd, he aimed, more or less, at the old man's knee. He kept his index finger pointed alongside the barrel, rather than on the trigger, just as he'd been trained to do when not intending to shoot. *Don't want to twitch a finger and . . .*

Moe handed the Taser to Todd, both men carefully avoiding the business end of the device.

"Thanks," Todd said. "I've splinted and elevated Irish's arm. Bound his jaw too, but I'm not sure how much good that'll do. And treated him for shock. Always treat for shock! But I think the other two . . . Well, I think they'd be better off if I were to tase them so I can rebind their wrists in front. Can't keep their arms pulled back that hard for long. I don't want to cripple them too." He sounded bright, almost cheery. "Besides, I don't want to get sued or anything. I don't suppose you know a good lawyer? So how's it going over here? You two getting acquainted?"

Moe chuckled mirthlessly. "You might say that."

"Well, don't take all night. Irish needs a doctor." And then Todd was gone again.

Tasing them is better than binding them? Well, if the alternative is permanent injury, I guess it makes sense . . .

Thurgood turned his face back toward his grandson. "Listen to me, Moses." His voice was earnest, almost desperate—all pretense of control gone. "What you are doing is incredibly dangerous. You are putting all of us—your entire family—in grave danger. You have taken up with the wrong people. You—"

An explosion of laughter burst from Moe, shaking his whole frame. It was all he could do to keep the gun and the flashlight aimed in the general direction of his grandfather. He could barely catch his breath. "Me? I've taken up with the wrong people? Are you completely delusional?"

Moe laughed again, but his laughter was filled with rage. "I just watched your precious client—your false goddess—murder a man and feed his blood to a-a-a . . . some kind of freakish, monstrous tree. And it grew! Right before my eyes! Then her dogs, they . . . How could you let this go on? No, you didn't just look the other way. You *helped* them. Keeping your hands clean? Your hands are *drenched* in blood! *I've* taken up with the wrong people? Are you insane?"

And for one mad, horrifying second, Moe was tempted—sorely tempted—to curl his finger around the trigger and pull.

But the old man's stricken expression stopped him cold.

He's not insane.

He's terrified.

Moe took a deep, calming breath. "We're going to end this. This whole monstrous cycle, this horrible curse—it ends now. With me."

"No!" Tears flew from the old man's wide eyes as he shook his head. "You mustn't! You can't! You don't know what they'll do when you cross them! You don't know what she's capable of! I—I had . . . to w-watch . . ." Thurgood Abbot's head drooped forward, and his thin, frail body quaked with heaving sobs. "P-please. Just let them go. They'll be gone. Halloween. It'll all be over. Then my family will be safe. Then I can die."

Moe shook his head. "No, Grandfather. It wouldn't be over. All you'd be doing is putting it off for the next generation."

"Please. Just let them go. Promise me you'll let them go. You must promise!"

"I made my mother a promise. And I mean to keep it. I'm ending this. I'm going to deliver my family if it takes my dying breath."

"Please." The barest whisper, barely audible. "Protect my family."

His family. Not our family.

Moe stared at the broken, terrified soul—the man he had hated all his life—the man his mother had sworn him to save. And though Moe still loathed the old man, in the ashes of despite, a small ember of pity glowed. *Forgive me, Father. Help me to forgive him. Strip this hatred from my heart.* "You've done horrible things, Grandfather, in the service of your false goddess. And you have suffered much at her hand. But you still have a chance . . . for redemption. Help me. Help me save our family."

Thurgood turned his face in Moe's direction. His eyes were streaked with red, and his craggy cheeks were wet with tears. His lips trembled. "How?"

Relief and compassion flowed through Moses Abbot, drowning the twin flames of bitterness and hatred. "Tell me everything. Confession—*true* confession is good for the soul."

And Thurgood Abbot opened his mouth. And he confessed.

◆ ◆ ◆

"You think the old man's okay to drive?" In the glow of the dashboard lights, Todd's expression appeared—for the most part— calm, emotionless. But to Moe's eye, the set of the man's jaw bespoke an underlying tension.

"He said he was," Moe replied. "He hasn't had a license in years, but . . ." Moe lowered the pitch of his voice, lampooning his grandfather's pomposity. "'I'm quite capable, young man.'" Moe had intended to elicit a chuckle, hoping to ease the tension.

Todd, however, merely nodded. Then he clucked his tongue and tilted his head to the side. "Shoulda driven Irish to the ER myself. Shoulda elevated his head, not his feet. His jaw was all swollen." He grimaced. Then he lifted his left hand off the steering wheel and shook it. "Already hurts like the dickens." Placing the hand back on the wheel, he growled. "Shoulda driven him myself."

Moe grinned sympathetically and shook his head. "You did what you had to do. Then you *succored* your enemy. That's more than *I* would've done."

Then again, I wouldn't have broken the man's bones in the first place. Wouldn't have been capable of it.

But then . . . well, I don't want to think of what might've happened if Todd hadn't done . . . what he did.

Todd shrugged. "So what'd you learn?"

Moe sighed and frowned. "Not as much I'd hoped — at least not that much more than I already knew or suspected. Half an hour of talking — that man can talk, let me tell you — half an hour, and not much to show for it. He's terrified — terrified for his family." *His family, but not me.* "But I did learn a few things and got confirmation on a few more."

"Such as?"

"Well, that ghastly tree is *all important* to the sisters. It *is* fed by blood. That's what makes it grow."

"Yeah. We saw that."

"Yes, but I suppose it helps — well, it helps *me* at least — to have that theory confirmed."

Todd nodded. "Yeah, okay."

"And you were right about it being suspended animation rather than time-travel. The fruit of the tree puts them to sleep. For sixty years. Apparently, the molossii sleep as well, guarding them."

Todd frowned dubiously. "What good does that do? I mean, a sleeping dog isn't much of a guard dog."

"My grandfather thinks maybe the scent of intruders might wake the dogs."

Todd nodded again, but rocked his head from side to side as he did so, indicating both agreement and doubt. "Well, I guess that works. But . . . what if the dogs *do* wake up? Let's say they defend Elaine and Morgaise, eat the intruders . . . then what? I mean, the

Morrigans sleep on, but the dogs are awake. Wouldn't they run off or starve or die of old age?"

"Oh, the sisters can be awoken. Physical contact—like a dog licking their faces."

"Or . . . a kiss." Todd nodded vigorously. "Yeah. Elaine freaked out at the Ren Faire when she heard the Sleeping Beauty story being told. Apparently, Elaine was the original—you know—the original Sleeping Beauty."

"Yes! And the original Snow White and Brunhilde too. That's what my grandfather said. Probably other 'sleeping maidens' or 'sleeping princesses' as well. She's probably the source of all those legends. But I don't know how Morgaise fits into that scenario. The fairy tales don't mention a disfigured older sister."

"What's with her face—Morgaise's face, I mean?"

"No idea." Moe shook his head. "What else? Let me see . . . Oh! There have been *breaks* in the cycle. There were a couple centuries where the Abbots were left alone completely. Apparently, the Morrigans were in central Europe during that period."

"Okay," Todd said. "But I'm not sure how that helps us now. What else?"

"Well, let's see . . . The house. Even my grandfather doesn't understand exactly why, but . . . there has to be a tower on the top." Moe counted off the requirements on his fingers. "Two stories, plus the tower. Twin staircases on either side. Two wings extending in front, and *only* in front. Oh, and lots of windows. With iron bars over all of them. Security, maybe?"

Todd scratched at his day's growth of stubble. "I don't know. There's something about the shape of that house that nags at me. It's like I should . . ." He shook his head. "Anyway, go on."

"The ravens. They have to be mated and named Bran and . . . Bov. But it's not spelled like it sounds. Gaelic, I think."

Todd waved a hand impatiently. "Interesting, maybe, but not helpful."

Moe chuckled nervously. "Sorry. Old scholar talking here. Fascinating, but . . . Let's see . . . Halloween. That's when the cycle ends. So we have a few weeks still. Um . . . my family only knows where the Morrigans will appear next—not where they sleep, *per se*. Next time, it's supposed to be in Montana. The land's already been purchased."

Todd's expression hardened. "Not gonna be a next time."

Moe frowned. "Agreed. It ends here. Now."

They drove in silence for a minute, each man lost in his own grim musings.

"The house," Todd said, breaking the silence. "You'd think a bizarre building like that would end up—I don't know—in *Architectural Digest* or something. So strange."

Moe slapped his forehead. "Yeah! I forgot! The house gets burned to the ground—same time as when the Morrigans disappear."

"Destroying the evidence?"

Moe shrugged. "Maybe so."

"So how did they track us after we pulled the battery out of Irish's phone?"

Moe chuckled. "Actually, that part was fascinating. It seems there's a small second battery in most smart phones—to preserve settings in case the main battery fails or gets pulled. So it never shuts down completely. That's how they were able to get a location on the phone."

Todd gave him a horrified look. "You've got to be kidding!"

Moe shrugged. "That's what my grandfather said. I don't know if—"

"Toss it out the window! Quick!"

"You don't think they're still—"

"Just get rid of it!"

Moe found the phone and hurriedly complied. "Sorry. I should've told you about that sooner."

Todd waved his hand dismissively. "Don't worry about it." He shook his head. "And I thought I was being so clever by pulling the battery." Todd thumped the steering wheel with his left hand in apparent frustration, then grunted in pain. He shook the offended appendage. "Well, that was dumb, Cavetto."

Moe grinned. "Maybe you should take it easy with that hand."

Todd chuckled once. "Tell me about it." He paused a second, then said, "Hey, do me a favor." He dug his own phone and its battery out of a pocket. "Put this back together for me, will you? I need to check in with Peggy."

"Sure." Moe took the phone and reassembled it. He pushed the power button, restarting the device. After it powered up, he handed the phone to Todd. "Here you go."

"Thanks. I sure hope they're not tracking my—"

The phone rang.

Todd glanced at the screen. "It's Peggy." He accepted the call, put the phone in speaker mode, and handed it back to Moe to hold. "Hey, pretty lady."

"Todd! Thank heaven!"

Todd glanced at Moe, his eyes narrowed with worry. "Peggy, what's wrong?"

"Where are you?" Peggy's tone was urgent, but not demanding.

"Just about to drop off Moe at his car in Springville. Then I'm heading up to the bishop's to pick you up. Be about—"

"No." Her voice was calmer, more measured. "I'm already home."

"What? Are you safe? Are you . . . alone?"

"I'm safe." She said the words slowly, guardedly, as if she was trying to communicate something else entirely. "I'm here with Derek. And Elaine is here too. They picked me up from the bishop's house. And we just got home."

She's with Elaine. And after what we saw tonight . . . Moe had met Peggy only the once, but he was frightened for her all the same. *And if I'm scared, Todd must be terrified.*

"I see." Todd drew out his words just as Peggy had. "You're on speaker. I'm with Moe. Say hi, Moe."

Moe glanced at Todd, who nodded once firmly. "Hello, Peggy," Moe said.

"I'm not," Peggy said.

Not what? Not on speakerphone? And I guess she doesn't want to let Derek and Elaine know I'm on the phone too.

"But Derek and Elaine are with me," Peggy continued, still using a slow, measured cadence. Moe could hear someone—he assumed it was Elaine—crying in the background. "Todd, you need to come right away. Elaine's upset. Something has happened. She says the harvest has come early. She says we're out of time."

Moe felt a chill shoot through him from his head to the pit of his stomach. *We're out of time.*

"We must flee!" Elaine screamed.

193

XXII

W e must flee!" Even with Myrddin's warm, strong arms encircling her, Viviane shivered as if with a midwinter chill. "We must escape."

Myrddin stroked her honey-colored hair with his clever fingers as if he were coaxing music from the strings of his harp. "Hush, sweet one," he crooned. "There is nothing to fear. You're safe. Safe with me, here in my cave. The way is secret. No man nor beast nor spirit of air, water, earth, or fire can find us here."

His voice was soothing, musical, like water in a merry brook. How many nights had his lyrical, magical voice calmed her fears, easing her into sleep? Viviane could not remember a time when he had not sung her from the waking world into the realm of dreams. *No!* screamed a part of her mind — like a virgin sacrifice struggling to free herself from a wicker prison. *It has not always been as this! There was a time — a time . . . before. A bad time.*

But Viviane attempted to block out the voice — so full of pain and trauma and terror. *Silence, Camorra. Are we not safe here?*

No! We are not! The Romans have returned! And the Saxons are coming!

Hush, Camorra. Myrddin loves us. He keeps us safe.

Viviane opened her eyes and gazed about Myrddin's hidden sanctum. The light of three candles, reflected and broken into thousands upon thousands of fractured fragments, showered the whole chamber in bright, magical green. Emeralds, both brilliant and clouded, large and small, made up the walls and ceiling of the small cavern. Packed earth covered the floor of the crystal cave, but Viviane well knew — for Myrddin had told her — that below the covering of dirt lay a floor of equally brilliant green beryl.

The chamber was furnished with simple, but well-fashioned furniture — a cistern filled with water from the sacred spring, a table, two stools, a workbench littered with pots, bottles, flasks, assorted bits of leaves, berries, flowers, roots, animal parts, the skull cap with its huge stag antlers—the tools of the healer, the mage, and the high priest of Cernunnos—and, of course, the sleeping pallet upon which she and Myrddin lay.

There was no brazier nor fire pit for cooking or warmth—the cracks in the ceiling were insufficient to allow that much smoke to escape—but the candles and their own body heat kept the cold at bay.

We would be warmer still if he would allow the dogs inside. But Myrddin insisted this space was theirs alone—Myrddin and Viviane's—and that the molossii remain in the tunnel outside the cave.

In a special place of honor and reverence, beneath a particularly large and dazzling emerald, there sat, of course, the small, wooden chest wherein was kept the dried fruit, leaves, and seeds—seeds which must be handled with the utmost care—seeds of Crann Beathadh, the sacred Tree of Life. Viviane's eyes lingered on the chest and the escape it promised—escape from this world into the next—a world in which there were no Romans.

We must flee!

Not yet, Camorra. I trust Myrddin. He is wise. He will keep us safe.

Viviane snuggled closer to her protector, nuzzling her face in his long beard. She felt as if she could rest in the safety of his arms for all eternity. *Centuries from now, some traveler will discover the cave and find our bones still entwined in a lovers' embrace.* She sighed happily at the thought and closed her eyes.

Myrddin pulled a bearskin over them.

Viviane shrieked and recoiled.

She tore at his arms and rolled out of his embrace. Scrambling to her feet, she drew the bronze dagger at her waist and brandished it at him. She backed away until the hard points of the crystalline walls pressed against her spine.

His eyes widened by shock and not a little fear, Myrddin drew a deep breath. His countenance appeared to relax, and he raised a placating hand. "I am sorry, my love. I know you are . . . not ready." He did not say it—not that time—but in her mind, Viviane heard him say, as he had once before, *Perhaps, you will never be ready. I am prepared to wait, my love, but not forever.* "I meant only to warm you."

Her breathing came in sobbing gasps. She dashed tears from her eyes, trying to clear them. Her hair hung before her face, further obscuring her vision.

And still she brandished the weapon.

Remaining on the bed, Myrddin lowered his hand. He gazed lovingly into her eyes. Then he smiled in that enigmatic way he did just before conjuring a bit of magic. He closed his brown eyes and, reaching behind, took the small harp from where it lay against the emerald wall. He plucked the strings experimentally a few times, twisted a peg or two, and then his skilled fingers created a song, crafting it out of the air of the crystal cave. And he sang.

Come, my dove, with me
Where sword and spear
Are but legend and song.
We will live in peace
Where cries of battle
Are but faded memory
And crows feast no more.
I will love you and kiss
Your honeyed hair and lips.

And as he sang, her fear turned to mist, like dew on morning heather evaporating in the light of the sun. He was her sun, and his light shone upon her, driving the dark terrors away.

She lowered the knife, and her shoulders slumped as the tension flowed out of her arms. The bronze blade nearly fell from her fingers. She slipped the weapon back into her belt, then sank to her knees, watching Myrddin with his sparkling, entrancing eyes.

And still he sang — of love and safety and peace.

In our cave of crystal
We shall taste the fruit
Of life eternal
And slumber together
Till the Romans be dust
And Saxons leave our shore.
And we will live in love
And you shall bear strong sons.

And his song drew her in like a magic spell. Without speaking a word, she gathered her skirt and crawled back to the bed, back to the shelter of Myrddin's warm embrace.

He placed the harp aside and drew her to himself. "I am sorry, my love. May I warm you?"

Viviane wiped away a tear and nodded.

In moments, the bearskin covered them. She laid her head on his chest. "I am sorry. I am . . . so afraid."

He said nothing, but he kissed the crown of her tawny head.

"Give me just a little more time," she said. "Another sleep. Then I will . . . give myself to you."

"Yes, my sweet one," he said. "But we cannot sleep just yet. I must help Artos. He can deliver our land from the Saxons."

"But Artos . . . He is a Roman."

He kissed her head again. "Roman blood runs strong here. There are few warriors who can claim to be of the People pure. His mother was of the People. His father? Yes, he has the Roman blood. But I have chosen Artos. He shall fight and protect us from the Saxons. I chose him the night I helped Ygraine take Uther to her bed — before our last sleep. We must stay a little longer. Do you understand, my love?"

Viviane nodded slowly, brushing her cheek against his beard. "When shall we flee then?"

"Soon, my love. Soon."

"And when will that be, *Master*?" The voice was hard, imperious — echoing around the chamber, invading their refuge.

Viviane stiffened. *Not now, sister. Leave us alone.*

Myrddin tightened his arms around Viviane, as if to keep the unwelcome interloper at bay. "You are not allowed in the cave, Nimue." His own voice was hard, matching Nimue's tone. "You must never enter. Never. That was our bargain."

"I must speak with you, Master," the older sister said, enunciating each word as she painstakingly forced them past her semi-immobile lips. "Meet me in the grove."

"As you wish," he said.

◆ ◆ ◆

Myrddin traversed the hidden path with all the speed stealth would allow. He had no desire to postpone the coming confrontation longer than necessary, but Nimue had named the place of meeting — the sacred grove, an hour's walk from the secret entrance to his cave. It was Nimue's place, where Myrddin instructed her in the mystic ways — far from the subterranean temple he shared with Viviane.

In his hand, he carried the cap adorned with the antlers of a stag. He always carried the Cap of Cernunnos, the Horned God, when he entered Nimue's place. It marked Myrddin as the master, the high priest, while Nimue was merely the disciple.

Illuminated by the moon waxing nearly to its fullness, the path, though little more than a deer trail, was easily visible. Myrddin took care to leave no tracks—no sign that might lead others to his home. He could not hear Nimue following, though he was certain she was there, most likely no more than a dozen paces behind him. *But where are the dogs?* he wondered. The beasts followed Nimue wherever she went, but Myrddin could not hear their panting, nor their heavy feet padding on the trail. *She left the beasts behind? I am nearby, so perhaps she feels protected.*

She should feel safe.

But he knew in his heart that fear—fear for her sister's safety—fear of the Romans who had abandoned the island long ago—fear of the Saxon invaders—fear colored Nimue's every thought and action.

By the Horned God! Both Nimue and her sister cloud my wisdom. Absently, he fingered one of the antler points of the cap. *Perhaps she left the molossii behind to guard the cave . . . and the chest.*

Yes, surely that must be the truth of it.

He thought of the maiden he loved more than his own flesh. She had beguiled him—he who had forsworn the pleasures of the flesh to gain the knowledge of the gods. Viviane had captured his soul, binding him with the soft fetters of unfulfilled desire.

And he thought also of her sister. He loved her as well . . . after a fashion. Nimue, though disfigured, was an eager student, adept in the ways, devouring all he had to teach her . . . except for the healing arts. For those, she had no inclination at all. And music. She would not learn music.

When he arrived in the clearing with its small ring of standing stones, he drew a wineskin from a pocket of his robe. He poured a small offering of wine on the ground for the god of the place—a god whose name Myrddin had never known, but then, did not every grove have its god?—and muttered a quick prayer to the unknown god. Then he entered the ring and sat upon the mould of the previous autumn's oak leaves. He placed upon his head the antlered cap of Cernunnos. He had no illusion that Nimue was there to be taught, but he meant to firmly remind her who was the master and who the acolyte. Even if she intended an argument, he would be in command. He closed his eyes, folded his hands in his lap, and waited, communing with the noises and spirit of the grove.

At the sound of Nimue's light footsteps on the rotting leaves, he drew a deep breath and offered another silent prayer—this time to the Horned God—for guidance and wisdom. *Wisdom? She drives it away.* Her footsteps stopped in front of him, but he did not hear her sit.

Opening his eyes, he looked up curiously. "You do not sit in the presence of the master?"

Half of Nimue's face, the living half, frowned down at him. The ravens, Bran and Badh, perched on her shoulders, their black eyes reflecting the moonlight, staring down at him as well. However, the birds' heads were cocked to the side, their stares indicating nothing more than avian curiosity. Nimue's good eye was narrowed in contempt. Her sagging eye, as always, conveyed nothing save death.

If she but had the dogs beside her, she would be the very image of the Goddess.

"Master?" Her voice dripped with an adder's venom. "You have nothing left to teach me, Myrddin Emrys. You have taught me the way of Cernunnos, the lore of the Tree, your magic, and your tricks. I know all your secrets."

Myrddin met her fierce gaze, forcing a kindly, beatific smile. "You still have much to learn, child."

"Much to learn?" she spat. "Healing? Physic? I have no use for such things. Music? I have no talent for it. Teach your songs to my sister."

"I have instructed her. But you could learn as well."

A tear threatened at the corner of her good eye. She looked away, the anger on the living half of her face fading into mourning. "I . . . cannot form the words. My face . . . my mouth . . . will not . . ."

He rose to his feet, then took her hands in his.

She started at the intimate, kindly touch. Disturbed by Nimue's sudden movement, the ravens croaked in protest and flapped away to perch in the branches of a nearby tree.

"Look at me," he commanded. "Wise, Nimue. Clever, Nimue. Look at me."

But Nimue would not meet his gaze. She blinked her good eye, and the tear slid down her cheek. Shaking her head, she said, "Artos cannot be trusted. He is a Roman."

Myrddin pursed his lips in irritation at the abrupt change in topic. "He is of the People. He is Welsh."

She snapped her face up and forward. She glared at him, anger smoldering in her good eye. "Welsh, is he? Then why is he now calling himself Artorius?"

Myrddin sighed. He had known this was coming. "The People fear the Saxons. So do the Celts. As much as they hated the Romans, they long for the safety the old Roman order provided, so Artos has taken a Roman name. Some of the People call him Arthur Pendragon, echoing his father's name." He paused and squeezed her hands gently. "Nimue, he can unite the tribes. And since his victory at Badon Hill—"

"I hear they call you Merlinus now."

He nodded. "Yes, Merlinus Ambrosius. And sometimes, simply Merlin. Names have power. You know that as—"

"Do you love me?"

Myrddin blinked, taken aback by this dizzying new question. His mouth gradually fell open as he struggled to find an answer. "Do I...?"

"You love my sister. Do you... *Can* you love *me*?"

He focused his gaze on her good eye, trying desperately *not* to see the right orb with its sagging lids and the drool stringing from the right side of her mouth. The living half of her countenance was hopeful, pleading.

"Yes," he said, "but ... not as you would wish. I love you as a pupil, as a sister, as a daughter—you are so many things to me—but not—"

"She will never take you to her bed. Not after the next sleep, not after a thousand slumbers. But I"—she pulled his hands and placed them on her chest, and he felt the thundering of her heart—"I will. I will give you the love you hunger for, the pleasure of the flesh you have been denied. Love me, Myrddin! Say you love me!"

A tremor of revulsion and horror shook him. "No. I cannot." He pulled his hands free of hers.

Nimue bowed her head. "You could ... close your eyes." Her voice was soft, as if she did not need to force her lips around the words. "You could pretend I am her. You could whisper her name to me in the dark."

Myrddin removed the antlered cap from his head. *This is no time for Masters and Acolytes. This is a time for pity.* "No, Nimue. I could not."

She stood with her head down, face turned to the side so that only the left half of her face—the beautiful half—was visible in the moonlight. "I would have been content. Half a love—even a false one—is better than an eternity of nothing."

He smiled for her then—a sad smile. "No, my adept apprentice, you would not be content. I know you." He ran a finger down her cheek, tenderly wiping away the tear.

She looked at him with her good eye. In the moonlight, that eye was beautiful.

"Go." His voice was kind, gentle. "I will follow in a moment. I must ... offer sacrifice." *To atone for the sin of letting you and your sister into my heart.*

Keeping her face turned, her good eye focused on him, the left half of her lips parted as if she would say more.

He lifted a hand in dismissal and looked away.

And Nimue turned and walked out of the ring of stones, her feet making hardly a whisper on the decaying leaves. After a few retreating footsteps, she was gone—Myrddin could hear her no more. Only the sounds of the sacred grove remained, the gentle stirring of the leaves, a mouse skittering across the ground, a small serpent tasting the air as it sought the mouse for a prey, the occasional chirping of a bird.

Placing the antlered cap back on his head, Myrddin prepared to make the offering the Horned God required—a token of blood. He drew the knife from his belt. Muttering a prayer to Cernunnos, Myrddin slid the tip of the bronze dagger lightly across the palm of his left hand, following the scar line left by past oblations. A line of crimson beaded there, thin and altogether inadequate for the offering.

He had not sliced deep enough into the scar. He had performed the ritual too many times of late. The scar was thick.

Old fool. Old, woman-besotted dotard! Retracing the first line, he sliced deeper into his palm. This time, the blood flowed more freely.

Too freely.

Cursing out loud, he let several drops fall to the ground. He sheathed his dagger even as he recited the remainder of the ritual. Then he squeezed his hand shut to staunch the flow of blood.

He does not require it all.

Bran, the male raven, still perched beside its mate on a branch above, croaked. "Myrddin," it said. "Love me."

Myrddin scowled at the birds. "Fly away. Go to your mistress."

"Mistress," Badh mimicked, cocking its head and eyeing him in the way of birds—both curious and detached at the same time. "She comes," the female raven said.

Myrddin heard a footstep behind him.

"Why have you returned?" He whirled about to face his pupil. "Come to plead for—"

The words died on his lips.

Before him stooped a crone, bent with age and wearing a cloak and hood of white after the ancient Druid fashion. The old woman's drooping countenance and doleful eyes fixed him, pinning him like a boar on the end of a lugged spear.

"Who are you?" he demanded of the aged figure. "What are you doing here?"

"Merlin." Her voice was the sound of dead leaves clinging to the fingers of skeletal trees, rubbing together in a winter wind. "They call you Vortigern's Prophet, do they not? You prophesied the Usurper's Doom—burned alive in his tower, no?"

Myrddin felt his tension ease. *Merely an old woman seeking a foretelling.* "Yes. I am."

She laughed then, a soft gurgling in her throat—a death rattle. "Well, prophet, I give *you* a prophecy. You shall be trapped for all time —imprisoned in a tree."

Myrddin blinked, staring at the lifeless face in utter incomprehension. "What?"

A small hand shot out from the sleeve of her robe, grasping him firmly by the wrist.

He tried to pull away, but her grip was powerful, like the inexorable grip of death. She squeezed hard, the pressure forcing his gory hand open.

In her other hand, she held, pinched between thumb and forefinger, a small black seed.

Myrddin knew that seed. "Take care! It must not touch blood! It is dangerous in the wrong hands."

"Then," the crone whispered, "let us put it in *your* hand."

She pressed the seed into his open palm.

His bloody palm.

Into his wound, into the flesh.

Into the blood.

And Myrddin felt the seed twitch.

With a squeal of terror, he wrested his hand from the hag's grip.

He clawed at the seed embedded in his palm, desperately trying to dislodge it. He succeeded only in drawing more blood.

Tendrils, like the legs of a wooden spider, erupted from his wound, quickly growing to encircle his hand, his fingers.

"No!" he cried.

He fumbled at his belt for his knife. *Cut off the hand! Cut it off before it —*

The thickening roots spread up his forearm.

He drew the dagger, hacking at the growing feelers.

Drawing more blood.

The wooden tendrils snaked up his arm, his shoulder. They bit into his flesh like a thousand groping thorns, piercing him, drawing even more blood, feeding on him.

He fell to the ground, thrashing, hacking, but the roots snared his knife hand, thrusting into his flesh.

"She would have loved you," the crone said.

Myrddin howled as the roots first encircled his chest, his neck.

He screamed as they stabbed into his eyes.

They pierced his pounding heart, seeking the blood at its source.

And then he was silent and immobile, imprisoned forever within a tree.

XXIII

Peggy, don't trust her." Todd's voice on the cell phone sounded deadly serious. "Don't trust Elaine."

Already struggling to remain in control, trying to ignore Elaine's frantic cries, Peggy felt as if her legs might collapse under her at any moment. She took a deep breath, held it, then exhaled slowly, forcing an outward calm to mask the terror squeezing her gut like a claw. "I understand completely. You know, I've always felt the same." *More or less.* "So, what do you suggest?"

"I get the sense that you can't talk freely."

He understands! Peggy thought. *Always depend on Todd.*

"Derek, please!" Elaine wailed from where she and Derek sat on Peggy's sofa. "You said we could go, just as soon as we got back to Peggy's place!"

Elaine pressed her face against Derek's chest. He held her close, stroking her hair in a—thus far—vain attempt to calm her. "I know, sweetheart. We'll go soon, I promise. Peggy says we should talk to Todd first." He looked up at Peggy, and their eyes locked. Derek looked terrified. "And I trust Peggy," he said. Elaine whimpered like a frightened child, and Derek kissed her head—but his eyes never left Peggy's. "You trust Peggy too, don't you, sweetheart?"

Elaine nodded, wiping a tear from her eye.

"Yes, Todd," Peggy said into the phone, forcing a smile. "You're right, of course. But I'm a very good listener. You can tell me anything."

"Roger that," Todd said. "Moe and I watched Morgaise and Elaine participate in a ritual human sacrifice. I don't think Elaine did the killing, but she was there. Do you understand? She was *there.*"

Peggy clenched her jaw, still maintaining an increasingly unconvincing smile. She broke eye contact with Derek. She couldn't bear to look at him—at Elaine and Derek. *Derek's in danger. And Elaine's at the heart of it. She may not be the cause of it, but . . .* "Yes, Todd.

I understand." *How could this frightened girl be part of human sacrifice?*

"Funny thing is," Todd continued, "I'm not absolutely certain Morgaise did the killing either. She was there, leading the ceremony, but I could've sworn there was . . . someone else."

Maybe someone's forcing Elaine . . .

"I think Todd's right," Moe said, his voice coming through the speaker phone. "In any case, Morgaise presided at the ritual. She must be the high priestess. She may even think she's a goddess. Her disciples . . . her worshippers—and there're a lot of them—they seem to think she is."

"I understand," Peggy said. *Only, I don't understand—not really. Elaine exudes sweetness and vulnerability. And she seems so incapable . . . of anything. She can't be a killer, can she?* "How soon can you be here?"

"Twenty minutes," Todd said. "I'm going as fast as I can. Try to stay put. Do you have your Glock?"

The semiautomatic handgun Todd had given her. In spite of the danger, Peggy felt a thrill at the memory.

He took her to a shooting range. It was the closest thing to a date they'd ever had—a time alone, away from home, without Derek and Elaine.

Not a recon mission. No intel gathering. Just the two of them alone.

He gave her the weapon—all black plastic and cold metal, smelling of gun oil. He said it was a present. It wasn't flowers, but it was a symbol of caring.

He was her protector, her friend.

Her truest friend.

Of that, she was certain—but was there . . . could there be . . . more?

And if there were . . . what then?

Peggy wasn't sure what her own feelings were anymore.

Could Todd have . . . those kind of feelings . . . for her?

He taught her to shoot the Glock—

Peggy could almost feel Todd's hands on hers, feel him standing behind her, breathing on her hair, her neck. She felt the fine hairs on the back of her neck stand up, and she trembled slightly.

A genuine smile on her lips, Peggy stepped over to the kitchen counter, and patted the large shoulder bag Todd had given her—the one with the built-in holster. She hadn't finished the lengthy process to obtain a concealed-carry weapons permit, but Todd thought the threat posed by the Morrigans and their followers justified the risk of carrying a hidden firearm. "Of course," she said. Peggy patted her jeans pocket, feeling the small can of pepper spray inside.

"Good," Todd said. "Keep it close. I'll be there as soon as I can. We both will. What *can* you tell me?"

Peggy forced herself to look at Elaine. Elaine in Derek's arms. "Elaine says the harvest has come early. She can't" —or *won't*—"give any more details. Just that she and Derek have to run away *tonight*."

"No!" Elaine cried, startling Peggy so badly she almost reached for her gun. Elaine broke out of Derek's embrace. She leapt to her feet and threw herself across the living room. Colliding with Peggy, Elaine almost knocked them both to the ground. Elaine threw her arms around Peggy's neck and squeezed her like a drowning woman clutching at a life-preserver. "No, Peggy! You must come with us!"

Acting out of some maternal instinct rather than conscious thought, Peggy put her arms around Elaine. "Me?"

Fear and confusion plain on his stricken face, Derek started to rise from the couch, then appeared to think better of it.

Elaine trembled in Peggy's arms. "Don't you see, Peggy? I love you. So—"

"What?" Peggy and Derek said together.

"You're like my s-s-sister!" Elaine sobbed. "I love you."

Derek actually looked relieved.

He thought—what?—some kind of . . . lesbian thing?

"Oh, Peggy!" Elaine continued. "After all w-w-we've done t-to you! You're so sweet to me." Elaine sniffed loudly. "You have every reason . . . every right to hate me, but—but you don't. You love me too. I *know* you do."

Peggy patted Elaine's back. "I . . . I do care about you." In spite of what Todd had said, Peggy couldn't deny an almost palpable need to protect the younger woman—the younger woman who had lived for centuries. *I can't hate you. I just can't. I just don't have it in me.* "I'll help you, if I can." And in the instant, she knew it was true. "But I can't just run . . ."

"No!" Elaine squeezed Peggy all the tighter and shook her head vehemently. "You must come with us! You must! If you don't—"

BOOM!

The front door shuddered. Peggy froze. Elaine screamed.

BOOM!

The door exploded inward.

White-robed-and-hooded figures poured in through the shattered doorway like water spilling through a breached dam. One of them carried a black, police-style battering ram.

Elaine released Peggy and spun around, placing her small body between Peggy and the intruders. She spread her arms protectively. "NO!"

Peggy dropped her cell phone and reached for her purse with its hidden gun, but she seemed to move with the maddening sluggishness of a dream. The purse, though barely an arm's length away, seemed hopelessly out of reach.

Druids streamed into the living room like the legions of the dead. And like ghosts, they said nothing.

An army of hands seized Elaine and yanked her away from Peggy. "No!" Elaine screamed. "Not now! Peggy!"

"Leave her alone!" Derek roared. "Let go of —" His voice cut off as if muffled.

Derek! No!

The illusion of slowed time vanished, and Peggy snatched her purse in her left hand. She shoved her right into the hidden side-pocket with the holster. Her hand found the pistol grip. *Got it!*

A male Druid, his hooded face cast in shadow, reached for her. In one hand, he held a wadded rag.

Chloroform?

And she understood why Derek had fallen silent.

She thumbed off the safety and turned the entire purse on the man. She pulled the trigger.

The blast, though muffled by the purse, was a thunderclap in her small living room.

Everyone froze.

The Druid's white robe blossomed with crimson. He stared at Peggy, a single emotion plain on his face.

Profound disbelief.

He opened his mouth. "G-Goddess?"

Then he dropped to the floor, knocking another white-robed man to the ground.

I killed him. Just like the Pagan.

Then another man reached for Peggy, and she turned the purse and fired again. *Don't shoot Derek or Elaine!* But she couldn't see either of them.

She emptied the clip. Surrounded as Peggy was, each bullet found a target, and each target—wounded or dead—crumpled to the ground.

And in the eerie silence that followed the final gunshot, the Druids still came.

The purse was wrenched from her grasp, and strong hands seized her, pinning her arms painfully behind her back.

Somewhere within the throng of Druids, Elaine screamed, "Morgaise! Stop this! You can stop it. Please!"

"Stop!" The female voice was not Morgaise's, but the throng of pagans stood still.

Peggy stomped backward, shoving her tennis shoe hard into a foot behind her.

The grip on her arms loosened. A man cursed.

Peggy ripped one arm out of his grasp, but other hands seized her.

"Try that again, bitch," snarled a voice in her ear, "and I'll break your damn arm."

She stomped again, missing this time.

Her right arm was yanked up hard behind her, causing Peggy to yelp in pain.

"Just use the chloroform," said another voice.

"No." The woman's voice again. "That won't be necessary. Let her see."

As if at the word of a pagan Moses, a sea of white robes parted.

Derek slumped between two robed men. His lolling head, slack jaw, and unfocused eyes clearly showed that he'd been rendered unconscious.

A third Druid held a knife to his throat.

Derek! "No." Peggy's voice was no more than a choked whisper. "Please. Please don't hurt him."

"You see?" said the woman. "Even a Mormon bitch can see reason when you rub her nose in it."

Peggy turned her eyes toward the speaker—a woman, and judging by her height, possibly the only woman among the mob of Druids.

Elaine was nowhere to be seen.

The female Druid pulled back her hood, revealing delicate, almost elven features, cold brown eyes, all framed by straight brown hair.

A familiar face.

For a second Peggy couldn't place it, then her eyes widened in recognition.

The Pagan's wife.

The Pagan's widow.

The woman bared her teeth in a malicious, predatory grin—a she-wolf having cornered an elusive and troublesome rabbit. "You know who I am. Good." She closed the distance between them slowly. She was shorter than Peggy, so she had to look up into Peggy's face. Her eyes burned with loathing and feral glee. "I've got you."

Terror ripped through Peggy like a jagged blade tearing through her guts. All the fear and panic of that horrible night returned in a moment, like the nightmares that still caused her to wake screaming.

Peggy could almost smell the dead man's sour breath again, feel his hands pawing at her — smell his blood everywhere.

I'm dead.

Derek's going to die. And there's nothing I can do.

Todd can't save me.

Not this time.

The widow's smile morphed into a frown of utter hatred. "You . . . killed . . . my . . . husband." Her lips twitched, then she spat in Peggy's face.

Spittle struck Peggy's cheek, and she gasped in shock.

The widow took a step back and grinned again.

She . . . spat on me? The act seemed so petty. And just as on that stormy night two months ago, Peggy let anger wash over her, drowning her fear. *Fight back, Peggy. Stall. Someone must've heard the shots. Someone must've called the police.*

"That's it?" Peggy forced a laugh. "I killed your husband — I gutted him like the *pig* he was — and you *spit* on me?"

The woman's grin vanished.

Still held tight by two strong men, Peggy straightened to her full height. She twisted her face into a contemptuous sneer. "Your *loving* husband tried to rape me."

The widow's eyes narrowed. "That's a lie. You're a lying Christian whore!"

She didn't know? Maybe, he told her he was just going to kill me.

Doesn't matter. Buy some time!

Peggy shook her head and grinned, trying to channel as much vitriol as she could into her smile and her voice. "I said he *tried* to rape me. But you know what? He wasn't up to the job. And yes, I killed him. Me. A girl. Your man — if you can call him that — was *pathetic*."

The woman's delicate features twisted in rage, her bottom lip quivering.

"Come on, Julia," said one of the men holding Peggy. "Let's go. Just drug her already, and let's get this over with."

"Yeah," said the other man. "Hurry up. The Harvest is here."

Peggy heard a distant sound.

Is that a siren?

Maybe Todd called the cops again.

Gotta keep them here just a little longer.

Summoning up all the high school theatre experience of her youth,

Peggy affected an expression of exaggerated pity. "What's the matter, Pagan-Lady? Not *woman* enough? Couldn't keep your pathetic man and his wimpy ponytail at home?"

Pagan-Lady snarled. She raised her hand and slapped Peggy hard across the cheek.

Peggy tried to turn her head, but the blow rocked her head back. Bright lights flashed behind her eyelids. As she fought through a haze of pain and shock, she heard the high-pitched wail again.

Louder. Closer.

Definitely a siren.

Peggy opened her eyes and turned her face back to the woman. "I bet prissy-boy liked it rough. Maybe that's the only way he could . . . perform. It seems he couldn't handle a woman who" — she shrugged — "fights back. He couldn't handle a *real* woman."

Pagan-Lady shrieked through clenched teeth. She hauled back and slapped Peggy again.

And again.

And again.

Peggy gritted her teeth and tried not to cry out. Tears leaked from her eyes, but she didn't care. *Just keep them here till help arrives.* She strained to hear the siren above the ringing in her ears.

And she did hear it.

She heard it fading — going away.

And with the retreating siren, Peggy's hope evaporated.

She looked for Derek, but he was already gone, swallowed up in an ocean of Druid white.

Derek!

"Rape her." Pagan-Lady's cold voice was calm, the rage gone.

The words hit Peggy like a fist to her gut. She forgot how to breathe. *No! No! No!* She opened her mouth to scream, but nothing escaped her clenched throat. *No!*

"When we get back," said one of the men holding Peggy's arms. "Let's get the hell out of here."

"Now," the woman said. "The Goddess put me in command, made *me* priestess. So I say, rape her. Rape her now." She leered at Peggy, making a sweeping gesture, encompassing the men in the room. "*All* of you."

Murmuring rose from the mob.

"We don't have time," said one man.

"Hell, yeah, we do!" cried another. A shorter man stepped out of the crowd, raising his robe, and unfastening his belt. "On your knees,

Mormon bitch. Hold 'er down, boys."

Peggy was forced to her knees, then yanked onto her back. "No!" She struggled, tried to fight back, but her thrashing was futile. They were too many and too strong. "Help!"

Heavenly Father! Help me!

Todd! Where are you?

Peggy shut her eyes tight, trying to block out her own panic and the leering face of the man who'd already dropped his pants. *Don't think about it. Think of something else. Anything else.* She opened her mouth, and mumbled the words of a Primary song.

"I am a-a child . . . of God . . ."

Rough hands clawed at her jeans, unfastening them. The zipper was pulled down.

"I am a ch-child of God, and —"

"ENOUGH!" boomed a commanding female voice.

The hands pulling at her jeans froze. "Goddess?"

"Stop this at once." Morgaise's voice — forcefully enunciating each word. "Get off her, you dog!"

Peggy opened her eyes.

Morgaise stood in the center of a small clearing in the forest of white robes. Though shortest in stature, she seemed to tower above her disciples. She was robed as well, but her hood was pulled back revealing the terrifying dichotomy of her face — one half sagging and pale, and the other livid with rage. "She is to be untouched — a virgin! Have I taught you nothing? A virgin! Do you hear me?"

"Yes, Goddess," the Druids said as one.

The color in the living side of Morgaise's countenance faded. "Drug her."

A rag was clamped over Peggy's mouth and nose. She smelled and tasted sweetness and decay — like rotten fruit.

And the darkness took her.

XXIV

62 A.D.: Glyn Cothi Forest, Wales

Crimson stained the snow.

Though fourteen years old, Camorra had never witnessed a human birth. She'd seen cattle, goats, and sheep birthed, but never a human baby.

However, even *she* recognized there was simply too much blood.

"Tasca!" Flinging away the armload of firewood she'd been carrying, Camorra dropped to her knees beside her younger sister. At a mere twelve summers, Tasca was too young to safely bear a child. "Oh, Tasca!"

Tasca, sitting with her back against a gray rock wall, was pale. Her breathing came in pants, as rapid as those of the great molossus lying beside her. The black dog snuggled against her as if attempting to share its warmth with the girl. Both the she-beast and the girl exhaled plumes of white.

The other black dog, the male, sat on its haunches just under the ledge of rock that served as poor shelter against the raging winter storm.

Tasca smiled weakly at her older sister. Tears had carved rivulets in the grime on her hollow cheeks. "I am"—she swallowed and seemed to choke before her shallow breathing resumed—"tired. And . . . thirsty. Did you . . . find water?"

Camorra fumbled for the waterskin at her belt. She couldn't make her numbed fingers loosen the thong holding the goatskin flask. "I got lost," she said, weeping. "The snow . . . I could not see my way. Phelan"—she glanced through her tears at the male dog, its black coat covered with the falling snow—"Phelan found our way back. Oh, Tasca, I should never have left you!"

At last Camorra got the waterskin free. She pulled the stopper and

212

handed it to her little sister. "Take it. Drink."

But Tasca didn't lift a hand to take the bottle. Both her arms cradled a small—too small—bundle, wrapped in part of her cloak.

Camorra put the flask to her sister's pale lips. Camorra's hands shook badly—both from fear and the cold—and she spilled a little of the precious water on her sister's breast. Tasca managed a few swallows, then turned her head weakly away.

"Drink more," Camorra urged.

Tasca shook her head. In spite of the cold, her golden-brown hair was drenched and steaming with sweat.

"I never should have left you," Camorra said again, her words coming out in a blubbering rush. "I could not find the river. Then I searched for wood to make a fire. I thought we might melt some snow. I—" She stoppered the waterskin, dropped it, and threw her arms around her little sister. "Forgive me!"

Tasca was shivering, but she laughed softly. "Camorra, I can barely . . . understand your speech when . . . you speak slowly and . . . carefully. But when you weep, I cannot . . . understand . . . you at all."

Camorra leaned back and dashed away her tears.

Tasca lifted an emaciated hand and laid it tenderly against her sister's cheek—against the lifeless side of Camorra's face. The younger sister's smile was sad and weary. "I am sorry. I know you find it difficult"—her shallow, rapid breathing hitched—"difficult to speak . . . to make your lips move . . . properly. That was a cruel . . . thing to say. Forgive me. You are . . . so good to me."

Camorra fought to quell her sobs and to speak more clearly. "I was gone too long. I did not know the babe was coming."

Tasca's smile faded. "Neither did I." Her gaze dropped to the bundle in her arms.

"Is it . . . ?" Camorra couldn't bring herself to force her half-dead lips to form the question.

"She is dead." It seemed that all the grief and weariness in the whole world was carried in those simple words. "She never . . . took a breath."

Tasca's head drooped forward.

"Tasca!" Camorra wailed. "Do not leave me!"

The younger sister lifted her head again and she shook it weakly. "I need to . . . rest. That is all. It is . . . so cold."

"I will build a fire!" *Please, Goddess! I cannot build a fire. I cannot blow on the embers. My mouth—my thrice-cursed mouth!* "Yes! I will build a fire." *Goddess, help me!*

Camorra turned on her knees and snatched up the wood she'd tossed to the snow. She selected a spot that was at least partially protected from the wind. As she cleared a space in the snow, down to the frozen dirt beneath, she saw the male dog pad over to Tasca. The beast sniffed at the blood on the snow, spread out from between Tasca's legs like a crimson fan. The dog took a few experimental licks, then raised its head to sniff at the tiny corpse in Tasca's arms.

"Phelan, *no!*" Camorra snapped at the dog. "*Accuba!*"

The molossus snorted in protest, then lay down next to Tasca, opposite Cahan, its mate. As if expressing agreement, Cahan snorted as well.

Camorra retrieved the flint and the small wooden tinderbox from her pouch, then unsheathed her iron knife. Her fingers were clumsy with the cold, but she worked with savage determination to force them to her will. "By the Goddess," she muttered, "I *will* warm you, sister."

As she prepared the fire, Camorra muttered a prayer to the Horned God. "Cernunnos! Spare my sister, o Master of Life and Death." Then she prayed to the Morrigan, addressing the Goddess in each of her aspects—Maiden, Mother, and Crone. "Please do not take Tasca from me!" *She is all I have!*

"I will never ... leave you," Tasca said. "I just need ... to rest a little. You are ... so good ... so good to me. You are always ... so good to me."

I was supposed to protect you!

I failed.

Camorra struck fiercely at the flint with her knife. A spark shot into the kindling, igniting hope within her breast. She bent quickly and blew desperately into the kindling, struggling to force her half-dead lips into the proper shape.

Miraculously, the spark caught. A small tongue of flame licked the twigs above.

Praise the Goddess!

In minutes, the small fire blossomed and grew sufficiently so Camorra could turn her attention back to her sister.

Tasca's head was slumped forward, her face hidden behind the sodden curtain of her hair. Her hands lay in her lap—empty.

The babe had tumbled out of Tasca's cloak and lay on her skirt, between her knees. The child's flesh was gray, the limbs askew.

But Camorra cared nothing for the stillborn child.

"Tasca!" she wailed. "No! Tasca!"

Camorra howled, giving vent to a grief and loss beyond words.

She snatched up the small corpse and flung the lot behind her, out into the storm.

As one, the two molossii jumped up and pounced upon the first meat they'd seen in days.

Camorra shook her sister, screaming her name.

Tasca gave no reply, her head flopping back and forth.

Mad with grief, Camorra stumbled to her feet and fled into the blinding storm.

◆ ◆ ◆

How long or how far Camorra wandered, she didn't know. She could see nothing except white. She stumbled blindly into trees, sometimes knocking yet more snow down upon herself. She tripped on hidden stones or roots, sprawling in the deep snow.

She could no longer feel her feet or her hands or the living half of her face.

She had ceased calling her sister's name into the howling gale, but in her mind she kept repeating it. *Tasca. Tasca. Why did you leave me?*

"Camorra! Wait for me!"

Tasca? You are alive?

No. It cannot be. It is some wraith of the storm. A wisp.

"Camorra! Look ahead!"

A black spot appeared before her — a single black spot in a world of white. Like a revenant, Camorra shambled toward it.

The spot grew as she approached. It grew until she was certain it was the mouth of a cave. She stopped at the threshold. One of the dogs, Cahan, slogged up beside her, its black snout pointing toward the darkness. The other dog continued past her and was swallowed by the blackness within.

"Into the cave, sister!"

Camorra started. "Tasca?"

"Inside!" It was most definitely her sister's voice. "Now!"

Camorra could not see her sister in the storm. Even Cahan was no longer visible.

Filled with a surge of hope and joy, Camorra drove herself forward.

Into blackness. Out of the storm.

She took several steps into the dark, caught a numb foot on a stone, and tumbled to the ground.

Exhaustion and cold had sapped all her strength. She felt, rather than saw, one of the dogs lie down against her, warming her, lending her strength and life.

"I thought . . . you were dead," Camorra croaked into the darkness.

"I told you," Tasca said, "I would never leave you. I only needed to rest a bit."

"How . . . How did you find me?"

"The dogs led me to you. Sleep now. We both need sleep."

"I love you, my dear, sweet sister."

"You are so good to me," Tasca said. "How could I ever leave you?"

A half smile crept over Camorra's half face.

And she surrendered to exhaustion and darkness.

◆ ◆ ◆

Somewhere in her slumber, Camorra dreamed. And in her dream, she heard her sister's voice . . . and the voice of a man, speaking in a tongue Camorra did not know. Camorra tried to open her eyes, tried to wake, but she couldn't—she could only listen.

"*Pwy wyt ti?*" the man said.

"I do not understand," Tasca said.

"Who are you?" the man said in Latin.

"I am Tasca," her sister replied—also in Latin. "And this is Camorra."

"Camorra?" The man sounded shocked.

"Yes," Tasca replied. "She is my sister."

The man said nothing.

"We were traveling in the wood and—"

"Tasca and Camorra, you said?"

"Yes. Thank you for saving us. We would have died without your help."

Again the man was silent.

"Where are the molossii?" Tasca asked. "Where are our hounds?"

"Your dogs are unharmed. I gave them . . . something to make them sleep." The voice was pleasant, kindly. "I have heard of you, Tasca—you and your sister. You are sought by the Romans." He paused. "There is a price on your heads. A high price."

Camorra at last was able to force herself from slumber. Her eyes snapped open, and she sat upright. In her weakened state, even that simple act caused her head to spin.

The man was thin—no warrior, he—with a dark-brown beard and long hair. He had dark, piercing eyes. He seemed surrounded in a soft, green aura.

"And you would sell us to the Romans?" Camorra cried. "Is that why you saved us?"

216

The man shook his head. His smile was warm and compassionate. "No. We have no love for the Romans here. Is that not why you fled to Wales?"

Camorra hesitated. They had been on the run for so long. And Wales had not yet bowed to Roman rule.

Not yet.

The man tilted his head to the side. "And you are Camorra?"

Camorra nodded carefully.

He bowed his head in greeting. "I am Myrddn. Welcome to my home. I have been expecting you."

Noticing her surroundings for the first time, Camorra stared in wonder at the cave. It was lined, floor to ceiling, with green crystal.

"Wondrous, is it not?" Myrddn said.

"H-how did you . . . You were expecting us?" Camorra asked.

"Yes, Cernunnos told me of your coming—in a dream."

"He told you?" Tasca asked. "The Horned God? You are . . . a prophet then?"

He nodded. "Among many other things."

"If you will not sell us to the Romans," Camorra demanded, "what then?"

He put forth his hand and touched Camorra's cheek—her good cheek. "I will shelter you—both of you. I will teach you, train you. I will protect you with my life. And so long as I live, you need not fear the Romans or any man."

And what will you demand in return? Camorra thought, her heart turning to stone within her. *Will you not take what all men take – what has already been stolen from us?*

But Camorra knew that, for the present at least, they had little choice but to trust him. They were both too weak, too helpless to resist.

"Praise the Goddess!" Tasca said.

"Are we to be kept hidden"—*prisoners*—"in this cave, never to leave?" Camorra asked.

Myrddn laughed then—a happy, guileless sound, full of mirth. "No, by the Goddess! No. You are free to come and go as you please— once you are rested and healed, of course. By command of the Horned God, my home is now yours. I ask only that you keep the secret of my home—but in my dream, Cernunnos did assure me that you will. Will you keep the secret of the cave?"

"We will!" Tasca said.

"Yes," Camorra said, "we will." She lifted a hand to the dead side of her face. "But my face is . . . known."

Myrddn nodded slowly. "Yes, Camorra. You will need to remain hidden. But you will be safe here in my cave and my forest."

Tears burned at the corner of Camorra's good eye. *The Romans have taken all, have they not?*

"But our names," Tasca said, "they are known throughout Britannia."

Myrddn smiled then. "That is a simple matter. We shall give you new names. You, Tasca, shall be . . . Viviane. And you, Camorra, shall be . . . Nimue. Those names shall—"

He inhaled sharply, and his eyes rolled up in his head so that only the whites showed. His mouth hung slack. In a flat voice, cold as the dead of winter, he began to chant.

And at his words—the words of the Horned God—Camorra felt a shiver which had nothing to do with the cold.

"Maiden shall bewitch me.

"Mother shall learn my secrets.

"Crone shall entomb me forever—forever within the Tree of Life.

"You shall steal the sacred emeralds of the Crystal Cave.

"And the Romans shall hunt you—hunt you and pursue you across the ages."

Myrddn turned his face toward Camorra, his blank, white eyes staring into the abyss of her soul. "And you shall never be safe."

XXV

It looks like she took out fifteen of them," Moe said after counting the bloodstains, arranged in a tight semicircle on the living room carpet. "But where the heck are the bodies?"

"I don't give a flying crap about the bodies!" Todd snapped. "Where's Peggy?" He knew he should be worried about Derek too, but his fear was focused on Peggy. And when he was afraid, his mind flooded with images of mutilated women and children. *Keep it together, Cavetto. You can't help her if you lose it now.*

The vivid memories of Afghanistan were replaced by an image of Peggy on her knees, a noose around her neck, a ceremonial knife at her throat. *Keep it together.*

"Where are the cops?" Moe asked. "You'd think after our nine-one-one call . . ."

Cops? They're probably in Morgaise's pocket – or your grandfather's.

Todd spotted Peggy's phone on the floor, near what appeared to be the origin point of the gunshots. He scooped it up. "You see any other phones anywhere?"

"No," Moe replied.

"Okay. Maybe Derek still has his. Did you get the old man's number?" *Please tell me you did!*

"My grandfather's?" Moe asked. "Uh, yeah."

"Call him. He can locate Derek's phone."

Moe nodded, grinning like the village idiot who just found a way to be useful. "Good idea! What's the number?"

Todd had to look up the number on his own phone. He grabbed a pen and a piece of paper from the kitchen junk drawer, scribbled Derek's number down, and handed it to Moe.

Moe reached into a pocket. A look of panic spread across his features as he hurriedly patted his other pockets. Then he groaned. "Left it in your car."

Todd tossed him the keys. "Hurry. I'll keep checking here."

But Moe had already disappeared through the shattered doorway.

Todd scanned the living room. The furniture was all tossed aside.
If she shot fifteen . . . There must've been a ton of them.

They must've taken her gun.

Then he spotted the purse, tossed into a corner, behind the overturned coffee table. He picked up the purse.

The side had been blown away.

She fired it . . . with the gun still inside, judging from the weight.

He reached into the hidden holster and pulled the weapon free. The slide was back and the chamber empty. He released the clip—empty as well.

He turned the purse on its side and shook it. Brass shell casings tumbled to the carpet.

He didn't have to count them to know how many there were.

Fifteen rounds. Fifteen hits.

And still there were enough of them left to take her and Derek, and remove the bodies.

Where are you, Peggy?

The image of the woman he loved, on her knees, noosed, and held at knifepoint by a Druid robed and hooded in white returned. Only this time, Peggy's nose had been bitten off, and her eyes dug out of their sockets.

Todd tried to force the waking nightmare from his mind.

Automatic gunfire.

Explosions.

The smell of gunpowder and blood and spilled intestines.

The screaming of women, girls, and boys being tortured, mutilated, and raped.

The smell of rotting and burned flesh.

The chanting of religious fanatics.

Helicopters overhead.

The screaming of A-10's.

The thunder of an AC-130 gunship's cannon.

Shouting in Pashto and Dari.

Or was that Gaelic?

"Freeze! Drop your weapon!"

Todd's eyes snapped open. He was on his knees, looking up into the business end of a semiautomatic handgun. And behind the weapon, a black-uniformed Orem Police officer.

◆ ◆ ◆

"I've got a bad feeling about this." Moe watched from the passenger seat of Todd's car as the second and third police cruiser pulled up in the parking lot. *Maybe we shouldn't have called nine-one-one. Or maybe we should've waited.*

"Assuming you're not making a *Star Wars* reference, what's going on?" From the sound of his voice over the cell phone, Thurgood Abbot seemed to have recovered from his ordeal on the mountainside—his dry wit was fully in evidence.

"The police are here," Moe said. "I mean—I called them, but we figured they'd be here when we arrived. But they're just now getting here."

"Have they detained you?"

"No. I don't think they know I'm here."

"Leave," said his grandfather. "Leave now, but don't make it look like you're in a hurry."

"But Todd's still in there."

"The barbarian?"

"Stop it," Moe snapped. "You're not helping."

"And *you* can't help your friend by remaining at the scene of a multiple homicide and abduction. You would only succeed in being detained as well."

"But Todd—"

"I will personally see to your friend's release, but it will take me one hour. Now get out of there."

"Why on earth should I trust you?"

"Moses, your question is a valid one. However, I'm risking *every-thing* to help you. I've already betrayed the Morrigans by talking to you this evening. My only hope, the only hope for my family—for *our* family—is that you are successful. Now, please get out of there!"

Moe hesitated. *Father in Heaven, what should I do? Should I trust him?*

"Moses," Thurgood said, "are you there?"

"Quiet," Moe muttered. "I'm praying."

"I didn't catch that. What did you say?"

Should I trust my grandfather and leave Todd here?

"Moses?"

Should I trust him?

A feeling of calm assurance started at the top of Moe's head and descended downward.

I thank thee, Father.

"Moses!"

Moe got out of the car, trying hard to act as if he didn't have a care in the world. "I'm leaving. I just have to get to the driver's seat."

221

"Very good," the old man replied, sounding profoundly relieved. "Make sure you at least look at the police cars as if you are curious, but don't be in a hurry—even though you must hurry."

Moe tried to look casually interested in the police activity as he walked around the car to the driver's side. "Did you get your men to the hospital?"

"I handed them off to . . . an associate some minutes ago. I can't be seen dumping assault victims at an emergency room."

Moe reentered Todd's car on the driver side and started the engine. He put his cell phone into speaker mode and set the phone on the passenger seat. "Do you have a location on that cell phone?"

"I have another associate working on that. I'll inform you as soon as I have the location."

Moe backed the car out of its parking spot. "They've probably just gone back to the house."

"Yes, that might be . . . Hold on. I have a message. One moment."

As Moe drove slowly down the road in front of Peggy's condo, another police car approached. The car slowed. Moe's palms began to sweat. *Look straight ahead. You're not fleeing a crime scene. You're just out minding your own business.*

The patrol car passed, and Moe let out a shuddering sigh of reprieve.

"I have a location," Thurgood said. "The phone is in Lehi, heading east."

"Lehi?" *That's north of here. But the house is south—in Mapleton.* "So they're *not* going back to the house?"

"It would appear not."

Moe turned in the direction of the interstate, forcing himself to drive the speed limit. "I'm going to need constant updates."

"Of course. Head north for now. I'll have my associate provide you with location updates. However, I must go rescue your barbarian friend."

"Okay, but . . . be nice to him. Todd's a good man."

The old man chuckled. "Oh, I'm going to enjoy having him at *my* mercy."

"I'm trusting you, Grandfather." *Even if I'm completely insane to do so.*

Thurgood Abbot uttered a most undignified and, for him, uncharacteristic sound.

Did he just growl at me?

"I'm an old man," his grandfather said. "You might at least indulge me with a moment of vengeful fantasy. But fear not, Moses." Thurgood sighed. "I will not betray your trust."

"Okay. I'm almost to the freeway."

"Moses?"

"Yeah?"

"I'm trusting you too." The old man's voice choked with emotion. "Moses, I'm . . . I'm frightened."

"Me too."

"You must . . . You must end this curse. You must save our family."

Our family. Save our family.

A small smile crept over Moe's face. "I will."

◢ ◢ ◢

"Peggy!" Elaine's voice — an urgent, frantic whisper. "Peggy! Wake up!"

Peggy's head felt fuzzy, her hands and feet numb. She tasted sweetness — sweetness and rot on her dry lips.

"Peggy! Please wake up!"

She opened her eyes . . . and saw only darkness. "E-Elaine?"

"Oh, Peggy! Thank the Goddess!" She paused. "No! No! *Curse* the Goddess!" Elaine's voice never rose above a whisper, but it was emphatic, filled with anger. "I reject you! Do you hear me? I reject you!"

What's she talking about? Peggy blinked hard, shaking her head to clear it. Elaine's silhouette slowly resolved out of the darkness, her pretty face cast in deep shadow.

"Derek," Peggy said. "Where's . . . Derek?"

"He's in the tower," Elaine whispered.

"Tower? What tower? Where . . . Where are we?"

"We're in the house — my house. Peggy, you must listen. There isn't much time."

Peggy realized she was sitting in a wooden chair, her hands bound behind her back, her ankles tied to the legs of the chair. She wore one of those white Druid robes over her clothes like the virgin in a pagan sacrifice. Terror ripped through her like a jagged blade of ice, instantly clearing the chloroform-induced fog. *The house! Those dogs! They're in the house!* She pulled against her bonds. "Elaine! Let me go!"

Elaine shook her head. "I can't! Not yet. And keep your voice down. She'll hear you."

"Who? Morgaise?"

"Yes!" Elaine hissed. "Yes! Morgaise, of course. Who else? She'll hear you."

"Okay," Peggy whispered. Her eyes were becoming accustomed to the darkness. Elaine's eyes dimly reflected what little ambient light there was. *Moonlight? Starlight?*

"Oh, Peggy!" Elaine sobbed. "I wanted to save Derek from all this. I wanted to run away with him, to escape. You know I did, but—"

"Untie me," Peggy whispered. "We'll all go together, Elaine—just like you wanted."

Elaine shook her head, dashing away tears. "No. It's too late. Too late for me. I can't go. Don't you see? Too late. It has begun again. But—but you! *You* can save Derek! You can save him, Peggy!"

"How?" Peggy pulled uselessly at her bonds again. "Elaine! Help me!" *The dogs! Where are the dogs?*

"No! If I let you go now, the others, the faithful ones—they'll just find you and stop you. And Suetonius—you know, my dog—he'll track you down. You have to wait. Then you'll have your chance. You're the only one who can save Derek. You have to listen to me!"

"What? How?"

"Are you listening?"

Peggy nodded.

"Okay," Elaine whispered. "Very good. Morgaise will be coming soon. She'll be bringing the fruit of the harvest—the fruit of the Tree of Life. She's going to put some of it in your mouth. If you resist, she'll simply have someone hold your mouth open while she forces the fruit past your teeth. They'll knock your teeth out, if they have to. Peggy, they'll force you to eat it. Do you understand?"

"N-no! I don't understand."

"Do you understand that you will be forced to swallow the fruit?"

Peggy nodded. "Yes."

"Good. The fruit will put you into a deep sleep, a sleep from which you will *not awaken* until it is too late. You will not awaken, unless . . ." Elaine held up something small and thin in her hand. "This is a leaf from the Tree. It is very bitter. But it . . . it *counteracts* the fruit. You must hold it in your mouth. Don't chew it or swallow it—not until you swallow the fruit. You must chew and swallow it *with* the fruit—not before. Do you understand?"

Peggy nodded.

"This is very important. Do not crush or chew the leaf until the fruit is in your mouth. You probably shouldn't hold it in your cheek or lip either—or under your tongue. I just don't know!" She put her fists to her temples as if her head hurt. "But the leaf by itself—Peggy, the leaf *ages* you. It ages you very quickly. The fruit is life, but the leaf is death. But the two together . . . Do you understand?"

Peggy shook her head. "No! I don't understand! Elaine, why—"

"To save Derek!" Elaine gripped Peggy's shoulder with her free hand. "And to save you too, my sweet sister! You must do as I say. Please, Peggy! Promise me!"

"Yes, Elaine, I-I promise. Just—"

Elaine made a sound between a sob and a laugh. She covered her face with her hand. "Thank you! Thank you!" Abruptly, she put her hands to her temples again. "Not yet. Not yet! No! No! No!"

Elaine shook herself, then focused on Peggy again. She held up a steak knife.

Peggy gasped. "Elaine, no!"

Elaine shook her head. "I'm not going to hurt you, sweet Peggy— kind, sweet sister. I'm going to put this into your hand. You can use it to cut your fetters—but only *after* you eat the fruit and the leaf. You must wait till Morgaise has gone. Do you understand?"

"Yes, I understand."

"Good. After you free yourself, go to the tower and free Derek. And you must not leave this room until you smell the smoke or see the flames."

"Flames?!" Peggy nearly shrieked.

Elaine nodded hurriedly. "Yes, the house will be put to the torch. It is part of the sacrifice. It is"—she paused as if in reverence—"the Burning Man."

In an instant, Peggy understood. *The house—it's shaped like a wooden man! The wings of the house in front—legs. The round staircases on either side—arms. The tower is the head. The old Druid ritual—a wooden man, filled with fruits, grains, and animals from the harvest. Set ablaze. Burned alive. Sacrificed to Cernunnos, the Horned God.*

The Burning Man.

And at the top, in the head . . .

A beloved one.

"Derek's in the head!" Peggy cried. Horror gripped her heart like an icy claw, crushing, drawing the breath from her.

"Yes!" Elaine nodded, and Peggy could see tears on her cheeks. "You understand at last. You, Peggy, are in the foot. Derek is in the head. You must save him! The leaf—it's your only chance."

Peggy opened her mouth to plead with Elaine, but Elaine inserted something into Peggy's mouth.

The leaf!

"Remember," Elaine said. "Do not chew it now. It will kill you. Hold it *gently* in your teeth."

Don't chew it? It was all Peggy could do to keep from spitting it out.

Elaine bent and kissed Peggy's cheek.

"Good-bye, my sweet, beloved sister. You have been so kind to me."

And then Elaine was gone.

And Peggy was left alone in the darkness with a poisonous leaf in her mouth.

◢ ◢ ◢

"You've got to let me go." Todd fought to control his panic, to keep the waking nightmares of Afghanistan from engulfing him again. "If you won't send someone to help my friends, at least let me go." Sitting in a chair in the kitchen, he pulled at his handcuffed wrists. "You said I'm not under arrest."

Orem City Police Officer J. Chen sighed. The half dozen other cops were "securing the scene." Their job was to keep curious civilians away from Peggy's condo. But Chen simply looked at Todd with weary annoyance. "I told you—you have to wait till the detectives arrive. You're a material witness to homicide and kidnapping. And you were found holding the murder weapon."

"But I'm the one who called this whole thing in!" Todd said for what felt like the hundredth time.

Chen shook his head. "Nope. You keep saying that, but it was one"—he looked at a small notebook—"Moses Abbot who made the nine-one-one call. And your ID says your name is Cavetto."

"But I was with him when he made the call! We've been over this! My friends are in danger!" *Peggy's in danger! She could be dead already!*

Chen wrinkled his nose as if detecting a nasty odor. "Now, you better calm down, Mr. Cavetto. You're already in restraints. Don't make me use more stringent measures to subdue you." He patted his holstered Taser. "We wouldn't want that, now, would—"

"You can't come in here, sir," said the officer guarding the shattered door.

"Officer, as I told your Neanderthal compatriots outside, I am Mr. Cavetto's attorney," said a familiar voice. "Now, out of my way, young man!"

Todd looked up to see Thurgood Abbot pushing past the officer and into the condo. "Abbot?" Shock momentarily overcame Todd's panic.

"Not another word, young man," said the old attorney, raising a boney finger and wagging it at Todd. Turning his withering gaze on

Chen, Thurgood said, "You will release my client immediately."

Chen snorted derisively. The cop, short on stature, but tall on bravado, took a step toward the gaunt old man. "Counselor, you can stick around, but we're holding him for questioning."

Thurgood took a step toward Chen. The old man stood at least a foot taller than the diminutive cop, and he took full advantage of his height. "Is he a suspect? Do you have any evidence to hold him? Do you have a body?"

Chen had to tilt his head back to look the nonagenarian in the eye. "We have a report of shots fired, a weapon, shell casings, and blood-stains."

"Ah." Thurgood smiled, exposing his impossibly white teeth. "So you don't have evidence of a *homicide*, merely of a shooting. My client reported the gunshots himself, and he was miles away when the report was made."

Chen, looking as if he was barely containing his rage, growled through clenched teeth. "He stays till my detectives arrive."

"And how long have you detained my client already?"

Chen uttered a short grunt, then muttered something.

"I'm sorry," Thurgood said. "I'm an old man. You'll have to speak up, Officer Chen. By the way, Officer Chen, what is your badge number?"

Chen's eyes narrowed in a murderous expression. "Zero-four-three-five," he said, enunciating each digit with venomous precision.

Thurgood gave the short policeman a deliciously malevolent smile, like a wolf grinning at a rabbit. "How long have you detained my client, Officer Chen, badge number zero-four-three-five?"

"It's been"—Chen checked his watch—"sixty-two minutes." His shoulders sagged, but his furious expression never wavered.

Thurgood's toothy smile would've rivaled the Cheshire Cat's. "Then you have detained him two minutes longer than is constitutionally allowed. In short, Officer Chen, you are violating my client's constitutional rights. Either arrest him—but you don't have probable cause for that, do you? Release him, or I will sue you—*you*, not your department—for far more than you make in a dozen years."

Chen turned his furious glare on Todd. "Don't leave town, Ca-vetto!" he snapped, as he unlocked Todd's handcuffs.

Thurgood chuckled. "Don't listen to the good officer, Mr. Cavetto. You are under no such restriction, not without a court order. Now, Officer J. Chen, badge number zero-four-three-five, you will return my client's effects, including his lawfully licensed firearm."

Moments later, after Todd had recovered his wallet, keys, and weapon, and had snatched Peggy's car keys from her purse—over Chen's strong objections—Todd and Thurgood strode calmly, but quickly past the police perimeter.

"You were the last person I expected to come to my rescue," Todd said.

"And I don't mind saying," the old man replied, "that you are the last person on earth I would wish to succor. However, my grandson needs you. He is in American Fork Canyon, pursuing your friends."

Todd almost missed a step. "The canyon? Not that house?"

"Yes, it is most curious, I must admit. My associates say there is unusual activity going on at the house, but—"

Todd's phone rang. "It's Moe," Todd said. He answered the call. "Moe?"

"Todd! Thank heaven!" Moe sounded frantic. "They're not here!"

"Where are you?" Todd asked.

"Up in the canyon. There's a cave. But Todd . . . there are some of those Druids up here, but they don't have your lady friend. Not Derek or Elaine either. Todd, I think this is where the Morrigans are going to sleep—you know, for sixty years. But the rest aren't here. They must be at the house!"

"On my way," Todd said as he sprinted toward Peggy's car, leaving Thurgood Abbot standing alone.

♦ ♦ ♦

Saliva filled Peggy's mouth.

Do I swallow it? If my saliva has already touched the leaf . . .

She tried to spit out the side of her mouth while still carefully holding the horrid leaf in her teeth.

She succeeded only in getting spittle down onto the front of her white robe.

Tears of frustration and terror welled at the corners of her eyes.

Hold it together, Peggy! For Derek!

You're pathetic, Peggy. Worthless.

Shut up, will you! I'm not worthless. I can save him. I have to save him.

The door opened, and three figures entered. In the gloom, Peggy could discern only that they wore white robes and hoods.

This is it, Peggy. Don't blow it!

The three robed figures stood before her. The shortest of the three, the one in the center, pulled back her hood. Peggy's eyes had become accustomed enough to the dim light to recognize the half-dead face of Morgaise Morrigan.

The living side of the woman's face curled up into a nasty smile. "I warned you, did I not? You should have stayed away."

Fighting down terror and the conflicting urges to swallow the saliva which continued to pool in her mouth or to spit it in the vile woman's face, Peggy forced a neutral, calm expression onto her face.

"Nothing to say, Miss Carson?" Morgaise raised one eyebrow.

Peggy kept her mouth firmly shut, watching as drool ran down from the dead half of Morgaise's mouth. *Focus on that, on her dead eye. Just not on the thing in your mouth.*

Morgaise sighed. "Very well." She waved dismissively. "I don't see what my sister ever valued in you. Kindness? Simple stupidity. Bravery? You are not brave. You are merely stubborn. Plain. Not worth another moment's thought." She motioned with a finger toward Peggy, and the two robed figures on either side of her stepped forward.

One of the Druids pinched the sides of Peggy's mouth, pressing mercilessly against her teeth, forcing her mouth open. The other figure shoved something into her mouth. Something sweet. Sickeningly sweet—like liquid saccharin.

The first Druid released the pressure on her teeth, then placed one hand atop her head and another below her jaw. He pushed, forcing her jaws closed, causing her to bite into the fruit . . .

. . . and the leaf.

An acrid, bitter taste flooded her mouth—bile mixing with the sweetness.

Death and life.

Peggy chewed quickly.

It will age you.

You're already too old.

It's not about me. I have to save Derek.

She swallowed.

What now? Do I pretend to fall asleep right—

Oblivion engulfed her.

🜄 🜄 🜄

Derek awoke to moonlight.

The ghostly radiance streamed in through a barred window, illuminating the room.

He lay on his back on a bed. At least, it felt like a bed. It was soft beneath him, but when he tried to sit up, he found that he was bound. His feet and ankles were restrained, and there was something across his waist.

229

"Elaine?" he called out.

There was no answer.

Derek struggled against his restraints. He lifted his head and looked down his body. Thick leather straps held his wrists, ankles, and waist.

"Elaine?"

In rising panic, he looked around the room. He could see nothing, except the round walls and the window with the moon shining behind the iron bars. He couldn't even see a door.

"Elaine?" *They took her!* "Elaine, where are you?"

"I'm right here, my love." Elaine's voice came from behind him.

He tried to twist his head around to see her. "Are you all right?"

She came into his field of vision. The moonlight caught her pretty face. She wore a white robe — just like those of the people who'd taken her.

She smiled sadly. "No, my love. I am not all right. I must go now. I must go with my sisters. I must leave you." Her tone was sad, resigned, calm.

Sisters? She said sisters? But she only has Morgaise.

"I love you, Derek," Elaine continued. "In all the ages, in all the centuries, I think I have loved you the most. Forgive me, my darling."

"Elaine, I don't understand," he said. "We were going to run away, to escape."

She shook her head slowly. "It is too late for that. I'm sorry, Derek. I truly am. I will . . . miss you." She shook her head again and placed her fists to her temples. She grimaced as if in pain. "No!" she wailed. "I will *not* remember you! I *never* remember. You will only be a wisp of dream to me. I-I took your phone, sweetheart. It's already in the place of sleeping. In the ages to come, I'll look upon it fondly and know that once — once upon a time, as they say in the bards' tales — I had a love like no other."

She reached behind her head and pulled up a white hood, casting her face in shadow.

"We must go now, sister." Morgaise's voice, speaking slowly and deliberately, forcing out every consonant.

Derek looked about in terror for the disfigured sister — the Evil Queen — but he couldn't see her.

Elaine shook her head. "But you said I could say good-bye."

"Then say it," said Morgaise, "and be done."

"Elaine?" Derek cried. "Don't leave! Don't leave me here!"

"I'm sorry, Derek," Elaine said. "I love you."

Still hooded, she bent and kissed him. The kiss was sweet and tender. Tears fell on his face. "Good-bye, my love." She straightened once more.

"Yes," said Morgaise. "Good-bye, sweet Derek."

Elaine pulled back her hood, bathing her face in moonlight once again.

Derek, his eyes wide in sudden horror, began to scream.

XXVI

61 A.D.: Verulamium (St. Albans), Britannia

Let us, therefore, go against them, trusting boldly to good fortune." Tasca's mother, Queen Boudicca of the Iceni Celts, stood atop her chariot and raised a bronze-headed spear. As she addressed her troops, Boudicca's voice was harsh, but then, Tasca had never known her mother to be a soft-spoken woman. "Let us show them that they are hares and foxes trying to rule over dogs and wolves!"

Sitting in her mother's chariot, Tasca watched as her mother released a rabbit from within a fold of her multicolored dress. The terrified animal bounded away. The rabbit turned sharply to the right and scampered out of sight.

To the right—a good omen, Tasca thought. *The Goddess will give us victory.*

Resting obediently behind the royal chariot, the dogs, Phelan and Cahan—gifts from the Roman governor—lifted their heads and sniffed in the direction of the retreating rabbit. Then the molossii rested their heads on their forelegs again. They had feasted well that day.

Tasca looked across the chariot and into the eyes of her sister—into the good eye, at least. Camorra tried to smile at her, but of course, only half her face moved.

And if we drive the Romans out of our lands, Tasca thought, *then perhaps this nightmare will end. But not for you, dear sister.*

Never for you.

The assembled Celts from the Iceni, Trinovantes, and other united tribes—more than one hundred thousand strong—cheered, raising their spears and swords in acclamation. The queen raised her other hand to heaven and prayed aloud to the Goddess of Vengeance, "I thank you, Andraste, and call upon you as woman speaking to woman! I beg you for victory and preservation of liberty!"

232

The Celts cheered again. They clashed their weapons upon their shields in a common rhythm, making a tremendous martial din. They chanted, "Kill the Romans! Kill the Romans!" However, the chant quickly changed to "Boudicca! Boudicca! Boudicca!"

Tasca had heard such speeches and acclamations before. Under Boudicca's leadership, the Celts had laid siege to Camulodunum, and then utterly destroyed it. The Roman colony had been poorly defended, but it was an important victory. They had destroyed the temple of the Roman Emperor Claudius, whom the hated invaders now deemed a god—and Boudicca had shown Claudius to be a false god.

Then they marched on Londinium, which Boudicca's forces burned to the ground. The Celts took no prisoners and showed no mercy—they slaughtered or crucified all the remaining inhabitants of the city—all those who had not fled before Boudicca's massive army. Word was that the Roman governor, Gaius Suetonius Paulinus, had ordered the evacuation of the city before the arrival of the Celts. The Romans didn't even tried to defend it. And the Celts had wreaked their terrible vengeance.

But Verulamium had been the worst by far.

As her mother basked in the adoration of her troops on the outskirts of Verulamium, Tasca reached across the chariot for her sister's hand. Rather than simply taking Tasca's hand in her own, Camorra sidled across the vehicle to sit next to her younger sister. Camorra put her arms around Tasca, and the girl accepted the embrace gratefully.

Tasca shivered in Camorra's arms, but not from the weather. Inexorably, her eyes were drawn back to the ghastly forest behind the chariot—a hideous forest of her mother's making.

Row upon row of wooden poles had been driven into the ground, each impaling the horribly mutilated body of a woman.

Mother appeals to the Goddess of Vengeance, woman to woman, yet she does this to these poor mothers and daughters? And they were not even Romans. How could she do this to our own people?

I do not understand.

Perhaps, I do not want to understand.

She felt the tiniest flutter in her belly.

The babe!

She laid a delicate hand on her abdomen. Tasca knew she should *hate* the child, but she could not bring herself to feel anything save love toward the tiny life growing inside her.

It is not your fault, little one. You are not to blame.
And I will protect you with my life.

Both her mother and the royal midwife thought Tasca too young to conceive. After all, Camorra did not get with child, and she was two years older.

And Camorra endured the same violence as Tasca.

But when Tasca failed to bleed, when it was apparent that she was indeed with child, her mother forced her to eat both laserpicium and wild carrot blossoms. Tasca bled and endured excruciating, cramping pains. She thought she had lost the baby—just as her mother intended.

But afterward, when she felt the movement for the first time, Tasca cherished a secret joy—the only joy she had known since her father's death.

Her mother had recounted the story many times.

The Romans invaded Britannia before Tasca and Camorra were born. King Prasutagus of the Iceni submitted to Roman rule. He was granted relative independence as a vassal king on two conditions—that he accept a rather large loan (which he did not need or want) from Roman bankers, and that upon his death, his kingdom would be annexed by Rome.

From that time forward, Tasca's father ruled without Roman interference, but he feared what might happen to his family and his people upon his death. He knew well that the Roman Procurator Catus Decianus coveted Prasutagus's rich lands and considerable wealth and that the Roman procurator would use any pretext to seize both lands and gold upon Prasutagus's death. So the old king devised a plan to secure imperial protection from the scheming procurator. He bequeathed his kingdom jointly to his daughters—Camorra and Tasca—and to the Roman Emperor Nero.

However, Prasutagus sorely underestimated Catus's greed. And that avarice had led them all to the horrors of Verulamium...

Her speech over, Queen Boudicca dismissed her warriors to their victory revels. The Celts dispersed to drink and rut with any woman available—their own wives or otherwise—amid the ruins of the town. Only then, when the eyes of her troops were no longer upon her, did Tasca's mother show any sign of weariness.

Dismissing even her handmaids to couple with whatever men were handy, the queen walked slowly in the direction of the royal pavilion, her head bent. Tasca and her sister followed their mother toward the tent. And the dogs followed after.

A rather bestial sound caught Tasca's ear. She turned to look...

and immediately regretted it. A warrior and one of her mother's handmaids were coupling right in the middle of the grisly forest of impaled women.

How could they? Right there? Amid those poor wretches?

Disgust and horror battled with nausea within her.

Nausea emerged victorious.

Tasca dropped to her knees and emptied her stomach on the ground.

In a moment, Camorra was at her side, holding her sister's hair away from the pool of vomit. Camorra laid a comforting hand on Tasca's back.

"On your feet!" her mother snapped. "Do not show them weakness. Get up and stop acting like—"

Tasca wretched again.

Clawlike hands gripped her upper arms and hauled her painfully to her feet. Boudicca shook Tasca hard. "Do not show weakness!"

The queen's piercing gaze lanced into Tasca's eyes, capturing her. "What is the matter with you?" her mother demanded.

Tasca clamped her mouth shut, fighting down the urge to be sick yet again. *She must not know about the babe. Not yet.*

"Please, mother!" Camorra tugged at Boudicca's skirts. "It is the impaled women. The sight frightens her."

The queen turned her fierce eyes on Camorra, and the older daughter bowed her head meekly. "It—it frightens me as well," Camorra said.

Tasca, briefly grateful that her mother was no longer glaring at her, swallowed the bile that had pooled in her mouth. "Mother," she began, fighting down a fresh wave of nausea, "forgive me. I understand we must take no prisoners—"

Her mother's eyes returned to Tasca. "We take no prisoners, because we have no time."

No time to take prisoners, but plenty of time to riot and rut. "I understand, Mother, but the women? Why not simply kill them? Why—"

"I do what must be done!" Her mother's voice was cold. Boudicca's face became a mask of rage, her normally beautiful features completely subsumed by murderous fury. Then it seemed to Tasca as if the queen's countenance sagged lifelessly, as if both sides of her face mirrored the dead side of Camorra's visage. Boudicca's voice dropped to a whisper, pregnant with malice and hatred. "Perhaps you wish to join those traitor whores?" Her voice dropped even lower. "No proper man will wed you now."

"If w-we are of n-n-no use to you," Camorra said, her voice shaking, "will you . . . c-c-cut off our breasts and imp-p-pale us as well?"

Boudicca's horrifying face turned toward Camorra. "No man will have you at all, marked one, not anymore. Your face is a curse from the gods — punishment for your failure to protect your sister."

Procurator Catus Decianus marched into Venta Icenorum with a small army. They were not proper soldiers. They were simply Roman veterans — former soldiers who had retired in Britannia or Gaul, taken Celt wives, and settled down to become farmers. They were men who were not above making a little extra money as mercenaries in deputized service to the avaricious Procurator.

Catus announced that, with the death of King Prasutagus, all Iceni lands were forfeit and the huge loans forced upon the king must be repaid immediately. He therefore proclaimed that the royal treasure of the Iceni was to be confiscated . . . in the name of the Emperor, of course.

When Tasca's mother, Queen Boudicca, objected, the queen was taken by the mercenaries. She was stripped, tied to one of the sacred trees in the center of the city, and flogged. The whip consisted of many leather thongs, each tipped with bits of bone. Tasca's mother screamed over and over as the flesh of her back and sides was flayed open. After more than thirty strokes, she mercifully lost consciousness.

But Catus Decianus was not finished with her.

He ordered the queen roused so she could witness the power and justice of Rome.

Before her eyes and in the sight of all the assembled Iceni, Boudicca's young daughters were dragged before her.

Camorra broke free of her captors and threw herself at the men who held her younger sister. Camorra clawed at them and bit them and struck them with her small fists, but she was seized and subdued once more.

Then the queen was forced to watch as her daughters were violated over and over by the procurator's men.

"It is no curse of the gods," Tasca cried, borrowing courage from her sister. "The Romans did this!" She pointed at the lifeless side of Camorra's face. "This happened when she was raped! This is *not* her fault."

Life returned to her mother's drooping face, and Boudicca's eyes softened.

"Mother," Camorra said, "it is not your fault, either."

Tears appeared in the fierce queen's eyes. She placed an arm around each of her daughters, drawing them close to her bosom. She bowed her head and wept aloud, apparently not caring if anyone else noticed.

And for a precious minute or two, Tasca and Camorra wept with her, hungrily returning the embrace. For a precious minute or two, they were not vengeful queen and raped princesses—they were simply mother and daughters, united in their grief.

They were a family again.

As sorrowful as she was, Tasca would have remained within the warmth of that embrace, within the shelter of her mother and sister's love forever.

Tasca heard the sound of running footsteps. "Your Majesty!"

Boudicca hugged her daughters more tightly. "Go away."

"Forgive me, Majesty," said the warrior, "but the Romans have been sighted."

The Romans? Tasca clung to her mother fiercely. *No more Romans. No more!*

"They are on the Roman Road," continued the warrior, "heading toward Viroconium. It is the governor, Gaius Suetonius Paulinus, himself! And, my queen, he has only a single legion—a mere ten thousand men! We can crush him!"

Boudicca released her daughters, and Tasca felt all the warmth drain from her body.

"Assemble the army!" the queen commanded. "Assemble the wagons. We march!"

🝋 🝋 🝋

"They are trapped, Your Majesty!" The Iceni captain's tone matched his face—triumphant and ecstatic. "We have them. There is no escape!"

"Order the attack," Boudicca said, her voice dropping to a terrifying whisper that made Tasca shiver.

Is it possible? Could we wipe them out with a single stroke?

Could this nightmare be over at last?

"My queen," said the man, bowing, "will you not oversee our victory?"

"We will be there." The queen motioned to Tasca and Camorra. "Into the chariot, girls. Today we avenge my honor and your stolen virtue."

Mother and daughters entered the chariot, and Boudicca took the reins. As they rode to the edge of a large natural bowl along the Roman Road, mother and daughters said nothing—not that they could have been heard above the roaring of the Celt warriors.

Tasca felt the tiniest movement of the babe within her. *Soon, little one. Then we will go home. And I will cherish you as no mother ever cherished a child before.*

At the top of the bowl's edge, the chariot stopped. Queen Boudicca stood in the chariot, arrayed in regal splendor — torc of woven gold at her neck, clad in cape and gown of many colors, her red hair flowing past her waist. She raised her spear and shouted, "Death to the Romans! And may Cernunnos, the Morrigan, and Andraste give us liberty and victory!"

"Boudicca! Boudicca!" roared the Celts, striking spears and swords upon shields. "Boudicca! Boudicca!" Their faces and bodies were painted blue with the juice of the woad plant. Most were naked to the waist. Almost all were barefoot. All wore torcs about their necks, though few of gold, and none so fine or large as the queen's. The magic of the torcs, they knew, would protect them in battle far better than the steel armor of the hated Romans.

The Celt army consisted of more than one hundred thousand warriors, perhaps two hundred thousand, perhaps more. And not all were men. Trained in sword, shield, and spear, a few thousand women fought beside and among their men.

Boudicca's army occupied one half of the natural bowl with its high sides. The Romans, barely ten thousand of them, were indeed trapped at the far end of the depression, their backs against a dense, impenetrable forest. The men of the single legion stood in their orderly formations, behind their oval wooden shields, awaiting their deaths and the death of any hope of holding Britannia.

And somewhere at the back of the hopelessly outnumbered Roman forces stood Legate Gaius Suetonius Paulinus.

How could there be so few of them? Tasca wondered. *And how could they possibly hope to stand against so many?*

Her mother's spies had confirmed that, although the Roman governor had pleaded for succor from two other legions, neither legion had appeared. Gaius and his tiny army stood alone, facing a force ten to twenty times their number.

Tasca looked around the edges of the bowl. The Celts had lined the entire edge with their wagons. Women and children sat and stood on the wagons, hoping for a good vantage point, a commanding view of the slaughter of the hated invaders and the end of the occupation. They cheered their husbands, fathers, sons, and even mothers and daughters.

But most of all, they cheered their queen.

"Boudicca! Boudicca! Boudicca!"

On either side of the chariot, the molossii, Phelan and Cahan, sat alert, ready to defend their mistresses. They drooled in anticipation of the coming feast.

What is Mother waiting for? Order the attack! The Romans have no hope.

As if hearing her thoughts, Tasca's mother pointed her spear toward the Romans.

And the Celts advanced.

The Romans had brought no archers, but when Celts were in range, the Romans hurled their *pila*. Ten thousand Roman spears arced up and rained upon the blue-painted warriors. After striking their targets—wooden shields for the most part—the *pila* bent under their own weight.

Tasca had never seen such a thing. *Why would they make a spear that bent after it struck its target?* But then she saw the wicked ingenuity of the Roman engineers. *A bent spear cannot be thrown back. And a bent metal spear protruding from a shield cannot be hacked off—it renders a shield useless.*

The Romans threw their second and final volley of spears. That time, a few hundred Celts fell—a few hundred in an ocean of hundreds of thousands. And still the Celts advanced.

A thrill of terror and exultation shook Tasca as the gap between the Celts and the Romans narrowed. *Soon, little one. Soon they will be dead.*

The Romans raised their shields in the dreaded formation known as the *testudo* or "tortoise." They braced for the attack. Tasca knew the men behind the front ranks would be digging their shoes into the ground and pushing against the men in front of them, holding them in place against the coming tidal wave of the Celts.

As if they could hold back the ocean itself. They are dead men.

With a roar of triumph, the Celts crashed upon the Romans.

But the Romans did not give ground.

❦ ❦ ❦

"How can this be?" Boudicca's spear fell from her limp hand. The queen stared slack-jawed at the battle. It was not a battle—it was a massacre. Camorra put her arms protectively around her sister as Tasca stared in horrified disbelief at the slaughter below.

The ground soaked with Celtic blood, Boudicca's army slipped and fell as they scrambled over the bodies of their own dead in a useless attempt to flee the inexorable Roman advance. A few hundred legionnaires lay dead or dying at the far end of the bowl, but many tens of thousands of Celts had been cut down by Roman swords.

Blue-painted men and women, now streaked with red and brown, threw down their weapons and ran for the sides of the bowl. But their bare feet slipped on the blood-soaked earth. They attempted to claw their way up the sides of the bowl, but even if they could get to the top, they were trapped inside—ringed in by their own wagons—their own women and children.

They will all be slaughtered like swine trapped in a pen.

"Mother?" Tasca tugged at her mother's skirt. "Mother, what do we do?"

Boudicca blinked as if awakening from a dream. "We must flee," she said, her voice unnervingly calm. "I cannot risk capture. Not here." She lifted the reins and guided her chariot away from the edge of the bowl, from the place of death—a place with no name. Taking her daughters with her, Boudicca, Queen of the Iceni and the united tribes, abandoned her warriors and fled.

♦ ♦ ♦

They took the Roman Road and headed east and south. They neither spoke nor ate—they had no provisions save their waterskins—as they traveled. The two sisters sat in the back of the chariot, sometimes holding hands, sometimes not—the mother sitting at the front or leaning on the railing, letting the horses follow the road. The dogs trotted tirelessly behind the chariot. The Queen and her daughters paused only occasionally to relieve themselves and allow the horses and dogs to drink.

Near nightfall, Boudicca spotted a forest south of the road. She reined the horses to a stop. Wordlessly, she took each of her daughters by the hand and led them out of the chariot and off the road.

Phelan and Cahan followed, flanking the girls on either side.

When they had walked a few dozen paces, they halted.

The queen bowed her head and broke her silence. "I have failed you, my daughters. There is but one thing I can do to protect you now. I will return to our home, to Veta, and there I will take poison—"

Tasca and Camorra opened their mouths to speak, but their mother gripped their hands hard, silencing them.

"I will take poison," she resumed, "and have a very public and lavish funeral. The Romans will hear of this and they will seek me there. They will find me—or at least my ashes—but they will not find you."

"But, mother," Camorra said in her slurred speech, "we want to—"

"No," said the queen. "You will enter this forest. You will travel by

240

night. You will make your way to Wales. The Welsh still resist the Romans. They share our gods. And the gods have not abandoned them—not yet. Take the molossii with you."

"No, mother!" Tasca wailed. "Let us *all* go to Wales!"

Boudicca shook her head. "No, I will draw the Romans away. You will flee. Find someplace where you can be safe. Safe with your sister. Safe from the Romans. Perhaps there is no such place. Perhaps the Romans will conquer the whole world. I do not know. And perhaps, someday, Cernunnos will allow us—the three of us and your father—to be reunited in the underworld. Perhaps."

She let go of the girls' hands and gripped Tasca's face. "Stay with your sister. Never leave her."

Tasca put a hand on her mother's, as if to keep it there, to never let her go. Tears streamed down her face, but she said nothing. Boudicca's hands lingered a moment longer, then withdrew.

Boudicca took Camorra's face in both her hands. "Protect your sister. She is your responsibility. You must be both sister and mother to her now. Never let her out of your sight. And when the Romans come at last, do what must be done."

She gripped Camorra's face, digging her fingers into the girl's living and dead flesh. The queen's face transformed just as Tasca had seen it do in Verulamium. Lifeless eyes in a dead face.

And Boudicca's voice dropped low and became as the sound of spiders crawling over grave clothes. "Do whatever must be done."

XXVII

Derek shook his head in horror and denial. "No!" he screamed, straining at his bonds. "No! It's not true!"

Morgaise stared down at him, half her face lifted in a mocking smile, her teeth gleaming in the moonlight. "Whatever is the matter, Derek? Am I not as lovely as my sweet sister? Or perhaps, *half* as lovely?" Drool leaked from the dead half of her mouth.

Derek twisted his head around, desperately seeking for Elaine. "It's not true! It can't be. Elaine? Where are you?"

Morgaise shook her head slowly. "Elaine is gone. We are"—she paused and closed her eyes as if listening for a voice only she could hear—"alone. It's just you and I now."

Derek felt a mad giggle clawing its way out of his clenched throat. *No-no-no-no!*

Morgaise extended a hand and caressed the side of his face, causing him to recoil in horror. She placed a finger on Derek's lips as if to silence him. "You have been chosen for a great honor, Derek. You are the *Grá Amháin*—the Beloved One. You will be sacrificed to the Horned God in thanksgiving for a bountiful harvest."

"Let me go!" he pleaded. "Please, let me go."

Morgaise lifted one eyebrow. "You wish to refuse this great honor?"

"It can't be. It's not true." He shut his eyes, squeezing out tears that spilled down the sides of his face.

"Very well then, sweet Derek. I offer you a choice."

He opened his eyes at that. "Choice?" His breath came in rapid gasps. He felt light-headed.

Morgaise leaned over him. Her mocking half-smile had vanished, replaced by an expression of longing. "Love me."

"What?"

"Love me, Derek. Love me as you would Elaine."

Derek's stomach clenched. He felt as if he might vomit.

"Love me." Morgaise sounded desperate, pleading. "You can close your eyes in the darkness and imagine her perfect face. You can call me by her name. I don't care. Love me—even if it isn't real. Love me, and we will leave this place, this time. We will live forever—you and I . . . and Elaine."

"Elaine?" The giggle threatened again—madness tearing at the crumbling walls of his mind.

"Don't you see, Derek?" The living side of her face smiled hopefully. "You can have us both. Both of us." The dead half shifted. The drooping lip straightened. The lifeless eyelid tightened around the eye. In a moment, the divided face was whole. Both sides matched.

Elaine's face.

"Derek?" Elaine said. She appeared frightened and confused. "I . . . I don't understand. M-Morgaise? What's going on?"

Half the face sagged again, lifeless as before.

"Kiss me," said Morgaise as she leaned over him.

The insane giggle escaped, ripping its way out of Derek's fracturing mind. Derek's howls of mad laughter echoed around the moonlit chamber.

◢ ◢ ◢

Peggy coughed, choking on smoke. Her eyes flew open.

Wavering orange light, shrouded by black haze, filled the room.

Fire!

The Burning Man.

Derek's in the tower!

Peggy opened her mouth, inhaled sharply, then clamped her mouth shut, stifling the scream.

You'll only alert . . .

Her breath exploded in a fit of coughing.

When she had regained control of her breathing, she tugged at her bonds, trying to get a hand free. Her hand tightened around something long and thin.

The knife!

With her hands behind her back, Peggy couldn't see the knife Elaine had given her, but she gripped the knife handle as best she could in fingers swollen from being bound. She tried to move it experimentally. She could feel it grating against the cords that bound her.

Frantically, she moved the knife up and down. She paused as another coughing fit seized her, temporarily driving out all thought except the need to suck in oxygen. Then she sawed again.

243

The cords around her wrists parted, and her hands were free. Grinning in fierce triumph, she flung her arms wide.

And the knife flew out of her tenuous grasp.

She watched helplessly as the knife landed a dozen feet away on the wooden floor — well out of reach. The blade reflected the yellow light of the flames.

"No!"

Panic almost overwhelmed her. It seemed as if flames covered every inch of wall, except for the window, which was open, but blocked by wrought-iron bars. The cooler outside air flowed into the room, feeding the fire.

Trapped. No way out.

Your hands are free. Untie your ankles.

She bent over and tugged at the leather strips binding her ankles to the legs of the chair. After a few moments of panicked clawing at the leather with no success, she looked over at the knife in desperation.

So go get the knife!

Peggy launched herself forward. The chair came with her, landing on top of her legs. The air was cooler and cleaner next to the floor, allowing Peggy to breathe more easily. Using only her hands, she crawled to the knife, seized it, then flipped onto her side. She slid the blade between one leather thong and the fabric of her jeans.

The leather wasn't thick and she quickly cut one leg and then the other loose.

Free!

She started to rise to her feet, then remembered to stay low.

Holding the knife, Peggy crawled toward the only door she could see. The room had no other furniture besides the chair she'd left behind. *Maybe this room's just here to be the "foot" of the Burning Man — no other purpose.* When she reached the door, she carefully touched it with her fingers, feeling for heat.

If it's hot, there's fire on the other side.

There's fire everywhere. And that door's the only way out.

The wood of the door wasn't any hotter than the air around her. The doorknob, however, *was* hot.

Peggy ripped off the white robe she'd been wearing when she awoke. She was still dressed in jeans, T-shirt, and tennis shoes. She wrapped part of the robe's white linen cloth around her hand to insulate it, and opened the door.

The room beyond was lit with flame and shrouded with smoke, though the flames were not as bad as in the room she'd left. The room before her appeared to be a wide hallway.

The leg.

Start the fire in the foot or feet, and it'll spread to the rest the house.

Maybe there's still time!

Four iron-barred windows lined each wall, and before each window sat a white-robed figure in a wooden chair. There were eight of them.

Peggy recoiled, expecting the Druids to turn toward her and seize her. The flickering yellow light made their robes and hoods seem to ripple. As one, the Druids turned in their chairs, reaching toward her with outstretched claws . . .

No! Not real!

She shook her head. The illusion vanished.

The Druids sat immobile, heads drooping forward.

Asleep! Drugged by that fruit?

They'll burn to death.

Save Derek!

Just leave them, Peggy. They're part of this. They're not even tied up! They chose this.

They were going to rape you.

Can't just leave them. I can't!

She got to her feet, but stayed bent low. The air was better in the hall.

The open windows?

She grasped the closest Druid by the shoulders and shook him. No response. Peggy shook harder.

The man simply slumped to the floor.

Peggy stifled a scream as the robed figure almost landed on her.

Her hands shaking, Peggy felt at the man's neck for a pulse. Nothing.

She tried and failed to wake two more of the robed figures before giving up. Carrying the knife and the wadded robe, Peggy headed for the open doorway at the opposite end of the hall.

Beyond the hallway, she found herself in a large and well-equipped kitchen. Along one wall, there were more open windows, more bars, and more insensate Druids.

The flames had barely reached that part of the house, tongues of fire licking greedily around the doorway as if tasting the wood. The dim light came mostly from outside.

To the left, an open arch led to a moonlit stairway. The doorway on the right opened into darkness. From her one previous visit to the house, Peggy surmised that way led to the foyer and the front door. *Left and up to Derek. Right to escape.*

For one brief and horrible moment, Peggy hesitated.

Get out! Now!

Derek!

He chose Elaine.

"I don't care," she said aloud . . . and turned to the left.

Just short of the stair doorway, she stopped, spun around, and ran for the twin sinks. *Please let the water still be on!* She shoved the wadded robe into the left sink and turned on the water.

Cool liquid gushed out, drenching the white fabric. Peggy trembled in relief. *Maybe I can use it to make a breathing mask, to block out the smoke.* She tucked the sopping linen bundle under her left arm and dashed for the stairway.

The steps of the spiral staircase were abnormally wide at the outer edge—so wide, they could accommodate a chair. Barred windows lined the curving, ascending wall, and in front of every window sat a robed Druid.

Peggy sprinted up the stairs.

The smoke pursued her.

As she climbed, she stayed to the center of the staircase, away from the human sacrifices seated at the windows. *Can't save them!* Tears coursed down her cheeks. *If I get Derek out, maybe I can come back for them. For some of them.*

Not if I get Derek out, she thought, gritting her teeth in fierce determination. *After.*

"I'm coming, Derek," she said, panting.

The archway at the top of the staircase emptied onto a long hallway. Windows, bars, chairs, robed pagans, and flames lined the right side—the side facing the front of the house.

On the left were three doors.

Turning her back on the flames, Peggy ignored the first door. *Tower's in the center.*

Reaching the second door, she gingerly touched the knob, testing to see if it was hot.

A loud thump behind her caused Peggy to jump.

She clamped her mouth shut, stifling a scream. *The dogs! Behind me!* Any second, she would feel hot, moist breath on her exposed skin—breath, and then huge, sharp teeth ripping into her neck.

She gripped the knife more tightly. It felt tiny and insignificant—like her.

But she felt no breath, no teeth—only the growing heat of the fire behind her.

Holding her breath, Peggy turned around.

No dogs.

One of the unconscious Druids—a woman—had fallen to the floor. The woman lay sprawled in her white robe, next to her fallen chair. Two of the chairs legs had broken when the chair toppled.

Peggy's knees almost gave out, and her breath escaped in a shuddering sigh. Her eyes went from the prostrate woman, to the broken chair, and to the flames spreading up the wall. Black smoke shrouded the ceiling.

Derek. Move!

Peggy turned back to the door. She turned the knob and yanked the door open.

The room inside was dark, lit only by the fire behind her. Peggy's own body blocked most of the light. She hesitated, trying to allow her eyes to adjust to the gloom beyond. She felt inside for a light switch and found one. She flicked the switch up and down twice, but nothing happened. Darkness prevailed.

She stared into the blackness, unable to make out anything.

What are you waiting for? The stairs to the tower have to be in there. It's the only way to Derek.

But I can't see. I'll break my neck or my ankle. Then I can't do anything. I'll be useless.

She whirled around once more.

Dropping the sodden robe she carried, then wiping her wet left hand on a dry area of her T-shirt, Peggy knelt beside the fallen Druid. She tore a long strip of the fabric of the woman's robe. Then she snatched up one of the broken chair legs. She wrapped the dry, white linen around the chair leg, tucking the end inside the roll of fabric. Then she thrust her makeshift torch into the flames.

She laughed nervously. *Careful! You might set the house on fire.*

You're losing it, Peggy.

Then she turned and entered the room.

After the light of the burning wall outside, the small light of her improvised torch didn't illuminate the room as well as she'd hoped. But she could see better than before. The room was narrow, but deep, and the back was still shrouded in shadow. There were no windows, but there were two more doors, one on the left and one on the right, both closed. The room contained no furniture. In fact, it contained only one thing—a stairway leading up, as narrow and steep as a ladder. It reminded her of the pull-down stairs which led into her parents' attic back home.

Behind the stairs, all was cast in blackness.

"Derek?" she called.

Peggy started for the stairs, almost dropping her torch and knife in her eagerness to get to him.

In the darkness behind the stairs, a patch of blackness stirred.

A dark shape rose, standing impossibly high. Peggy couldn't hear the breathing, but she saw two large orbs of white—white eyes with black pupils.

The molossus stepped into the light of Peggy's feeble torch.

🔸 🔸 🔸

"What do you mean, they're not responding?" Todd was doing at least ninety on the freeway, weaving in and out of late-night traffic. His cell phone, operating in speaker mode, lay on the passenger seat of Peggy's car. "Your agents say the house is on fire, but you say the fire department won't come?"

"Mr. Cavetto," Thurgood Abbot said, "I made certain . . . arrangements at Morgaise Morrigan's request." The old man spoke in the slow, slightly weary tone of a patient teacher explaining something painfully obvious to a particularly slow student. "The intention was always for the house to be burned down at the end of the harvest—usually on Halloween—and the Client does not wish this to be prevented."

"Then call someone and fix it!" Todd snapped.

"I can't, not at this point. And even if I did, it wouldn't trickle down to the fire station in time to do anything. Even if they did respond, with the house already engulfed in flames, they'd let an isolated building like that burn." The lawyer's tone softened. "I'm . . . truly sorry, but there's really nothing I can do."

Todd growled in frustration and panic. *Engulfed in flames!* He wanted to shout at the old man. He wanted to hurl words he'd never, ever said aloud. But he knew that wouldn't help Peggy. And he realized the old man was probably right.

"Do what you can to help Moe," Todd said curtly.

"On my way, young man."

Todd ended the call and floored the accelerator, narrowly missing an SUV.

I'm the only help that's coming.

No. Not the only help.

"Father in Heaven, please protect Peggy."

✦ ✦ ✦

Peggy alternated between brandishing the tiny knife and waving the dim torch at the massive beast. Her hands shook so badly, she thought she might drop her puny weapons. Her legs trembled as well. She was certain that, at any moment, they would fail her, and she'd fall to her knees before the predator. She fought to control her breathing.

Why did it have to be a dog? I hate dogs!

The molossus, apparently heedless of the flames and the smoke—and of Peggy's insignificant weapons—padded toward her casually. It did not growl or bark. It merely sniffed the air.

And it drooled.

The Roman war dog, bred to be immune to the sights, sounds, and smells of the battlefield, was unafraid . . . and it was hungry.

Peggy, on the other hand, was terrified.

This dog ate Jerry. And it's going to eat me.

If we don't burn to death first.

"G-go away." Her voice sounded tiny, pathetic. "The house is on fire, you stupid dog. You'll burn. Go away."

The beast stopped suddenly a few feet away from her.

For one insane moment, Peggy thought maybe it had heard her, understood her.

Then the dog licked its lips. It growled at her then, baring fangs that would've made a lion proud.

Why doesn't it attack? What's it waiting—

The dog lunged, and Peggy shrieked. The molossus stopped short of her, its huge jaws snapping closed on empty air mere inches from Peggy's extended knife hand.

She blinked in incomprehension.

Then she saw the chain. The molossus was chained to the foot of the stair.

To make it stay, to make it guard the only way to Derek.

The dog snapped at her.

Peggy stabbed at the beast, but her hand trembled so badly, she couldn't put much force behind the blow. The knife struck the dog on the side of its massive neck, but the blade snapped off at the hilt, not even piercing the tough hide.

Peggy jumped back before the dog could attack again.

Get out of here, Peggy! You can't save him. You tried.

You failed.

"Shut up," she said aloud.

249

She swiped at the animal with her torch. The beast didn't shy away from the small flame. It merely growled at her again.

Meanwhile the heat from the hallway behind her was increasing. Her back was plastered with sweat.

What am I gonna do? I can't fight this thing! I've got nothing to fight with.

Then Peggy remembered the small canister of pepper spray. Not taking her eyes off the molossus, she patted her pocket.

Still there!

She fished the canister out, fumbled the top open and aimed the nozzle at the dog.

The massive jaws snapped at her again. Peggy flinched and dropped the pepper spray. She watched helplessly as the small canister fell to the floor, bounced, and rolled toward the dog.

No!

The molossus dropped its head and snatched the canister up in its jaws. Peggy heard a pop as the dog bit into the canister. The contents, pepper spray and propellant, exploded inside the dog's maw.

The dog yelped once, and shook its head savagely. Then it turned its malevolent eyes, now streaked with red, on Peggy. It snarled and snapped at her.

Peggy almost dropped the torch and ran.

No! I have to save Derek!

The dog's mouth was foaming now. The beast might be in pain, choking and half-blinded from the pepper spray, but it wasn't giving up.

Not just pepper spray. There was propellant in that can.

Peggy bared her teeth and snarled back at the dog. "Hey, dog! Guess what?" She grinned savagely. "Propellant's flammable."

She thrust her guttering, makeshift torch at the beast.

The monster's head was instantly engulfed in flame.

Peggy stepped back as the molossus howled in agony. The sound was horrifying—not like a dog's howl, but more like an inhuman shriek. The beast thrashed about. It ran back toward the stairs, then off to one side and then the other, trying frantically to escape the flames.

With a massive jerk, the dog broke its chain, then ran howling past her, out the door, and into the burning hallway beyond.

Peggy stared after the dog in astonishment and horror. *What a horrible way to die. Poor thing.*

Poor thing? That thing ate Jerry!

And I beat it.

I beat the molossus!

Triumph and adrenaline pounding through her veins, Peggy turned and climbed the stairs, toward the hole in the ceiling which lead to the tower. The stairway was steep, but there was a hand railing on the left side. The railing appeared to extend beyond the hole. Peggy hesitated near the top, before she could poke her head into the room above.

Where's the other one? The other dog?

Just go! Get Derek! The house is burning!

Peggy stuck her head through the hole and peered around. Moonlight filtered through the single window. The circular room was empty except for a single bed in the middle of the floor.

Peggy climbed off the stairs and onto the floor. She got to her feet and moved quickly to the bed.

Derek!

He lay on his back atop the mattress. He was dressed in a white robe. His hands were folded on his chest. His eyes were closed, his face pale. He lay unmoving, like a corpse, and the robe was his burial shroud.

"Derek!" Peggy cried.

She ran to him.

Peggy grabbed him by the shoulders and shook him. He didn't respond. "Derek! Wake up!" She felt his neck for a pulse. Nothing — and his skin was cold.

She shook him again, tears streaming down her face. "Derek, please wake up!" Her voice dropped to a pleading moan. "Please. Please don't be dead."

Peggy threw her arms around Derek's shoulders. "Please wake up. Please. I—I can't carry you out of here. You're too big, too heavy. I'm not strong enough. You have to wake up. Please, Derek. Wake up!"

She sobbed, closing her eyes and hugging him tight.

He's dead!

No, he's drugged. Just drugged!

Doesn't matter. He's gonna die here.

We're both gonna die here.

Smoke filled her mouth, and she coughed. Opening her eyes, she saw smoke wafting up from the stairway.

What'd you think you were gonna do? Scoop him up in your arms?

You're pathetic, Piggy-Peggy. You can't do anything. Ugly, fat, and worthless.

Shut up, Gollum. I beat the molossus.

251

"No!" Peggy snarled. "We're not gonna die." She released Derek's limp form and stood up straight.

"You know why we're not gonna die? Because I'm not fat. Not Piggy-Peggy. Never been fat." She shook her head. "Nope. I'm just *big-boned!*"

She rolled Derek onto his side and dragged him to the edge of the bed. She swung his legs off the bed, then yanked him to a slumped sitting position. She grabbed Derek's arms, turned her back to him, and pulled his arms over her shoulders. She planted her legs, hoisted Derek onto her back, and stood.

"Come on, Sleeping Beauty. We're getting out of here."

And carrying Derek, Peggy staggered toward the stairs.

At the edge of the opening, she stopped. Smoke billowed up through the hole, blocking her view of the stairs. She glanced over at the barred single window, then focused on the stairs.

Only way out.

She carried Derek over to the side of the hole where the stairs should have been, turned around, reached blindly into the smoke, and grasped the hand railing. She had to clamp her right arm down tight over Derek's arms to keep him in place, to keep him from sliding off her back.

Heavenly Father. Help me. Guide me.

Peggy sucked in a deep breath and held it. She closed her eyes and bearing all of her own weight and Derek's weight as well on one trembling leg, she lowered a foot into the smoke.

Her questing foot found a step. She almost gasped in relief. She took another step down. And another. She could feel heat on the backs of her legs.

Room's on fire.

Doesn't matter. Keep going.

She took another step.

How many steps are there?

Just keep going.

The air in her lungs burned. *Gotta breathe!*

Keep going.

I don't remember this many steps. Too many steps!

Gotta breathe!

Her foot struck something more solid than a stair.

Floor!

She collapsed to the floor, landing hard on her chest. Derek's dead weight crashed atop her, knocking the breath from her lungs. Peggy rolled him off her back and sucked in air.

Hot, but free of smoke.

She lay gasping for a moment, catching her breath.

I did it! I got Derek out of the tower.

She laughed weakly.

Now just have to get us out of a burning house. No big deal.

Opening her eyes, she saw that the room wasn't entirely filled with smoke. *Because the smoke has somewhere to go — up into the tower.* She looked toward the door. The open door and doorframe were ablaze; the hallway beyond, lost in fire and smoke.

The wet robe she had dropped in the doorway steamed and bubbled, charring at the edges. With the doorway aflame, there was no way to get back to the stairs.

They were trapped.

XXVIII

As he scrambled out of Peggy's car, Todd watched in shock and horror as a large section of the roof collapsed. The entire front half of the house was ablaze, a yellow wall of flame lighting up the night. The intense heat struck him like a blast from a furnace, driving him away from the house. He sprinted toward the rear. The back wasn't all in flames . . . yet.

Please, God, get Peggy to the back of the house!

As he rounded the corner of the inferno, he searched for a way in. Parts of the rear wall were burning. Smoke billowed from the windows, all of which were open, each one covered with wrought-iron bars. But nearly half the back side of the house was not yet ablaze.

He spied the back door, ran to it, and tested, then tried the knob. *Locked!* He kicked door—hard. The doorframe splintered. He kicked again, harder, and the door flew inward. Smoke rushed out and up the wall. Through the doorway, Todd could see nothing but blackness.

"Peggy!" he yelled. "Peggy!"

The only responses were the roar of flames and the cracking of wood.

Downed helicopter blazing on an Afghani mountainside.

Dragging an injured crewman from the inferno.

The man's face —

"Not now!" he growled. "Focus, blast you!"

Stay low. He took a deep breath, held it, and bent to a crouch. *I'm coming, Peggy.*

The instant he entered the house, smoke stung his eyes, causing him to clamp them shut. He swung his arms wide, left and right, up and down, blindly feeling his way.

Guide me to her, Father!

His right hand brushed against cloth. Todd turned to his right. He reached out with both hands and felt a shoulder, a head, the soft, yielding flesh of a breast. *A woman! Sitting on a chair? Peggy?*

254

Looping an arm across the woman's chest and under her armpit, he lifted her up and hauled her toward the door. He felt his way along the wall, found the splintered doorframe, and dragged his burden into the open air.

He opened his eyes and looked at the woman. The soot-grayed hood had fallen away from her face.

Not Peggy.

He carried her a few yards from the house, laid her on the ground, and ran back into blackness.

◆ ◆ ◆

The roof came crashing down in front of Peggy.

With a thunderous *CRACK-CRACK-BOOM*, flaming timbers fell in the hallway, tearing through the floor. For a moment, the full moon shone through the doorway, surrounded by the dark sky. A rush of cool night air hit Peggy, refreshing as a summer rain. Then the flames leapt up all the higher, cutting off her brief glimpse of a world beyond the inferno.

Peggy and Derek were trapped. There was no longer any way forward, through the fire or otherwise.

Peggy scrambled back, crablike, away from the roaring blaze. She grabbed a fistful of Derek's robe and shirt collar, and hauled him away from the flames as well.

No way out!

Can't go forward.

So, left? Or right?

Running out of time!

"Heavenly Father, show me the way," she muttered in fervent, urgent prayer.

Left! Peggy wasn't sure if the thought was her own or the whispering of the Spirit, but she didn't question it.

She flipped over onto her stomach. Still dragging Derek by the collar, hoping she wasn't choking him—*He's not breathing, remember? He's not dead!*—Peggy crawled toward the left door.

When she reached the door, she raised a hand to test the knob. A few inches from the knob, she paused.

So what if it's hot? Nowhere else to go!

She grabbed the knob—which, thankfully, was no hotter than the air around them—and twisted. The door opened a crack and stopped.

Smoke and flames did not burst out of that crack, so Peggy pushed at the door. It didn't budge. *Stuck! Maybe the doorframe shifted?* She twisted around on her back and brought her foot to bear. She kicked at the bottom of the door. It moved, but no more than an inch or two. She kicked with both feet, and the door swung open. Spinning around again, Peggy crawled through the open doorway, tugging Derek's dead weight behind her. The chamber wasn't as hot as the room they'd just left, so Peggy kicked the door repeatedly to close it again.

She glanced around. Flames ate hungrily at the wall closest to the front of the house, but the rest of the room was free of fire . . . for the moment. The room—a bedroom—was spacious, almost palatial, with a huge canopied bed, sofa, vanity with a lighted mirror, two chairs, two dressers, standing bird perch, and massive armoire. An open door at the other end of the room led to what Peggy assumed must be a bathroom. There were two barred, open windows. However, unlike every other window she'd encountered, there were no sacrificial victims sitting in front of them.

Elaine's room. Peggy felt sure Morgaise wouldn't sit before a lighted makeup mirror.

With a *whoosh*, the bed canopy erupted in flames. Ash and embers swirled and drifted down through the air like flurries of gray and orange snow.

Peggy jerked away from the burning bed. *Running out of time!*

The back wall wasn't aflame yet, so Peggy dragged Derek toward the nearest window. Standing up, she could see the yard outside, with its ring of standing stones. The spooky tree, however, had been cut down. Only a stump remained.

Peggy tugged futilely at the bars, shaking them with all her strength. But they wouldn't budge. She tried the other window, but had no more success there.

She looked around the room, fighting panic. *There has to be a way out! There has to be!*

Smoke poured from the bathroom door.

Not smoke.

Steam!

Peggy dashed to the bathroom door. She ducked low to avoid the steam and peered inside. She found the normal accoutrements of a bathroom—toilet, sink, and tub. The tub was old-fashioned, metal and free-standing, perched on cast-iron claws. A shower curtain hung from the ceiling. The floor below had broken partway and the tub canted downward toward the back wall at an angle of twenty degrees or so. Flames licked up through the fractured floor. A shower pipe, running from the floor, was bent at a more severe angle than the tub itself.

And water sprayed from a kink in that pipe.

The water sprayed in a declined fan, hitting the metal tub and the flames beyond it, generating the steam she'd seen.

A fierce grin split Peggy's face.

She went to the tub and turned on the cold water faucet. The water came out hot, of course, but it wasn't scalding. *Not scalding . . . yet.*

Water pooled at the lower end of the tub.

Peggy turned back to get to Derek.

The bedroom was ablaze now. The bed and half the room were enveloped in flame and smoke.

Peggy dropped to her hands and knees and crawled quickly toward Derek. She grabbed him by the collar and dragged him as fast as she could toward the bathroom, keeping as much distance between them and the flames as possible.

By the time she had dragged Derek through the bathroom door, the tub had tilted down even more. It dropped into the floor at a forty-degree angle.

Faster, Peggy! It'll go any moment.

Only gonna get one shot at this.

She lay beside Derek and pulled him onto her back. Holding his arms around her neck as she'd done in the tower, she struggled to her feet.

"Either you're gaining weight, pretty boy," she said with a grunt, "or I'm just running out of steam." She chuckled, and to her own ears, it sounded more like a sob. "Steam. Get it?"

You're losing it, Peggy.

She stepped to the edge of the hole where the tub, its lower end now filled with steaming water, slanted downward into the flaming cauldron below. "This is nuts."

With Derek on her back, Peggy leaned forward, twisted around, and fell into the tub.

With a creak, a pop, and a groan, the floor gave way, and the tub, with Peggy and Derek inside, slid forward and down into the fiery jaws of Hell.

🌢 🌢 🌢

Todd's lungs burned from the strain of holding his breath. Five times he'd gone into the house, going a little deeper each time, holding his breath longer and longer. Five times he'd returned with a robed figure. And none of them was Peggy.

Please let this one be her!

He hauled his sixth rescue out of the house. The breath exploded from his lungs, and he sucked in air. Then he got a look at the face of the woman he carried, and groaned in frustration and panic.

Every few feet — another one. Could be dozens of them.

Don't think about it, Cavetto. Just keep going.

I'll find her.

I have to find her.

He laid the woman next to the five other unconscious Druids, then sprinted for the house, ignoring his exhaustion, dehydration, and terror at the almost certain knowledge that Peggy was still inside, burning alive.

A loud *CRACK* stopped him from plunging back into the smoke. He wheeled to his left, panting hard.

With a *BOOM* like a thunderclap, the wall at the far end of the house exploded. Something long and white flew out of the house, crashing onto the lawn a couple of yards from the wall.

Todd stumbled toward the long, semicylindrical object.

A bathtub?

The tub lay on its side, its claw-feet pointing at Todd. Something moved at the top rim of the tub.

A hand.

The hand was followed by a head. Then a woman climbed shakily to her feet. She bent down, almost disappearing behind the tub again.

"Peggy?" he yelled.

No response.

He ran toward her, calling Peggy's name.

She reemerged from behind the tub, dragging the limp figure of a man.

A burst of flame illuminated her face.

She was drenched from her stringy hair to her soggy sneakers. Steam rose from her body. Soot streaked her face.

And she was beautiful.

"Peggy!" he roared.

Still she seemed oblivious to him, all her attention focused on dragging an unconscious man away from the tub, away from the fire. She had barely made it a couple of yards before dropping her burden on the lawn. She stumbled backward and toppled toward the grass.

Todd caught her, scooping her up in his arms as if she were a child. He spun around, dancing, staggering with unbounded joy and mind-cleansing relief. All the exhaustion and horror of the past several minutes evaporated as he laughed and wept in delight. "You're alive!"

Peggy gaped at him. "Todd?" Her face split in a wide, heart-stopping smile. "Todd!" She threw sopping wet arms around him and hugged him, pressing her cheek to his.

He wanted to kiss her, to smother her soot-streaked face in kisses. *Derek can . . .*

"Derek!" they both cried at the same time.

Peggy struggled out of his arms. She dropped to her knees and bent over the man lying on the grass in a soaked robe.

Derek?

Todd knelt beside Peggy. "You . . . got him out!"

She looked up at Todd with a ferocious, triumphant grin. "Yes!"

Todd shook his head in awe. *Incredible woman.*

Peggy's grin vanished, and she bent once more over Derek. "He's not breathing! He's drugged. The fruit of that awful tree. It's what they use to go to sleep for—" Her voice broke. "Please! He can't be dead!"

Todd pushed her aside as quickly and gently as he could. He bent his ear to listen and feel for breathing. Nothing.

"Do CPR!" Peggy urged.

"Hold on." *If I start CPR, I'll probably break his ribs.* He put two fingers to Derek's carotid artery.

Nothing.

He's so cold.

No! Wait!

One pulse—faint, almost imperceptible.

Todd waited a few seconds more.

Another pulse.

Todd licked his fingers with an almost dry tongue. He held the moistened fingertips under Derek's nostrils . . . and detected a slight cooling.

"He's alive."

"Thank you!" she whispered. "Thank you, Heavenly Father. Thank you!"

"I think he's okay," Todd said. "Moe said it's something like suspended animation."

Peggy caressed Derek's brow and cheek. "Yeah. Elaine said something like that too." A sound somewhere between a sob and a laugh burst from her. "He's alive! You're going to be all right, Derek. Just . . . Just hold on."

An ugly wave of jealousy ripped through Todd. He stared down at the man for whom Peggy had braved even the raging inferno

What's wrong, Cavetto? Wish he'd died in there?

He shook his head. *No.* Then his whole body trembled. *No. I'm glad he made it. I just . . . envy him.*

He turned his gaze on Peggy as she ran her fingers through Derek's wet hair. She looked at Derek with unabashed love and longing. *I wish you'd look at me that way. Just once.* Then Todd smiled. "You're amazing. You know that?"

Peggy turned her face toward him. She looked confused. "What?"

Todd smiled and shook his head. "Nothing." He pointed in the direction of six prone figures he'd rescued. "Drag Derek over there, with the others . . . if you can. He should be safe enough there."

She turned her head toward the unconscious Druids. "Okay. Those people—you got them *all* out?"

Todd got to his feet. "Yeah."

"Why?"

The corners of Todd's mouth twitched, forming the ghost of a sad smile. "I thought . . . they might be you."

"Where're you going?" she asked in a voice filled with panic.

"Back inside."

He turned and ran toward the inferno.

◢ ◢ ◢

Todd's first foray back into the house yielded no one. He'd been cut off by flames, and been forced to make his way outside, empty-handed, to breathe. He bent over and put hands on his knees, sucking in air to fill his burning lungs.

He looked over at Peggy. She'd gotten Derek over with the others and was cradling his head in her lap. Todd waved at her.

She yelled something, but Todd couldn't hear it over the roar of the flames. She waved frantically with both hands and shook her head vehemently.

Probably telling me not to go back in.

Sorry, pretty lady. Gotta go. Gotta save as many as I can.

It's what I do.

He smiled. "I love you," he whispered, and turned and reentered the house.

Todd went to the left this time, feeling his way, desperately searching for another door or another victim. He stumbled over something. He dropped to his knees and probed with his hands.

A woman!

He picked up the limp form, slung her over his shoulder, and staggered back the way he'd come. He felt the house tremble around him.

This is it! The whole thing's coming down.

He bumped into something, backed away, suddenly uncertain of the direction. *I'm lost!*

His lungs ached. *Gotta breathe.*

No!

He forced himself to keep moving, his hand questing blindly in the dark for a wall, a door—for anything familiar.

A rush of cooler air hit him. He turned to follow it . . . and felt the doorframe.

Todd stumbled out the door and collapsed on the grass, his human burden dropping beside him. The air in his lungs exploded out his mouth, and he greedily breathed in huge gulps of air.

He allowed himself only a moment's rest, then got to his knees, hoisted the woman onto his shoulder, and rose to his feet.

That's the last one. Can't go back.

As if in confirmation, he heard the house crashing down behind him, but he didn't look back.

He had eyes only for Peggy.

But Peggy wasn't there.

He spied the prostrate forms of the other Druids he'd saved, but he couldn't see Peggy or Derek. He broke into a lurching run.

When he reached the bodies, he stopped. He laid the woman on the ground and stared at the Druids. All six were there, all the people he'd risked his life to save.

And they were all dead. Their throats had been sliced open. Crimson stained their once-white robes.

"Peggy!" He looked around, frantically searching for her. He ran all the way around the huge pile of burning wood that had once been a house.

But he saw no sign of Peggy . . . or Derek.

Todd saw no evidence of any living person, except for the last victim he'd pulled from the flames.

Peggy was gone. Derek too.

But Todd knew exactly who had taken them.

Morgaise.

He dashed toward Peggy's car.

I'm coming, Peggy.

XXIX

Moses Abbot was normally not a man to jump at shadows. However, the wavering, smoky light from a trio of braziers seemed to make everything in the cavern tremble, gave every shadow life. Twice he'd been certain he'd seen something moving just at the edge of sight, but nothing moved except the shadows.

Moe wasn't exactly alone in the cave—a pair of white-robed women lay comatose on the cavern floor near a rock wall, each still clutching a piece of round, golden fruit—two pieces of fruit, each missing a single bite. No, he wasn't exactly alone, but a pair of pagan Snow Whites didn't count.

They still gave him the creeps.

This whole place gives me the creeps.

Low flames provided dim illumination in the deep chamber. The braziers, with their smoke that smelled of charcoal, rendered animal fat, and cloves—like an Easter ham that'd roasted too long—gave the place an air of Dark Ages mysticism. Against the far wall, in the deepest, darkest shadows of the cave, lay a large wooden bed. The fires, the smoke, the smell, and the deathlike Druids would've been more than sufficient to unnerve Moe.

But there was also the gibbet.

The massive wooden structure, not unlike the frame of a child's backyard swing set—a swing set proportioned for giants, only without the swings—stood in the middle of the floor. The heavy crossbeam was equipped with a sturdy hook and a noose. The hanging rope ran through a system of pulleys and then to a winch anchored to the A-frame sides of the gallows.

And beside the gibbet, sat an old-fashioned metal washtub, ready and waiting to catch blood.

This is where Todd's friend Jerry must've died. This is where the Morrigans strung up a warrior and drained his blood.

Moe shuddered at the image.

What was that?!?

He spun around, his handgun at the ready. *Could've sworn . . . Something moved.*

Just shadows, Moses.

You're jumping at shadows.

Moe wiped fear sweat from his brow with a clammy palm. Then he wiped his hand on his shirt.

He forced himself to examine the gallows once more. The frame was held together with carriage bolts and nuts. *It's meant to be disassembled and moved — moved to the next location. My grandfather said it was gonna be Montana. Then why are they planning on sleeping here? Why not Montana?*

Could it have something to do with the harvest coming early?

A low moaning sound.

Moe uttered a decidedly unmanly squeak. He whipped his weapon from side to side.

The Druids?

Double-checking that his index finger was pointed safely down the barrel of the gun and not poised on the trigger, Moe calmed his frenzied breathing and approached the two sleeping women.

Neither had moved.

He prodded the nearest with his foot.

No response.

He knelt beside the woman and shook her shoulder. When he entered into the chamber from a long, unlit tunnel and found them sleeping, he tried to wake them. He wanted to question one of them, but had no more success at waking them this time than he had the first time he tried.

He tweaked the Druid's fine nose.

Still no response.

The Druids were still alive — Moe was certain of that. Earlier, he'd checked for a pulse and discovered a faint and regular — if extremely slow — heartbeat. He frowned in annoyance and frustration. *I thought human touch — skin-on-skin contact — was supposed to "break the spell," but . . . nothing.*

He heard the low moan again.

Moe leapt to his feet and scanned the cave. The urge to put his finger around the trigger was nearly irresistible.

Keep it together, Moses.

His gun hand shook so badly, he was afraid he'd drop the weapon. *Gotta be the wind. Wind across the mouth of the cave. That's all it is.*

Keep it together.

He took a deep, shuddering breath and held it. When his lungs screamed for oxygen, Moe exhaled. He breathed in again, his breathing steady once more.

Moe resumed his examination of the chamber.

How do they keep this place a secret? Sure, there are the dogs . . . Hold on — where are the dogs?

He whipped around again. *The last moan sounded almost like a growl.*

A shadow moved, just on the edge of his peripheral vision.

Moe spun toward it. Nothing. *Just a gallows shadow.*

Could've sworn it looked like a man . . . or an animal.

Just finish scouting this place and then get the heck out. Call Todd, report what you've seen. Figure out what to do next.

He walked over to the bed. The wooden bed frame was ornate, carved with pagan symbols and animals figures, and wide enough for three — but only a single pillow lay at the head. A luxurious, emerald-green comforter covered the thick mattress.

I half-expected glass coffins.

But just one *pillow?*

At the head of the bed, Moe found a small wooden box with a rounded lid, reminiscent of a stereotypical pirate treasure chest. The box was unlocked, so Moe knelt and opened it. A cursory glance inside revealed a curious collection of small objects — a pen knife, a silver pocket watch, a fife, a man's ring. But on top of them all sat a cell phone.

This must belong to young Derek.

I'd bet these are Elaine's treasures — mementos of past lovers.

Best to leave these undisturbed for now.

Moe closed the lid and checked out the other end of the bed.

At the foot of the bed sat another wooden box — about a foot square and eight inches deep. Moe bent to examine the small, flat chest. It appeared to be ancient, the wood well-oiled, with leather hinges at the back and a simple leather-and-wood latch at the front. Engraved on the lid was a stylized likeness of a tree.

A thrill of horror and fascination shook Moe.

I know what this is!

With trembling fingers, he undid the latch and lifted the lid.

The box was divided into three compartments. The center compartment contained slices of fruit, white on the inside with golden skin. The left compartment held green leaves — the right, small dark seeds.

This is from that horrid tree.

Moe reached into the box to extract a couple of the seeds, but stopped himself abruptly. He recalled his grandfather's warning and what he, himself, had seen first-hand earlier that night. He checked his hands for even the tiniest spot of blood.

His hands weren't precisely clean, but he hadn't scratched himself during his climb up the hillside to the cave. He wiped his hands on his jeans just to be sure.

Then he carefully picked up two of the small seeds. He examined them — they looked like apple or pear seeds — and tucked them into his left breast pocket, securing the pocket's button.

I know a botanist at BYU who'd love to examine these.

On impulse, he took one of the leaves and stuck it in his breast pocket as well. He left the golden fruit alone.

The fruit might be missed, but I doubt they'll notice the absence of a couple of seeds and a leaf.

He closed and relatched the lid.

The low sound, halfway between a moan and a growl, returned, startling him. Moe spun around, brandishing his weapon.

Still nothing.

But something in the shadows moved.

No. The shadow itself moved. Man-shaped, with stag horns growing out of its head, the thing of darkness advanced, looming larger as it approached, reaching for him with hands of midnight.

Moe fired into the black shape. The muzzle flashes lit the chamber like a strobe light, but the dark thing did not fade.

Moe screamed as the shadow enveloped him.

♦ ♦ ♦

Thurgood Abbot clamped a trembling, bony hand over his own mouth. White jets of steam shot from his flaring nostrils — the stifled, tortured wheezes of an old man of ninety-five who had labored to climb a mountain path in the cold night air.

But he *had* to quiet his labored breathing. He had to be silent.

Silent as the grave.

The grave? He almost laughed at the absurdity.

I should've been in my grave long ago.

And why aren't you in your grave, counselor? Why didn't you just blow your brains out like your son did? You could've done that. Then you never would've had to live through a second, damnable Covenant year. So, why didn't you, you old fool?

Because I'm a coward. I'm more of a coward than my son. He abandoned

life to escape. But I'm too afraid of what awaits me . . . on the other side.
I'm too afraid to pay the price of my sins.

He saw them again—five hooded figures toiling up the path Thurgood had just left. He'd scrambled off the path and into the scrub. The old man tried to shrink in on himself as he crouched behind a bush.

And he watched them come.

Four of the figures, walking in pairs, carried stretchers between them, and there appeared to be a body on each stretcher. However, Thurgood couldn't be sure they were human bodies. The moon was bright, but not bright enough for Thurgood—even with his sharp eyesight, undimmed by age—to see everything, especially through the branches of the bush.

The figure trailing the procession was not burdened with a litter. Two black shapes, one on each shoulder, bobbed and flapped dark wings as the figure climbed.

Morgaise. With those ravens. It has to be. But where's Elaine?

In spite of centuries of strict instructions and whispered tales, much about the Client was still a mystery to Thurgood. However from what he'd seen and been told, he was certain of one thing at least—Morgaise Morrigan would never allow her younger sister to carry anything heavier than a purse, much less half the dead weight of a human body. Hideous Morgaise doted on the pretty Elaine.

Maybe Elaine's already in the cave.

With Moses.

What a pathetic joke! You came to help your grandson. You, Thurgood Abbot. You couldn't save . . . Just what were you hoping to do?

Thurgood had no answer.

For perhaps the hundredth time that night, he cursed Todd Cavetto.

If not for that barbarian, there'd be other strong hands to help me, to do this for me.

Oh, really, counselor? Is it not true that without Mr. Cavetto's intervention, you would simply be burying your aged head in the sand like a geriatric ostrich, passing the Abbot curse along to yet another generation?

And just what is the likelihood of success? Not likely at all.

Especially if I'm caught pissing my expensive suit pants on this mountainside.

The dogs would surely sniff me . . .

Where are the dogs?

Thurgood was almost as frightened of those monstrous beasts as he was of Morgaise.

266

Almost. Nothing in this world frightened the old lawyer more than the evil woman climbing the path below.

Not even those damnable dogs.

Then a black shape passed in front of Morgaise, the beast nearly as tall as she was. And once Thurgood was able to see one dog, he spied them all—black shapes moving in the darkness.

A fresh thrill of terror nearly made him yelp.

There must be half a dozen of them!

Thurgood shuddered and fought to control his bladder.

Don't wet yourself, old fool! They'll smell urine for certain.

They'll likely smell you anyway. Smell your cologne, your old-man odor.

Thurgood almost turned to crawl farther into the scrub like a frightened rat scurrying for cover, to flee from the monsters—canine and human—approaching his pathetic hiding place.

Stop! They'll hear you!

He closed his eyes, shutting out the sight of the fiends—the fiends, but not his own memories. In an instant, he was back in 1955, back digging that grave for his friend, Father Hank Malloy. He could feel the hot breath of the dog, smell its reek as it watched him, drooling over him.

He remembered the alien feeling of that evil seed twitching in his fingers as it touched the priest's blood.

In his mind's eye, he saw the Druids, the Morrigans' disciples, invading his home, tearing him and his wife from their bed, forcing him to watch as they stripped his wife and flogged her, as they raped his . . .

Trapped between the nightmares of the past and the horrors of the present, Thurgood opened his eyes.

They were nearly upon him.

He held his breath as the first pair of figures, a pair of women, passed his position. The litter borne between them did indeed carry the supine form of a woman. She wasn't wearing a robe. Black grime streaked her face. Steam rose off her body as if she were wet.

Be careful, missy. You'll catch your death.

He suppressed an insane giggle. *I'm going mad.*

As they passed, he slowly released his pent-up breath, quietly drew in another, and held it.

The second pair passed his position—two men, this time, bearing an unconscious man on their litter. The sleeping man was clad in a filthy robe, but it was wet and steaming as well. The man's face was dirty too, but Thurgood had seen enough surveillance photos to be certain this was Derek Rasmussen.

Wasn't he supposed to die in the house fire? A sacrifice to their blood-thirsty god? That's what happens to all Elaine's beaus, isn't it?

Perhaps so, but there he is, presumably still alive.

Morgaise's plans must have gone seriously awry.

The best laid plans of Morrigans and men . . .

And when things do not go as planned, people make mistakes.

Thurgood did not have time to take another breath before Morgaise Morrigan approached. Her hood was thrown back, and the setting moon caught her face, illuminating it with a ghostly light.

Thurgood heard a sound as of a child whimpering.

The whimpering issued from his own quivering lips.

He forced himself to be silent.

As the grave.

In the moonlight, Morgaise appeared to be smiling — with only half her face, of course. She laid a hand against her cheek, tilted her head, and sighed.

She's . . . happy about this . . . unexpected development?

The dogs trotted around her.

No, not all of them. One walked dutifully at her side. The others capered about, playfully nipping at each other as if they were —

Puppies? But they're nearly fully grown!

Thurgood counted six of the demon spawn, in addition to the adult beast.

Seven of them!

One of the giant pups broke away from the pack and trotted right up to Thurgood's hiding place, sniffing as it came.

No, no, no, no, no! Please, just go away!

Thurgood fought the urge to reach for his Taser. *Wouldn't even faze that thing!*

Upon reaching the old man's hiding place, the man-eating puppy sniffed the bush. It froze, alert. The dog seemed to stare right through the puny plant, straight into Thurgood's eyes.

Mary, mother of God . . .

The dog turned, lifted its leg, and urinated on the bush, barely missing the quaking old man hiding behind it. Then the dog huffed as if to say, *Your meat's too tough and stringy for my taste,* and then it scampered away to catch up with its siblings.

Thurgood stared after the beast and the procession of human and canine demons as they climbed up and away from him.

At last, he let out his breath. His aged heart pounded in his thin chest. The sour stench of urine filled his nostrils. He wasn't entirely certain if all the smell was due simply to the dog. And he didn't particularly care.

No hope! Can't do anything. Just a worthless, old man. Old slave. Old fool.

Can't even make the climb.

And what would you do if you could, counselor?

Nothing.

I can't help Moses. Only God can.

And the barbarian.

Thurgood's hands quaked as he fumbled his phone out of his suit coat pocket.

◆ ◆ ◆

The world had turned to blood.

Moe fought to make sense of a world cast entirely in shades of crimson—a world turned upside-down.

Where am I?

But he knew exactly where he was—hanging from the gallows, strung up by his feet, the blood pooling in his head, in his eyes . . . in his hands. His ears pounded—he could hear his own labored heart beating. He could hear other things too—panting, growling, the sounds of something—or rather *somethings*—feasting.

He shut his eyes, trying to ignore the grisly sounds. Then he opened his eyes again and looked up, or rather down, toward his throbbing hands. They dangled over the metal washtub, which had been placed right below him. "No," he moaned. "Not that!" He tried to lift his swollen arms. The pain was excruciating.

"Are you all right?"

Moe let his arms drop. He recognized that voice. "E-Elaine? M-Miss Mo-Mor-rigan?"

She came into his field of view. Her pretty face was cast in dancing shadows. Dressed in a robe, which appeared red to Moe's blood-engorged eyes, Elaine stood before him—upside-down—wringing her hands. "You're that Roman—the centurion. Not really a Roman. It was just a mummery . . . a play . . . for the faire. You . . . you spoke kindly to me . . . and after I nearly . . ." She buried her face in her hands.

Moe heard a muffled sob. *She's weeping?*

"Miss Morrigan . . . Elaine, p-please." Moe struggled to keep the panic and terror out of his dry, rasping voice. Breathing was so difficult. It felt unnatural. "Please . . . let me down."

Elaine snuffled, and wiped her eyes and nose with the sleeve of her robe. She shook her head. "I can't. I'm sorry. My sister won't let me."

She beat her tiny fists upon her thighs. "Everything has gone so wrong! I tried to save them! I did! I love Derek, don't you see? I truly, truly love him. And I love Peggy so dearly too. She is so kind to me. So sweet." Elaine wiped at her eyes again. "Nobody has ever been so sweet to me, n-not even . . . not even Morgaise. Peggy" — Elaine sobbed — "would have given up Derek for me. She would've let me run away with him. She would've saved me too if she could. And she *loves* him! Why would she give him up if she loved him?"

Elaine put her fists to her temples as if her head ached. "Why is Peggy so kind to me?"

Moe tried to nod. The movement sent a spike of agony shooting through his spine. "She's" — he grunted with the pain — "a good woman. Elaine, please let me down."

Elaine shut her eyes tight and thumped her temples with her fists. "I can't! Morgaise is letting me take them with us. She's letting me take Peggy and Derek with us!" She opened her eyes and stared at him sadly, shaking her head. "I'm sorry. I truly am. But I have to save them. I can't save you too. I would if I could. I truly would. Please believe me! Say you believe me, please?"

And in that moment, in spite of his own peril, in spite of the pain, Moses Abbot understood, on a level he couldn't have articulated, how this beautiful, vulnerable creature had captured the hearts of so many men across two millennia. He understood how she had ensnared his ancestor, Lucius, so many centuries ago. *Helen of Troy.*

Not Helen.

And Moe knew he still had one card left to play.

"I know . . . I know who you are," Moe rasped.

Elaine froze. Then her hands dropped to her sides, the fists uncurled. Her eyes were frightened, but wary. "What? What do you mean?"

Moe had come across two names in his brief research that afternoon. *Was it really just this afternoon?* He wasn't even sure if he was right, but the time period fit, as did Elaine's fear of Romans. *But they could be anybody. They don't have to be someone famous from history, but . . .*

"Tasca," he said.

Elaine's eyes opened wide in shock.

Or rather, one of them did.

Half her face twisted with rage.

The other half sagged, drooping lifelessly.

Morgaise?! Elaine and Morgaise are —

"NO!" Morgaise screamed. She leapt toward Moe and slapped him hard across the face.

Pain exploded in his blood-engorged head, red and white lights flashing before his eyes. Moe spun and swung on the rope like a worm bobbing at the end of a fishing pole. A wave of nausea descended from the pit of his stomach.

"Never speak that name!" Morgaise screamed. "Never! Do you hear me? NEVER!"

Moe opened his eyes.

The chamber whirled and jerked around him like a spinning kaleidoscope where all the colors were shades of blood. He caught glimpses of parts of the cave he hadn't been able to see since he'd regained consciousness.

And he wished he'd kept his eyes closed.

A woman and a man lay on their backs upon the huge bed. He'd seen them only once—and in better light—but he recognized them— Peggy and Derek. They were asleep, like the Druids he'd seen before.

But it was the Druids themselves that he wished he could erase from his memory. There were more of them now. Perhaps half a dozen lying on the floor of the cavern.

And they were being devoured by the molossii—eaten alive. Blood and body parts were everywhere.

"*I* protect Tasca!" Morgaise shrieked. "It is *my* duty!" She swung again at Moe as he bobbed—and missed. She swung once more, still failing to connect.

Morgaise screamed in wordless fury. She spun away from him.

As Moe turned and swayed on the rope, he caught a glimpse of something else, a black shadow on the cave wall, man-shaped and antlered—a shadow cast by nothing and no one.

What is that thing? What did it do to me? He remembered only overwhelming cold and darkness and absolute despair from when the shadow attacked him.

A cold voice whispered in Moe's mind. *I am Cernunnos, the Horned One. I was ancient before your God was born. Look on me, Christian, and despair.* The shadow raised its arms, and grew till it seemed to fill the cavern. *You have entered my place, my temple. You shall nourish me with your blood. And the dogs shall consume your flesh.* And in that voice, Moe sensed an undying hatred of all living flesh, a profound envy of any mortal who had ever possessed a physical body. *And in exchange for your sacrifice, I will guard my consort during her long sleep.*

"*I* protect Elaine," Morgaise snarled. She seemed oblivious to the presence of the dark entity she worshipped. *"I protect my sister — not you, interloper."*

Moe ripped his attention away from the enemy of shadow. He focused instead on the enemy of flesh and blood. His spinning back and forth had slowed — almost stopped — and he was facing toward Morgaise, more or less.

However, Morgaise wasn't looking at him, wasn't even speaking to him. She had turned toward the bed, toward Peggy. "I don't know how you escaped the Burning Man. But you have defied the gods. For that alone you should die. However, I promised my sister I would bring you here and let you sleep. I have fulfilled that promise. But I did not promise you would come with us into the next life. You thought to steal my sister from me, woman, to steal Elaine's love. You will not!"

Morgaise drew a knife from her belt and raised it. It gleamed red in the brazier light through Moe's blood-tinged vision.

No! Stop her!

"Camorra!" Moe's voice was hoarse. It wasn't loud, but it had the desired effect.

Morgaise froze.

"Camorra, don't do it!" Moe croaked.

Morgaise turned toward him, knife still raised.

But the woman who gazed upon Moses Abbot was no longer Morgaise, no longer Camorra. Both halves of her face sagged, devoid of expression — a mask of death and decay. "You will not speak that name." The harsh voice was a whisper — the hissing of vipers.

"Wh-who are you?" Moe asked. His head felt as if it might explode. *It's like an extreme case of MPD — with physical manifestations!* "Are you . . . Queen Boudicca?"

Expressionless eyes glared at him from lifeless lids, but the knife hand lowered slightly. "I do what must be done to protect Tasca and Camorra. And just who are you, Roman?"

The dry voice sent a fresh tremor of fear ripping through Moe's spine. "I'm the man who's going to stop you."

How?

I don't know. He almost shook his head. *I don't know, but I trust in my mother's dream.*

The crone laughed — a harsh, evil sound like the cracking of dried bones. "You? Stop me? You're going to die, Roman. You're going to feed my god."

Moe tried to force a laugh. It came out as a choking gurgle. "I've seen your god. He's just" — Moe attempted to swallow, but couldn't — "just a shadow."

"He bested you, Roman. I will drain your blood and pour it like wine on the ground as an offering. But first, I will deal with the sister-stealer." She turned back toward the bed . . . and Peggy.

Moe fought to ignore his growing nausea, the horrible sounds of the molossii feasting on Druid flesh, the horned shadow on the wall, and the pain in his arms and head. He focused on one thing — stopping the crone from murdering Peggy.

Confront her with her delusion. "Boudicca, you have no sisters, no daughters, no mother."

The crone stopped, turning about to face him again.

"It's just you," he said, doing his best to fall back into the role of priest, counselor, bishop. "You're too young to be Boudicca. Besides, Boudicca had red hair. You must be one of the daughters — Camorra or Tasca. Today, we call it multiple personality disorder — MPD. You couldn't face what happened to you, to your mother, to your sister. You failed to protect your sister, didn't you? You lost her, so you *became* her. Which one are you really? Tasca or Camorra?"

"You lie." She didn't even sound rattled. The crone turned back toward Peggy and poised the knife against the sleeping woman's throat.

"One comes!" The voice came from nowhere and everywhere. Moe heard the demon in his mind, but the crone seemed to hear it as well that time.

She spun around and cried, "Gaius, *interfice!*"

The sounds of dogs ripping and gobbling flesh abruptly ceased — to be replaced by deep-throated growls.

Moe rotated his throbbing head toward the mouth of the chamber just in time to see a man enter, bent in a wary crouch.

Todd.

The molossii attacked.

XXX

Todd fired his Glock into the pack of giant dogs, trying to pick specific targets and to aim chest-high at each beast. The first shot dropped its intended target. The second and third had no visible effect.

The gunshots were deafening in the close confines of the cave, the muzzle flashes burning white spots on Todd's retinas. Most of the pack paused, confused and frightened by the booms and the flashes. Two winged, black shapes screeched and flapped past Todd, toward the exit, distracting him for an instant.

The largest molossus lunged forward, heedless of the havoc of battle. Todd fired twice into its chest. The dog barely flinched. Todd fired twice more, and the beast collapsed mere feet away.

"Gaius!" came an anguished cry. "No! No!"

The other dogs charged. Todd fired eight times more, emptying his clip. Three more hounds fell.

Two remained.

Still holding the weapon by its grip, Todd swung it like a bludgeon, striking at the nearest dog. Sharp fangs sank into his left forearm from above and below. He roared in pain and crushed the animal's skull with the gun barrel. The beast held on still, its jaws locked about Todd's arm, even as the dog twitched in its death throes.

The final molossus lunged for Todd's throat, its maw wide and filled with huge, gleaming teeth. The dead weight of the dying molossus clinging to Todd's arm pulled him down. And that saved his life — for the moment. The attacking molossus missed Todd's throat, its slobbering jowls brushing his face while its jaws snapped on empty air.

Even as he fell, Todd swung his Glock. He struck something, but didn't feel the solid connection of forged steel hitting hard bone.

He landed atop the dying dog. The impact ripped the beast's jaws open, and fresh agony shot up his arm.

Todd struck blindly behind and above himself as he scrambled to

274

roll to his feet. He connected with the remaining molossus and heard a satisfying yelp.

Todd lurched upright and spun around. The dog crouched a yard away, growling, fangs bared. Blood flowed from somewhere near the beast's neck, splashing to the ground.

Todd bared his own teeth as he faced the monster. "Here, doggy," he growled. "I've got a treat for you." His left arm screamed at him, and he could feel his own blood coursing down it, falling freely from his left fist.

The molossus lunged. Todd sidestepped, bringing the gun down.

He missed.

Todd pivoted, but the beast was on him in a heartbeat, bearing him to the hard cave floor. Todd landed on his back with the snarling molossus atop him. As he hit the hard floor, the air whooshed from his lungs. His gun struck a rock, knocking the weapon out of his hand. Todd clutched at the beast's neck, locking his hands around its throat, as the dog's massive jaws snapped at him. Todd's weakened left arm quivered, and he felt it failing under the weight of the colossal dog.

Drool hit Todd's face as the chomping teeth got closer and closer. Huge, bloodshot eyes glared at him in savage triumph. The teeth snapped inches from Todd's throat. Todd's arms quaked with the strain.

Can't hold it!

The wounded arm gave way first. As he felt his left arm cave, Todd shoved hard with his right, twisting and rolling to the left.

The dog's head struck the stone floor with a crack. Grabbing a rock, Todd swung it around, bringing it down on the monster's skull with a sickening crunch. He struck again, then raised the rock a third time —

"Todd!" Moe croaked. "Behind you!"

Todd twisted, barely getting his shaking right arm up in time to deflect a bronze knife as it sliced through the air in a lethal arc. He caught a glimpse of a ghastly face, sagging and lifeless, like the visage of a corpse. The creature shrieked at him.

Todd swung his left fist around. The wounded arm missed the thing's head, connecting instead with the attacker's shoulder. The impact sent the enemy staggering back, even as a fresh spear of agony ripped through Todd's arm.

He cried out, wincing with the pain. The smell of blood and smoke filled his nostrils, and for a moment the waking nightmares of Afghanistan threatened to overwhelm him.

NO! Not now!

He forced his eyes open and searched for his assailant.

Where did that thing go?

He glanced quickly around the chamber. He saw Moe dangling upside-down, strung up by his feet from a wooden framework.

"Where is it?" Todd demanded.

"I don't know!" rasped Moe, twisting his head wildly about. "I lost her. Can't see much."

Todd continued to scan his surroundings, looking for the threat. He saw the dead molossii, a mass of mangled, half-devoured human corpses lying in a vast puddle of gore, the smoking braziers, the bed—

"Peggy!"

Todd leapt to his feet, pain and fatigue vanishing at the sight of her. He dashed toward the bed.

Peggy lay there, asleep, just as the Druids had been, her hands crossed over her chest. And she wasn't alone. Derek lay there as well, dressed in a white robe. And between them, lay Elaine, still clutching a round piece of golden fruit. Elaine wore a long white dress that went down almost to her bare feet.

They look dead. He shook his head quickly. "Just drugged," he tried to assure himself. "That bloody fruit." *Please don't be dead. Father in Heaven, please let Peggy be okay!*

Todd scanned the chamber again. Nothing moved . . . except the shadows.

But the shadows set Todd's teeth on edge. The desire to snatch Peggy up and haul her out of there was almost unbearable. But he couldn't—not while that knife-wielding horror was still on the loose.

And I can't abandon Moe and Derek. Or Elaine.

He quickly examined his wound. *Bleeding, but not spurting — not arterial.*

Lucky. Not gonna bleed out. Not yet.

Maybe that thing ran away.

Moe called it a "her." Might've been a woman. Didn't look like Morgaise, though. Well, sort of, I guess — if both halves of her face were dead.

Probably was Morgaise after all.

He moved swiftly around the perimeter of the chamber, looking for his assailant. He found his empty Glock and picked it up. *Not much of a club, but better than nothing.*

Good enough to kill two of those blasted dogs.

But he did not find the knife.

Okay, so she's got the knife.

276

However, he did find a white robe lying next to a dead molossus. *She must've dropped it.*

"You okay, Moe?" he asked without looking at the man.

"Been better," Moe croaked. "You're wounded."

"I'll live."

Keeping a wary eye peeled, Todd snatched up the robe and ripped off one of the sleeves. He wound the linen around his injured arm. With the gun still clutched in his right hand, he couldn't tie off the bandage, so he simply tucked the ends in.

That'll have to do for now.

"Can't believe" — Moe coughed — "you took out all *seven* of them."

Todd shook his head slightly and grimaced. "Maybe if I'd been a better shot, I wouldn't be wounded."

"You did good enough."

Todd strode to the wooden frame, noticing the metal tub resting below Moe's dangling, blood-swollen hands. Todd's eyes traced the rope around Moe's ankles, running from the hangman's noose up to the hook, then back down to the winch. *Like a gallows . . . or a slaughterhouse.*

Is this where Jerry died?

"Keep an eye peeled," Todd said. "I'm gonna get you down." He unlatched the winch, grunting as the throbbing in his arm flared, and began to lower Moe toward the floor.

"Sure thing," Moe said. "Can't see much, though."

"You just watch my six," Todd said. "I'll watch yours."

"Roger that." Moe groaned. "Todd, there's . . . *something* in here."

Todd froze, then quickly scanned the chamber again. *What was that? Could've sworn I saw something.*

No. Nothing.

Just shadows. "Something? What do you mean?"

"It's a demon. Says it's Cernunnos." Moe hissed as his hands hit the rocky floor. "You know — Morgaise's god?"

"A demon? Here?" Todd looked around warily. His hands trembled. He wasn't sure if it was the presence of a pagan god or just his adrenaline wearing off.

"Yeah, a demon." Moe hissed again sharply. "Oh *boy*, that hurts!"

"Sorry. I'll have you down in—"

"Watch the shadows," Moe croaked. "They . . . move . . . when you're not looking."

Todd kept scanning the cavern as he finished lowering Moe to the floor. His arm throbbed miserably, and his hands shook. *Yep. Adrena-*

line's gone. At least the bandage isn't soaked through. Yet.

Once Moe's feet were down, Todd knelt beside him and loosened the noose.

"Thanks," Moe said. "I don't suppose you brought any water."

"Negative." *He's thirsty. Probably in shock. Need to get him out of here. I need to get them all out of here. But if I leave any of them alone . . . Best chance is to wake Peggy and Derek up. And Elaine.*

Please, God, let Peggy be alive! "You probably can't walk, can you?"

Moe groaned and shook his head.

"Okay. You're on lookout, then. I'm—" *What was that?* "That shadow—could've sworn I saw . . . like a man . . ."

"That's him!" Moe cried.

Todd lurched to his feet again.

The dark shape shuffled toward them, then paused. "Moses?"

Todd let out a shuddering breath of relief and lowered his weapon. "Abbot?"

Thurgood Abbot stumbled into the brazier light. The elderly lawyer looked much the worse for wear—bent and wheezing. His expensive suit was torn in several places, the knees ripped and filthy. Blood dripped from the old man's left hand.

He must've crawled the last part of the way. Say what you like about the old creep, Cavetto—it took a lot of guts and determination to climb the rest of the trail in his condition.

Todd shook his head. "I thought you were going *down* the path to wait for help."

The old man didn't answer. His eyes were wide with naked terror as they moved from the dead molossii to the piles of blood and tissue that used to be Morgaise's disciples.

"Grandfather?" Moe croaked.

The old man's head spun on its spindly neck. "Moses!" Abbot quickly shuffled over and knelt beside his grandson. The two of them conversed in low, rasping voices.

Todd couldn't make out what they were saying, but it sounded as if they were arguing. "Abbot!" Todd said. "Did you see someone as you came in? An old woman, maybe?"

Abbot coughed and shook his head. "No."

Blast it! Means she's still in here somewhere. Maybe not in this chamber, but—

"No!" Moe rasped, shaking his head and waving a puffy fist at Thurgood. "It's my task. My mother—"

"You've done enough, Moses." Using his right hand, the old man

278

forced his grandson's curled, bloated fingers apart, removing something from Moe's fist. "Let an old man—"

Moe's head snapped toward the entrance, his eyes wide as saucers. "There! It's him!"

Todd looked up just in time to see an enormous, sinister silhouette —man-shaped and antlered. The dark shadow filled the chamber, consuming the light of the braziers. Blackness enveloped Todd—darkness, cold, loathing, envy.

And despair.

Todd couldn't move, couldn't breathe. *Dying. Peggy will die.* He had failed.

The demon's cold voice filled Todd's mind. *I am Cernunnos, the Horned One. I was ancient before your Christ was born. Look on me, Christian, and despair.*

There was no hope. Todd was certain he had never known hope in his whole life.

Hope did not exist.

All those people—pulled them out of the fire.

Couldn't save them.

Failed.

Can't save Peggy either.

No hope.

There was only darkness, cold, and death.

The dark entity laughed, and its mad glee filled the chamber, filled the whole world. *Your god cannot save you, Christian.*

"No," Todd moaned. "NO!"

Christian. Todd seized on that word. *Christian. Christ. Priesthood.*

"In the name of Jesus," he whispered. *Just give in. No hope. Lost. Embrace the darkness. Let go.*

No! Peggy!

Heavenly Father, help me! Help me save Peggy.

Todd forced his lips to move even though no sound came out. "In the name of Jesus . . . just . . . just go away."

The demonic laughter rose and transformed into an ear-splitting shriek. The cry echoed and reechoed around the cave.

And then it was gone—the laughter, the unearthly cry, the darkness—evaporated as if it had never been.

Todd could breathe again.

"Thank you," he whispered. "God, thank you."

He drew in deep, cleansing breaths—savoring and relishing life and light . . . and hope.

"Peggy," he said aloud.

Todd realized he was on his knees. He got to his feet and turned toward the bed and Peggy.

And he froze.

Morgaise stood next to the bed. She wore the same white dress as Elaine.

And she held the bronze knife to Peggy's throat.

However, Morgaise looked shaken to her core. She stared at Todd in dismay, her good eye wide. "What . . . did you do?"

Moe laughed from where he lay under the gallows. The sound was harsh, forced. "He banished your god, lady. And he slaughtered your giant, scary dogs."

Thurgood knelt beside his grandson, quaking like a yellowed leaf barely clinging to a tree in a windstorm. The old man held his fists to his ears as if to block out the voice of the demon.

The look of horror and shock on Morgaise's half-face dissolved, hardening into a flint of contempt and loathing. She glared at Todd with her good eye. "This woman, this . . . sister-thief—she means something to you, Roman? She is precious to you?"

Todd glanced from Morgaise's face to the knife poised at Peggy's neck, ready to sever her jugular vein.

Lie to her, Cavetto. Do your crazy shtick. Make her think you don't care.

But Todd knew he couldn't do it. He couldn't take a chance with Peggy's life. *With just a flick of her knife . . .*

"Please," he begged, as he slowly bent and carefully placed his empty sidearm on the cave floor, "please don't hurt her. I'll do anything. I'll . . . Tell me what you want. Just, please, don't hurt her."

Moe grunted as he forced himself into a sitting position. "Morgaise, listen. Elaine doesn't want you to hurt Peggy. You promised Elaine."

Elaine? Todd noticed the space on the bed between Peggy and Derek, empty except for the single piece of golden fruit. *Where's Elaine?*

The fruit — there's no bite taken out of it.

The same dress.

A shiver rocketed up Todd's spine.

Could it be?

Morgaise's lips twitched. She looked confused, uncertain. She shook her head slightly. "No, we can't."

Can't what? Who's she talking to?

Morgaise shook her head more vehemently. "We don't need her. We have Derek. I'm allowing you to take him with us. We haven't done that since Myrddn. Isn't Derek sufficient?"

Another shiver of understanding shook Todd. *She's talking to Elaine.*

A small, crimson bead of blood welled on Peggy's neck where the cold, sharp tip of the knife pressed against her soft flesh.

Do something! "What do you want, Morgaise? Tell me what you want."

Morgaise's good eye pierced him, like a dagger of hatred. "What do I want? I want my molossii back. You killed my dogs, you *madra salach*! They were . . . the last of their kind. Now they are gone. Gone! Can you give them back to me?"

She shook her head, never taking her eye off Todd. "You desecrated the Burning Man, ruined our sacrifice." Her voice rose in pitch and volume. "Your Roman whore has robbed me of my sister's love! *I* protect Elaine! *I!* I have spent my whole life—hundreds of lifetimes—protecting Elaine. Can you give me back Elaine's love?"

"Morgaise," Moe said, "where is your sister?"

The woman's good eye blinked in confusion. "She's . . . She's right here—with me."

"Where, Morgaise?" Moe asked. "Is she on your left, or on your right?"

"She's right here!" the woman snapped. "You can see her."

A trickle of blood slid down Peggy's neck.

"Y-Your Highness." Thurgood's voice shook. "Of course, we can see her. Of course, we can. H-how may I serve you, Your Highness? Please, my Lady, surely we c-can find a resolution that will—"

Contempt replaced confusion on Morgaise's half-face. "I will deal with you later, Thurgood. Your family will pay a high price. Again."

Thurgood Abbot bent and began crawling toward her, groveling. "P-please, Your Highness! Please, spare my family. I beg of you. Spare them. I have served you faithfully all my life."

The old man quaked as he crept closer to his mistress. Pain and exhaustion were plain to see in the trembling of his arms, barely able to support his gaunt frame. His gnarled hands were clenched into arthritic fists, the left fist wet with blood. His frail, thin frame quivered as he crawled. "Forgive me, Princess Morgaise. Forgive a foolish old man. I have served you faithfully. Take my life. Just spare my family. Please. I beg you! Have mercy, Your Highness!"

What is he doing? Stay back, you idiot!

"Grandfather!" Moe reached a swollen hand toward the old man. "Stop! Don't do this."

281

Thurgood ignored Moe. And as the old man approached her, half a malevolent smile curled Morgaise's lips. Her good eye gleamed wickedly. "Very well. I will take you with us, Thurgood. I will take you with us . . . so you can watch your progeny suffer for your transgression." She licked her lips in anticipation. "Oh, how they will suffer!"

Thurgood prostrated himself at her bare feet. "Mercy!" He raised his trembling hands in supplication, clasping them together. He rotated his hands until the right was atop the left. Then the old man gasped, and his eyes widened.

Thurgood's bloody left hand shot out and clutched Morgaise by the ankle. Thurgood howled as if in torment, and Morgaise recoiled, but she couldn't pull out of the old man's grasp.

"No!" she screamed. "NO!"

Black, wooden tendrils sprouted from Thurgood's clutching hand, wrapping themselves around his hand and his forearm. The tendrils snaked up Morgaise's leg like a writhing army of black, wooden serpents.

Morgaise shrieked. She bent and hacked frantically at the lattice of roots as it spread up her leg.

Todd sprang toward her. *Get her away from Peggy!*

"Todd, no!" Moe cried. "Stay back!"

The wooden tentacles pierced Morgaise's leg, seeking more blood. She let loose a howl of agony and terror.

Todd lowered his shoulder and drove into the woman, knocking her down and away from the bed—away from Peggy. As Morgaise fell, a dark tendril shot out and wrapped itself around Todd's bloody forearm like a wooden python.

Todd stumbled back, wrenching his arm free, snapping the root off from the rest of the ghastly plant. He landed on his backside, then grasped the twitching root, ripped it off his arm. He flung the quivering thing away into the darkness.

Todd scrambled backward, putting some distance between himself and Morgaise, Thurgood, and the carnivorous roots. In shoving Morgaise, Todd had only managed to separate the squirming, writhing mass from the bed and Peggy by a couple of yards.

Please, God, let that be enough!

The hideous web had spread all the way along the old man's arm and was rapidly encasing his torso and head. Thurgood screamed as a tendril pierced his eye. He convulsed once, then his body went limp.

The roots now encased Morgaise's abdomen, chest, and arm. The knife fell from her fingers and hit the cave floor with a brazen clang.

Ignoring the questing roots, Todd lunged for the weapon. He snatched it up, then scrambled to put his body between the monstrous tree and the bed where Peggy lay.

A root snaked toward him.

He hacked it off.

Morgaise screamed. "Cernunnos! Deliver—"

When her voice abruptly cut off, Todd looked up at her.

Her half-dead face had shifted. Both sides of her face sagged, lifeless. The murderous crone looked back at him with the expressionless eyes of a living corpse. The next moment, Elaine's pretty face twisted in agony. "Help me!" she cried, reaching toward Todd with her free hand and pleading with her wide, terrified eyes.

A root, thick and straight like the stinger of a huge spider, punctured her chest. She uttered a piercing shriek. The shriek choked off into a wet gurgle. Blood poured from Elaine's delicate lips.

And then she was silent.

The roots, however, continued to creak and groan. They grew, expanding and consuming until both corpses—Thurgood's and Elaine's—were encased in a wooden cocoon. Only then—when Todd could see nothing but rough shapes that had once been human—only then did the horrible roots cease to squirm.

For a moment, all was still. Then with a pop, a thin tree trunk erupted from the wooden mass. It shot straight up till it was more than a foot tall. Branches sprouted from the sapling—and from the branches, leaves.

And when at last Morgaise's deadly Tree of Life had consumed her and Thurgood Abbot, it ceased to grow.

An eerie quiet filled the cave. The only sounds were Todd's own labored breathing and Moe's unabashed weeping for a grandfather he'd barely known.

Todd got to his feet.

He shoved aside all questions and thoughts about Elaine and Morgaise and the surprising, heroic self-sacrifice of Thurgood Abbot. He didn't care about giant, man-eating dogs or vampire trees or ancient demons.

There would be time to process it all later.

At that moment, one and only one thought filled his mind—

Peggy.

XXXI

It was the kiss that woke her, the soft brush of lips against hers—skin on skin, flesh on flesh. Love's first kiss. And it was sweet.

But just as Peggy began to open her eyes, she hesitated, then squeezed them shut again.

Who was it? Who kissed me?

The more important question is, who do I want it to be?

"Peggy?"

Todd.

Yes, Peggy. That's Todd's voice, but you didn't answer your own question. Who do you want it to be?

She opened her eyes.

Todd was leaning over her, his face barely six inches from her own. And he looked frightened. Not just frightened—he looked scared out of his mind. Peggy had never seen Todd look scared—not for one second.

Then his eyes opened wide, and he gasped. "Peggy!" His face split in a grin wide enough for two happy men.

He pulled back for a second, then quickly slid his arms under her back and knees. In a moment, he had scooped her up in his strong arms. He danced around, holding her as if she were a child or a bride at a threshold. He whirled and laughed with unrestrained joy. "Peggy! You're alive! You're okay!" Then he laughed some more.

Peggy could only put her arms around his neck and hold on.

She had no idea where she was—a cave of some sort, lit by smoky fires. But for that moment, she didn't care where she was. She was disoriented and confused . . . and happy.

Todd's laughter was infectious, and Peggy laughed with him—not her embarrassing, "goofy" laugh, but laughter born of pure joy.

She smiled up at him as he slowed his exultant spinning. He stopped, lowered her gently to the ground, and hugged her close.

She returned the embrace, melting into the comforting power and protection of Todd's strong arms, exulting in the warmth and firmness of his body pressed against hers. She closed her eyes and sighed contentedly. "You came for me."

He chuckled, squeezing her so hard she could barely breathe.

And even that felt nice, comforting. "I knew you would," she managed to say.

He eased the pressure around her. "Always," he whispered, and to Peggy, it seemed as if a whole world of hope and promise and commitment was contained in that one, simple word.

"I knew you'd come for me," she whispered, her lips brushing his ear. "Even when you went back into that burning house, I knew you'd . . ."

And memory crashed on her like a tidal wave.

The Druids took her from behind, hands grasping, clawing at her — just as in her condo, just as when they were going to gang-rape her. All the terror of that moment slammed into Peggy as she was forced onto her back. They held her down, one white-robed figure seizing each arm or leg.

She screamed for Todd. Then she felt sharp, cold metal at her throat.

Peggy froze.

The familiar face of the Pagan's widow leaned over her, the pretty, delicate features twisted into a leer of savage triumph and murderous need. "Remember me, bitch?"

"STOP!" cried an imperious voice.

The widow frowned, took a deep breath, then spat in Peggy's face.

"Stop this at once," Morgaise commanded. Her voice was quieter then, but no less demanding.

The knife was withdrawn.

Morgaise's half-face leaned over Peggy's. In the light from the blazing house, only the living side was visible. At that moment, Morgaise looked just like Elaine would — if Elaine were angry. Morgaise scowled at Peggy. Then she nodded, and Peggy had the oddest impression that Morgaise was listening to someone else — someone Peggy couldn't hear.

Morgaise shook her head. "We don't need her." A pause. "She was kind to you? Am I not kind to you?" Another pause. "Very well." Morgaise breathed a sigh tinged with bitterness and resignation. "I can deny you nothing, can I, my sweet sister?"

Morgaise motioned at Peggy with an authoritative hand. "Open her mouth. Quickly!"

The Pagan's widow pried Peggy's jaws open, then Morgaise shoved a bit of that evil fruit past Peggy's teeth.

Peggy tried to spit it out, but her mouth was forced closed, her teeth crushing the morsel of sleeping death. She tasted overwhelming sweetness.

Todd will come, *she thought. But as the darkness took her once again, her thoughts turned briefly to the man she'd rescued from the fire.* Derek.

"Derek!" Peggy ripped herself out of Todd's sheltering embrace. "Where's Derek?"

In the light of the braziers, pain seemed to cloud Todd's eyes for a moment. Then his lips tightened into a hard, thin line. He nodded, pointing with an arm which only a second before had held her tight. "Over there. On the bed."

Peggy spun in the indicated direction. As she turned, her eyes took in many strange and disturbing sights—an amorphous, grisly mass of blood, bone, tissue, and red-stained linen; dead molossii; a bulk of dark, crisscrossing, wooden roots with a tiny tree sprouting from the top; a familiar-looking man with salt-and-pepper hair and a kindly, tear-streaked face; braziers alight with smoky, yellowish-orange fires; a large, ornate bed.

And lying at the far side of that bed, on a coverlet of green—Derek.

He was clad in that dirty, white robe, still damp from their escape from the burning house. His hands were folded across his chest as if he were dead.

"Derek!" she cried and bounded the few steps it took her to reach the bed. She crawled onto the emerald comforter and across the bed until she could kneel beside him.

Peggy grasped Derek by the shoulders and shook him. His hands slid off his chest to rest limply at his sides, but he didn't respond. "Derek! Please, please wake up!"

Behind her, someone coughed—an oddly polite and disturbingly normal sound, interrupting her panic and terror.

Peggy turned her body slightly and looked over her shoulder. She recognized the man with the kindly face. *The centurion at the Ren Faire —the one who unintentionally freaked Elaine out.* The man grinned sheepishly at her. "You might try . . . kissing him."

In confusion, Peggy turned her face toward Todd. He stood beside the bed, his expression unreadable. He nodded and shrugged. "Yeah. It . . . worked on you." He swallowed, and his mouth twitched. Then he cocked his head, and his lips curled into a grin that didn't reach his eyes. "And *I'm* not gonna do it."

Peggy felt awful—she really did—but Derek needed her. She turned her gaze away from the man who'd come for her—who'd always come for her—and back to the man lying on the bed.

She had dreamed of this moment, fantasized about it for years—ever since the day she'd met Derek at work.

Gorgeous, dreamy Derek.

Derek, who went with her to all the comic book, sci-fi, and fantasy conventions—Kili to her Tauriel. Derek, who went to lunch with her dozens of times, who listened to all the geeky stuff she was into and out-geeked her right back. Derek, who watched a *Doctor Who* marathon with her as they munched on popcorn, and shared secret, knowing smiles at the ridiculous, silly bits—but never, ever laughed.

Derek, who never had a clue how much she loved him—not until that awful rainstorm in the parking lot.

He chose Elaine over you.

Doesn't matter, not right now.

Right now, Derek needs me.

Peggy gathered her hair in one hand, pulling it aside, so it wouldn't fall onto Derek's face.

Yuck! My hair's so filthy!

Who cares? Certainly, not Derek.

She bent, hesitated for a moment . . .

And kissed him.

His lips were soft, but they were cold as death.

"Please, Derek," she whispered. "Please, come back." *. . . to me.*

Derek's eyes fluttered open. And they were gorgeous.

Peggy flashed him her best smile. *See me, Derek. See* me.

Derek opened his mouth, inhaled sharply . . . and screamed.

🙢 🙢 🙢

The moon had set long ago, and the eastern sky was just beginning to lighten, as Peggy and Derek sat together on a large rock near the path, well below the cave. Derek's trembling hands clutched her tightly about the waist, as he rested his head against her chest and sobbed like a lost and abandoned child. Peggy had one arm around his back, as she gently patted his head.

A tumult of thoughts spun through Peggy's mind as she tried to comfort Derek.

Elaine and Morgaise were . . . the same person?

That man—Moe . . . He said . . . some kind of split-personality thing.

Elaine wasn't real? Never really existed?

No! That's not true. It can't be. Elaine was sweet and kind. She had to be real . . . at some level. She had to be.

But she's dead. Morgaise is dead. They're both dead.

Back at the house, in the yard, Morgaise was talking to Elaine. I couldn't hear it, but Elaine said I was kind to her.

Elaine . . . spared my life.

"Elaine!" Derek sobbed. "Oh, Peggy! I loved her. I loved her so much!"

A tear spilled from Peggy's eye. She stroked Derek's hair. "I know."

Derek shook his head against her chest. "She wasn't real. She wasn't . . ."

Peggy shushed him. "She *was* real." Her own grief leaked from her eyes and flowed down her cheeks. "She . . . she loved you too. Morgaise wanted to kill you . . . kill us. But, somehow . . . part of her . . . the Elaine part, I guess . . . well, she saved us . . . in a way. Elaine saved us both. I don't understand it, but . . ." *Because I was kind to her?* "Morgaise brought us here . . . to the cave. Then Todd came." *Todd always comes.* "And he saved us."

Derek's sobbing diminished into a quiet snuffling. "Todd said *you* saved me. *You* got me out of the burning house. He said you were awesome. So brave." He shook his head again. "And after I treated you like . . . like crap. You saved my life."

"It's okay." *I saved you, because I love you. And I know you don't love me back, but I —*

Derek shook his head more forcefully. He sat up and looked her in the eyes. Peggy couldn't ever remember Derek looking her directly in the eye, not like that — not as if he were really *seeing* her.

"No," he said, "it's not okay." He smiled sadly. "You were always there . . . always there f-for me. It was always you. Peggy, I . . . I just didn't see it. It was always you. Peggy, I . . . I'm sorry. I was such . . . a jerk."

Peggy put her arms around him and hugged him. He hugged her back, whispering into her hair, "I'm sorry."

Peggy closed her eyes and shivered in Derek's embrace. In spite of the cold, predawn air, in spite of their damp clothes, Peggy felt warm. "It's okay. Really. I'm just . . . I'm . . . so happy you're okay."

"Can you ever forgive me?"

She squeezed Derek tight. "Always."

Always? That's what Todd said.

Todd came for me. He's always there, always watching over me, always protecting me.

Always.

He kept running into that burning building, pulling people out. "I

thought they might be you." *That's what he said.*
And he never asked me for anything. Never expected anything.
And now, now that the danger's past . . .
A sob gurgled out of Peggy's throat.
Now Todd will go away. He'll leave.
He'll leave . . . and he'll never know . . .
"Peggy," Derek whispered, "Peggy, I love you."

◢ ◢ ◢

Todd watched the chamber entrance. It was a hopeless vigil, he knew, but he couldn't help himself.
She's not coming back – not back into this abattoir.
Not that I blame her.
Todd didn't want to remain in the cave either, but Moe wouldn't leave, not yet at least. The ex-priest sat on the edge of the bed, glaring with moist, bloodshot eyes at the massive, tangled roots of the evil and incongruously tiny tree.
At least the cloves in those fires mask the stench of blood and guts. Man! There has to be gallons and gallons of blood in here! Not to mention all the other gory bits.
The gore lay pooled around the mangled bodies of the Druids and around the dog carcasses. Todd didn't want to think about Morgaise's disciples and the way they died. Unconsciously, he patted his holstered, empty Glock, as if the weapon could protect him from visions of mayhem and death. *Eaten alive by those monsters. I wonder if they felt anything. Or were they so drugged they just . . .* His wounded forearm throbbed. And itched. A shudder of revulsion ripped through him at the memory of the tree root seizing his arm. *Or devoured alive by a bloodthirsty tree. Don't know which is worse.*
Think about something else, Cavetto.
And he did. His thoughts kept running back to Peggy – back to Peggy and the tempest of emotions that thoughts of her always evoked.
She'll wait outside. With him.
Give her space. Derek needs her right now.
But I need her too. I ache for her.
I loved Christie. I did. Once. But Peggy – she's so . . .
Not now, Cavetto. The timing sucks.
A soft, bitter chuckle escaped him. *My timing always sucks.*
Peggy's an adult. She can make her own decisions.
She made her decision a long time ago. And she chose him.
He doesn't deserve her.

And you do, Cavetto? You're still stuck in Afghanistan. You're still . . . broken.

Peggy deserves a whole man, not an emotional cripple.

"It was supposed to be me," Moe said, interrupting Todd's troubled thoughts. Moe wiped tears from his eyes as he stared at the half of the wooden cocoon that used to be his grandfather. "Why, you stupid, old man? I would've done it! Mama said *I'd* be the one to deliver the family. She had a dream!" He slammed an impotent fist against the mattress in grief-borne anger. "It was supposed to be me!"

Todd sat down beside Moe and put an arm around the man's shoulders. "You know, Moe . . ." *That sounds stupid – two rhyming words in a row.* Todd cleared his throat. "I think . . . I think it *was* you."

Moe shook his head and snorted in derisive, bitter dismissal—then wiped at his dripping nose.

"Seriously," Todd continued, "if not for you, he . . . your grandfather would've just . . . passed the curse on to future generations. You showed him the way out."

Moe barked a bitter laugh. "He barely knew me. We just met tonight. Was it only tonight? I barely knew him! What was he doing here anyway?"

"He came to help you."

Moe looked at Todd with skeptical, red-rimmed eyes. "Why would he do that?"

"I think you—I don't know—got through to him somehow."

Moe shook his head and glowered at Thurgood's root-woven sarcophagus.

"Think about it," Todd went on. "He had people who worked for him. He called them 'associates,' but they seemed like just hired muscle to me—especially judging by those rocket scientists up on the mountainside. I'm sure he had more goons. He could've sent them. You said there was another grandson, your cousin, right?"

Moe nodded. "Winslow."

"Okay. Somehow, I don't think the old guy would've hesitated to wake up your Cousin Winslow. No, I think this was something he . . . felt he had to do himself. I think . . . he wanted to . . . redeem himself."

Moe shrugged. "Maybe. Maybe."

"He called me," Todd said, "told me where to find this place." Todd shook his head and smirked. "I had to stop for gas. I mean, that never happens in the movies. The hero" —*Is that what you think you are, Cavetto? The hero?* – "has to stop for gas? Then I got a little lost. I don't know this area worth beans." He shrugged and sighed. "When I met old Thurgood on the path, he looked scared enough to die on the spot — too scared, I thought, to come up here. Alone. He came alone. It took courage for him to do that. A *lot* of courage. *You* did that, my friend. *You* inspired it. You saved him."

Moe let out a shuddering sigh, then wiped his eyes and nose once more. "I had the seed . . . in my hand. I was going to do it."

"Where'd you get it? The seed, I mean?"

Moe fished in his breast pocket with fingers that were still swollen and clumsy. He pulled out a small black seed and a crumpled, green leaf, then displayed them on his open palm. "Here. I was going to show them to a botanist at the Y."

Todd looked at the seed and leaf, but made no move to touch them. *Could be some small bit of blood on my hand.* "Where'd you get those?"

Moe stood, carefully avoiding the tree, and walked past Todd and over to the foot of the bed. "Over here."

Todd rose and followed him.

Moe bent down and retrieved a wooden box from the cave floor. Todd caught a glimpse of an image carved into the lid—a tree. Moe's clumsy fingers fumbled with the leather-and-wood latch. He turned around, caught his foot and stumbled.

And lost control of the box.

With a cry, Moe tried to catch the chest, but it went tumbling out of his hands.

As it fell, the box disgorged its contents. Leaves spilled and fluttered, slices of fruit flew out in arcs of white and gold . . . followed by a spray of tiny, dark pips.

Tiny, dark seeds.

Dozens of them landed in one of the several pools of blood.

The seeds exploded, shooting forth hundreds and hundreds of roots, like a horde of giant, wooden spiders thrusting out legs and pincers.

Todd grabbed Moe by the arm, yanking him away from the rapidly expanding cluster of wooden death. "Run!" Todd yelled over the horrid din of creaking, snapping wood.

Todd dashed for the exit, hauling Moe behind.

When they reached the chamber entrance, Todd felt the rock tremble under his feet. The tremor tripped him, and he spun around as he fought for balance.

Roots thick as tree branches dug into the rock of the floor and walls. Stone cracked and split, making a racket like a battalion of thunderclaps, and the walls of the chamber began to shatter and collapse.

Moe dragged Todd backward.

Todd turned, and the two men scrambled out of the cave—out of the chamber of death and darkness and into the breaking dawn.

Todd and Moe slipped and skidded and blundered their way down the path as the ground heaved and pitched beneath them. Todd spied Peggy and Derek halfway down the path. Derek and Peggy stood. Derek had his arm around Peggy as if to protect her.

Todd waved at them frantically. "Go! Run!"

Peggy grabbed Derek's hand, and they turned and ran down the path.

When the four of them reached the road, gasping and out of breath, the ground had ceased to tremble. Todd turned his face back toward the cave. The hillside around the cave entrance had collapsed in a great cascade of broken rock and mangled vegetation—a tomb of wood and stone—a crypt for Elaine and Morgaise, Thurgood Abbot, and the Druids.

Todd, Moe, Peggy, and Derek stood, bent over, hands on knees, and mutely panted as they stared in wonder at the devastation.

We made it. We're alive. Todd looked at Peggy—Peggy standing next to Derek. *Peggy's alive. Thank you, Heavenly Father. Peggy's alive.*

After a long minute, Moe bowed his head in prayer. "Heavenly Father, please have mercy on him . . . on my grandfather . . . on Thurgood. He . . . He sacrificed himself to save us all. 'Greater love hath no man than this,'"—his voice broke—"'that a man lay down his life for his friends.' Especially those friends . . . he barely knew."

Moe paused, and the pregnant silence extended long enough that Todd stole a peek at him. Moe wiped his eyes and nose with a dirty hand, then continued. "And please have mercy on those other . . . misguided souls in there . . . and on all the other victims down through the millennia." He paused again. "And, Father, even on Camorra, daughter of Boudicca . . . she whom some of us knew as Morgaise a-and Elaine. Father, please . . . help her . . . help her find peace. And help us who have survived by Thy good grace to—"

A choking sob interrupted Moe's praying. Todd opened his eyes and turned around. He found Derek weeping like a child, his arms locked around Peggy, with his face buried in her hair.

Peggy held Derek close, swaying from side to side as she cooed and shushed in an effort to comfort him. Her own eyes were shut tight, though tears leaked from them.

Todd turned away. He wasn't sure if it was to give Derek and Peggy privacy in their grief—or because he couldn't bear to look at Peggy in Derek's arms.

She's made her choice.

◆ ◆ ◆

After some tense discussion, the three men—Peggy hadn't taken part in the discussion, remaining oddly reticent with her eyes on the ground—had decided how they would split up for the drive back. Moe would drive Todd's car, and Todd, since he'd driven Peggy's car up there—and had to stop for gas—would drive her vehicle, with Peggy and Derek riding together in the back. They would all rendezvous at the restaurant where Moe had passed the Mexican Chicken Test the previous evening—it *had* been only the previous evening, though it seemed as if whole days had passed—so Moe could retrieve his own car, hopefully before it got towed.

After that, the plan was for Moe to go on home, and for Derek to drive Todd's car back to Peggy's condo so Derek could then pick up his own car. This was the part of the plan that Derek objected to most strenuously. He didn't want to be parted from Peggy. However, Todd was adamant.

"I'm not going to assume," Todd said, "that every single cultist is dead. I know at least one survived the fire—at least she was alive when I left her lying on the lawn—and there could be others out there."

Todd still felt guilty about that, leaving the woman defenseless— even if she was a member of a murderous cult. He called nine-one-one as soon as he peeled away from the house, but it still gnawed at him.

Derek opened his mouth to argue—again—but Todd shut him down hard. "I'm not leaving her side," Todd said with the same hard-edged precision he used on an aircraft radio, "not until I'm sure—absolutely sure-she's no longer in danger."

The lines of Derek's face hardened into a scowl. "And just how long is that going to be?" The younger man didn't even try to keep the sarcasm out of his voice.

Todd's intense eyes bored like lances into Derek's, as if daring the younger man to try to stare him down. "As long as it takes," he said, enunciating each word carefully. But after a moment, Todd lowered his eyes. He didn't care if Derek thought he'd won the staring contest. "Or until the lady asks me to leave."

Peggy said nothing.

Thurgood Abbot's car was left abandoned at the side of the canyon road. The old man's car keys were assumed to be buried under tons of wood and stone anyway.

An awkward, deafening silence filled Peggy's car as Todd drove through the morning. Derek sat in the middle of the back seat, pressed next to Peggy. He had an arm around her shoulders in a manner that was both protective and—to Todd's eyes, at least—territorial.

Todd kept his eyes studiously on the road, the side mirrors, the dashboard—anywhere but on the rearview mirror.

Peggy's alive. She's okay. Nothing else matters.

Nothing.

Keep telling yourself that, Cavetto. You love her.

Yeah, I do. And if I really love her, I'll want her to be happy.

And Derek makes her happy.

Derek's the one she wants.

A sudden sound from the backseat caused Todd to reluctantly check the rearview mirror. Derek's head lolled to the side, his mouth open and slack.

He was snoring.

Todd rolled his eyes. *You'd think after pulling a "Snow White," the guy wouldn't be sleepy for a year.*

Peggy wasn't sleeping, however. As she looked into the mirror, her eyes locked with Todd's.

Such pretty eyes. Like a doe's eyes.

Eyes like that could steal a man's soul.

You've stolen my soul, Peggy Carson, and my heart.

I'm yours if you want me. Just say the word.

Those beautiful, heart-and-soul-stealing eyes, however, now brimmed with grief and weariness and trouble.

Todd flashed her what he hoped was a reassuring grin. He didn't know if she could see the smile in the mirror or not. In either case, she didn't smile back. And after a lingering moment, she looked away, staring out the window.

Todd snapped his focus back to the road.

She's made her choice, Cavetto. And it's not you.

You didn't sign up for this mission to win her heart—you signed up to protect her. That's the mission—protect Peggy.

His jaw hardened in determination.

Protect Peggy until you're sure the danger's past—or the lady tells you to leave.

XXXII

Like a stalking molossus, a dark cloud of foreboding dogged Todd's steps as he walked swiftly from his car back to the north-facing entrance of the Payson Temple. Something momentous and—for him—devastating was coming. He could feel it in his bones.

You knew this day would come.

He wanted with his whole soul to slow down, to take his time—to put it off just a minute longer. But he couldn't leave Peggy waiting.

Focus on the mission.

He patted his suit coat where the Glock rested in its shoulder holster. He wasn't comfortable bringing the weapon inside the temple, so it was his habit to escort Peggy to the entrance, then return to the car, drop off the semiautomatic handgun in the glove compartment, and hasten back to join Peggy inside the lobby. That was what he did when they arrived at the temple. After a temple session, he'd reverse the procedure, just as he was doing now.

Peggy would be waiting for him, safely ensconced in the entryway. And under normal circumstances, there would be a spring to Todd's steps as he hurried back to her. He'd see her standing inside the doors, smiling that heart-stopping smile of hers, her beautiful, brown eyes sparkling. Then he would grin and say, "Hello, pretty lady! May I have the honor of escorting you safely home or wherever else your heart may desire?" It was corny, he knew, but that was him—cornball to the core. And Peggy always seemed to appreciate it—or at least tolerate it with her usual good grace.

And besides, corny or not, he meant it—every word.

But he sensed in his heart that Peggy was probably not in the mood—not today.

She'd been quiet all morning, and that was potentially a bad omen. Normally, on Saturday, she was relaxed and fully able to just be herself. And for Peggy, that meant she liked to chat about anything and nothing. But not today.

Last night, Derek took her out to dinner. Friday night was Derek's night—Derek and Peggy's date night. It was one of those Japanese steak houses, where they grilled the food right at the table—one of Peggy's favorites. Last night was special.

As usual, Todd kept a discreet distance, never intruding or eavesdropping on their conversation. In fact, most of the time, he avoided looking at them—at least directly. He was there to watch for danger. He was there to protect Peggy, not watch Derek wooing her—not watch Peggy basking in the glow of Derek's attention. They knew he was there, of course, but he stayed out of the way and gave them their privacy.

He focused on the mission—always on the mission. The mission was about all he had left.

But even as he studiously avoided looking at them, out of the corner of his eye, he saw a sparkle of white and a flash of gold in Derek's hand.

Last night, Peggy came home smiling—a secret, knowing smile.

But she wasn't wearing a ring. And until she did come back with a ring, there was still hope.

Not much hope, but a little. Maybe she turned him down.

Keep telling yourself that, Cavetto. You know where this is going. Even if she's not wearing a ring . . . yet.

Peggy had wanted, *insisted* on going to the temple that day. Going to the temple together on a Saturday—just Peggy and Todd—wasn't out of the ordinary, but this particular Saturday was also Halloween.

Tonight would've been the "Harvest," if it hadn't "come early."

You know that's not it, Cavetto.

She's done with her mourning.

Even Derek seems to have completely forgotten Elaine. He's focused on Peggy.

Can't say as I blame him.

Peggy occupied almost all of Todd's waking thoughts.

She haunted his dreams too.

She'd been planning on wearing the princess gown from the Ren Faire for Halloween that night. They weren't planning on going anywhere, just staying at home, watching a scary movie and passing out candy . . . in costume. He'd been looking forward to it all week. To be honest, he'd been looking forward to seeing her in that dress again . . .

But that was before this morning, before Peggy's unusual reticence.

Peggy sat for a long time in the temple, thinking and praying. That wasn't unusual, either. But she sat alone, away from him. Then she stood up and whispered to Todd she was ready to leave.

And that was the last thing she'd said to him.

There she was, standing inside the temple doors, wearing one of her best dresses—solid red, mid-length, and very flattering—Todd's favorite. Peggy would never be petite, but she didn't have to be. She looked fantastic in that dress.

And when she smiles . . .

But Peggy wasn't smiling. Her countenance bore the same somber expression she'd worn all day. And there was something else to her expression now—fierce determination. It was there in the set of her jaw, in the hard lines around her eyes.

This is it.

Todd stepped inside, his guts writhing like a pit of snakes. He forced a grin and offered Peggy his arm. "Hello, pretty—"

Peggy pushed past him and stomped out of the temple, out into the crisp autumn air.

Todd followed her. There was nothing else he could do.

She strode quickly to the steps beside the large fountain at the front of the temple, her high heels clicking on the concrete, her hips swaying in that way which normally inspired less-than-temple-appropriate thoughts in Todd's mind—thoughts he fought so hard to keep in check. But now, all he could think about was catching up with her—and the dread of what would happen when he did. Peggy kept going, down the steps toward the base of the fountain.

When we get to the bottom of those steps, to the front of the fountain . . .

Todd had endured Christy's betrayal, and that had nearly destroyed him. He had survived the horrors of Afghanistan. He'd faced armed thugs, a burning house, giant hell-hounds, vampiric trees, a demon, and Morgaise herself. And he had been terrified.

But at that moment, he was more frightened than he had ever been in his life.

When she reached the front of the fountain, Peggy stopped abruptly. She spun about, her skirt flaring around her. Todd halted a few feet away. Instinctively, he scanned about them for threats. Then he focused on Peggy.

She folded her arms under her breasts as if shielding her vital organs—or her heart—and for the first time that day, looked him in the eye. Her lips were drawn into a tight, resolute line.

"Todd, I need you to leave. You need to move out. You need to go. Today."

Todd felt as if his heart had been ripped from his chest. He swallowed hard, not trusting himself to speak. He couldn't clear the lump in his throat. Instead, he did the only thing he could think of—he looked around for threats again.

But of course, there were no threats. No Druids. No molossii. No Morgaise. Nothing.

Nothing except Peggy and the emotional bridge burning between them.

"Stop it!" she snapped. "Stop looking around as if you have to protect me. There hasn't been anything—not in weeks. No stalkers. No rapists. They even arrested that Druid woman you pulled out of the fire. Todd, there's nobody left to save me from."

Todd nodded, still unable to find words to answer her.

When he said nothing, Peggy went on. "So I want you to leave. You said you'd go when I asked. So . . . I'm asking."

Todd nodded again. "Okay." His voice came out in a croak, the word ripping from his throat like sandpaper. "I'll pack up as soon as we get home." *Home. No. Not home anymore.* "Sorry. As soon as we get back to . . . your place."

She glared at him. Her nostrils flared, and her mouth worked as if she were about to say something more. Then she spun around, her arms still folded protectively, and stomped quickly back up the stairs —away from him.

Todd hesitated a moment longer, standing beside the fountain, hearing the water splash and gurgle and drain. The water would run through the fountain in an eternal cycle of renewal—like living water promising eternal life. But there would be no eternity with Peggy.

You can't make her love you, Cavetto. And even if you could have, it's too late now. She's made her choice.

Peggy reached the top of the stairs and turned toward the south parking lot. Todd realized with a start that she was headed the wrong way.

He hurried after her. "Hey, Peggy! The car's over—"

She wheeled around so abruptly, he almost ran into her.

Almost.

He stumbled back, nearly losing his balance.

Peggy was livid, her cheeks flushed with anger. "You are the most infuriating man, Todd Cavetto!" Her eyes brimmed with tears.

Todd was completely flummoxed. "I-I don't get it. I said I'll go. That's what you want."

"No!" She dropped her arms to her sides, her hands curled into fists, and stomped a foot. "That's not what I want at all!" She squeezed her eyes shut, forcing out tears.

"I don't understand." He wanted to take her in his arms, to dry her tears. But he held back. "Tell me what you want me to do, Peggy. I'll do anything you want. Just tell me."

She opened her eyes and shook her head. "That's just it. You'll run into a burning building to save me. You'll fight molossii and pagan gods and who knows what else for me."

He gripped her shoulders gently. "Always."

She jerked back out of his grasp as if his touch burned her. "'Always,' that's what you say. I used to think—I used to hope it was . . . some sort of *Princess Bride* thing—like that was your way of saying . . ." She shook her head again, biting a trembling lower lip. "But you don't! You don't love me. You don't *want* me. And I just . . . can't . . . take it anymore."

She turned her head away. "I can't stand being near you, having you sleeping in the next room, dreaming about you . . . knowing you don't—"

Todd enfolded Peggy in his arms, squeezing her tight. He kissed her, smothering her cry of protest.

He wasn't tender, not at first. His kiss was rough, bursting with need and longing.

After a moment's hesitation, she kissed him back, just as hard, just as passionately. Her arms went round his back, clutching at him, clinging to him, as if she were drowning and his kisses were the very air she needed to breathe.

And then they slowed, the passion of the moment giving way to gentleness. Todd realized he was weeping. They were both weeping.

She was the first to break off the kiss. She put her lips to his ear. "I love you. Oh, I love you so much. Do you really love me? Really?"

He pulled his head back and gazed into her lovely, red-rimmed eyes. He sighed with a relief so profound it made his whole body tremble. "Always."

She smiled back, and her face lit up like a thousand stars.

"Peggy," he said, "you are so beautiful when you smile."

Her smile widened, and Todd thought his heart would melt in the radiance of her smile.

Todd bit his lower lip. "What about . . . Derek? I saw a ring."

Peggy shrugged. "I turned him down. I don't . . ." He voice trailed off, and she smiled sheepishly.

Todd gently pulled out of their embrace. He took both her hands in his and dropped to one knee. "Peggy Carson, princess fair, queen of my heart, goddess of my dreams, please do me the honor of being my eternal bride."

Still smiling, Peggy cocked her head. "You know how corny you sound, right?"

He grinned impishly. "Hey, pretty lady, that's how I roll." Then his grin vanished, and he looked up at her hopefully and earnestly. "But I mean every single word. Always."

She smiled down at him, but she said nothing.

"So," said a woman's voice, "are you gonna answer him?"

Todd's head snapped to his left. They were surrounded by a small crowd of men and women—couples, of various ages. They were all smiling. The woman who had spoken was white-haired and possessing a face as sweet as Todd's own grandmother. She was holding hands with an elderly, balding man who leaned on a cane.

Some bodyguard you are, Cavetto! We're surrounded.

"Well . . ." Peggy drew out the word playfully. "He hasn't actually said the words." She gazed down at him. And this time, it was her turn to flash him an impish grin. "I need to hear the words."

The words? And then he understood.

"I love you." He enunciated each word deliberately and unambiguously. "Always. Now, please? Be my wife?"

Peggy's beautiful, doe eyes sparkled. "Always."

Todd jumped to his feet, scooped her up into his arms as if she were a bride at a threshold. Peggy wrapped her arms around his neck.

He bent his head, she lifted hers, and they kissed.

And the crowd cheered.

The End

Acknowledgements

As much fun as this project has been, it would not have been remotely possible without the help of numerous individuals. First and foremost, my wonderful eternal companion inspired and encouraged me, and painstakingly proofread every word. She also allowed me to use her as a sounding board for all my harebrained ideas. Thank you, my beloved Cindy. Mable Belt also proofread and critiqued every word. Bryan Belt provided medical and biological expertise as well as much-needed critique. And then there are the wonderful members of the LDS Beta Readers group who provided feedback, corrections, critique, and encouragement: most notably, Jenny Flake Rabe, Amber Hall, Jacque Stevens, Michael Young, Loury Trader, Lori Widdison, Emily Soloman Bogner, Jean Newman, Rebecca Charlton, and John Kammeyer. Steve Devenport, M.D. and Evan Black, M.D. provided medical expertise. John Murdock, LCSW, imparted a wealth of knowledge on abnormal psychology. Dr. Eric D. Huntsman was enormously helpful with Latin and history. Randy Marshall allowed me to consult with him on legal matters (and didn't even charge me). Christian Belt provided essential law-enforcement expertise. Alison Barton and Staci Meacham were very helpful as consultants and beta readers. Blaine Stewart provided technical expertise on surveillance equipment. Devin Asay, Major USAFR (ret.) was my expert on USAF SAR and helicopter aviation. John Abercrombie was also a loyal beta reader. Teri Crockett, Layne Miller, and Dr. Luke Howell were also invaluable consultants. "Red" Dawn Johnston graciously proofread my Gaelic. David Belt (my father, not me) allowed me to bounce ideas off him during our many forays to Home Depot. Elizabeth Bentley, my amazing editor, vastly improved this work. And last, but not least, to the nearly five hundred fellow members of the Mormon Tabernacle Choir and Orchestra at Temple Square, you have inspired me.

To each and every one of you, please accept my sincerest, heartfelt, bone-deep gratitude.

About the Author

C. David Belt was born in Evanston, Wyoming. As a child, he lived and traveled extensively around the Far East. He served as an LDS missionary in South Korea and southern California (Korean-speaking). He graduated from Brigham Young University with a Bachelor of Science in Computer Science and a minor in Aerospace Studies. He served as a B-52 pilot in the US Air Force and as an Air Weapons Controller in the Washington Air National Guard. When he's not writing, he sings in the Mormon Tabernacle Choir and works as a software engineer. He collects swords, axes, spears, maces, crossbows, and other medieval weapons and armor. He and his wife have six children and live in Utah with an eclectus parrot named Mork (who likes to jump on the keyboard when David is writing).

C. David Belt is the author of the trilogy, *The Children of Lilith*, and of *Time's Plague*. For more information, visit www.unwillingchild.com

CPSIA information can be obtained
at www.ICGtesting.com
Printed in the USA
FSOW02n0703021016
25558FS